Larissa Ione is a *USA Today* and *New York Times* bestselling author. She currently resides in Williamsburg, Virginia, with her husband and young son.

Please visit her website at www.larissaione.com
www.facebook.com/OfficialLarissaIone
www.twitter.com/Larissa Ione

Also by Larissa Ione

Demonica series:
Pleasure Unbound
Desire Unchained
Sin Undone

Lords of Deliverance series:
Eternal Rider

PASSION UNLEASHED

LARISSA IONE

PIATKUS

First published in the US in 2009 by Grand Central Publishing,
A division of Hachette Book Group, Inc.
First published in Great Britain as a paperback original in 2011 by Piatkus

A CIP catalogue record for this book
is available from the British Library.

ISBN 978-0-7499-5572-4

Typeset in Times by M Rules
Printed and bound in Great Britain by
Clays Ltd, St Ives plc

Papers used by Piatkus are from well-managed forests
and other responsible sources.

MIX
Paper from
responsible sources
FSC® C104740

Piatkus
An imprint of
Little, Brown Book Group
100 Victoria Embankment
London EC4Y 0DY

An Hachette UK Company
www.hachette.co.uk

www.piatkus.co.uk

To Brennan, because without you, I would never have known the joy of being a mother, and I don't think my characters would, either. You're my world, Goob!

ACKNOWLEDGMENTS

Special thanks to the fabulous staff at Grand Central Publishing, from the cover art department to my copyeditor and editor, Amy Pierpont. I'm so very lucky to be working with such talented people.

And a huge thank you to Justin Knupp of Stonecreek Media, for being so great to work with and for being such a big, visible part of the Demonica world.

Finally, a big 'love ya, gals,' to the Writeminded Readers Group and the Writeminded blog ladies, Jaci Burton, Maya Banks, Amy Knupp, and Stephanie Tyler. You are my much-needed support group!

GLOSSARY

The Aegis – Society of human warriors dedicated to protecting the world from evil. See: Guardians, Regent, Sigil.

Carceris – The jailors of the underworld. All demon species send representatives to serve terms in the Carceris. Carceris members are responsible for apprehending demons accused of violating demon law, and for acting as guards in the Carceris prisons.

Council – All demon species and breeds are governed by a Council that makes laws and metes out punishment for individual members of their species or breed.

Dresdiin – The demon equivalent of angels.

Fakires – Derogatory term used by vampires to describe humans who either believe themselves to be real vampires or who pretend to be vampires.

Guardians – Warriors for The Aegis, trained in combat techniques, weapons, magic. Upon induction into The Aegis, all Guardians are presented with an enchanted piece of jewelry bearing the Aegis shield, which, among other things, allows for night vision and the ability to see through demon invisibility enchantment.

Harrowgate – Vertical portals, invisible to humans, which demons use to travel between locations on Earth and Sheoul.

Infadre – A female of any demon species who has been impregnated by a Seminus demon.

Maleconcieo – Highest level of ruling demon boards, served by a representative from each species Council. The United Nations of the demon world.

Orgesu – A demon sex slave, often taken from breeds bred specifically for the purpose of providing sex.

Regent – Head(s) of local Aegis cells.

Renfield – Fictional character in Bram Stoker's *Dracula*. Also, derogatory term for any human who serves a vampire. A vampire groupie.

S'genesis – Final maturation cycle for Seminus demons. Occurs at one hundred years of age. A post-s'genesis male is capable of procreation and possesses the ability to shapeshift into the male of any demon species.

Sheoul – Demon realm. Located deep in the bowels of Earth, accessible only by Harrowgates.

Sheoul-gra – A holding tank for demon souls. The place where demon souls go until they can be reborn or kept in torturous limbo.

Sheoulic – Universal language spoken by all demons, though many species speak their own language.

Sigil – Board of twelve humans known as Elders, who serve as the supreme leaders of The Aegis. Based in Berlin, they oversee all Aegis cells worldwide.

Swans – Humans who act as blood or energy donors for vampires, either actual undead or fakires.

Ter'taceo – Demons who can pass as human, either because their species is naturally human in appearance, or because they can shapeshift into human form.

Therionidryo – Term a were-beast uses for a person he or she bit and turned into another were-beast.

Therionidrysi – Any survivor of a were-beast attack. Term used to clarify the relationship between the sire and his therionidryo.

Ufelskala – A scoring system for demons, based on their degree of evil. All supernatural creatures and evil humans can be categorized into the five Tiers, with the Fifth Tier comprised of the worst of the wicked.

Classification of Demons, as listed by Baradoc, Umber demon, using the demon breed Seminus as an example:

Kingdom: Animalia
Class: Demon
Family: Sexual Demon
Genus: Terrestrial
Species: Incubus
Breed: Seminus

PASSION UNLEASHED

ONE

'When you are dining with a demon,
you got to have a long spoon.'
– Navjot Singh Sidhu

There were three things Wraith did well: hunt, fight, and fuck. He was going to do all three tonight. In exactly that order.

Crouching on the rooftop of a shop run by immigrants who had probably come from such a shitty country that the violence in the streets of Brownsville, Brooklyn, didn't faze them, Wraith waited.

He'd spied the gang members earlier, had scented their aggression, their need to draw blood, and Wraith's own need to do the same stirred. Like any predator, he'd chosen his target with care. But unlike most predators, he didn't go for the weak or the aged. Screw that. He wanted the strongest, the biggest, the most dangerous.

He liked his pint of blood with an adrenaline chaser.

Unfortunately, Wraith couldn't make a kill tonight. He'd already met his one-human-kill-per-month limit set by the Vampire Council, and no way in Sheoul would he go over.

Strange that he worried about it, given that ten months ago Wraith had happily gone through his *s'genesis*, a change that should have made him a monster who operated only on instinct – an instinct to screw as many demon females as possible, with the goal being to impregnate them. An added bonus of the *s'genesis* was that male Seminus demons became so focused on their sex drives that they cared little for anything else. But in Wraith's case, he was also a vampire, so killing things was in his blood. So to speak.

Eager to get started with his new life, Wraith had found a way to bring on The Change early. Unfortunately, it didn't *change* a damned thing. Oh, he wanted to screw and impregnate females, but that was nothing new. The only difference was that now he *could* impregnate them. Oh, and he also had to shapeshift into the male of their species to do it, because no female on Earth or in Sheoul, the demon realm in the planet's core, would knowingly bed a post-*s'genesis* Seminus demon. No one wanted to give birth to offspring that would be born a purebred Seminus despite the mixed mating.

So yeah, a few things had changed, but not enough. Wraith still remembered the horrors of his past. He still cared about his two brothers and the hospital they had all started together. Sometimes he wasn't sure which was worse.

Wraith scented the air, taking in the recent rain, the rancid odors of stale urine, decaying garbage, and spicy Haitian cuisine from the hovel next door. Darkness swirled around him, cloaking him in the shadows, and a cold January breeze ruffled his shoulder-length hair but did nothing to ease the heat in his veins.

He might be the epitome of patience while waiting for his prey, but that didn't mean that inside he wasn't quivering with anticipation.

Because these weren't your typical gangbangers he was hunting. No, the Bloods, Crips, and Latin Kings had nothing on the mercilessly cruel Upir.

The very name made Wraith's lips curl in a silent snarl. The Upir functioned like any other territorial street gang, except those pulling the strings were vampires. They used their human chumps to commit the crimes, to provide blood – and bloodsport – when needed, and to take the falls when the cops busted them. For their service and sacrifice, the humans believed they would be rewarded with eternal life.

Idiots.

Most vampires adhered to strict rules regarding turning humans, and since a vampire was allowed only a handful of turnings in his entire lifetime, he didn't waste them on lowlife gangbangers.

Of course, the gangbangers didn't know that. They played the streets, their fangs-dripping-blood tats and crimson-and-gold gang colors screaming warnings others heeded. No one messed with the Upir.

No one but Wraith.

The Upir came. Seven of them, talking trash, swaggering with overblown arrogance.

Showtime.

Wraith unfurled to his nearly six feet, six inch height, and then dropped the fifteen feet to the ground, landing right in front of the gang.

'Hey, assholes. 'Sup?'

The leader, a stocky white guy wearing a bandanna wrapped around his bulbous head, stumbled back a step, but hid his surprise behind a raw curse. 'What the fuck?'

One of the punks, a short, fat, crooked-nosed troll – not literally a troll, which was unfortunate, because Wraith could have killed him, penalty-free – drew a blade from his coat pocket. Wraith laughed, and two other punks produced their own knives. Wraith laughed harder.

'The dregs of human society amuse me,' Wraith said. 'Rodents with weapons. Except rodents are smart. And they taste terrible.'

The leader whipped a pistol out of his droopy-ass pants. 'You got a motherfucking death wish.'

Wraith grinned. 'You got that right. Only it's your death I wish for.' He smashed his fist into the leader's face.

The leader rocked backward, clutching his broken, bleeding nose. The scent of blood jacked up Wraith's temp a notch . . . and he wasn't alone. The two gangsters at the rear zeroed in on the scent, heads snapping around.

Vamps. One black male, one Latino female, both dressed like the others in baggy jeans, hoodies, and ratty sneakers.

Jackpot, baby. Wraith was going to get some kills in tonight, after all.

Before any of the stunned humans could recover, Wraith sprinted down a side street.

Angry shouts followed him as they gave chase. He slowed, drawing the gangsters in. Nimbly, he leaped on top of a Dumpster and then swung up to a rooftop and waited until they passed. Their fury left a scent trail he could follow blindfolded, but instead, he dropped to the ground, used his infrared vamp vision to see them in the darkest shadows ahead. He hated using any of his vampire skills, including super speed and strength, but vision was the one he truly despised.

Despised, because he hadn't been born with it. Instead, it had come twenty-two years later, with the eyes Eidolon had transplanted into his head nearly eighty years ago. Every time Wraith looked into the mirror at the baby blues, he was reminded of the torture and pain that had preceded the new peepers.

Kicking himself for letting the past distract him, he silently started the hunt. Normally, he'd take out the vamps first, but the troll was just ahead, huffing and puffing and trailing far behind the others.

He pounced, squeezed the breath out of the squat human, and left his unconscious body behind a pile of boxes. Next, he tracked the male vamp, who thought he'd gained the upper hand by swinging around behind Wraith.

Wraith feigned distraction, standing in the open beneath the bright glare of a street light as the vamp crept forward. Closer . . . closer . . . *yes.* Wraith spun, pummeled the massive male with a flurry of fists and feet. The vamp didn't have a chance to throw a single punch, and once Wraith had hauled him into the darkness beneath an overpass, he took him down. With a knee in the male's gut and one hand curled around his throat, Wraith drew a stake from the weapons harness beneath his leather jacket.

'What,' the male gasped, his eyes wide with shock and terror, 'what . . . are . . . you?'

'Buddy, sometimes I ask myself that same question.' He slammed the stake home. Didn't wait around to watch the show as the vampire disintegrated. There was another one to take out.

Anticipation shimmered through his veins as he stalked the female through side streets and alleys. Like the male, she believed *she* was the one doing the hunting, and Wraith caught her off guard as she crept in the shadows behind a building. He shoved her into the wall, lifting her by the throat so she dangled off the ground.

'This was too easy,' Wraith said. 'What is the Vamp Council teaching younglings these days?'

'I'm no youngling.' Her voice was a low, seductive purr, and even as she spoke, she lifted her legs to wrap them around Wraith's hips. 'I'll show you.'

The scent of lust came off her in waves. His incubus body responded, hardening and heating, but he'd rather kill himself than screw a vampire – or a human, though he had different reasons for not bedding human females.

He leaned in so his lips brushed her ear, which was pierced all the way around. 'Not interested,' he growled, but still, she arched against him, affected by his incubus pheromones.

You shouldn't play with your food. Eidolon's voice rang in his ears, but Wraith ignored it the way he ignored pretty much everything his brothers said to him. He had no intention of making a meal of this female.

'Could've fooled me,' she said, rolling her hips into his erection.

'Maybe you need some convincing.' Wraith pulled back and gave her an eyeful of wooden stake.

Her eyes went wild. 'Please . . . ' She swallowed, her throat convulsing beneath his palm. Her body wilted like a dying flower, and that fast the temptress was gone. 'Please. Just . . . do it quickly.'

He blinked. He'd expected her to beg for her life. He met her wide, haunted gaze, and slowly, with a sick sense of dread, he shuffled his fingers on her neck. A raised pattern peeked from beneath the collar of her hoodie. *Damn.*

He shoved his stake into his pocket and tugged her sweatshirt aside to reveal a welted pattern the size of his fist.

A slave mark. Not just any slave mark. The cross-bones brand of Neethul slavemasters, the cruelest of the demon slave traders. This female had been forced to live in hell for gods knew how long. Somehow she'd gained her freedom, probably by escaping . . . and now she was doing what she had to in order to survive.

She'd suffered. Was probably suffering even now.

Something clawed at his gut, and it wasn't until he lowered her to the ground without realizing it that he identified the strange feeling. Sympathy.

'Go,' he said roughly. 'Before I change my mind.'

She got the hell out of there, and so did Wraith. Rattled by his uncharacteristic display of mercy, he ruthlessly shoved aside the incident. He needed to get back on track. He needed to feed. He needed to cause some pain.

The punks had split up, and one by one, he tracked them down with almost mechanical efficiency until only the leader was left. Somewhere nearby, a gunshot rang out, a familiar sound in this part of the city, so familiar he doubted the cops would even be called.

The leader was ahead, pacing in front of a boarded-up shop front, his voice crisp with agitation as he barked out orders on his cell phone.

'Yo, scumbag,' Wraith yelled. 'I'm over here! Would it help if I wore a neon sign?'

Red-faced with fury, the leader bolted into an alley after Wraith. Halfway in, Wraith pivoted around. The gangster pulled his gun, but Wraith disarmed him before he could so much as blink. The weapon skidded across the wet pavement as Wraith put the guy's back into a wall and jammed his forearm across the human's thick neck.

'This is disappointing,' Wraith drawled. 'I expected more of a fight. I seriously wanted to tenderize you before I ate you. When are you guys going to learn that a gun is no substitute for learning hand-to-hand combat techniques?'

'Fuck you,' the guy spat.

'Guy like me?' Wraith smiled, leaned in so his lips grazed the guy's cheek. 'You. Wish.'

An outraged bellow made him smile even more. He inhaled the man's aroma, anger tainted by a tantalizing thread of fear. Hunger roared through Wraith, and his fangs began to elongate. Playtime was over. He sank his teeth into the gangster's throat. Warm, silky blood filled his mouth, and after a couple of spasms, his prey went limp.

Wraith could have used his Seminus gift to fill the guy's head with happy, pleasant visions, but this dude was scum. The things he'd done slapped at Wraith's brain in rapid-fire succession. Sure, Wraith was no angel – though he'd screwed a false one or ten – but with the exception of Aegis Guardians, he didn't harm human women or children.

This guy . . . well, Wraith wished he hadn't blown this month's kill quota on the Sumatran poacher. Still, tormenting the gangster could be fun. Swallowing the human's alcohol-laced blood with relish, Wraith used his mind power to feed the guy gruesome images of what Wraith would do to him if he ever found out that he'd committed a violent crime again. For the most part he couldn't care less if a human lived or died, but this guy got off on preying on the weak and the old.

There was no sport in that.

Power surged through Wraith, power and adrenaline and flashes of heat lightning under his skin. His *dermoire*, a history of his

Seminus demon paternity, pulsed from the tips of the fingers on his right hand to his shoulder and neck, and all the way to the right side of his face, where the swirling black glyphs marked him as a post-*s'genesis* Seminus. Humans thought it was a tattoo – some thought it was cool; the rest were appalled.

Humans were so freaking uptight.

His prey's pulse picked up as his heart tried to compensate for the blood loss. Wraith took two more strong pulls, disengaged his fangs, and hesitated before licking the puncture holes to seal the wound. He'd never minded drinking from his victims, but he hated licking them, tasting sweat, dirt, perfume, and worse, their individual essence. Cursing silently, he swiped the holes with his tongue and tried not to shudder, but the shakes wracked his body anyway.

'You should kill him.'

The male voice, deep and calm, startled him. No one snuck up on Wraith. Ever.

He released the gangbanger, letting the guy hit the pavement with a thud. In a fluid, easy movement, he faced the newcomer, but too late he saw a flash and a blur, felt the sting of a dart in his throat.

'Shit!' Wraith ripped the dart from his neck and threw it to the ground, even as he charged the guy who had shot him with it. He was going to gut the bastard.

Wraith grabbed for the male's shirt, some sort of burlap tunic, but his fingers only brushed the collar. The guy was unnaturally fast – unnaturally fast for a human. This male was demonkind, species unknown.

The male didn't make a sound as he whispered through the night, moving toward a sewer grate.

Awkwardly, because his left side had begun to weaken, Wraith drew a throwing star from his weapons harness. He hurled it, catching the newcomer in the back.

The male's ear-shattering, high-pitched scream rent the night as he fell. Wraith slowed, a sudden sense of dread weighing him down, turning his limbs sluggish and uncoordinated.

He stumbled, attempted to catch himself on the side of a building, but his muscles had turned to water. His vision grew dim, his mouth went dry, and with every breath it felt as if he was taking flames into his lungs.

He tried to reach his cell phone, but his arm wouldn't work. And then his mind wouldn't work, and all went black.

൭

Throbbing pain in Wraith's head woke him, and a serious case of cotton-mouth made him gag. He smelled sickness. Blood. Antiseptic.

Shit, what had he done last night? He'd been clean for months ... well, he hadn't fed on a junkie just for the sake of getting high, anyway. He'd eaten his share of humans and demons who had drugs in their systems, but that hadn't been why Wraith had chosen them as food. At least, that's what he'd told himself.

In any case, he hadn't woken up with a drug or alcohol hangover in months, but this ... this was one mother of a hangover.

He peeled open his eyes, the pain convincing him his eyelids were coated on the inside with sandpaper. They watered, and he had to blink several times before he could focus. Through blurry vision he saw chains hanging in loops from a dark ceiling. Low, muted voices blended with the sound of beeping hospital equipment and ringing in his ears. He was at Underworld General.

He should be relieved, comforted to be safe. Instead, his gut wrenched. Clearly, he'd screwed up again, and his brothers were going to chew his ass but good.

Speak of the demons, he thought, as Eidolon and Shade entered the room. Wraith tried to lift his head, but the room spun in a nauseating swirl of dark colors.

'Hey, bro,' Shade said as he grasped Wraith's wrist. A warm, pulsing sensation shot up Wraith's arm. Shade was doing his body probe thing, checking his vitals and whatever other crap needed to be checked. Maybe he could do something about the spins.

'What's up?' he croaked. 'You boys are wearing your grim faces.' Which meant he'd fucked up even more royally than he'd thought.

Eidolon didn't smile, not even the fake, doctorish, it's-going-to-be-okay smile. 'What happened the other night?'

'*Other* night?'

'You've been out for two weeks,' E said. 'What happened?'

Wraith levered up so fast his head threatened to fall off. 'Oh, no. Fuck, no. E, did I kill someone?'

His brothers both pushed him back on the bed. 'Not that we know of. Yet. But we need to know what happened.'

Relief made him sag into the mattress as he searched the black hole that was his memory. An alley. He'd been in an alley. And in pain. But why? 'I'm not sure. How did I get here?'

Shade grunted. 'I felt your distress. Grabbed a medic team and took a Harrowgate to you.'

'What do you remember?' E asked, jacking up the head of the bed so Wraith could sit up.

He sifted through the fuzzy memories, but piecing them together was like trying to do a jigsaw puzzle while blindfolded. 'I was eating a gangbanger. Tasty, surprisingly free of drugs.' He frowned. Had he killed the guy? No, he didn't think so ... remembered closing the punctures. 'I felt a sting in my neck. And there was a male. Demon, I think. Why?'

The pulses down his arm stopped, but Shade kept his hand where it was. Even though he was no longer using his healing power, his *dermoire* continued to writhe. 'You were attacked by an assassin. Sent by Roag.'

'Ah ... did you guys miss the bulletin that said Roag is gone?' Wraith eyed his brothers, waiting for the punchline, but they didn't look like they were jacking with him. 'Oh, come on. Roag is as good as dead. For real this time.'

Their older brother had plotted a gruesome revenge against the three of them, had nearly succeeded. If Wraith never saw the dark depths of a dungeon again, it would be too soon.

Eidolon ran his hand through his short, dark hair. 'Yeah, well, he hired the assassin to handle his revenge on us in the event of his death. You must have injured him, because he was in bad shape. Tayla tracked and caught him while Shade was bringing you back here. He confessed everything before Luc ate him.'

'*Ate* him?'

E nodded. 'The assassin was a leopard-shifter. Nothing scares them more than werewolves, so we chained him up in Luc's basement to get him to talk. We thought we'd secured him far enough away from Luc.' He shrugged. 'Apparently not.'

'I love werewolves,' Wraith said, shooting Shade a sly grin. 'Guess you'd better not piss off Runa. She might eat you.' Shade had bonded to a werewolf last year, and had been disgustingly happy since. 'Why are you here, anyway? Shouldn't you be helping her with the monsters?'

'You mean the ones you haven't bothered to come see yet?'

'Shade.' Eidolon's voice held a soft warning, which was odd. Usually Shade was the voice of reason when it came to handling Wraith.

But ever since Runa had delivered their triplets, Shade had been seriously overprotective and easily offended. He just didn't get that not everyone went as goo-goo over his offspring as he did.

Wraith shoved the sheet off his body and saw that he was naked. Not that he cared, but his coat had better not have been ruined when they stripped him. Knowing Shade's love of trauma shears, Wraith figured odds were good that he'd have to buy another one.

'So why all the doom and gloom? The assassin failed.'

Shade and E exchanged glances, which set Wraith on high alert. This wasn't good.

'No, he didn't fail,' Shade said softly. 'The guy has a partner. He's still out there, and he's after all of us.'

'So I hunt his ass down and kill him. I don't see the problem.'

Shade's pause made Wraith's gut do a slow slide to his feet. 'The problem is that the first assassin shot you with a slow-acting poison dart.'

Wraith snorted. 'Is that all? Just shoot me up with the antidote.'

'Remember Roag's foray into the storeroom?' E asked, and yeah, Wraith remembered. Last year during Roag's bid for revenge, he'd helped himself to E's collection of rare artifacts and crap Wraith gathered for him. 'One of the things he took was the mordlair necrotoxin. That's what the assassin used.' E exhaled slowly. 'There's no antidote.'

No antidote? 'Then a spell. Find a spell to cure it.' Panic started to fray the edges of his control, and Shade must have sensed it, because his grip grew firmer.

'Wraith, we've consulted every text, every shaman, every witch. ... There's nothing that can flush the poison from your system.'

'So, bottom line. What are you saying?'

E handed Wraith a mirror. 'Take a look at your neck.' He brushed Wraith's hair back to reveal his personal symbol at the top of his *dermoire.* The hourglass, which had always appeared full on the bottom, had emerged following his first maturation cycle at the age of twenty.

Wraith inhaled sharply at what he saw now: The hourglass had been inverted, the sand flowing from top to bottom, marking time.

'You're dying,' Eidolon said. 'You have a month, maybe six weeks, to live.'

TWO

Serena Kelley was dying. Well, not literally, but it felt like it, what with the way the air was being sucked from her lungs by an extremely hot vampire who was kissing her senseless.

She wasn't one to hang out in Goth clubs, but tonight's nose-bleed-Euro-Goth music at Alchemy had promised to bring in the vampires – both the wannabes of the human variety and the actual undead.

The music echoed off the walls of the old slaughterhouse so loudly it messed with her heart's ability to beat, shocking her pulse into an uneven, chaotic rhythm. The smell of perfume, sweat, and sex was thick in the air, ratcheting up her libido. She moved with the crush of bodies on the dance floor, going with the tide as the vampire whose name she'd just learned guided her.

She sensed his hunger, his dark need, and yes, it was wrong of her to lead him on like this. Wrong to let him think he was going to get a meal and a notch in his coffin from her.

But what the hell. Every girl needed to flirt now and then.

Especially when flirting was as far as she could go with a guy.

'Come,' Marcus said, in that low whisper vampires could somehow make audible above any racket. 'My table waits.'

Marcus was an old vamp, his formal, stiff speech part of his allure, and Serena's hormones ran amok as he led her to a shadowed corner where several human groupies quivered like excited lapdogs at his approach.

Like so many older-generation vamps, he dressed in tasteful, conservative clothing beneath a midnight trench coat that helped him blend among the Goth and punk fashion in the bars. Glossy black, waist-length hair and ruby-red lips on a severe, pale face completed the look.

He waved his hand, and the lapdogs scattered, some of them cutting her jealous glares. She wondered how many knew he was a real vampire. Few who were deep into the vampire lifestyle actually believed in the undead. Those who did had a tendency to become Renfields – scraping, bowing hangers-ons who offered themselves up to be used in any way a vampire wanted.

Serena might have a thing for vamps, but she'd never stepped over the line to become a meal or a throwaway bedmate.

They sank into the booth, her black cargoes sliding across the faux-leather seats. Marcus wrapped his arm around her waist and tugged her into him.

Perfect. Because yes, she had a vampire fetish her boss, benefactor, and personal Aegis Guardian, Valeriu Macek, would have seizures over, and yes, she liked to live on the wild side. But she also liked to mix business with pleasure, and at this very moment, her business as a treasure hunter involved stealing Marcus's very valuable, very antique bracelet off his wrist.

Slowly, carefully, she slid her hand over his so her fingers rested on the ancient Macedonian bauble. Marcus didn't notice – his heavy-lidded gaze focused on her throat, and his erection prodded her hip.

'Shall we go outside, or stay here?' he asked, and she wondered if he knew she was fully aware of what he was.

The way he kept his fangs concealed told her he probably didn't know. Then again, after hundreds of years of being undead, keeping them hidden had probably become second nature to him. And really, vampire canines weren't all that obvious unless the vampire became excited, and then they'd erupt from the gums, elongating, growing . . . *so* erotic.

Serena tilted her jaw, exposing her throat enticingly. Distractingly. 'Here,' she purred, working the bracelet with one hand, and running the other up his chest.

Powerful muscles flexed beneath her palm, and for the thousandth time, she wished she weren't celibate. Wished she could let herself do all the stupid, risky things humans did when they were in their twenties.

Marcus's smile revealed just the tips of his fangs as he leaned in, wincing when his chest crushed her pendant between them. He frowned at the grape-sized crystal. 'That's one hell of a jewel.'

'Gift from my mom,' she said easily, even though the necklace was far more than that.

The bracelet slid free. She slipped it inside a leg pocket in her pants and glanced at her watch. 'Oh, would you look at the time! I'd better go. Don't want to turn into a pumpkin.'

Marcus's hand squeezed her biceps. 'I am not finished with you.'

She smiled sweetly. 'Oh, but you are. I'm no swan,' she said, using the term for humans who offered up their blood or psychic energy to vampires, though they usually believed the vampires were of the breathing, human variety – what true undead jokingly called *fakires*.

Rage iced over his dark eyes, and his lips peeled back to reveal daggerlike canines. Any sane human would be terrified, but not Serena.

She had a little secret. She'd been protected by a divine charm for eighteen years, since the day it was bestowed upon her at the age of seven, and no harm could come to her.

Not so long as she remained a virgin.

Marcus lunged for her throat. Serena angled away, and for no apparent reason, the vampire lost his balance, slipped off the seat, and landed in a heap on the floor. The groupies hovering nearby either backed away or rushed in to help him up, but he came to his feet in an explosion of anger.

His eyes narrowed and his fists clenched, but he hadn't avoided being slain by Aegis Guardians for centuries by causing scenes. Wisely, he did nothing more threatening than curse at her, and then he whirled away in dramatic vampire fashion, the crowd swallowing him and his Renfields as they followed on his heels.

Before Marcus figured out she'd lifted his bracelet, she needed to haul ass—

Something flashed in front of her. No . . . *inside* her. A crisp pop burst in her ears, echoing from somewhere in her head. A wash of nausea made her break out in a cold sweat. Instinctively, she reached for her pendant, let the cool, smooth orb comfort her.

Except, the comfort was short-lived. The pendant glowed. A warning. Her cloak . . . compromised. She was exposed.

Jerking to her feet, she stumbled toward the exit on wobbly legs. She needed to get home. Back to Val's mansion.

Because for the first time in eighteen years of living a carefree, sheltered life, Serena was afraid.

ණ

Byzamoth fell back in his seat, panting, body shuddering. Orgasmic waves of power pumped through him, the name he'd just learned breaking softly from his lips.

Serena Kelley.

He hadn't known the identity of the human he'd been seeking, but everything about her was now as clear as a witch's crystal ball.

Too quickly, the power fizzled, leaving him weak, but no less ecstatic. His palm burned, but it was a lovely pain, easily endured. He opened his fist, where the cause of the discomfort, a golf-ball-sized orb known as Eth's Eye, glowed red. Red instead of gold, because it had been used for evil rather than good.

Exhausted, he let his head fall against the seat rest and gazed up at the ceiling of the Israeli house he'd commandeered this morning. The family who'd inhabited it lay at various angles around him, dead eyes staring blindly. The youngest female virgin had volunteered herself as the blood sacrifice Byzamoth had needed to activate the evil capabilities of Eth's Eye.

'Volunteered' was probably too strong a word, but in any case, Byzamoth had gotten what he wanted. He'd found the most important human in the universe, the one who would be instrumental in kicking off the most significant event in demon history.

'It's started,' he said to the demon standing in the living room entrance.

Lore entered, a massive male covered from neck to toe, including his hands, in black leather that matched his short hair. He was one of the most efficient killers Byzamoth had come across, a male whose touch killed everything his bare hand came into contact with.

Byzamoth might be immortal, but even he gave Lore a wide berth.

'I don't give a shit about your war. I want my money.'

'Why the rush?'

'My partner failed to kill the vampire demon. I need to finish the job.'

Byzamoth waved his hand. 'You'll get your payment, but it won't matter. Soon, money will be worthless. Pain will be the new currency.'

'Yeah, well, right now cash buys beer, so hand it over.'

Byzamoth smiled. Even now, the underworld would begin to stir with the sense that something was coming, even if that something was still a mystery to them. Few would understand the significance of what Byzamoth had just done, which was to lift the divine cloak of invisibility that had shielded Serena from demon eyes for so long.

For years she had walked the Earth disguised as a normal human, and few, if any, were the wiser. Until now.

Fortunately for her, she was still charmed and still the keeper of the necklace, Heofon, and no one could take either away from her – not against her will.

No one but a select few individuals. Like Byzamoth.

He had every intention of taking them against her will.

And when he was done with her, he'd be in possession of the most powerful weapon imaginable, and demons would finally rule the world.

ൟ

Doctor Gemella Endri sat in UG's conference room with her sister and Eidolon's mate, Tayla, at her right side and Shade at her left. Eidolon and doctors Shakvhan and Reaver sat across from them. Tension thickened the air, growing more oppressive as the night went on with no new, feasible ideas for how to save Wraith.

Who had been sedated after Shade and E told him he was dying. Wraith had taken the news surprisingly well, but neither Shade nor Eidolon had trusted him to not immediately take off after the second assassin. They wanted him here, where they could monitor his health, though they had to know that their little brother wouldn't be held immobile for long. That demon couldn't sit still, and doing nothing wasn't in his DNA.

Making matters even worse, the hospital had been plagued by odd equipment and structural failures. All of the windows lining the inside of the administrative area had cracked, the lights in the cafeteria flickered constantly, and the third-wing lava bath had leaked, destroying the sulphur-steam room next to it. Eidolon had been kept too busy with the problems to concentrate on medicine, because every time he fixed one thing, something else would go wrong.

'I had a consult with an Orphmage this morning,' Gem said, 'but he was no help.'

She hadn't expected the powerful Cruentus mage to be of assistance, but it had been worth a shot. Cruenti had a bloodthirsty love of killing that didn't stop even at their own species, so she'd thought that maybe a Cruentus mage capable of the vilest of death magic would know something about how to interrupt mordlair toxin.

He'd been more interested in how to get some for himself.

'I could try again—' She broke off with a gasp.

A sinister wash of energy rolled over her, followed by several smaller concussions, as if a stone had been dropped into tainted water. She was about to ask if anyone else felt it, but from their expressions, she definitely was not the only one at the table to experience the ... *whatever* it was. Even after the tiny waves stopped, the uneasy feeling remained, a sense that something evil had ripped into the very fabric of life.

Something bad, something very, very bad had been set into motion.

'What the hell was that?' E rasped, seeming more affected than Gem, but then, he was full-blooded demon, and she was half human, less sensitive to the tides of evil.

Gem shook her head, which did nothing to get rid of the impending feeling of doom.

'Reaver?' Tayla leaped to her feet. 'Shit!'

All heads turned to the fallen angel, who sat in his high-backed leather seat ... convulsing. Instantly, the doctors and Shade, a paramedic, had him on the floor and were assessing his condition, but this wasn't a medical issue, and both Gem and Tayla knew it.

'Leave him alone.' Tayla's voice shook as badly as Gem's hands.

Thanks to their half-Soulshredder parentage, the sisters could see that Reaver had split wide open along the seam of an invisible scar that ran from his throat to his groin.

Soulshredders possessed the ability to see scars, both physical and emotional, that no one else could. Their species used their ability to expose old wounds, exploit them, make them worse. Gem had spent twenty-six years battling her nature, sometimes unsuccessfully. But her nature also gave her a lot of advantages when it came to her job.

Gem moved in, crouched next to Reaver as he seized, sapphire eyes rolled back in his head. The other docs were still crowded close, and as Tayla joined Gem, she shoved them all aside. Dimly, Gem heard E ask what the hell was going on, but her full attention was on Reaver.

He grabbed Gem's wrist with one hand, squeezing so hard she had to clench her teeth to keep from crying out. 'Someone found . . . her.'

She placed her hand on his chest next to the emotional scar that had come apart as if he'd been unzipped. As a Soulshredder, she could use her power to mend scars as well as make them worse, though her mixed blood diluted her ability, and something this big was way too much for her to handle. Still, she had to try.

'Who, Reaver? What are you talking about?'

He didn't seem to hear, was muttering, mostly incoherently. 'Serena . . . Sentinel . . . exposed . . . *fuck.*'

Gem was confused as hell, but Tayla leaned in, placing her hand next to Gem's. 'Reaver? What about Serena? Do you mean she's charmed?'

Reaver didn't answer, but his convulsions eased into mildly spastic twitches. Something ugly reared up inside Gem, made her want to keep the scar open, to probe harder and deeper. The impulse to dig and cause pain terrified her, and she jerked her hand away, only to have Tayla grab it and put it back.

'This is important,' Tay growled, her own Soulshredder instinct surfacing. 'We need to learn more.'

Gem took a deep, ragged breath and demoned up. Ruthlessly, she dug her fingers into his scar and tugged, as Tayla did the same. Reaver screamed, but Gem ignored the sound, got into his face.

'Who is Serena?'

'Kelley . . . ' Reaver groaned, muttering in a language Gem didn't know.

'She's a Marked Sentinel?' Tayla asked, and Reaver froze. Then, suddenly, in a blinding flash of light, he flew across the room as if he'd been knocked senseless by a Gargantua demon and landed in a crumpled heap against the wall.

'Shit.' Eidolon hit the intercom on the wall and called for a stretcher, and in moments, nurses and another doctor had arrived to wheel Reaver into the emergency department. Doctor Shakvhan went with him, leaving Gem with Tayla, E, and Shade.

Shade was pacing the length of the room, fists clenching reflexively. 'Someone want to explain what the hell just happened? Anyone else feel that weird vibe right before Reaver turned into Seizure Boy?'

'I did. Freaked me out. I can still feel it.' Tayla rubbed her arms, as if she were suddenly cold, and Eidolon tucked her protectively against his chest.

Pain and a sense of longing bubbled up through an old wound. Gem was happy her sister had found love, but she couldn't snip the thread of jealousy that had woven its way into her heart after Kynan had left her ten months ago – just when they'd finally found their way to each other.

'Me too.' Gem cleared her throat of the bitterness that lingered in her voice. It wasn't Tayla's fault Gem had lost the love of her life. 'Something is stirring in the underworld.'

'I don't like it,' Eidolon murmured. 'This could be bad.'

'Or,' Shade said, crossing his arms over his broad chest, 'it could be nothing.'

'Right,' Eidolon said wryly. 'Because Reaver often collapses into seizures and speaks in tongues.'

Tayla broke away from Eidolon. 'Reaver said something I think could be important. For Wraith.'

E and Shade went taut, and Gem tugged on one of her black-and-pink braids. 'The Marked Sentinel thing?' When Tayla didn't answer, Gem put a hand on her sister's arm. 'Tay?'

Tayla nodded. 'There are stories – rumors, really – in the Aegis ... about humans charmed by angels. No one knows why, or if it's even true, but the stories say that these humans are invincible. Immortal.'

'How does that help Wraith?' Shade asked.

Tayla hesitated until Shade cleared his throat. She shot him an annoyed glare before speaking. 'According to legend, Marked Sentinels can give up their charm to someone else.' She shuffled her feet, clearly uncomfortable sharing intimate Aegis secrets even with her own brother-in-law. 'If we can find this Serena Kelley, Wraith might have a shot at survival. All he has to do is take her virginity.'

THREE

It took less than a day for Gem and Tayla to track down Serena Kelley, but their discovery came at a high cost. They'd had to consult a Darquethoth shaman, who had, after casting a seek spell, taken a strong interest in the human. Too strong. Eidolon had a feeling that the shaman would gladly reveal the charmed human's location to the highest bidder.

Wraith needed to get to Serena immediately, because not only was his life at stake, but so was the entire hospital's future.

But before Eidolon unloaded all the details on his brother, he was going to have a little chat with Reaver, who had recovered from his ordeal and was about to be released.

E entered Reaver's hospital room, where the dripping wet angel had just stepped out of the shower.

'We need to talk about Serena Kelley.'

Eidolon swore Reaver's hands shook before he clenched them into fists at his sides. 'Who?'

'The charmed human you told us about yesterday. We think she may be the cure for Wraith—'

In the span of a heartbeat, Reaver's fist was wrapped in Eidolon's scrub shirt and he'd been yanked into the fallen angel's face. 'Keep Wraith away from her.' Reaver's voice was a low, dangerous growl, but the writing on the walls – a ward against violence – hadn't begun to pulse, so he didn't intend harm.

Shade entered the room, black brows raised at Reaver's nudity. 'Am I interrupting a private moment?'

Eidolon met Reaver's heated gaze with a glacial one of his own. 'I suggest you release me,' he said coolly. 'Now.'

Reaver uttered a curse and stepped off. 'Eidolon, you can't let this happen.'

'Wraith will die.'

'I'm sorry for that,' Reaver said, pulling on a pair of scrub pants, 'but he got himself into this mess. Serena is innocent.'

'He's not going to hurt her. He's going to have sex with her. And you know he can't rape her if she's protected by the charm, so she'll be going into it willingly.' Eidolon was bluffing, performing a little exploratory surgery with the fallen angel. What information Tayla had gotten from The Aegis about charmed humans was mostly speculation, but so far, it seemed as though her information was dead on.

Reaver jammed both hands through his golden hair, kept them there as though he was trying to hold his head on. 'Why her? Why not one of the other half-dozen charmed humans?'

'There are only six of them?' When Reaver didn't answer, Eidolon shrugged. 'You gave us her name. Gem and Tay consulted a shaman who performed a locator spell. She lit up like a cheap beer sign.'

'Dammit,' Reaver breathed. 'The cloak that keeps all charmed humans invisible to demon eyes has been broken. It's what caused my ... condition. Someone must intend to use her for great evil.' Before Eidolon could ask more, Reaver shook his head. 'You've got to forget about Serena. Wraith can't touch her.'

The persistent headache E had been suffering for days kicked up a notch on the pain scale. 'That's not your call.'

'Don't do it. I mean it, E. She needs the charm.'

'Why?'

'Because,' Reaver said, his voice as cold as a grave, 'the charm is all that's keeping her alive. If she loses it, she'll die.'

ᘐ

Reaver watched the expression on Eidolon's face fall. Shade just looked pissed. As usual.

'What the hell do you mean, she'll die?' Shade demanded. 'Does that happen to all charmed humans who give up their charm?'

Reaver didn't want to answer any of their questions, didn't want to talk about something so sacred, and he really wanted to kick his own ass for spilling his guts about Marked Sentinels at all. The existence of charmed humans had been a carefully guarded secret for thousands of years, and if it got out . . . Reaver's stomach turned over violently.

'Answer the question.' E was all cool Justice Dealer calm, which was deceptive; the guy could go from sub-zero to scorch in a heart-beat. He'd been raised by the Judicia, demons who meted out justice, and his icy, detached disposition only made him that much more lethal, because he was rarely swayed by emotion.

'Serena is a unique case.' Reaver's voice was guttural, the instinct to protect the charmed human something he couldn't sup-press even though he was no longer worthy of doing so. Technically, no angel could interfere in a Sentinel's life – not directly. That job fell to their human Aegis Guardian.

He rubbed his temples, considering how much to reveal. He couldn't do anything about whoever broke her cloak, but if he wanted to save her from Wraith, Reaver would do well to appeal to his brothers' medical sides, the parts of them that saved lives.

'Serena's mother, Patrice, was the keeper of the charm until Serena was seven, and Patrice gave it up to her.'

Shade interrupted. 'Wait. Patrice had to have been a virgin, right? So Serena was adopted?'

'Patrice was a virgin,' Reaver said, 'but she was Serena's biolog-ical mother. She was impregnated through in vitro fertilization.'

Eidolon propped his hip on the sink and watched Reaver with the intensity of a hawk. 'How do you know this?'

'When there are only a handful of charmed humans in the world, you know everything about them,' he said, though it wasn't entirely true.

'And why was she gifted?'

'It doesn't matter.' Reaver was telling the demons far too much as it was. Eidolon and Shade were about as decent as demons could be, but if Reaver had any hope of getting back into Heaven, he didn't want to blow it by handing over vital information to demons. Consorting with demons, working in a demon hospital ... he was walking a fine line as it was.

'What matters is that shortly after Serena was born, a Mara demon somehow learned the truth about Patrice. He bit Patrice's parents ... and Serena.'

Being bitten by a Mara was bad news. Each one carried a unique disease within its body, to be spread through a bite, and only that demon possessed the antidote to its individual disease.

'He wanted the charm in exchange for the cure. Patrice had a terrible choice to make, and she chose to kill the demon. As a result, her parents suffered for months before they died. Serena spent years in and out of hospitals, and doctors could do nothing. Just before her seventh birthday, her time ran out.' Reaver's voice was scraped raw after being dragged down memory lane. 'When it became clear Serena was going to die and no cure could be found, Patrice passed her charm to Serena in order to keep her alive—'

'How?' Shade interrupted. 'I thought sex was the key.'

'Serena was a special case,' Reaver said shortly. The truth, that the transfer never should have happened, was something he didn't care to discuss.

Or think about.

Shade took the hint and steered the conversation in a new direction. 'So what happened after Serena got the charm?'

'Her health improved instantly, but if she loses her charm, the disease will progress. She'll die in a matter of days. Hours, maybe.'

'Oh, fuck,' Shade muttered. 'We can't tell Wraith.'

Eidolon's dark brows shot up. 'He needs to know.'

'If he knows, he might not take her charm.'

Reaver stared. 'Are we talking about the same Wraith who screws and eats everyone he meets?'

'Wraith won't kill human females.'

'That's a character flaw I didn't see coming,' Reaver muttered.

'If it makes you feel any better, he does make exceptions for female Aegi,' Shade said, and turned to E. 'She's just a human, so I don't know what your deal is.'

'Your own mate is human.'

'*Was* human. She's cured of that now.'

Reaver rolled his eyes. It was a stupid argument; werewolves, both born and turned, had human souls, and were therefore technically human. Vampires were, as well, though the fate of their souls was more complicated than that of humans, weres, and shifters.

'Find another way to cure Wraith,' Reaver said, 'because I won't allow this to happen.' It was a bluff; under no circumstances were angels, especially fallen ones, allowed to interfere in a Marked Sentinel's life.

Then again, he'd done it before when he'd facilitated the transfer of the charm from Patrice to Serena.

And he'd paid dearly.

Shade got right up in Reaver's face. 'You interfere, and I'll make you sorry.'

'You can't kill me, incubus.'

'I sure as hell can try. And if I fail, I can still drag your sorry ass down to Sheoul for a little eternal fun.'

Sweat dampened Reaver's temples. Right now Reaver was stuck between realms, tossed out of Heaven but not completely ruined. A fallen angel who stayed in the human world still had a chance of getting back into Heaven, but one who entered Sheoul was lost forever.

'Shade.' Eidolon clamped down on Shade's thick biceps. 'Back off. This isn't helping anything. Wraith will do the right thing.'

Wraith? Do the right thing? Reaver couldn't believe that had come out of Eidolon's mouth.

Reaver willed his heart rate to slow down so he could hear through the roar of blood in his ears. He didn't care about Wraith's survival, or even Serena's, no matter how much he liked her. Because this wasn't truly about her life or death.

Every Marked Sentinel was charmed for a reason. Every one of them was in possession of an object vital to the well-being of humanity.

And what Serena held was the most important of all.

Shade hung his head. 'We tell him. Gods help us, we tell him.'

ᘏ

Darkness closed in on Serena as quickly as the demons surrounding her. Four of them, ugly toadlike creatures that came no higher than her waist, had ambushed her when she'd stopped the car at the mailbox outside Valeriu's mansion's main gate.

Yesterday she'd depleted her entire savings to pay a sorceress to repair her cloak, but clearly, the word was out.

She still hadn't told Val. There was no reason to at this point, and besides, he was already on edge, because an alarm had been sounded within The Aegis, of which Val was a high-ranking, card-carrying member.

According to Val, The Aegis was gearing up for what they thought might be a demon incursion. Demon sightings by the general human population were on the rise, skirmishes between demons and The Aegis were taking place much more frequently, and they were taking heavy losses.

In an effort to combat the growing threat, the demon-fighting organization had lowered their standards for recruitment, put former

Guardians on alert for recall, and were deploying current members on research and reconnaissance missions.

Serena was itching to help, had been hoping Val would send her on her own assignment, and if the text message she'd gotten from him telling her to get home immediately was any indication, her itch might just get scratched.

After she got away from these demons, anyway. Their creepy, overly wide mouths gaped open, rows of sharp teeth disappearing far down their throats. A tremor of excitement shot through her, because she rarely got to handle things like this. Her specialty was treasure hunting, and normally her only challenges consisted of layers of dust, poisonous insects, and the occasional booby trap of either the physical or magical variety.

She supposed she should be cautious – after all, if her cloak had failed, maybe her charm could too, but she didn't think so.

There's a way around every charm, spell, and curse. Val's constantly uttered words, spoken with a Romanian accent, rang in her head. The guy was seriously paranoid.

One of the demons hissed and leaped for her. She nailed it in the face with her purse, and it tumbled backward, bowling over two others. Whirling, she opened the Land Rover's driver-side door, whacking a demon as it came at her. She jammed the SUV into gear and drove over the things, squashing them like bugs.

Though she'd never killed a demon before, Val had assured her that they disintegrated aboveground, and sure enough, as she idled in the driveway and watched through the rear window, they shriveled up and disappeared, leaving greasy stains on the road.

She was so not telling Val about this.

Her phone beeped. Val again. Stepping on it, she sped up the drive. She parked at the guest quarters, where she'd lived for the last six years, and jogged to the main house. She found Val and his son, David, in the lavish library, which was lined with shelves of books about archaeology, anthropology, world history, and demonology. Val might be an Elder, a high-ranking member of The Aegis, but he'd also been an archaeology professor for years, one of the few who specialized in paranormal archaeology and demon artifacts.

Neither man bothered with a hello. Val didn't even look away from his computer. 'Where have you been?' He waved his hand. 'Never mind. You're here now. I'm sending you to Egypt. You leave tonight.'

'But I thought you wanted to finish research on the Philae project before we went.'

'Actually,' Val said with a sly smile, 'I believe I may have found something.'

A thousand questions formed on her lips, tangling together until only one slipped out in a tentative whisper. 'The Temple of Hathor?'

'Yes.'

'And the other artifact? The coin?'

'Alexandria. The catacombs of Kom El-Shuqafa – the Hall of Caracalla, specifically.'

'Oh, my God.' Her fingers trembled as she tugged her amulet back and forth on its gold chain. 'Of course.'

This was amazing news. The two artifacts he'd been seeking were of historical importance, but more than that, Val was certain they would be critical in a battle between good and evil. A battle The Aegis believed was brewing at this very moment.

The artifacts, an ancient Gnostic tablet and a bronze coin, were, by themselves, capable of powerful protection against evil. But together they could strike a critical blow to demonkind.

'Can you be ready to go in two hours?'

'No problem.' She moved to the wet bar in the corner and scooped ice into a highball glass. 'I can't wait. I love Alexandria.'

'Yes,' Val said, reaching out to run his finger over the intricate designs etched into the bracelet she'd stolen from the vampire the night before. 'I know. But there's no time for sightseeing. You'll get in and get out as fast as you can.'

She froze as she tipped the bottle of bourbon toward her glass. 'Alone? You aren't coming with me?'

'Unfortunately, no. The Sigil has called all Elders together. David and I will leave for Berlin tomorrow night.'

David, a handsome, thirty-four-year-old version of Val, with his dark hair and eyes, finally looked up from the map he was studying. 'No one to hold your hand on this one.'

He was teasing – he often gave her a hard time about Val's constant hovering, but he was right; this *was* highly unusual. Val rarely let her go on trips longer than a night without him. Her safety wasn't an issue; he was more concerned about the possibility that some man would sweep her off her feet, and she'd finally give in to her desire for a relationship that included all the normal things, like sex. Lots of sex, if she had anything to say about it. God, her body was a powder keg ready to blow, and Val knew it.

He was like an overprotective father with a shotgun.

In many ways, she was glad for that. She'd grown up without a father, without a male influence at all.

After her mother died, she'd been raised in a convent, educated by nuns who had hoped she'd become a nun as well. But Serena had been too adventurous, had desired travel and excitement, and she'd left the good sisters to follow in her mother's footsteps and become a female Indiana Jones.

She smiled at that, because she'd done the Indiana Jones thing, all right, but not in the way she'd expected.

Eighteen years old and hungry for life, she'd gone to college, her days filled with archaeology and anthropology courses. Which were bo-ring with a capital B. It had taken only a year of working part-time in the archaeology department and falling asleep in class to realize that becoming an archaeologist might not be the right career for her. Too much research, too few ancient curses and speeding bullets.

And that was when Val had stepped in.

He'd been an assistant professor of anthropology at Yale University, and had, in fact, been the reason she'd chosen the college. She'd remembered him as the Guardian who had watched over her mother until she died, and who had visited Serena occasionally as she was growing up.

He'd encouraged her love of archaeology, from the moment she demonstrated an uncanny ability to find pretty much anything anyone lost, and then later during college, when he took a few select students on a field trip to a historical Revolutionary War battlefield.

A gut feeling had led her away from the group, to a forested area just beyond the battleground. There near the remnants of a stone fence and three feet under the soil, she'd discovered a shoebox-sized chest containing a few coins, a pipe, and a letter detailing a heinous betrayal by the leader of the Americans. A leader who had gone down in history as a hero, but if the letter could be authenticated, history would be turned on its ear.

That very day, Val had offered her a position with his private archaeological contracting company, a place to live in one of the two guest houses adjoining his mansion-slash-museum, and pretty much squat for pay. Not that the pay truly mattered – she wanted for nothing, in part because Val paid for the essentials, and in part because he kept her so busy traveling that she didn't have a lot of spare time.

He'd left the university right after that – solely so he could keep an eye on her, which he still did with annoying frequency.

So yes, she had everything – a great life and the career of her dreams. She had almost everything she wanted and no fears save two: years of illness and time spent in hospitals had given her an irrational fear of death – irrational because as long as she was charmed, she couldn't die. Well, she couldn't die unless she fell victim to her other fear – that she would someday give in to her desire for a relationship.

Right now she was strong, but she was terrified of the day she met the man of her dreams, because as strong as she was, she was also curious and hungry, and temptation was an evil mistress.

'I'm assuming all my travel, hotels, and entrance into the catacombs have been arranged?'

Val pushed a file on his desk at her. 'It's all here. An ex-Guardian named Josh Nichols will meet you in Alexandria to give you an item you may need to gain access to the chamber I believe holds the coin.'

Setting aside her drink, she picked up the folder and thumbed through it. 'Does he know about me? What I am?'

'No.'

Very few humans did. As far as she knew, only a handful of the twelve Aegis Elders, including Val and David, knew. 'What am I supposed to tell him?'

'You don't need to tell him anything. He's used to people borrowing the artifact, which we think is a key of sorts.'

She raised her eyebrows. 'Why would people borrow it?'

'It's been in his family for centuries, but no one knows precisely what it does. Only that it has been associated with the catacombs, and whenever a new section is excavated, his artifact becomes an object of interest.'

'And now that you know the location of the coin, you think his artifact is significant?'

'Exactly.'

'Okay, then. I'll get going.' Giddy, because this might be the find of a lifetime, Serena headed for the door.

'Serena.' Val's voice stopped her in her tracks, and when she turned, his dark gaze sent a chill of foreboding up her spine. 'Be very careful.'

'Always,' she lied.

'You can't be too careful,' he said. 'Don't ever forget that, Sere. Never.'

FOUR

The worst thing about dying slowly wasn't the dying part. It was the fact that the poison the assassin used had all but killed Wraith's libido.

He used to require sex a dozen times a day. Since last week when he'd awakened from the drugged stupor his brothers had put him in, he'd been lucky to feel a stir every couple of days.

Yep, dying sucked. Dying slowly sucked, anyway. He'd made a few valiant attempts to accelerate things a bit since he'd escaped the hospital without his brothers' knowledge, had put himself in some seriously shit situations in demon pubs, had antagonized entire nests of vampires just for fun, and had interrupted a Nightlash demon hunt – never a good idea to get between a dozen Nightlashes and their meal. The battles had been exhilarating, brief, and bloody. Wraith had been outnumbered but never outclassed, and he'd limped away from every one of the fights.

Whether or not he'd truly won was the question.

E had been calling several times a day, calls that Wraith had ignored, though he had gone into UG last night and what he had seen there shocked him.

The hospital had been severely understaffed. As he'd stood in the emergency department, a section of the ceiling had collapsed. Every demon he'd come across seemed agitated; rumor had it that an army was starting to gather in the outer reaches of Sheoul, but no one could confirm it. Besides, a demon army was always gathering somewhere, each time some territorial warlord started something up with another.

Wraith didn't bother knocking on E's door. He opened up and immediately Tayla's ferret Mickey scampered down the hall, his tiny nails clicking on the hardwood floor. The critter climbed Wraith's jeans-clad leg and waist until he was happily tucked in the crook of Wraith's right arm.

'Hey, buddy,' Wraith murmured. 'Where's my brother?'

He headed for E's office, nodded at Tayla and Gem, who were baking something chocolate in the kitchen, but who looked pretty damned grim as they stood there with tall glasses of orange juice in their hands. Their Soulshredder species was tropical, and they required large amounts of vitamin C, especially if they were stressed out.

Wraith wondered how many gallons they'd already gone through this morning. Hell, Gem had been downing the stuff like vodka ever since Kynan had quit the hospital and gone back to the military. Whatever. The guy was decent – he'd volunteered his rein to Wraith a time or two – but when it came down to it, Wraith could kill Kynan as easily as he could look at him.

'Eidolon's in the den with Shade,' Tay said, and *oh, great* ... this was a family get-together. Must be really bad.

Cursing to himself, because he really didn't need this shit, he stepped into E's study, where Shade was lounging on the leather sofa with E's dog Mange at his feet. Eidolon sat at his desk, nose buried in a medical text. He looked up as Wraith closed the door, and for the first time since telling Wraith he was going to die, E didn't look at him with sorrow in his dark eyes.

'What's up?' Wraith said, taking a seat. Mickey chattered

indignantly and scrambled onto his T-shirted shoulder, then draped himself around Wraith's neck like a fur stole.

'I think we've found a way to save your life.'

Wraith's pulse went double-time, but he forced himself to stay level. What E had just said sounded great, but there was still a serious set to his mouth, so something wasn't all blood and fun here. 'Lay it on me.'

'You're going to have to steal a charm from someone.'

'A charm? Like a dangly little bracelet thing?'

'Not exactly,' Shade said. 'This charm is a divine blessing that makes the recipient immune to harm. You'll have to take it from the owner.'

Wraith narrowed his eyes at Shade. 'Something tells me that stealing this charm won't be as easy as getting up an *Orgesu*'s skirt.'

'Depends on how you look at it.' Shade shifted on the couch, his leather pants squeaking on the cushions. 'I mean, it involves sex.'

'Well, then, things are looking up. So what's the challenge?'

Shade exchanged glances with Eidolon before saying, 'Ah, well . . . you'll have to seduce the owner. The charm can only be transferred through sex. Willing sex. Obviously, if she's charmed, she can't be forced.'

'Seduction isn't a problem.' Hell, no. Females came to him willingly. At least, they had until he'd gone through *s'genesis* and gained the facial markings that flashed warnings to all demon things female. Now he had to resort to trickery to get laid.

If he were like every other mature Seminus demon on the planet, the deception wouldn't bother him. *Thanks for the human DNA, mommy dearest.* The human part of him hated being unable to have sex in his true form, hated having to resort to tricks to get a female to lay with him. The demon part of him required it.

'Hold up.' Wraith had been petting Mickey, but now he froze, his hand hovering over the weasel's spine. 'There's a catch, isn't there? There's always a catch.'

E nodded. Stalled. Finally blurted, 'She's human.'

Wraith rocked backward, earning a sharp scold from Mickey. 'No.'

'Wraith—'

'I said, no!' He swore, robustly, in several languages. 'What kind of fucked-up charm-release spell requires sex?' Unless ... *oh, shit.* 'She's a virgin, isn't she? Damn it to Hades, she's a fucking virgin.' E said nothing, which was confirmation enough. Wraith shoved to his feet. 'Not only no, but *fuck* no. In fact, let me count the ways I can say no.' He started to tick off his fingers, but Shade stood, slowly, as if he was afraid sudden movement would make Wraith bolt.

'Bro. Chill. It's no big deal. Once it's done, you'll be charmed, and the Seminus Council won't be able to punish you. Even if they could, it's not that bad.'

'Not that bad? It took E a full day to recover after he popped that hippie chick's cherry.'

Deflowering humans was forbidden for most species of demons, and E had accidentally taken a woman's virginity nearly fifty years ago. Guardian angels were serious tattletales, and E had been forced to endure a severe flaying by Seminus Council members.

Wraith's reluctance to take a virgin had little to do with the punishment, and both his brothers knew it. 'I swore I would never screw a human again, let alone a virgin—'

'I know,' E interrupted. 'But this is life or death.'

Flashes of the past blinked in his head, the years he'd spent in a cage, held there by his own evil mother. Innocent female humans had been stripped and tossed into his cage after their virginity had been taken – brutally – by the vampires who had brought them to him. Vamps, since they were technically human, weren't subject to the can't-deflower-virgins rule. So they'd gotten off on waiting until Wraith was nearly mad with lust, and then they'd raped the females in front of him, tossed them in the cage, and sat back to watch and wait.

Even now, eighty years later, he still broke out in a cold sweat when he thought about it. Going through the *s'genesis* was supposed to have made him forget. Not care. No such luck.

'Who is this chick? Why is she charmed?' Wraith paced, trying desperately to outrace his nervous energy. 'And how did you find her?'

E closed the book he'd been reading. 'Long story. But between Gem, Reaver, and Tayla's Aegis connections, we were able to get a bead on Serena.'

Mickey nuzzled Wraith's ear, as though trying to comfort him. 'I wouldn't think information like that would be available to Aegis grunts.'

'Tay isn't exactly a grunt.' E leaned back in his desk chair, looking annoyed.

No, Tayla was definitely more than a grunt. She headed up the New York City cell of slayers, and since taking command, the demon body count had gone down, and so had demon-on-human violence. A fragile truce had been declared between the New York cell and peaceful demons, which left the slayers more time to concentrate on taking out the harmful species. In addition, the friendly demons were more willing to give up intel. The symbiotic relationship had worked well so far, but with the unrest in the demon underworld lately, Guardian-demon relations were once again on shaky ground.

Wraith rubbed his palm over his face. 'I don't like this. I need to think about it.'

'You don't have time,' E said. 'And there's something else you need to know.' He trailed his finger along the gold-embossed spine of the book in front of him. 'She was bitten by a Mara before she was charmed. After you take her, the disease will progress rapidly, and she'll die.'

Wraith paused mid-step. '*What?*' He looked at Shade. Then E. Then Shade again. 'This is such bullshit. I'm not doing this.'

'You have to—'

'No!'

E stood, knocking his chair into the wall and startling Mange to his feet. 'Then you doom the hospital.'

'What the fuck are you talking about?'

Eidolon planted his fists on the desk and leaned forward, nailing Wraith to the wall with the intensity of his gaze. 'We built it with our blood, sweat, and tears.'

Literally. When the foundation had been laid, each of them had given up one of the elements in order to make the hospital strong, enchanted, and undetectable to humans. Wraith had given his blood. E, tears. Shade, sweat.

'Yeah, and?'

Shade scrubbed a hand over his face. 'I can't believe we didn't see this coming.'

'See what?' Wraith snapped, at the end of his patience.

'Our life forces are bound to the hospital,' E said softly. 'You're dying. . . .'

Ah, fuck. Wraith exhaled slowly. 'So the hospital is dying. That's why strange shit is happening there.'

'Yeah.'

Nausea rolled through him. 'Is that also why it's running half-staffed?'

E shook his head. 'Whatever is shaking up the underworld is shaking up the staff. They aren't showing up for shifts. Quitting. They're terrified. Things are a mess. And, oddly enough, it all coincides with the charmed human's appearance on the scene.'

'Dammit,' Wraith breathed. He might not give a crap about much, but the hospital had given him a purpose in life, at a time when he'd been directionless and self-destructive. Not that he wasn't those things now, but he'd mellowed a lot. He was probably still alive only because of his brothers and the hospital.

More important, it meant the world to E and Shade. More than anything except their mates and Shade's offspring. Wraith might not give a shit about his own life, but he couldn't let the hospital die just because he didn't want to bang and kill a human.

He was really a piss-poor excuse for a demon.

It was time to let that particular childhood trauma go. If he didn't, his mother would win. She'd wanted him dead from the moment he was born, thanks to the horror his father had inflicted on her. Not that Wraith could blame her – she'd been a human on the verge of turning into a vampire when his father had raped her, then kept her just this side of alive with the same gift Shade possessed. For nine months he'd kept her in a horrible stasis, raping and abusing her until she gave birth.

Not surprisingly, she'd gone insane. His father had taken off after he was born, as all unmated Seminus demons did – although usually they abandoned the female immediately after sex and conception.

His mother had completed her transformation into a vampire, becoming vicious as well as insane, and had taken out her anger on Wraith. He'd fought to live, and though he'd done some incredibly stupid things to get himself killed as an adult, something deep inside always kept fighting.

So fuck it. He was going to live. He was going to find the charmed human, take what he needed, and rock on.

And once he was nicely charmed and invincible, he was going to start taking out vampires in a way he'd wanted to do since he'd broken free of his cage. Starting with the Vamp Council.

Oh, yeah. Let the good times roll.

Wraith's plan to find and seduce the human woman hit a roadblock right away.

The fancy shmancy New Haven mansion where she lived was warded against demons.

For hours, Wraith was forced to lurk in the woods that hugged the expansive and well-tended grounds, but when a middle-aged man came out, loaded his Mercedes with luggage, and climbed behind the wheel, Wraith struck.

He tore across the paved drive and slipped into the back seat.

'What the—' The man's breath cut off as Wraith's arm went around his neck. The guy flailed, landing a blow on Wraith's chin before Wraith wrenched his head between his palms. A second later, Wraith was using his Seminus gift to get inside the dude's mind and do a little probing.

The man, Valeriu, possessed some impressive mental blocks that hindered Wraith, but not for long. Soon, he learned that Serena had left for Egypt the night before, and that she was supposed to collect some sort of key from a man named Josh in ... shit, an hour.

Quickly, Wraith filled Valeriu's head with new memories, ones that would cover up the fact that he'd been attacked on his own grounds. Once he was done, he put the guy to sleep, so although Valeriu might wonder why he'd fallen asleep behind the wheel, he wouldn't remember.

Wraith slipped out of the car and sprinted to the nearest Harrowgate. He had to get to that Josh guy. Now he knew that the key to the treasure Serena was hunting was also the key to her.

ൾ

Serena had always liked Egypt, and Alexandria was her favorite of all Egyptian cities. Known as The Pearl of the Mediterranean, it boasted beautiful residential districts, elegant gardens, and a Mediterranean, rather than Middle Eastern, atmosphere.

She'd spent the day trying to locate the first of the two objects she'd come for in an ancient vault beneath the city. Just as the sun began to set, she found it. Its resting place, anyway. Unfortunately, Kom El-Shuqafa's visiting hours forced her to give up for the day. Val had managed to finagle special access to off-limits areas of the catacombs, but apparently visiting hours were not negotiable.

Besides, if Val was right, she'd need a key to access the vault, and she was already late to meet Josh at her hotel.

She caught a cab, but as usual traffic was a tangle of cars, donkey carts, bikes, and pedestrians. The narrow streets, minor accidents, and non-functioning traffic lights made for extremely slow progress. Ancient Egyptians could have built an entire pyramid in the time it took her taxi to go a single block.

Fed up, starving, and a nervous wreck after watching several pedestrians nearly get run over, she scrambled out of the cab several blocks from her hotel, figuring she could walk faster than the cab could get her there.

Dressed conservatively in tan cargoes and a long-sleeved, white cotton blouse, she didn't draw much attention, although her blond hair and blue eyes screamed 'foreigner.' No woman should walk alone on these streets, but Serena was safer than if she'd been traveling with an entire army of guards.

The uneven, cracked sidewalks posed no problem for her as she walked, caressed by a light breeze off the harbor. All around, shopkeepers and restaurant owners hawked their goods, which ranged from clothing to fresh vegetables to roast pigeon that scented the air with spice as Serena passed.

Ahead, a man approached, his flowing brown dishdasha flapping around his ankles, his white, bucketlike taqiya cap soaking up the evening shadows and the pale lights from the nearby buildings. He walked with his head down, but when he stepped in front of Serena his head came up, and she drew in a startled breath. The man was beautiful. So beautiful it hurt to look at him. He radiated a glow as fierce as the sun's reflection off the gold dome of the mosque of Sultan Omar Ali Saifuddin, and his features were so perfect he could have been drawn with a camel-hair brush.

'Serena.'

She didn't stop to think how he knew her name, because his musically lilted voice had mesmerized her. She didn't recognize the accent, but it sounded familiar in an ancient sort of way.

'Yes,' she breathed, and his lips curved in a smile that turned her brain to mush.

He cast a furtive glance around them, and it was then that she noticed the normally bustling street was deserted. Her self-preservation and survival instincts were rusty from disuse, but now they stirred, as though awakening from a deep, dark sleep. The sensation was strange, but she recognized it for what it was – danger.

Still, she wasn't afraid. Nothing could touch her. Even so, she automatically brushed her fingers over the pendant beneath her blouse. It was a stupid habit, but one she couldn't break any more than she could break the enchanted chain from which it hung. Oddly, the necklace felt hot against her skin.

'Hey.'

Another deep male voice came from behind her, and she turned to the newcomer, a man casually dressed in faded jeans and a Guinness T-shirt, with a backpack draped over his shoulder. He was tall, close to six and a half feet, with blond hair that fell nearly to his shoulders and a tattoo that extended from the fingers of his right arm all the way up to his face, where the swirling black pattern stretched from his jawline to his temple.

It struck her that *this* man was the source of the danger vibes. She could feel it in the way her body flushed with warmth, the way her skin tingled, the way her pulse leaped.

'Y-yes?' *Dolt.* Not only had she stammered, but she'd sounded all breathless, like a Renfield meeting her first vampire.

The dishdasha guy turned to the other man. 'Leave us.' His commanding tone made her jump, but the T-shirted guy merely held up his hands.

'Hey, dude, I'm supposed to be here. What's your deal?'

She eyed the blond. 'Josh?'

'Yup. I was just heading to the hotel to meet you.' He gave Dishdasha a pointed look, and wow, Val could have mentioned that his buddy was movie-star hot and bore the physical confidence of a freaking Navy SEAL. 'This asshole bothering you?'

'Uh . . . ' Yet another intelligent response. God, she was lame.

The air seemed to shimmer with aggression, and there was that danger sensation again, making her skin tingle and her heart race. Something was going on here, but what, she didn't know. All she knew was that two impossibly gorgeous men were staring each other down like rival tomcats, and she was in the middle of it all.

Something primal and feminine in her got excited, overriding her brain, which screamed that there was no way anything so abnormal could be good. After a long, tense moment, the man wearing the dishdasha bowed his head and turned to Serena.

'My name is Byzam al-Majid. Val sent me to assist you in your search.'

Josh snorted. 'You gonna to buy that? Because this guy has scam written all over his strangely smooth forehead.'

The situation was weird; she couldn't deny that, and she knew damned good and well that if Val was going to send someone other than Josh, he would have contacted her.

Smiling politely, she clutched her knapsack closer to her body. 'I don't mean to be rude, Mr. al-Majid, but you understand that I'll need to contact Val about this.'

'Of course.' He bowed and backed away. 'I'll be in touch.'

She felt a strange sense of relief as he melted away into the night . . . until she realized she was now alone with the other man, the one who emanated erotic strength and fierce sensuality.

Swallowing, she looked up as he towered over her, one corner of his lush mouth tilted in the cockiest grin she'd ever seen. She dropped her gaze to broad shoulders that tested the limits of his tee's elasticity, let herself admire his deep chest and narrow waist, made for a woman to wrap her legs around.

Val had said Josh was an ex-Guardian, and she could imagine him making the most of his warrior build to battle demons and satisfy a woman's needs in bed.

He wasn't wearing a wedding ring. . . .

Normally she'd take the opportunity to flirt, to let her wild side have a little fun. But just standing next to him brought the sensation of danger flaring to life within her. She had no doubt that he was dangerous in a lethal, animal way . . . and that the true menace was to everything that made her a woman. Especially her virginity.

Oh, yes, this man was scary, in more ways than she could count, or probably imagine.

FIVE

Wraith allowed himself a moment to revel in his victory but he didn't get cocky. This wasn't over yet. Still, the evidence of Serena's attraction surrounded him: a faint, musky aroma of arousal mixed with her own clean, vanilla-almond scent. Oh, yeah, she wanted him.

So much for not getting cocky. But hey, were-leopards couldn't change their spots, right?

Shadows had swallowed up Byzam – what a bullshit name – but Wraith kept his eyes peeled. 'We should go before he comes back. Something about him wasn't right.'

Serena narrowed her gaze at him, but her tone was teasing when she said, 'How do I know you're any safer?'

Winking, he turned on the charm. 'You don't.'

'Well, at least you're honest.'

'Not nearly as often as I should be.'

She cocked a blond eyebrow. 'Good to know. I'll keep my guard up, even if you are a friend of Val's and an ex-Guardian.'

Guardian. Yeah, that had been an interesting revelation. He'd had to leave Val too quickly to extract much detail from his mind, but once he got to Josh in his hotel room, he'd spent a little extra time learning what the guy's deal was. Then he'd made Josh believe he'd already met with Serena and needed to head home. Hopefully, the real Josh was already checked out of the hotel and on a plane bound for Italy.

Serena would be all his.

Wraith's eyes went to the V of her blouse, which was buttoned too conservatively for his taste, and then down, to her tiny waist that flared into hips she probably thought were too wide but which excited both the primal male and the horny incubus in him. Her body was made to buffer a male's lust, and for carrying his offspring.

The former would happen, the latter would not. He could sense fertility in any female, and Serena wasn't ovulating. Besides, no self-respecting Seminus impregnated a human. Offspring born of other demon species would be purebred Seminus demons; those born to human women would be half-breeds, and of no use when it came to carrying on the Seminus breed.

Wraith reluctantly dragged his gaze back up to her face and tried to forget she was human. 'Honey, as hot as you are, you shouldn't trust any man.'

Her easy laughter cut through the cool night, and through his gut. He liked the soft, feminine sound in a way that left him feeling vulnerable . . . and *that* he didn't like.

'You're smooth,' she said. 'I'll give you that. Something tells me you leave a trail of broken hearts in your wake.'

He crossed his fingers over his own heart. 'I promise not to leave any on the way to the hotel.'

She snorted and started down the sidewalk. 'Gee, thanks, Josh.'

'My friends call me Wraith.'

She grimaced. 'Wraith? That's a horrible nickname. I'll call you Josh.'

Great. Just great. Bad enough that he had to pretend to be nice. Now he had to do it while being called *Josh*.

Wraith stayed cocked and ready as they hoofed it toward the

hotel. He wasn't sure what was up with the creepy Byzam dude, but he knew without a doubt that the male wasn't human. Which meant he was up to no good. Maybe he was after Serena's charm, maybe he'd learned why she was in Egypt and wanted whatever she was after. Either way, his presence was a thorn in Wraith's side. The last thing he needed was interference.

Wraith's gaze returned to Serena's lithe, graceful body. Her breasts were smaller than he liked, but when it came down to it, he didn't have to like her. He was after one thing. Still, he'd be stuck with her for a few hours at least, so he might as well observe. And it wasn't as if she was hard on the eyes. Far from it.

She was short, maybe five-feet-five, with wavy blond hair she'd pulled into a high ponytail that stuck through the hole in her beige baseball cap. Long eyelashes framed big brown eyes shot through with gold. High cheekbones added definition to a slightly rounded face, and her generous mouth tipped crookedly to the right when she smiled.

'Are you staying at my hotel?' she asked as they halted at the corner of a busy street. He loved the natural, sultry rasp in her voice that made everything sound as if she'd added 'in bed' to the end of every sentence.

'Yup. Flew in this afternoon. I'm already checked in.'

'You live in Italy, right?' She had to yell over the sound of a honking horn.

He nodded, recalling what he'd extracted from Josh's mind, and said, 'I'm originally from Ohio, but I've been in Perugia for the last six months.' He had no idea why Josh had moved there, so he hoped she didn't ask.

'I love Italy.' *In bed.* Her smile grew dreamy, and he really wished she wouldn't do that, because it made him want to kiss her.

Which was crazy, because he'd never kissed a female before, not in his hundred years of life. But suddenly he wanted to put his mouth on Serena's and see what all the fuss was about.

She watched him, her eyes glittering with curiosity, and he

wondered if she felt the static crackle of awareness between them. When her gaze slid to his mouth and she swayed, he knew she did.

In an almost dreamlike state, he drew closer to her. His vampire senses picked up her sweet scent, the sound of her pulse rate increasing. His own went erratic and off the charts as he leaned in. Anticipation made his skin tingle, but out of nowhere a foul scent like burning flesh hijacked the air.

He started, shaken out of his insanity. Oh, he was going to kiss her – Tayla had given him a damn primer on what human women liked, and she insisted kissing was part of seduction – but pouncing on Serena out in the open was probably not the way to go.

'Do you smell that?' He swung his head around, zeroing in on the odor. There, behind a truck parked on an incline between two closed-up shops . . . eyes. Red, glowing eyes.

'I don't smell anything—'

'Stay here.' He peeled off toward the threat, his body revved for battle, adrenaline pumping hotly through his veins.

The creature behind the truck growled, a chilling sound that made the hair on the back of Wraith's neck stand up. This was a *khnive*, a summoned demon tracker bound by its master to do his bidding until the spell controlling it timed out.

'What is it?'

Wraith paused at Serena's voice. She was right behind him. 'I told you to stay where you were.'

'Last time I looked, you weren't my boss.'

So she was sexy *and* spirited. An admirable yet annoying combination.

'Stay.' He sprinted toward the creature. It screeched and skittered down the street toward a drainage hole. If it escaped, it would report to its master that it had found Serena. 'Oh, no you don't.'

Wraith grabbed the creature, which looked like a mastiff-sized skinned opossum, by its ratlike tail. It wheeled around, snapping razor-sharp teeth.

'Bad monster.' Wraith flipped it with a flick of his wrist. It landed awkwardly on its side with a snap of bone, but the injury didn't stop it. The demon came at him, a drooling, fire-eyed abomination—

A backpack smashed into its face and the *khnive* yelped, rearing backward and clawing at its eye, which had been impaled by a pencil. Serena clobbered the creature again, and it struck out at her with venom-laced claws, but somehow missed despite its close proximity.

Bright lights blinded Wraith. A swerving vehicle bore down on them, its driver apparently drunk, the vehicle's tires bouncing off curbs.

'Serena!' Wraith caught her around the waist and threw them both into an empty vendor's cart. Brakes and tires squealed. The compact car smashed into the truck the *khnive* had been hiding behind, and the creature leaped into the back of the pickup as it rolled forward, gaining momentum on the hill.

Serena tore free of Wraith's grip, darted toward the truck, and vaulted nimbly into the back with the demon.

Unbelievable. The woman had *no* sense of self-preservation. Wraith chased after them, landing next to Serena as she pummeled the thing. With a curse, he darted around behind the demon, wrapped his arm around its neck, and snapped hard. It went limp, sinking to the pickup bed.

The truck hit a bump, catapulting Wraith backward. He grabbed for the roof with one hand, and for Serena with the other. Horns blared, and a busy-ass intersection loomed ahead. Shit. He dove on top of Serena, covering her as chaos exploded around them. The truck T-boned a bus, and then at least two more vehicles smashed into its rear quarter panel and the driver's side door, spinning it wildly into other cars. The sound of metal crunching, glass shattering, and people screaming pierced the veil of smoke and steam that rose up all around them.

'You okay?' He pulled Serena to her feet. Though she looked a little dazed and had lost her cap, she smiled sheepishly.

'I'm fine.' She shook shards of glass out of her hair. 'Stuff like this happens to me a lot.'

'Your dates must love you.' Sirens warbled in the distance. 'Let's get the hell out of here before people start asking questions. Or before a plane lands on you or some shit.'

Keeping hold of her hand, he leaped out of the truck and they both ran, weaving through the tangle of smashed cars and the crowd of people. She kept up easily, her strides quick and graceful, a gazelle in flight. The predator in him wanted to give chase, to take her down to the ground. The male in him wanted to ravage her while she was there.

Right now, the best he could do was keep other predators away.

They didn't slow until they reached the hotel. He pulled her to a stop in front of the door.

'What was that thing?' Serena panted, looking back over her shoulder as though afraid it would come after them, even though it had started to disintegrate before they'd even jumped out of the truck.

'Don't suppose you'd buy that it was a rabid dog?'

'Hardly. I know it was a demon.'

'A tracker.' He watched her closely, wondering how much she was willing to say. 'What do you think it's tracking?'

She lifted her chin and looked him straight in the eye. 'No idea. But thank you for killing it. I'm glad your Aegis skills haven't rusted.'

Well, good. He'd earned her gratitude. Tayla had told him to be nice, but maybe killing things for her would be even better. Not to mention, more in character. And more fun.

Tayla had also said human females liked polite men, so he opened the hotel door, releasing an aromatic breeze of coffee and spicy lamb coming from the restaurant. He entered behind her, and speaking of behinds ... hers was *nice.*

'I could use a drink,' she said, gesturing toward the bar. 'Want to join me for one before we talk business? You have the artifact, right?'

'It's in my room.'

'Excellent.' She gave him a smile that made his insides quiver. Weird. No female had ever made his insides do that. His outsides, yes, but that didn't take much.

Maybe the poison was affecting him in yet another way. Besides the libido-dampening, he'd been intermittently nauseous and dizzy, and sometimes his muscles and organs cramped as they slowly died.

Fun stuff, that mordlair necrotoxin.

'I could definitely use a whiskey.' Which didn't affect Wraith, unless taken through the veins of a human who had imbibed. He eyed Serena's throat. He didn't suck human females, but he'd love to latch on to Serena's long, slender neck and drink his fill, maybe settle between her thighs. . . .

'I could use a few more than *a* drink.'

'My kind of female.' Wraith could really like this chick if he ever allowed himself attachments, which he didn't.

Find an excuse to touch her. Tayla had told him that. She'd said something about how he had to start small. Light, innocent touches.

He was *not* good at light and innocent. Pounce and pillage . . . that was his style.

Cursing to himself, he cocked out his arm in a foreign-feeling gentlemanly gesture to escort her. To his surprise, she hooked her dainty hand around his forearm and allowed him to walk her to the bar, where they were greeted by a middle-aged Egyptian man who wrinkled his nose at Wraith's facial *dermoire.*

Wraith itched to shove the guy's head up his ass, but he kept himself in check and ordered a double whiskey, neat.

'I'll have what he's having,' Serena said, and Wraith felt the slow burn of admiration creeping up on him. He'd expected her to drink something sweet and fruity.

This chick was not what he'd expected, and he wasn't sure if that was a good thing or a bad one.

He put his hand on her knee.

She picked it up and put it back in his lap.

Crash. And. Burn.

As though Wraith didn't exist, Serena braced her elbows on the bar top and played with her napkin, grinning at the bartender when he set her drink down in front of her. *Goddamn.* The sensual glow that radiated from her when she smiled was downright unholy, and he felt an erotic surge rise up like a tide in his veins. And in his jeans.

He despised that reaction to humans. It made him feel dirty, and he ruthlessly tamped down his urges, even though those urges were what were going to win him the prize.

He'd planned to meet her, whisk her someplace private, take her, and be done with it without ever having to exchange names. He was a freaking incubus, after all. Effortless sex was what he did. No female had ever resisted him. It figured that the one he needed to not resist him would be the one he would have to work at seducing.

This situation had been poorly planned on his part, which was unacceptable. He usually spent weeks, if not months, researching his missions, his prizes, his targets. It wasn't that he liked research, but better to know every detail than to spend too much time chasing his tail when he could be chasing some female's tail. He liked a quick in and out. Smash and grab.

Serena was not going to be a quick in and out, though there *would* be some of that.

'I wouldn't have taken you for liking the hard stuff,' he commented as the bartender slid his glass toward him.

She downed her whiskey like a shot and pushed her glass at the bartender for a refill. 'Love the burn.'

Burn. Yeah. Because that's what she was doing to him right now.

'You probably think that's pretty unladylike, don't you?'

He shook his head, which had begun pounding at the temples. The poison again. 'I think it makes you pretty damned hot.'

'Well, aren't you a charmer.' She frowned. 'Are you okay?'

'Fine.' He hooked his foot through one of his backpack straps and tugged it closer to the leg of his stool. His meds were in there, and he wanted to keep them close. 'Slight headache.'

'That thing didn't hurt you, did it?' She put her hand on the side of his head, running her fingers through his hair. His scalp tingled and his body coiled and he hissed in a breath. She jerked her fingers away. 'Sorry. Didn't mean to hurt you.'

'It's okay.' His voice was humiliatingly hoarse. 'I have aspirin.'

She nodded at his lame response and trailed her finger along the rim of her refilled glass, circling it almost lovingly. 'So, when do you head home, Josh?'

Josh. Man, he wasn't going to survive this. Wraith downed his drink, welcoming the smoky bite and the burn, just like she did. He signaled for more whiskey.

'Whenever I feel like it. I decided to make a vacation out of this trip. One of those one hundred and one things to do before you die.'

She slammed another shot, and a railroad spike of lust hammered into his groin. 'So you've never been here then?'

'I've been here.' Hundreds of times, actually. Egypt was a treasure trove of useful artifacts for Eidolon's magic collection. 'But always for work, never for . . . pleasure.'

'Ah. What kind of work do you do?'

Here was where he needed to play his cards right. Too much information might make her suspicious, especially if it didn't jibe with what she'd been told about the 'real' Josh. But he needed to tantalize her, reel her in with common interests.

'My brothers and I run a medical center that uses nontraditional cures to treat patients, and I'm in charge of collections.'

'Collections? As in, getting people to pay?'

'Collections, as in assembling the ingredients and mystical objects the doctors sometimes use in the cures.'

'Your medical center sounds very new age.'

'You might say that.' He leaned back on his stool and stretched his legs, letting his calves 'accidentally' brush hers. Her heat shot straight to his dick. 'And what brings you to Egypt? Obviously, something to do with the artifact I brought.'

Serena practically bounced in her seat. 'Val didn't tell you?'

'He just told me you needed the key. I'm guessing you're searching for something in the catacombs?'

'Possibly.'

Wraith watched her over the rim of his glass. 'So evasive,' he murmured as he put the glass down. 'Why?'

'Well . . . ' She braced her forearms on the bar top, leaned in, and lowered her voice with dramatic, conspiratorial flair. 'I don't know if I should be telling the competition what the prize is. I wouldn't want you taking it from under me.'

Oh, he'd be taking the prize, from under her or from on top. Either would work for him. 'No worries. I'm on vacation, and if I don't get paid, I don't do the work.' He shot her a stern look. 'And why are you traipsing around Egypt by yourself? That's dangerous, you know. As tonight should have proved.'

'Isn't that the pot calling the kettle black?'

He shrugged. 'I can take care of myself.'

'And you think I can't?'

He grinned, enjoying playing clueless when he knew damned good and well that, thanks to her charm, she could take care of herself. 'Does Val know you have demons after you?'

Her eyes flared. 'They aren't after me—'

'Bullshit. I saw how the *khnive* watched you. Why is that?'

'I have no idea.'

'Then I think Val should know,' he said. 'He'd be pissed if he knew you were in danger.'

'You can't tell him!'

Her panic gave him the opening he needed. 'Then I have a proposal. You let me tag along on your little treasure hunt, and I'll keep my trap shut.'

'Absolutely not.'

He took a swig of whiskey. 'I guess you don't want the key that badly.'

Angry red splotches put color in her cheeks. 'That's blackmail.'

'Yep.'

'Why?'

'I'm intrigued,' he said, and it wasn't a lie. 'It's not often I find someone who does the same job I do. I mean, you've got the stuffy archaeologist types, but they do everything so slowly. So carefully.' He took her glass from her, took her fingers in his, and studied her fingernails. Short, square, strong. Not manicured, and kept in the perfect condition to be functional instead of pretty. 'But you don't do slow and careful, do you? You like the hunt. The chase. You like to jump in. Use your hands. You crave the rush. The *burn*.' His own adrenaline pumped through him at the mere thought of the rush of the hunt and chase, whether it be for blood, sex, or an ancient artifact.

A slow flush worked its way up from her neck to her scalp, and yeah, she was getting excited too. Aroused. He waited for her denial, but she surprised him by leaning in aggressively, mischief dancing in her chocolate eyes.

'You're wrong about one thing,' she purred.

He angled inward so their faces were only inches apart. 'And what's that?'

'I don't *like* it,' she said, her voice breathy and husky and bed-me-baby hot. 'I *love* it.'

His eyes were riveted on her, his heart pounding hard. 'Then it looks like we have even more in common than I thought.'

Taking her hand out of his, she sat back and studied him, seeming far more composed than he was. 'I still don't get why you want to do this.'

'Like I said, I'm free with my schedule. And why wouldn't I want to hang out with someone I find so interesting? Not to mention beautiful.' Gods, he might as well be reading poetry to her, as foreign as his flattery was sounding. Foreign, but not insincere.

Something passed over her face, an emotion he couldn't name. 'Look,' she sighed, 'I should warn you now that I'm not available. Romantically.'

'That's okay. Neither am I.'

Her brows rose. 'You're married?'

'Nope.'

'Girlfriend?'

'Uh-uh.'

'Boyfriend?'

He shuddered. Any Seminus who had a thing for males would be in a lot of trouble, since they could only orgasm with a female, and if they didn't get that release daily – several times daily – they would die.

'Not even close.'

'Then what?' She grimaced. 'Or is that something I shouldn't ask?'

'Depends. I'll tell you why if you'll tell me why.' He knew, but he wanted to see how she explained herself to men, wanted to get a read on how she felt about being celibate. As for his excuse, he couldn't very well tell the truth, that his goal for the last eighty years had been to go through *s'genesis* so he could be as recklessly free with females as possible, with no ties he cared about and no worries other than where he was going to find his next fuck.

That hadn't turned out so well.

He just prayed that this turned out better.

SIX

The bartender made himself scarce in that way they instinctively did when customers sank deep into conversation. Serena sat there in silence, wondering how much she should tell Josh. She had, after all, asked him to explain the rationale behind his romantic unavailability, so it was only fair that she should share her own motives. But she'd always kept the virgin thing to herself, figuring it was nobody's business but hers.

Guys who knew she was a virgin either viewed her as a challenge or they figured she was nothing but a tease, and they had a tendency to get real pissy.

Only once had she let herself believe she could have a workable relationship, had thought she could handle intimacy without intercourse. That had been a disaster.

Matthew had been a senior in college and working part time for Val while finishing up his archaeology degree. They'd grown close over months of working together, and she'd insisted that they could have a romantic relationship without sex. For a while, they'd done well, a normal couple who went to dinner and picnics, movies and hikes in the woods. They held hands, hugged. Kissed.

But eventually, she'd wanted more. The touching turned to hot groping sessions in which they both gave as good as they got, but something had been missing, and one night after a Christmas party when they'd both been drunk, she'd nearly given in to the desire to make love.

It had been a wake-up call for her, especially when he'd started talking marriage. How was she supposed to explain the fact that even after marriage she'd have to remain celibate?

'Serena? You don't have to talk about this if you don't want to.'

Josh swirled the whiskey in his glass, and she shook herself out of the past, which was one of the most unpleasant places she could be.

'Right. No, um ... it's okay. I just feel sort of silly telling people this.'

'Telling people what?'

'I'm celibate,' she blurted.

There. She'd said it. She tossed back her drink.

'And?'

'You're not going to ask why?'

'Does it matter? I said I wanted to join you in your treasure hunt. Not get into your pants.' He winked. 'Though I won't lie and say that I won't fantasize about it.'

The idea that he might have her naked in his head made her wildly hot. But that didn't change the fact that his mind was the only place he could see her naked. 'Why should I believe that you're on the up-and-up?'

'Why wouldn't I be?' he asked, and she must have been wearing her skeptical face, because he snorted. 'Hey, if I was on the hunt for a piece of ass, I'd be prowling some loud, obnoxious bar in Rome, not strolling around Alexandria, Egypt. Right?'

She blinked at his candor. 'I suppose.'

'So, you'll let me tag along?'

He stared at her with his piercing blue eyes, the light of victory already dancing in them. He thought her acceptance was a given, and God, it was tempting. Especially if he was serious about ratting her out to Val. But she wasn't one to cave in to blackmail or smooth lines no matter how drop-dead gorgeous a guy was.

'I don't think so,' she said. 'I work better by myself.'

The utter shock on his face nearly made her laugh. He was a man not used to rejection, and he had to be smarting.

She glanced at her watch, felt a stirring of disappointment that it was so late, because between the demon, the multi-vehicle pileup, and the banter with Josh, tonight had been rather enjoyable. 'I should be going. I have an early morning ahead of me.'

'At least let me try to convince you on the way to your room.' He pushed smoothly to his feet, a panther uncoiling from rest. He held out a hand, and for a ridiculously long moment, she hesitated.

'You're very serious about wanting to go with me, aren't you?' She finally took his hand and allowed him to help her to her feet.

He looked at her, the intensity in his expression so overwhelming that she took a step back, but he tightened his grip and brought her against his hard body. 'When I say I'm going to do something, I do it.' His thumb skimmed over her fingers in lazy strokes, making her breath hitch, making her hyperaware of the contact between them. 'And when I want something, I get it.'

Oh ... God. The dark, seductive tone in his voice reached deep inside her and just grabbed at her womb. And wow, his eyes said, 'I'll take you to bed and take you to Heaven.'

'You're very sure of yourself, aren't you?'

'When you can't be sure of anything else in this crapped-on world, you have to be sure of yourself.' He let go of her hand but only to touch her shoulder in a move that was innocent, but still stirred her dangerously. 'Let's go.'

The walk to the elevator seemed to take forever. Serena was acutely aware of Josh's presence, his light touch, the hot brush of his jeans against her leg when he bumped up against her. By the time they reached the elevator, her mind was so scrambled that she actually had to concentrate in order to remember her room number.

The moment the doors closed Serena wished they'd taken the stairs. The tiny, enclosed space seemed to magnify the erotic energy pulsing off him, until the entire car was charged and her skin was tingling. As Josh's fingers drifted over her shoulder in a lazy up-and-down motion, the very air became thick with sensual awareness. She might be a virgin, but she wasn't naive or innocent, and she recognized sexual tension when she saw it . . . and felt it.

He waited for her to exit before he joined her, his long strides bringing him alongside her in half a dozen steps. A secret, wicked part of her wished he'd walk ahead of her so she could watch that extremely nice rear, encased in well-worn jeans.

'Your steps are very light,' she said, stupidly and for lack of anything else to say, but it was true. He moved like a cat on the prowl.

'I'm a hunter,' he said simply, and then he came to a sudden halt in the deserted hallway.

Startled, Serena froze. The last time he'd done this, a demon had been stalking her. 'What's wrong?'

He was looking at the floor, hair falling forward so she couldn't see his expression.

'Josh?'

He lifted his head, and a predatory gleam sparked in his eyes. 'I want to kiss you. I'm *going* to kiss you.'

When I say I'm going to do something, I do it.

The unexpected declaration made Serena's mouth drop open, but not a single sound came out even as he moved toward her. Her feet remained frozen in place, even though her pulse pounded and her mind screamed at her to run in some sort of fight-or-flight response. But neither was going to happen, because she couldn't flee, and neither could she fight.

His hands came down on her shoulders, his grip firm and unyielding as he pushed her back against the wall. 'You want this, don't you?'

She wanted to say no, but that would be a lie. She'd never wanted anything more, which, at the moment, made this man the most dangerous person on the planet. 'Yes.'

His smile was pure male triumph as he took his hands from her shoulders and braced them high above her head so he was caging her in but not touching her. She had to tilt her head back to look at him, and she wondered if she looked the way she felt, like a mouse trapped by a cat.

Slowly, he leaned in, sinking to his forearms against the wall. He was close, so close she could feel the heat radiating from him, could hear the soft intakes of each breath even over the pounding of her pulse in her ears.

His mouth descended. Her knees shook, and thank God she was propped against the wall, because she felt like she could fall over at any moment. Panic wrapped around her chest like a steel band, and no, she couldn't do this. Something told her she'd never be the same—

His lips claimed hers, not gently. Ravenously. Unapologetically. As if he did this all the time, and she supposed he did.

'Open for me.' His voice, a husky, resonant command, had her obeying without a second thought, and in an instant, he took what he wanted. His tongue slipped inside her mouth to stroke her teeth, the roof of her mouth, and then it slid against her tongue in a fierce, wet caress.

Her body ached, arching without her consent as though seeking his, but he still didn't touch her – the only physical contact between them was where their mouths connected. He was seducing her with nothing more than his tongue, giving her a taste of what she was missing in her life.

God, she wanted more. Right here, right now.

Even so, she found herself murmuring against his lips, 'I can't do this. . . .'

Josh pulled back slightly. Too far, yet not nearly far enough. 'I'm scaring you,' he whispered. 'But you aren't afraid of *me*. You're afraid what I'm doing will lead to more.' He let his lips brush hers, barely, but with such passion that she gasped. 'Don't worry, Serena. If I wanted more right this moment, you'd know. My hands would be sliding up under your shirt so I could caress your breasts. I'd pinch your nipples, just a little, until they peaked so I could swipe my tongue over them.'

Oh, yes. Her body sagged, but he caught it with his, pressing up against her and pinning her to the wall.

'I wouldn't stop there.' His lips skimmed her ear. A shiver went through her, and heat licked between her legs. 'I'd drop one hand to your waist, but I don't know if I could be patient enough to unbutton your pants, or if I'd just rip them open. Either way, I'd get in. I'd find that sweet place between your legs with my fingers, and I'd play until we were both panting. You'd be wet and ready for me when I dropped to my knees and replaced my hand with my mouth.'

She made a noise, something between a squeak and a moan as she pictured everything he was saying. No one had ever spoken to her like this, and the thrill shot straight to her core, which was going wet for him just as he'd said.

'Please . . . ' She trailed off, unsure if she was begging for him to stop talking like that or to continue, because her mind had gone fuzzy and her body had gone liquid. But it was time to turn the tables.

Hooking her leg around his calf, she tugged while pushing against his chest. The unexpected movement caught him off guard, and she spun him around, easily putting his back into the wall – though she got the impression that he could have stopped her if he'd wanted to. His breathing was steady and even, while she was struggling for each breath. She'd almost think he was completely unaffected by the searing sexual tension between them, but his gaze was sleepy, heavy-lidded, and when she dropped her eyes, she saw the impressive evidence of his arousal behind the fly of his jeans.

'Look,' she croaked, 'this has to stop. You might have stepped out of the pages of *Playgirl*, but I can resist even you—'

Josh drew her hard against him and kissed her again, a possessive, yet gentle meeting of lips that once again left her breathless and reeling. He thrust his muscular thigh between hers. His hands dropped to her hips, and he held her steady as he rocked his leg against her.

The pressure was incredible, and she knew without a doubt that she could come like this. Easily. Maybe she should. The pleasure streaking upward from her core was overwhelming, and she was arching into him all by herself now, taking what she wanted . . .

He ended it. He broke off the kiss and just watched her with that damned cocky lift to his mouth. 'What was that about resistance?'

Unquenched desire and irritation at both his arrogance and her own weakness tangled up into a knot of fury.

'Give me the key,' she snapped.

He waggled his brows. 'Come to my room and get it.'

'What part of celibate are you unclear on? I will not change my mind. I will never change my mind.' She stepped back so she didn't have to crane her neck to look at him. 'Don't think you can blackmail me into sleeping with you for the key, because I promise you it won't happen.'

'I know it won't happen,' he said, taking her hand and bringing it to his lips, where he nipped the pad of her finger. 'But we can do other things. And I want to do other things. Make no mistake about that. As far as the artifact is concerned, you want it, you let me tag along.'

Outraged by his manipulation, she jerked her hand away. 'Fine. You can come with me. But the rest? You couldn't handle *other things* with me. Guy like you, settling for heavy petting? *Please.*'

It was the wrong thing to say, because the erotic light in his eyes became something hotter and more intense . . . the light of challenge, of battle.

She'd just thrown down the gauntlet, and suddenly she was afraid that of the two of them, she'd be the one to break.

ꩮ

As Wraith watched Serena flee down the hall, his body buzzed like he'd eaten a junkie, only this was way better. This was like the really good shit running through a Wall Street executive or a Hollywood star's veins. So, yeah, better . . . and worse. Because he wasn't going to be able to satisfy his body's needs. Not yet. What he'd assumed would be a smash and grab with Serena was turning out to be anything but. Although she sure as hell seemed to be affected by the incubus fuck-me pheromones that came standard-issue in his species, he had a feeling the poison was affecting their potency. Which sucked.

On the other hand, the toxin was also allowing him to get turned on without feeling the irreversible, driving need to have sex or suffer, which was always a concern for his breed. Seminus demons couldn't relieve their lust by their own hand, and once they were aroused, their lust had to be slaked, or they'd suffer intense agony or even death.

Gods, she had fire. Fire and fight and she might very well be his match in every way. But his life was on the line, and he was going to fight until he won. Her resolve was strong, but with the Grim Reaper – or one of his *griminions* – on his heels, Wraith's resolve was just as strong. And right now, he had to make sure she believed he could be with her because he wanted to be with *her*, not because he wanted to pop her cherry.

Still, it was becoming clear that being sweet and charming wasn't going to work, not only because it just wasn't him, but because she didn't believe he was a choir boy. He'd have to be himself as much as possible if he wanted to have a shot in hell of seducing her.

He just had to get through this without letting himself get attached, which shouldn't be a problem. The ability to care about anyone or anything had been tortured out of him long ago.

Sure, he'd reluctantly admit to caring for his brothers, and his mates-in-law weren't total wenches. And then there was Gem, who was pretty cool for being half human, but to say he actually cared about her . . . that would be an exaggeration.

He continued to watch Serena as she let herself into her room. Wraith had no idea what was going through her head, but he knew what was pinging around in his. He'd enjoyed that kiss, and he wanted to kiss her again. He tried to tell himself the desire to do so came from necessity, the need to seduce her, but if that was true, why did his breath come a little faster and hotter in his throat when she turned to glare at him one last time?

He held her gaze, and even across the distance she got the message, the flare of her eyes giving her away as she caught his silent declaration of intent. Tomorrow, she was his.

௵

The Feast Moon was out tonight. The new moon always brought out the crazies of the underworld. The deaths. It would be even worse now that Army intel had determined that a battle was coming, a confrontation between good and evil that threatened every human life on the planet.

Kynan Morgan had always been sensitive to the tides of the night, and the vibration in his blood told him this was going to be a bad one. His stomach churned as he stepped out of his car in Underworld General's underground parking lot, knowing the ER would soon fill up.

He missed the rush of treating trauma patients, of working while hopped up on adrenaline to save a life, and not for the first time he wondered why he'd spent the last ten months in an Army facility getting poked and prodded when he could have been back with The Aegis, battling demons and then patching up Guardians.

Or he could have been back here, working in a demon hospital to save their lives.

Either way, he was no longer conflicted by his loyalties to humans and demons. He was working both sides, because neither was wholly good or bad, and he'd discovered that the good on both sides wanted the same thing: peace.

He threaded his way through the vehicles, stopping short as Gem exited the hospital through the sliding doors. His heart did a flip and settled into a rapid-fire machine gun rhythm.

She was even more beautiful than he'd remembered. She'd changed her hair – still black and falling to her shoulder blades, but she'd replaced the blue streaks with a hot pink that suited her.

She walked toward her red Mustang, keys twirling on her finger. He'd planned to find her after he spoke with Eidolon, but what the hell. He opened his mouth to call out to her, but snapped it shut when a huge male approached her. Where had he come from? His short, dark hair reminded him of Eidolon, and his head-to-toe black leather, including gloves, brought Shade to mind. The deadly aura was pure Wraith.

He couldn't hear what they were saying, but Gem smiled, her teeth flashing white against the contrast of her black lipstick. He'd kissed that mouth, had wanted to do a lot more before they were interrupted in her apartment by the U.S. Army's paranormal unit, the Ranger-X Regiment. They'd barely given him a chance to say good-bye.

That had been nearly a year ago. Last week he decided he'd had enough. The R-XR had determined that he was descended from a fallen angel, and they were pretty sure he was part of a prophecy, but they'd stalled out.

And he born of man and angel shall die in the face of evil and may yet bear the burden of Heaven . . .

What a bunch of bullshit. Was it too much to ask that a prophecy actually make sense?

He'd left the R-XR with two goals: getting Gem back, and being reinstated as a Regent in The Aegis.

The Aegis thing hadn't gone well – they hadn't been happy that he'd walked away from the organization after his wife died, and worse, he'd left The Aegis to work in a demon hospital. But with trouble looming – not to mention his distant fallen-angel relative and link to a prophecy – they'd been willing to give him another chance.

If he'd use his demon connections to find out all he could about what was brewing in the underworld.

Basically, they wanted him to spy for them.

So no, The Aegis thing hadn't gone as smoothly as he'd have liked. But there was still hope with Gem.

He started toward her, stumbled to a halt when the guy took her hand and led her to his Hummer.

Feeling as if he'd been run over by a tank, he watched helplessly as the asshole held the door open for her, his hand brushing casually over her butt as though it had been an accident. *Accident, my ass.* She actually grinned at him. *Grinned.*

Tell her not to wait. The message he'd given Runa to relay to Gem came roaring back. When the R-XR had taken him, he hadn't known when, or if, he would return, and he'd wanted Gem to be happy.

Maybe not *that* happy.

The urge to pound Mr. Gropey Hands into a pulp even Eidolon couldn't heal made him twitch. And wouldn't that just impress the hell out of Gem. *Hey, babe, I want you so bad I'll kill anyone who comes near you, even though I cut you free.*

Yep, he could say 'Restraining Order.'

With a nasty curse, he watched Gem ride off with the guy who was, no doubt, a demon. The gate leading to the aboveground parking garage flashed open, and the Hummer had to pull aside for one of UG's black ambulances to come through, its lights flashing.

Things were about to get chaotic. Kynan would come back tomorrow to talk to the Sem boys, Tayla, and Gem. Gem, especially, because this wasn't over, not by a long shot.

SEVEN

The sound of knocking woke Serena at three a.m. Groggy, she climbed out of bed and stumbled to the door. A sense of foreboding shivered across her flesh. She knew she shouldn't open up, but for some reason she couldn't stop herself.

Josh filled the doorway, his facial tattoo shifting like waves on lake water, eyes glowing gold, and it struck her that she wasn't awake. This was a dream. A dream where the sexiest man she'd ever seen, the sexiest man she'd ever kissed, was staring at her as if he was a lion and she was an antelope. Her first thought was that, like an antelope, she should run for her life. Her second thought was that she wanted to get caught.

'You're mine,' he said, his voice rumbling through her in a muscle-deep caress.

It didn't occur to her to argue. Not when this was something she'd waited for all her life, had hoped for, had daydreamed about . . . and now it was coming true. Well, it was coming true in her dream, which was the only safe place for it to happen.

Still, as he approached, she wrapped her arms around herself and backed up, realizing too late that he was herding her.

Toward the bed.

'Josh—'

'Wraith. In your dreams, you will call me Wraith.' He stripped off his T-shirt, and oh, yes, she'd call him anything he wanted as long as he kept undressing. His chest was smooth, the thick pads of muscle rolling beneath tan skin. And his abs, dear Lord, his abs . . . his eight-pack could be cut from fine Egyptian granite.

The backs of her knees hit the bed, and she sat down awkwardly. When she looked down at herself, she sucked air. Gone were her shorts and tank top. Instead, she wore a sexy black and crimson teddy, garters with black stockings, and no panties. She tried to cover up, but Josh – Wraith – whatever – tumbled her back on the bed and raised her hands above her head.

'Never hide your body from me. I want to look at you.' He brushed his lips across hers and kissed a trail down her neck. 'You're so beautiful. You taste so sweet.'

She trembled, felt the bed shaking beneath her as his fingers stroked her hip.

'Don't be afraid,' Wraith murmured against her skin. 'I'll be gentle.'

Gentle? No. She'd waited too long for this. Suddenly, her trepidation melted away, because this wasn't real, no matter how lifelike it all seemed. This was her chance to take what she'd been denied, and it might be the only opportunity she had.

Wriggling, she worked her legs from where he'd pinned them with his, until he was nestled against her, the hard ridge of his arousal rubbing her core. 'Do it now. Please. I want to do it before I wake up.'

His head came up, his eyes still glowing magnificent gold. 'Don't worry about that. We can take all the time we want.' His fingers found the hem of her teddy and slowly pushed it up. 'And I definitely want.'

She jerked one hand out of his grip and brought it down to his waistband. 'This is *my* dream,' she growled, 'and I want it now.' She emphasized her words by tearing open his fly, and he hissed when her fingertips brushed the head of his erection.

'You're a greedy little thing, aren't you?' His voice was husky with appreciation as he cupped her breast. 'Let's see just how greedy you are … oh, yeah.' His fingers found her nipples tight and sensitive, ready for attention.

Her entire body arched upward, seeking his touch. Smiling wickedly, he focused on her breasts, and suddenly the top was gone, leaving her bare-chested and open to his hungry gaze.

'I'm so going to suck on those,' he whispered. 'Maybe nibble … bite … '

'Yes.' She writhed beneath him, needing him to do what he was describing.

His mouth came down on her throat instead, and she shuddered at the scrape of teeth over her skin. Slowly, he dragged his mouth lower, sometimes nipping, sometimes licking. Desire scorched her, easing only when he finally took one nipple between his lips.

But the sweet relief was temporary. His tongue flicked over the hard nub as his mouth drew deeply and his hands caressed and massaged both breasts. Her breath left her, leaving her gasping for air and bucking beneath him. God, if this wasn't a dream she'd be humiliated by the way she'd clenched one of his thick thighs between hers and was pumping against him, on the verge of orgasm already.

She clung to his massive shoulders, and when she dug her nails into his skin he let out an erotic, encouraging growl. 'That's it,' he murmured against her breast. 'Take what you want.' He shifted his hips and let his hand drift down, flattening over her abdomen and then dipping between her legs. '*Oh, damn* … you're wet. So fucking wet.'

His fingers slid back and forth through her cleft, and on each upstroke, he gently rolled her clit between his fingertips, bringing her to the edge each time.

He was cruel. Skilled. Devious. She wanted it all and then some.

Still working her breasts with his tongue, he pushed a finger inside her, and they both groaned. He began a slow, steady rhythm with his hand, working the ring of her entrance with his finger, working tight circles around her clit with his thumb. He brought his lips to her ear and nipped her lobe gently. 'Do you like to be touched like this?'

Her hips bucked, and she had to bite her lip to keep from crying out. 'Yes,' she said. 'Oh, yes.'

'Good. I want to touch you a lot more.'

She thrashed wildly, wanting more but unable to voice her desire because she was caught in a maelstrom of pleasure so intense she couldn't speak. Could barely breathe.

'That's it. Let go, Serena.' He added another finger and slid them in and out, faster, but his thumb stopped circling. He applied steady, vibrating pressure to exactly the right spot, and commanded her, 'Let go *now.*'

She did, with a scream he captured with his mouth. Colors exploded behind her eyes as she shattered. Before she even came down, he ripped open his fly the rest of the way and entered her hard. She knew there should be pain, not just because of her hymen but because he was huge, and not gentle. But this was a dream, a perfect, wonderful dream that felt so real she wondered if she'd be sore in the morning.

She grasped his shoulders, soft skin stretched tight over steely muscle, and clenched her thighs around his waist, taking him deep and making the ache inside throb.

'You still don't want slow and gentle?'

'No. Please . . . just *move.*' This felt so good, so right, and when he began to pump his hips, the aftershocks from the first orgasm turned into the forewarnings of a second one.

'Ah . . . fuck.' His head fell back, the tendons in his neck straining, his mouth open in male ecstasy, his canines elongated into fangs.

Fangs?

He dropped his head forward again, eyes focused like gold lasers on her. 'I'm a vampire, Serena.' He thrust into her so forcefully she banged her head on the headboard, but she didn't care. She was lost to sensation, pleasure, wonder, and wow – he was a vampire. How cool was that?

'Will you bite me? I mean ... are you going to?' *Please say yes.*

'Hell, yeah. I want to take you inside me, like you've taken me inside you.' He licked her neck in a brief, wet stroke. 'Does that scare you?'

Unease flickered in her belly, because it didn't scare her, and what did *that* say about her? 'No,' she moaned, 'it doesn't.'

He nuzzled her throat where he'd tasted her. 'Did you know some vampires can orgasm if their teeth are stroked? Would you do that? Run your fingers up and down my fangs until I came?'

'Yes ... ' She wanted to touch them, lick them ... but he didn't give her the chance. In an instant, he was at her throat, his fangs cutting into her flesh. There was no pain, only the most amazing pleasure as he began to suck.

Her orgasm tore through her, a stinging pleasure so intense it nearly hurt. He joined her, his body convulsing, his mouth pulling until she felt dizzy. But it was a good dizzy, and as his weight settled on top of her, she couldn't imagine not knowing this kind of bliss again.

'I don't want this dream to end,' she whispered, as she sifted her fingers through his hair.

She felt the warm caress of his tongue over the bite, and then he lifted his head and peered at her through sad blue eyes. 'I don't, either.'

He seemed surprised at his own admission, and then he was gone, and she was alone.

She was awake. This time, she was really awake. She sat up in bed, slapped a shaking hand over her neck. There was no pain. No wound. But her body tingled and her sex throbbed with the sensation of a recent release. Could women have wet dreams? Obviously, because that had been the most intense, realistic dream she'd ever had, and she was definitely wet.

Wet, and now, more than ever, craving the one thing she could never have.

൭

The floor beneath Wraith fell away. Groaning, he dropped to his knees in front of Serena's hotel room door. He kept one hand braced on it for support, but that didn't help the fact that he could barely suck air into his lungs, his fangs pulsed, and his dick was so hard it might break.

Breathe, motherfucker. Breathe.

Pain rocketed from his throbbing balls into his groin, and he doubled over, waited for the agony to pass. This was the dark side of his ability to get inside someone's head and make them think anything he wanted them to. The Seminus gift was intended to be used on females in order to make them receptive to sex, and it worked . . . but he was supposed to actually be in the same room with them so he could get out of their heads and into their bodies to make the imagined sex a reality.

But he'd fallen victim to his own gift, something that had never happened before. He'd been so into the dream sex he'd planted in Serena's mind that he'd not only finished it in her dream, but he'd revealed his vampire self. And asking her if she'd fangjerk him? He couldn't come like that any more than he could with a handjob.

Has to be the poison. Making him sick. Weak.

He ached. He throbbed. He was jonesing so hard for sex that he was a danger to both himself and any female who might be unlucky enough to walk down the hall. At this point, he had two choices: He could hunt down a female or he could stumble back to his room and inject himself with the libido-relieving drug Eidolon had developed to keep Wraith level while he was on this mission. Eidolon had tested the drug on himself, and though it hadn't worked on him, he'd been certain that in Wraith's weakened condition it should suffice.

It had to. Eidolon had suspected that in order to seduce Serena,

Wraith would have to get both her and himself worked up multiple times, and it would look suspicious if he kept having to excuse himself to find a female to screw.

Wraith had figured he'd have Serena in bed before debilitating pain became an issue, but he'd seriously underestimated her willingness to hang on to her virginity.

And the charm.

And her life.

Head spinning, he lurched to his feet and somehow made it to his room at the end of the hall. Once inside, he dug through his backpack to the nylon med kit E had stuffed full of a variety of pill bottles and pre-filled syringes full of medications to help relieve the pain and nausea he experienced as the poison ate away at his organs – and his life.

He found the bottle of the libido drug, drew two ccs with a shaking hand, and jabbed himself in the thigh. Almost instantly, the maddening desire to find a female melted away, though he really could go a round with one. The images of being inside Serena kept playing through his mind in agonizingly slow motion, every detail as real as if it had been a true memory. He could smell her, taste her, feel her.

He'd never, ever wanted to bed a human before. Not like this. They'd been forced on him, and he'd nearly taken one – Kynan's wife, no less – during a fit of bloodlust, but he'd never actually allowed himself to be attracted to one. How could he, after what he'd been forced to endure … after what he'd been forced to do to them. There were too many memories gnawing away at him, too many nightmares lurking in his sleep.

He tossed the syringe into the trash and stumbled to the bathroom for a glass of water. When he looked into the mirror and saw his reflection, he dropped the glass, shattering it on the counter.

His personal symbol, the hourglass, had changed. Oh, it was still an hourglass, still inverted. But more of the sand had drained to the bottom, marking time he didn't have.

EIGHT

'He's crashing!' Gem moved away from her patient's head, where she'd been securing a Sora male's breathing tube, and quickly crunched a set of compressions into his broad chest. 'Page Shade,' she snapped, and Chu-Hua, a Guai nurse who resembled a wild boar on two legs, dove for the intercom.

'It's not working!'

'Shit! Then get him.'

Chu-Hua lumbered off, and Gem cursed under her breath. Things were breaking all over the hospital, always at critical moments – Murphy's Law in action. Wraith had better get into that human's pants, and fast.

'I've got a pulse.' Shawn, a vampire physician assistant, didn't bother to hide the relief in his voice. This Sora was a victim of an Aegis slayer's stang, and no one wanted to see a demon die at the hands of the enemy.

'We need to get him into surgery. That hole in his gut needs to be plugged.' Gem hit the intercom button, remembering too late that it didn't work. 'Anyone know if the OR is ready?'

Chu-Hua stepped into the room. 'I can't find Shade, but Dr. Shakvhan is ready in OR two.'

Within moments, Gem had the patient, whose normally bright red skin had faded to a bleached brick color, wheeled to the operating room. She volunteered to assist, but Shakvhan and Reaver could handle things more expertly there than Gem could. She was better at adrenaline-fueled emergency patch jobs and routine, minor medical procedures than she was at surgery, which required stamina, patience, and a steady hand.

Exhausted, she tossed her bloody gloves and gown and headed back to the emergency department. She'd been working for sixteen hours straight, and still there was no end in sight. The hospital was seriously understaffed, and naturally, the slayers had been extra busy.

The only break she'd had since the underworld had gone nutso was last night, when she'd met an impossibly handsome demon named Lore, and he'd asked her out for coffee. Apparently, he'd been heading into the hospital because he was interested in a medical career, so he'd picked her brain about the hospital, how it got started, the staff . . . anything she cared to share.

Afterward, she'd invited him to Vamp, the Goth club where she liked to hang out, and he'd agreed. They'd spent the evening doing some rather daring dirty dancing, though he'd never taken off his jacket and gloves.

She wondered if he was scarred beneath his clothes, or maybe if he was hiding some demon feature unique to whatever species he belonged, like scales or quills.

Maybe next time she saw him, she'd get him undressed.

It was about time she got over Kynan and got back on the dating horse, and Lore, with his off-the-charts danger-and-sex vibe, might be just the guy to ride.

And this time around with a guy, *she* was calling the shots.

The doors to the ambulance bay slid open, shaking her out of her thoughts. She hoped like hell whoever entered wouldn't be another patient.

'Hey, Gem.' Kynan Morgan walked into the ER like he owned it, halting mere feet away, so close she could smell the leather of his jacket and the natural male spice that made her world tilt, and she had to catch herself on a crash cart.

With spiky dark hair that begged her to run her fingers through it, eyes the color of new denim, and tan skin stretched over perfect, angular features, Kynan was as handsome as ever. Beneath his jeans, black henley, and bomber jacket, he had a lean, powerful athlete's body to freaking die for. She'd seen it back when he used to come into the human hospital where she'd worked, way back when she thought he was nothing more than a married man who took in street kids and put them on the path to a good life.

The truth, that he and his wife had headed a local Aegis cell, hadn't changed her feelings for him. Sure, he'd killed demons for a living, but her heart hadn't cared about that. Especially after his wife died and he quit The Aegis to work at UG. She'd actually believed she had a shot at him.

Fool.

'What are you doing here? When did you get back?' And why did her heart have to jump around like it was excited to see him even after he'd broken it?

She could still remember the day that Runa, whose brother also worked for the R-XR, had invited her to the house she shared with Shade, handed her a margarita, and then said, 'Kynan gave me a message for you. I'm sorry . . . but he said to tell you not to wait for him.'

God, Gem had been devastated. She'd waited anyway, until last night, when Lore had caught her on a particularly bad day. She'd been exhausted, worried about Wraith. To top it off, that morning Runa had brought the babies by the hospital.

Gem was thrilled for Shade and Runa, but their happiness had been like a blow. Kynan was gone, probably for good, and she wasn't sure she'd ever have children. She wanted them, but she was half demon, stuck between two worlds, and she refused to subject any child to what she'd gone through.

'I got back last night,' he said in his gravelly voice, a result of a battlefield injury he'd suffered years ago while serving as an Army medic in Afghanistan.

'So why are you here?' She tried to keep her hopes in check because while she wanted to hear that he'd come back for her, she'd been stomped on hard enough to know she needed to be realistic. Not that realistic was a possibility when his masculine scent swirled around her, embracing her like a lover.

'I can't get into that right now, but we need to talk.'

'I think you said it all with the message you gave to Runa.' She spun on her heel, intending to leave him high and dry like he'd left her.

Which might have been a good plan had he not grabbed her arm and hauled her around.

'Why are you being like this?'

'Why?' she asked, incredulous. '*Why?* Because you broke my heart. A dozen times. And I finally decided I'm tired of being stomped on.'

'I'm just asking for a talk, Gem.'

Of course, *a talk*. He couldn't ask for more than that, could he? No, not Kynan Good Guy Morgan. Mr. Honorable. Though, if she could calm down for a second and be honest with herself, she could admit that much of his honor and purity and just plain *goodness* had been scoured away by the betrayals he'd faced nearly two years ago. He'd gone through a period of darkness, had taken wounds and let them fester.

She knew, because her Soulshredder self had seen them. She'd helped to heal them, though she'd had to be careful, because when she was angry, hurt, or jealous, the wicked desire to exploit weakness and pain grabbed hold of her like a powerfully seductive drug.

And right now, her inner demon wanted out something fierce.

'Sorry, Kynan,' Gem said, 'but you can't just pop back into my life after so much time and expect me to fall at your feet.' She brushed past him and headed for the staff break room, mainly to get away from him. 'I'm over you. Leave me alone.'

The next thing she knew, she was against a wall and he was covering her, his big body pinning her so she could hardly move. He moved between her legs as his mouth came down on hers. She was furious, spitting mad, so why had she grabbed his jacket and tugged him as close as he could get while still being clothed?

He kissed the hell out of her, and when he was finished, they were both panting. 'That,' he said, 'doesn't feel like you're over me.'

'Fuck you,' she breathed.

'Maybe,' came a low, controlled voice that had them both whipping their heads around to Eidolon, 'you could find a private room before the fucking starts?'

Groaning, Gem let her head fall back against the wall. There would be no fucking, but she certainly was fucked.

ꟹ

Busted.

Kynan pushed away from Gem and faced Eidolon. The guy looked like he'd been dragged through a knothole backward, and Kynan wondered what the hell was going on. The hospital appeared to be seriously understaffed, and were those cracks in the walls?

'Hey, E. I need to talk you. Your brothers around? And Tayla?' He glanced at Gem, who was glaring at him. 'You too.'

'Oh, so the fact that you need to talk to me didn't really mean you needed to talk to *me*.'

'We'll talk,' he swore. 'In private. But business first.'

Eidolon gestured for Kynan and Gem to follow him into the break room. Inside, Eidolon and Kynan sank onto the couch, while Gem staked a claim near the coffeepot, which was usually Wraith's territory. 'Where's everyone else?' Ky asked.

E studied the ceiling fan. 'Shade is with Runa. Tay's at work.'

'And Wraith? He out getting into trouble?'

'He's already done that,' E said quietly, and Ky listened in shock as the demon filled him in on the shit that had gone down with Wraith and the hospital.

'Damn.' Ky's voice was strangely raw. There had been a time – right after Ky had witnessed Wraith feeding on Lori – that he'd wanted to kill the demon. Ky had loved his wife, and Lori's betrayal had stung to the bone. But Ky had learned to like Wraith, liked all the brothers in fact, and this had to be hitting them hard.

'Yeah. Then there's always the fun uncertainty of another assassin being after me and Shade. Haven't seen any evidence of it so far, but we're keeping our backs to the wall.' E shoved his hand through his hair. 'So now you're caught up on the latest episode of Underworld General Hospital. What's your deal? Why are you here?'

Gem crossed her arms over her chest and tapped her foot. Her green eyes sparked, but her twin black-and-pink pigtails softened her furious expression.

'You're probably aware that something is happening in the demon world.'

'Aren't you a rocket scientist,' Gem muttered.

Eidolon gave her an exasperated look and turned back to Ky. 'Its come to our attention, yes.'

'Do you know what's going on?'

'Why?'

'The Aegis sent me to find out what I can. Besides Tayla, I'm pretty much the only Aegi with contacts in the demon realm, and Tay can't tell them anything without giving herself away.'

Gem snorted. 'So they expect you to gather intel from demons . . . so they can fight demons?'

Kynan bit back a sigh. 'Come on, Gem. Whatever this is . . . it's going to be bad. We'd rather stop it than fight it.'

'Agreed.' Eidolon kicked his feet up on the coffee table. 'But right now, we don't have much information. Mostly rumors. Some are saying that the Reclamation is starting. Some are saying it's not the Reclamation, but more of a takeover – demons swarming out of Sheoul. Still others think humans are leading the charge to break into Sheoul. The ones who aren't excited by the prospect of war are going into hiding. We're losing staff members every day.' The demon's eyes blazed – the hospital was his baby, and the fact that it was falling apart and staff were deserting must sit on his broad shoulders like an elephant. 'What do humans think is going on? I don't get much from Tayla but rumors.'

He wouldn't. Only the Sigil would be privy to the true goings-on, and even then, their info would be sketchy if *demons* couldn't get all the facts.

'Worst-case scenario? Armageddon. What you call the Reclamation. Best case? Some kind of attack. Religious leaders and world governments are going nuts behind the scenes, spinning damage control, because no one wants the truth about demons to get out. Talk about mass chaos scenarios.'

Gem snagged a soft drink from the fridge. 'You said The Aegis sent you. Why aren't you still with the military?'

'Got tired of doing nothing. They were fine with me leaving as long as I went back to The Aegis.'

'Don't suppose you can use your contacts at R-XR to find out everything you can about Marked Sentinels,' she said.

'I thought Wraith was already after one.'

E nodded. 'Yes, but we're pretty sure there's a link between her and what's going on in the underworld. Reaver is holding something back, but we do know that at the same time we felt the first stirrings of unrest, her cloak was blown.'

Interesting. 'I'll see what I can find.'

Eidolon's beeper went off. He checked it and shoved to his feet. 'I have an incoming trauma. Slayers have been busy.' He moved toward the door, his gait curiously devoid of the usual snap. He was dragging ass. 'Good to see you. If you get bored, we could use a hand around here.' He took off, leaving Kynan alone with Gem.

'I should go, too.' She pushed away from the counter.

Kynan blocked the door. 'Not so fast.'

'I said no.'

'Give me an hour, Gem. That's all I'm asking.'

'Are you going to tell me why you left? All of it?'

'All of it.'

She gave him a single nod. 'Be at my place tonight at six.' She shoved him out of the way. 'And do *not* be late.'

NINE

Serena had just thrown her backpack over her shoulder when someone pounded on her hotel room door.

'Serena! Open up!'

Josh. Unsure whether she was excited or not, she opened up, a sensation of déjà vu washing over her at the sight of him standing in the doorway. Like last night, he wore jeans, but over his Hard Rock T-shirt he wore a well-worn leather duster that suited his rugged masculinity and made her breath come a little faster.

The dream she'd had last night was still so vivid, so real, that her face heated with a morning-after awkwardness. At least, what she imagined morning-after awkwardness must feel like for someone who had indulged in a one-night stand with a stranger.

'You'd better have the artifact,' she said, but he ignored her, grabbed her hand, and tugged her through the doorway.

'We're leaving. Now.'

'What the—'

'There's a demon in the hotel.'

'Damn,' she breathed.

'Damn*ed*, anyway,' he muttered. 'Come on. We're taking the stairs.'

A low rumble started up, sounding distant, as if it were coming from outside, but then the floor at the end of the hall began to ripple . . . toward them.

Josh swung around in a sinuous, effortless movement. The carpet snapped upward with such force it sliced a twenty-foot gash in the wall. 'Shit.' Josh stepped back as though reconsidering his stance. 'Yeah . . . run.'

They sprinted to the stairwell. Josh tore open the door and shoved her inside. She took the stairs two at a time. The building shuddered, and she lost her balance, coming down awkwardly at the second-floor landing – the charm protected her from injury, but it didn't make her graceful. Above her, Josh held the steel door against something that was bashing into it, leaving massive dents.

'Go!'

She couldn't. This was wrong. Whatever was chasing them was after her, not Josh, and she was protected by the charm. He was the one in danger, not her.

'I'm not going without you,' she shouted. 'Don't argue or I'm coming back up there.'

His curse echoed through the stairwell. He hesitated, and then he leaped down the flight of stairs and landed lightly in front of her in the most amazing feat of athleticism she'd ever seen.

Not to be outdone, she launched herself to the next landing and grinned up at him.

'Show-off,' he grunted, joining her.

They exploded out of the door at the bottom of the stairwell and into the lobby. People milled in alarm, disturbed by the shaking building, but she and Josh cut swiftly through them, out the front entrance, and into the blinding sunlight. At the curb, a man was just opening a cab door.

'Sorry, dude,' Josh said, slipping in front of the guy and pushing her into the back seat. 'Medical emergency. My wife here is having a baby.'

The guy blinked, mouth dropped open, no doubt because Serena looked about as pregnant as a Popsicle stick, but he backed away as the cab pulled out into traffic, nearly side-swiping a bus. Though her heart raced and she was more than a little rattled, she gave instructions to the cabbie and tried to ignore the blaring horns outside and Josh's heat as he settled next to her on the seat.

'I really, really want to know why you're a demon magnet,' Josh said.

'I want to know what that thing was.'

'No idea.' He swiveled around to watch out the rear window, menace rolling off him in dangerous waves. He was still poised to fight, and she got the feeling he'd go right through the window if he had to.

'How did you know it was in the hotel?'

'Smelled it when I stepped into the hall.'

She watched him, slightly distracted by the way the hourglass tattoo on his neck seemed to be draining sand. 'Your sense of smell is pretty amazing.'

'Leftover from Aegis training.' He shifted to face forward, sitting back and spreading his legs wide so his knee touched hers. 'Looks like we're clear. Were you okay last night?'

Very. 'What do you mean?'

'Any visits by demons?'

'Oh. No. Everything was fine.'

'Did you sleep well?'

Her heart shot into her throat, which was insane, because he couldn't know what they'd done in her dreams. 'Why?'

His eyes took a bold, leisurely ride down her body and back up. 'Just wondering if you dreamed about me.'

'Why in the world would I dream about you? Just because you kissed me? It wasn't even that great of a kiss.' *Liar.* He'd kissed her into an aching frenzy.

'You've had better kisses?'

No. 'Yes.'

'In that dream you're denying you had about me?'

She huffed. 'You're really full of yourself, aren't you?'

He shrugged. 'Hey, every guy wants a gorgeous woman to dream about him.'

Gorgeous? He was buttering her up, and even though she recognized the flattery for what it was – an effort to get her to do those *other things* he wanted to do with her – she still got warm and fuzzy. But two could play at that game.

'Fine,' she said, with a saucy bat of her eyelashes, 'I confess . . . I did dream about you.'

He cocked an eyebrow. 'Was it good?' He leaned in and whispered against her ear, 'Tell me.'

Desire shivered over her skin. 'It was crazy,' she whispered back. 'I dreamed you were a vampire. A very sexy vampire.'

'Huh.' His teeth latched on to her earlobe, nipped tenderly. 'You have a thing for vamps?'

More than a thing. She'd indulged her curiosity even before she'd learned vamps were real, reading everything – fiction and non-fiction – she could get her hands on. She'd even spent months in several European countries, including Hungary, Germany, and Romania, researching Dracula and the Vlad Tepes origins.

'They fascinate me,' she admitted.

Josh withdrew. 'They're monsters. There's nothing fascinating about them at all.'

She glanced out as they passed Pompey's Pillar, the tallest ancient monument in Alexandria, but today the impressive granite structure failed to move her. 'You sound like Val.'

'Val's right.' He shifted his gaze out the window at the palms lining the street. Beyond the trees, new, modern buildings contrasted with older, pockmarked structures, between which she caught glimpses of the Mediterranean. 'Tell me you aren't one of those nut jobs who dresses up like an Anne Rice character and hangs out in vampire bars.'

She tried not to squirm, because she *had* done that. Only once, and it had been in the name of research. Really.

'You are, aren't you?' Josh grabbed her by the shoulders and turned her to face him. His bright gaze drilled into her. 'Stay away from those places, Serena. There are people there who aren't . . . right. They're dangerous. I don't want you getting hurt. Or worse. Because there *is* worse.' His expression went as dark and haunted as his voice, sending a shiver up her spine.

'I know,' she said. 'And I'm careful.'

Out of the blue, he kissed her hard. 'That is the biggest lie I've ever heard,' he said against her lips.

His kiss gentled, his lips becoming soft velvet as he delivered an unspoken apology before settling back in the seat. And yes, she should be irked by his arrogant insistence that she heed his warning, was still a little annoyed by the fact that he'd basically blackmailed her into joining her treasure hunt. But God, she'd been alone for so long, had been so lonely she sometimes ached.

No matter how attentive Val was, how many people she surrounded herself with, she still felt that yearning she couldn't banish no matter how busy she kept herself. Now she understood the shadows in her mother's eyes. At the time, Serena had been too young to know what made her mother cry when she thought she was alone, but the closer Serena got to Josh, the more clearly she understood.

The only person who had ever made her mother's shadows recede was Val. Serena's heart thudded against her rib cage at the sudden suspicion that threaded its way into her mind. Her mother . . . had she been in love with him?

Val had been married, living only a few miles away. Serena didn't remember any inappropriate contact, but her mom definitely lit up when her Guardian had come to visit.

'Hey,' Josh said, tilting her face up to his with a finger beneath her chin. 'We're here. Where are you?'

The taxi had pulled to a stop halfway up the curb, and she'd barely noticed. Seemed her trip down memory lane was bumpier than the streets of Alexandria.

'I guess I was spacing.'

Josh paid the taxi driver and reached for her knapsack. She figured that since he'd bullied his way along, he most certainly could carry it. With a grunt, he heaved it over his shoulder alongside his own.

'What do you have in this thing? I think it weighs more than you do.'

She laughed as she got out of the vehicle, glad she'd thrown on a light sweater to counter the cool morning. 'Maps, tools, water, snacks.'

'You're one of those always-prepared people, aren't you?' He made it sound like a bad thing.

'Maybe. I also brought my flask. Never leave home without it.'

He cocked an eyebrow. 'Whiskey?'

'Of course.'

'That's my girl.' He dug into the pocket of his backpack and pulled out a pair of sunglasses. Squinting into the sun, he popped them on. 'Guess this proves I'm not a vampire, huh?'

God, he was perfect. Even the aura of danger that surrounded him appealed to her basest feminine instincts, because this was a man made to protect what was his, and what she wouldn't give to be his . . .

Well, she'd give anything but her virginity.

'It was just a dream,' she muttered.

'Did I bite you?'

She swallowed, the memory heating her far more than the Egyptian sun. 'Yes.'

He gazed out over the tops of the palms lining the horizon, not looking at her. 'Did you like it?'

'Yes,' she whispered, her mind replaying the moment his fangs had penetrated her. God help her, she'd loved it.

'Then I'll have to remember that.' He turned to her and smiled, a dark, erotic smile that took her breath. 'Because make no mistake, Serena. I do bite.'

൭

Serena hurried ahead of Wraith to the catacombs entrance, and he hung back a little, mainly to keep an eye out for danger, but the view wasn't bad, either. From her hiking boots to her olive drab cargo pants and fitted T-shirt, she was sin in adventure gear. She'd pulled her hair into a ponytail, and all he could think about was winding the thick hair around his fist while he kissed her. Undressed her. Pounded into her as he had in the dream.

Afterward, he'd take her again, feed from her, and take her once more. Twice more. He could spend days with her . . .

His gut clenched. He couldn't spend days with her, because she might not have days after he took her charm. There was an expiration date on her life, and he was the one stamping it there.

He shoved the thought aside, because thinking about the consequences of his actions was a waste of energy and time, and besides, why should this be any different from anything else he'd done?

It wasn't.

She looked back over her shoulder at him, her full lips parted in a sultry smile.

It wasn't.

It didn't take long for Serena to arrange access into a private area of the catacombs of Kom El-Shuqafa. The man she'd spoken with had been hesitant to let Wraith tag along, until Wraith explained that he was her assistant, though he had to admit that the way she'd flirted with the guy had probably helped. And it had torqued the shit out of Wraith. Why, he had no idea.

He glued himself to her side as they walked the cavernous passages marked by Roman and Egyptian art. Though he'd been all over Egypt and the Middle East, he'd never been inside the catacombs. As a demon, he was attuned to malevolent undercurrents, and the closer they got to the Hall of Caracalla, the stronger the feeling became. He hadn't studied up on the history of the catacombs, but he knew all the way to his bones that something evil had taken place here.

'There are several tombs within the Hall of Caracalla,' Serena said quietly, so the guide wouldn't hear them. 'Many haven't been fully explored or excavated. There's a specific area I'm interested in, closed to the public, but we've been given special access.'

Wraith let out a low whistle. 'Val has some connections.' In Wraith's opinion, The Aegis was way too powerful for its own good. He gestured at their guide, who was descending into a stairwell ahead of them. 'Will he be watching us the whole time?'

'I hope not.'

Wraith had ways to deal with the guy if he decided to hang out, but after last night's jaunt into Serena's head, he was in no hurry to use his gift to get inside anyone else's mind. He'd never had a problem with recovery time before, but thanks to the whole dying thing, he felt a hell of a lot weaker than he should.

The fact that he hadn't eaten anything solid since the night before wasn't helping.

Last night after kissing Serena, he'd fed on a local shopkeeper, and this morning he'd thought about getting some breakfast in the hotel restaurant, but keeping down solids was becoming harder and harder. Seemed like, lately, blood and whiskey were all his stomach could tolerate. Even coffee didn't appeal to him anymore.

No coffee. He might as well be dead already.

The narrow staircase opened up into a square room, around which were a hivelike series of arched brick tunnels. Serena gestured for him to follow her, and they moved to the right, through an archway that led to a tomb that had been roped off. The guide stood aside, watching warily as they slipped beneath the rope.

The chamber was like every other ancient chamber on the planet. Dark. Dusty. Smelled like the air had been filtered through a dried corpse.

It was the scent of adventure, and already adrenaline was trickling into Wraith's system.

Wraith turned to the guide, speaking in Arabic. 'Why is this chamber off-limits to the public?' The guy just stared. Wraith waved a hand in front of his face. 'Hel-lo.'

Serena pinched Wraith's waist, and he yelped. Her eyes conveyed a private message: Don't antagonize him. Probably wise. But more boring than necessary.

Wraith let her lead him around the corner to an even smaller chamber. Holding her finger to her lips in a gesture for silence, she eased into a dark recess. Wraith lowered her pack next to her and moved to the corner, where he leaned casually against it to keep an eye on the guide. Behind him, he heard Serena scrounge through her backpack. A moment later, the familiar sounds of digging began.

A few minutes later, the guide yawned and glanced at his watch. He shot Wraith a look of utter distrust before disappearing up the stairs.

'Nothing,' Serena muttered. 'There's nothing here.'

'Need some help?'

'Couldn't hurt.'

He found her on her knees in front of a fist-sized opening in the limestone wall. On the ground was a pile of excavated stone and a small brick marked by writing and timeworn etchings in a language he didn't recognize.

'Was there supposed to be something inside the hole?'

'I thought so.'

Wraith crouched next to her and tried not to get distracted by the feminine scent of sun on her warm skin. 'What does the writing say?'

'It's a prayer, of sorts.' She sank down, tucked one leg beneath her, and stared at the brick. A couple of wisps of hair had fallen forward across her bronzed cheeks, and Wraith reached out to brush them back, an excuse to touch her. She rewarded him with a sinful smile before turning back to the brick.

'See, in the year two hundred and fifteen, the emperor Caracalla became enraged at the citizens of Alexandria, and he supposedly slaughtered twenty thousand of them. Many of the dead were brought here. The writing is a wish for any Christian souls to find their way through the mass of heathen souls surrounding them.'

The slaughter explained the feeling of malevolence that crawled on Wraith's skin like a million stinging ants. 'So why did the dude freak out?'

She ran a finger over the text, almost lovingly. He imagined her doing the same to his *dermoire*, tracing the symbols, caressing the lines with her hands, her tongue . . . he stifled a groan.

'There are a lot of theories, but Val believes that the Alexandrians insulted him with a satirical play about some of his actions, including the murder of his own brother.'

Fratricide hit a little too close to home, and Wraith quickly brought the subject back to their search. He really wished she'd stop fingering the brick.

'Tragic, but what does all of this have to do with the artifact you're looking for?'

She cast a sideways glance at him as though she wasn't sure she wanted to talk, but after a moment she shrugged. 'According to some ancient Gnostic texts, there are people walking the earth who are charmed by angels.'

'You're talking about Marked Sentinels.'

'I didn't think The Aegis was open about that.'

'They aren't,' he said smoothly, 'but I was slated for the Sigil, so I was privy to some classified information.' Actually, he had no idea if that was true for Josh, but it sounded good.

'Okay, then you know they can't be killed, but they can take their own lives. Supposedly, one of these charmed humans sacrificed himself to be buried along with the slaughtered Christians. He thought he could help guide their souls to Heaven.'

'Why did he think that?'

'It's said he was in possession of a coin imbued with special powers.'

'And you thought this coin was hidden behind a brick?'

'I'd hoped so.' She frowned. 'If it's here, I'll find it. I always find what I'm looking for.' She cocked an eyebrow at him. 'Kinda like how you always get what you want.'

'Remember that.' With a wink, he stood, offered her a hand, and helped her up. 'So, let's think this through. Anyone who was charmed by an angel and was in possession of a magical artifact wouldn't do something as hasty as shove the thing behind a brick. He'd put it someplace special, maybe where it could be found by the right person. Did you reach into the hole?'

'Yes, but I was looking for an object ... ' Bending over, she squeezed her hand into the crevice again. *Niiice.* Her pants were molded to her ass like shrink-wrap, and his entire blood supply rushed to his groin. No panty lines. Not. One.

'I've found something ... a slight indentation.' Her tongue slipped between her lips as she concentrated, and Wraith casually used his palm to adjust his aching erection.

'How are you doing?' His voice had gone husky, but she didn't seem to notice.

'I'm trying to turn it ... maybe I should push it ... darn. Nothing. Now might be a good time for your artifact.'

Wraith dug into his backpack and removed the bone carving he'd acquired from Josh.

She took the oval disk, a jeweled Roman pendant that hung from a leather thong. Carefully, she inserted the pendant into the hole. He heard a click, followed by another, louder click. Nothing happened. Disappointment put shadows in the hollows of Serena's cheeks, and dammit, Wraith wanted to do something to make it better.

He didn't have time to analyze the oddity of that particular feeling, because a rumble shook the floor, followed by a rain of pebbles and a poof of dust. A demon? No, the taint of evil hadn't strengthened, but a crack had appeared in the far wall.

A doorway.

'Eureka,' she breathed. 'I think we might have found it!' She darted to the fissure, but Wraith grabbed her before she could pry open the stone slab.

'Wait. Let me do it. It might be booby-trapped.'

'Really,' she said, 'it's safer for me.'

'Why is that? Are you one of those charmed people?'

Her eyes flared, but she recovered quickly, with a blinding smile. 'Don't be silly. It's just that I'm smaller than you are. Less of a target.'

'Humor me.' Sure, she was charmed and all but invincible, but this kind of thing was what he lived for. Except . . . he was dying, so really, he had nothing to lose anyway.

'Josh—'

He shoved the stone aside before she could argue, grimacing at the sigh of stale air that escaped as though the Hall of Caracalla had been holding its breath. Wraith's natural night vision allowed him to see perfectly, but Serena flicked on a flashlight. The rough-carved passage was dusty and full of cobwebs, slanting slightly downward on a floor of packed earth.

Here the walls were chipped and grooved, bare of artwork, evidence that the area had been closed off soon after construction.

It ended in a round, unfinished cavern no larger than one of UG's exam rooms. It was empty except for a crude pillar in the center and a clay jar in one corner. Serena brushed past Wraith and sank down on her knees in front of the plain brown pot. Carefully, she reached inside and withdrew a fist-sized leather pouch.

Her sharp intake of breath accompanied a flash of gold as she drew a coin from the bag. Her thrill was a shock of energy that danced across his skin. Wraith knew exactly what she was feeling. He only felt alive when he was fucking, fighting, or hunting, and hunting relics could be as big a rush as hunting food.

'Is that it?' he asked, sinking down beside her.

'Yes. Oh, yes.' She turned the coin over and over, finally running her thumb over the back, on which words were etched. There she went with the rubbing again. His *dermoire* writhed as though it wanted the same attention. '*Let that which is open, close. That which is closed, remain.*'

'Man, I hate the cryptic shit.'

Her eyes shone with excitement as she returned the coin to its pouch. 'I love it. Solving the mystery, finding the hidden meaning . . . there's nothing like it.'

'Oh, I can think of something like it,' he said, letting his gaze linger on her lips. 'Something that'll get you just as dirty. Sweaty . . .' Gods, he was turned on. Who'd have thought that searching for treasure could be an aphrodisiac?

'You're hopeless.'

He reached out and traced her bottom lip with his thumb. 'I've heard that once or twice.'

Serena tucked the pouch containing the coin into her backpack. 'I'm sure you have,' she said dryly.

'Grave-robbing offal.' The booming, musical male voice echoed through the tomb with an evil resonance Wraith felt to his soul.

He leaped to his feet and whirled in a single motion. Standing at the entrance to the hidden area was Byzam. A black hooded robe obscured his body and his hair, but his unnaturally handsome face peeked out from the cowl. The hair on Wraith's neck stood on end in a way it hadn't the first time he'd seen the other male.

This wasn't your average evil scum. Death would think twice before standing in the way of this demon.

Serena stood and calmly brushed the dirt from her pants. 'It's true that I'm more of a treasure hunter than an archaeologist,' she said, apparently unconcerned that the male who had snuck up on them might be a threat, 'so I have a bit of a mercenary finders-keepers attitude. But offal? That's a little strong.'

Byzam moved in a smear of light that even Wraith's vampire

vision barely tracked. In a blink, he had Serena's arm twisted behind her back and she was kissing the wall.

With a roar that shook dust from the ceiling, Wraith plowed into the demon, sending him careening off the pillar. A sound like a gunshot rang out as the stone column cracked, chips of stone peeling away from the fissure that spread upward from the dent Byzam's body had made.

Wraith got right up in the male's face. '*Get the fuck out. Now.*'

Byzam leaned close, so close Wraith could smell his foul breath as he whispered, 'I know what you're up to, Seminus.'

Wraith rocked his head forward, smashing his skull into Byzam's mouth. 'That's because you're up to the same thing.'

The bastard smiled through bloody lips, but kept his voice low. 'She won't give it up to you, so you might as well go home to whatever hole you crawled out of.'

Wraith bared his fangs. 'If I see you again, I'll bleed you out.'

'When you see me again, you'll be calling me god. For now, you can call me Byzamoth.' He bowed to Serena and swept out the door. Wraith gave chase, but Byzamoth had disappeared into thin air. Wraith stood outside the chamber for a moment, waiting for the battle high to subside, for his fangs to retract and his eyes to return to blue from the angry red he knew they'd turned.

When he returned to the chamber, Serena was waiting for him, her backpack slung over her shoulder, her face ashen.

She was shaken, and truthfully, so was Wraith. Had her charm failed, or did it not activate unless she was in mortal danger, and Byzamoth hadn't intended to kill her?

The scent of blood was in the air, faint and human. Serena had been hurt. He went to her, took her wrist, and shoved up her sleeve. Four deep crescents scored her forearm, beading with blood. Hunger roared through him and his fangs began to throb, his mouth to water. Shit.

Pulse racing, he released her and forced himself to take a step back. 'You're hurt,' he ground out.

Gods, he wanted her in a way he'd never wanted any female, human or demon. He wanted to lick her from her arm to her throat, sink his fangs into her and take her like he had in the dream. He could pump into her as her blood pumped into him—

'I'll live,' she said, her voice stronger than he'd have expected, given what had just happened. 'What did he say to you?'

He took a moment to get his shit together before answering. 'That his name is Byzamoth. And he wanted the treasure.' True enough, except Serena was the treasure. And for some reason it pissed him the hell off that the sonofabitch treated her like nothing more than a prize.

Which was exactly how Wraith was treating her, and when the fuck did he gain the guilt gene? Ruthlessly, he summoned an emotion he was far more comfortable with.

Extreme anger.

'So that's what he's been after all this time?' She frowned. 'How did he know about it? And how did you convince him to go?'

'I don't know how he knew about it, but I told him I'd kill him if he came near you again.'

Her hand went to her necklace, and he caught a whiff of blood again. She was killing him. 'He isn't human, then.'

'Would it matter if he was?' His voice was bitter and rough to his own ears. She didn't deserve his anger, but he was pissed at Byzamoth, at Roag, at the assassin who'd poisoned him, at himself, at the entire fucking world, and he was tired of playing nice.

'Would it matter to you?'

'No. He's a threat. Period.'

'You've lived a hard life, haven't you?' Her words were softly spoken, but they echoed around the tiny chamber and inside his skull.

'What? Yours has been charmed?' The words flew out of his mouth before he realized the irony of what he'd said.

She smiled – he knew the look. It was the one Tayla and Runa gave to E and Shade when they wanted to humor his brothers. Might as well give him a nice pat on the head, too. 'I have. I've always been lucky.'

'Luck runs out, Serena.'

'So you're a pessimist?'

'I'm a realist.'

She walked over to him and punched him in the biceps. 'Stick with me, baby. You'll learn to be an optimist.'

Fat chance of that, but this was the opening he needed. 'Oh, I'm sticking with you.'

She handed him the Roman pendant he'd taken from the real Josh. 'I don't need you anymore.'

'Yeah,' he said, 'you do. You have demons after you, and I have a shitload of experience fighting them.'

He wondered how she was going to argue her way out of this, but to his surprise, she merely said, 'I'm going to Aswan. If you think you can keep up with me, you're welcome to tag along.'

She poked him in the chest with a finger and strutted off, leaving him standing there staring after her like a dolt. When she reached the exit, she threw him a cocky grin over her shoulder.

'You coming?'

Not nearly soon enough.

The thought came naturally, easily, but for the first time, it was followed immediately by shame. Because Gods, she was better than that, standing there in the dim glow of the flashlight, dirt smudged on her cheek and nose. She had a purity about her, a good, wholesome energy that seemed to repel darkness and capture light. He figured, being a demon, that he should be repelled, but she drew him, and even now he felt himself drawing closer to her.

He needed to resist, because getting emotional with her meant regretting what he had to do to save his life.

He nearly laughed out loud at that. He'd never denied himself, had never resisted his desires or regretted much of anything. Now, suddenly, he was trying to exercise some control, something even his brothers hadn't gotten him to do.

But this spirited little human had him by the balls, and some small part of him liked it.

Hell's bells, as Shade would say. *Hell's fucking bells.*

TEN

I don't need you anymore.

That's what Serena had said to Josh after the demon left them in the catacombs, but it wasn't true. Something was wrong with her charm, because that demon shouldn't have been able to hurt her.

Not that it had hurt her a lot, but when he'd wrenched her arm behind her back, his nails had dug into her skin ... and drawn blood. It was a minor injury, but it never should have happened, and as much as she hated to admit it, she was a little frightened.

Josh had handled himself like a pro, and as an ex-Guardian, she supposed he was. Until she figured out what was wrong with her charm, she could use his protection.

They caught a quick bite at a deli near the hotel before hurriedly – and cautiously – grabbing their remaining belongings from their rooms and catching the 17:20 train to Aswan.

They'd each purchased a large private sleeping compartment and agreed to meet up in the dining car for dinner. She had a few minutes, so she changed out of her dusty clothes, took two swigs from her flask for courage, and put her time to good use, calling Val while she still had a signal.

'Hey,' she said when he picked up.

'Serena? It's David.'

'Oh.' She strained to hear David's voice over the crackle of static in the cell phone and the rumble of the train on the tracks. 'Is Val there?'

'Yeah, hold on. Did you get the coin?'

'It's in my pack.'

'Good. Keep it with you,' he said, as if she was an idiot who would let it out of her sight. 'Here's Dad.'

She heard the transfer of the handset. 'David said you got the artifact,' Val said by way of greeting. 'Any problems?'

'Maybe. Last night a man approached me on the streets of Alexandria. He said you sent him.'

'*What?* Josh was supposed to meet you, but I didn't send—'

'I know, Val. Calm down. I got rid of him.'

'Why didn't you tell me last night?'

'I figured he was gone for good.' She took a deep breath. Val was going to hit the roof. 'But today he showed up at the catacombs . . . and it turns out he's a demon.'

Val inhaled sharply. 'You okay?'

'You know I am.' She hesitated, considering how much she should say. If he knew Byzamoth had hurt her, he'd send every Aegis cell within a day's travel after her. 'But my secret is out.'

'What are you saying, Serena?' Val's voice was low, controlled, and for the first time, she heard the Aegis warrior he was.

'My cloak was compromised,' she admitted. 'I didn't tell you because I didn't want you to worry. It's repaired now, but it was down for a time.' Now she had to hope whatever was wrong with her charm would be as easily fixed.

'You need to come home. Forget about the Aswan artifact.'

'I'm already on the train.'

'You will get off in Cairo and catch the first flight back.'

She gazed out the window at the harsh yet beautiful landscape, a mix of golden sand and graceful trees, and shook her head. 'I'm perfectly safe. And Josh is with me.'

'Josh? Why?'

'Val, come on. He was a Guardian. Who better for me to travel with?' She could practically hear the top of Val's head blow off. Time to go. 'Wow, the static is terrible. I should hang up. I'll call you when I get the tablet.'

'Wait—'

She severed the phone link by mashing the End button with her thumb. Just to be safe, she turned off the phone completely and headed for the dining car.

Nerves, from the tense conversation with Val and from the anticipation of seeing Josh, turned her stomach into a churning cauldron. But when she saw Josh smiling at her from a table, she wondered why she'd been anxious.

Something about that devastating smile just made her go all mushy inside. She'd never been one for tattoos, but the swirling design on his face suited him, with its angular twists and whorls and dark, sharp edges. One pointed end kissed the very corner of his mouth, and she pictured herself putting her lips to his and following the tattoo until it ended at his fingertips.

He stood – awkwardly, almost as though doing so was an afterthought – and waited for her to sit before taking his own chair again. He was already halfway through a glass of whiskey, and he'd ordered her one as well. Very thoughtful.

She downed it. 'I called Val.'

'Did you tell him you have demons after you and your artifact?' He took a swig of his drink, and as his throat muscles worked the liquor down, Serena realized for the first time that a man's neck could be damned sexy. Maybe she could have one of those dreams like she'd had last night, only this time, *she* could be the vampire.

'Yes, I told him.' She shot him a wry look. 'So your blackmail material is ruined.'

His grin made her pulse leap. 'Don't need it. Now you want to hang out with me all on your own.'

'Are you even aware of how cocky you are?'

'Do I really need to answer that?' He stroked his long fingers up and down the glass, and she suddenly wanted him to do the same to her. After a moment, he pushed the whiskey at her. 'I think you need this more than I do. What did Val say?'

'He wants me to come home.'

'Are you going to go?'

'Heck no. Val's paranoid.'

'Maybe he's smart.'

She rolled her eyes. 'Not you, too.'

He leaned back in his chair, his sinfully toned body sprawled out as though he didn't have a care in the world, but the way his alert gaze kept checking out their surroundings said otherwise. She got the impression that a gnat entering the dining car wouldn't escape his notice.

'So . . . what's his story? Why does he act more like a father than a boss?'

She watched the liquor in the glass slosh around from the motion of the train. 'He was a friend of my mom's. After she died, he kept in contact with me, encouraged my love of archaeology. He's an archaeologist,' she explained. 'I went to Yale, where he taught, but college turned out not to be my thing. I was getting sick of school, ready to drop out, and he hired me for his private archaeology foundation. He offered me a place to stay at his mansion, and I would have been stupid to turn it down.'

Josh's eyes narrowed into slits. 'What's the catch?'

'Catch?'

She could have sworn she heard a low snarl come from his side of the table before he spoke.

'No man offers a tight young bod like yours a place to stay without wanting something in return.'

Tight bod? She laughed. 'Trust me, he has no interest in me. Not like that. You said it yourself: He's like a father.'

'Why?' he repeated.

She shrugged. 'I think it's partly because we have a lot in

common.' Namely, she was the only person working for him who knew the truth about his and David's Aegis connections, and he was one of only a handful of people who knew the truth about her. 'And partly, it's because he's kind of felt obligated to watch out for me.'

'What does your real dad have to say about that?'

'I never knew him.'

'Was he a tomcat who ran around impregnating every female he saw, and your mother was unlucky enough to get taken in by him?'

'Do I sense some paternal issues?'

'Nope.'

His overly laid-back tone gave him away – he was lying, but Serena didn't push. 'Well, no issues here, either. My mom couldn't conceive naturally, so Pops was a sperm donor – literally.' She pushed the glass of whiskey back at him, because it was obvious that now he needed it more than she did. 'I miss my mom, though. What about you? Do you have any family?'

'Two brothers. Both older. Three baby nephews.'

'Three? Wow. I'll bet they're adorable.'

He downed the liquor. 'I wouldn't know.'

'Do they live far away?'

'Not really.'

'So . . . do you want children of your own?' When he peered into his empty glass and didn't answer, she murmured, 'I'm sorry. That's too personal.'

'S'okay.' The train had slowed to a crawl, and he looked out the window at a shepherd with a herd of goats. 'I'm not capable of raising a kid.'

'Of course you are. Kids don't come with instructions – everyone learns as they go.'

'Trust me, I have no business being in a child's life.'

His earlier comment came back to her. 'Does this have something to do with your father?'

'Didn't have one.'

'What about your mother?'

His bitter laughter rang out. 'She wasn't exactly a shining example of parenthood.'

Serena took his hand in hers. 'A lot of mothers aren't what they should be.'

He pulled his hand away as though he suddenly couldn't bear to be touched. 'Do a lot of mothers keep their children in cages and torture them?'

Serena stopped breathing. 'Tell me that *cage* is metaphorical.'

'It was a cage in the basement.' His voice dropped to a low, tense growl. 'And if you can conceive of the torture, she did it. Fun was had by all.'

Serena had no idea what to say. Didn't want to imagine it or believe that things like that truly happened. Her life had been blessed . . . with the exception of her mother's death.

'That's . . . horrible,' she finally managed.

'Fuck.' Josh scrubbed a hand over his face. 'Let's just trash all that, 'kay?'

Except there was no putting that particular cat back in the bag. How could a mother do that to a child, and how could a child come out of an experience like that and still be whole?

'What about your brothers?'

'Why?'

She blinked. 'Why what?'

'Why do you want to know about them? About me?'

'Because I like you.'

Surprise and another emotion she couldn't name flitted across his face before he closed his eyes, as though he couldn't decide if he wanted her to like him or not. 'Different mothers,' he said, his voice so gravelly she barely understood. 'We had different mothers.'

'And where the hell was your father?'

A young couple walked past the table, and he waited for them to take seats on the far side of the car before saying, very quietly, 'He's the one who drove her to it. But her cla – ah, family, hunted him down and killed him a few months after I was born.'

She'd never been speechless before. Ever.

'Look,' he said. 'I don't usually—' He clutched his belly. 'I . . . oh, damn.'

'Josh? What's wrong?'

'Must be . . . something I ate.' He lurched to his feet, and she came to hers. 'Need to get to my room.'

'Let me help you.'

'No,' he moaned. 'I can do it.'

'You can barely stand. Now shut up and let me help.'

One corner of his mouth tipped up in the tiniest of smiles before he sucked in a pained breath and nearly fell over. 'Shutting up, ma'am.'

'That must be a first for you.'

'Funny,' he gasped.

The rocking of the train didn't help his balance as she guided him to the sleeping car. She nearly buckled under his weight a couple of times, and he would mutter, 'Sorry,' and try to stand upright, which would send him careening into a wall.

'You're not looking good, Josh. Maybe there's a doctor on board.'

'*No.*' His voice was practically a shout, and when she flinched in surprise, he lowered his voice. 'No. This has . . . happened before.'

She wanted to argue, but he seemed adamant, and besides, they'd arrived at his room. His hand was shaking so badly he couldn't get his fingers into the handle slot in the door. When he cursed softly and gave up, just resting his head against the door, her heart nearly broke. He was powerful enough to break the thing down, but opening it normally was beyond his ability.

Wordlessly, she opened the door and helped him inside the tiny compartment.

The seats had been made into a bed already, and he collapsed onto it with a thud. A shudder wracked his body, followed by violent shivers. 'C-cold.'

She palmed his forehead, which was on fire. How had he gone

from merely warm to inferno in a matter of seconds? Something was seriously wrong. Quickly, she grabbed a blanket from the top bunk and covered him.

'I'll be right back. I'm going to my room to get another blanket.'

He didn't seem to hear her, but the sound of his teeth chattering followed her all the way down the hall.

ꟹ

Wraith waited until Serena closed the door behind her to roll ungracefully off the bed and drag his duffel from beneath it. His stomach heaved and his muscles had locked up so hard he could barely move. Motherfucking poison was kicking his ass.

It took forever to open his bag and find the medic kit. He spilled half of his pills but didn't care. He finally swallowed the three he needed – one painkiller, one antibiotic, and one anti-seizure capsule. The painkiller wouldn't actually work for the pain – for vampires, oral painkillers needed to be filtered through human blood and ingested to work – but it would reduce his fever.

There was a way to treat the pain – UG's one human nurse had volunteered to take a high dose of Vicodin, and once it took effect, Shade had drawn as much blood as the human could stand losing. He'd then sealed the blood in small packets for Wraith to drink as needed.

Right now he needed – boy-howdy, he needed – but the effort involved in opening the insulated bag that held the medicated blood and the half-dozen units of food blood E'd packed was beyond his abilities. Instead, he shoved his duffel away and wondered how he was going to climb back onto the mattress.

The door opened, and he groaned as warm arms came around him. He felt himself being lifted, but Serena couldn't get him onto the bed by herself, so he mustered the last of his strength to drag his sorry, freezing ass up. It was humiliating the way he couldn't stop shivering, even after she covered him with three blankets.

Agony wracked his insides, and shooting pains stabbed his

brain. The poison was eating away at him, killing his insides, just like E said it would. He heard Serena talking, but his hearing had dimmed, so he couldn't understand. Her tone was enough to soothe him, though, and he just let himself listen to the gentle drone of her voice.

'Wraith?' His name floated down to him. *Wraith?* No, wishful thinking. She'd called him Josh. But what he wouldn't give to hear his name on her lips.

Gods, if he wasn't in so much pain he'd laugh. Clearly, he was delirious. Which was why, when he felt the bed sink and her warm body stretch out next to him, he closed his eyes and enjoyed the sensation. She was fire against his ice, a delicate furnace that eased his shivers almost immediately.

She stroked from his shoulder down to his hand and back up, lulling him, easing the chill and the pain. He didn't know how long she petted him like that, but three hours later he woke up with her still curled against him, her light, delicate snores as comforting as anything.

She'd stayed with him. She barely knew him, and yet she'd taken care of him, held him, and was now sleeping next to him as if she belonged there.

He almost started shaking again. This time, though, he couldn't blame the poison. With the exception of his brothers, no one had ever cared for him like that. And even with them, most of the time he suspected they cared more out of obligation than out of affection.

Carefully, so as not to wake her, he rolled over in the narrow bunk to face her. The darkness didn't hinder his ability to admire the way her hair fanned out over the pillow, a silky curtain of gold. She was so peaceful in her sleep, her breathing soft and steady, her nose scrunching up every once in a while as though she were smelling something delicious in a dream.

He could get into her dreams and find out what she was thinking, like he had last night, but doing so now seemed wrong. An invasion of unforgivable proportions.

What. The. Hell.

He'd never given a shit about 'wrong' before. Human morals did not apply to him. But suddenly, he was feeling squeamish about doing what he'd been born to do – get inside a female's head and seduce the hell out of her.

Idiot.

He should get inside her right now. Get her so hot that when she woke up, she'd still be in a partial dream state, would willingly give herself to him. He was, after all, a predator, and it was time to take down his prey.

Closing his eyes, he concentrated, punched through the barrier between the conscious mind and the subconscious one.

He found her in a bedroom, and he got the impression it was hers, at Val's guest house. *Val.* There might not be anything between Serena and the old guy, but he still wanted to rip the dude's limbs off and beat him with them. Serena was hot, and no way was Val not noticing that.

'Josh?'

Wraith started. He hadn't inserted himself into her dream yet, but she was asking for him? She was kneeling on the bed, naked except for a pair of fuck-me-baby high heels. A door near the foot of the bed opened, and . . . *he* walked out. Not his true self, but a dream Wraith she'd conjured.

Holy shit, she was dreaming about him. All on her own.

As Wraith watched, mouth open, his naked dream-self stalked across the room, fangs bared, body hard and primed for sex. And that naughty girl, she'd endowed him nicely.

Which, of course, was accurate.

Serena met him at the end of the bed, thighs spread, head thrown back, and the dream Wraith didn't wait. He sank his teeth into her throat as he sank into her body.

The sex was raw and rough and when it was over, Serena held him.

And he held her.

Wraith's gut wrenched. This was what she wanted. What she dreamed of on her own. What he could never give her.

Oh, he could give her the orgasms of her life, but the warm touchy-feely cuddles afterward? No, all he had for her was death's cold embrace.

Guilt pricked at him like a needle, and shame tightened like a band around his chest. He pulled out of the dream and came back into the train compartment.

Fuck. Maybe the toxin was affecting more than just his body. Maybe it was fucking with his mind, too. And wouldn't that just figure. Roag's perfect revenge didn't stop at killing him slowly. Oh, no. He had to saddle him with a conscience as well.

Serena stirred, gave a little yawn. She was so small against him, but she was strong. He could feel it in the taut firmness of her muscles, the hard lines of her body, all the way to the force of her will. And yet, there was a vulnerability to her that brought out a protective side he hadn't known he possessed.

He ran his hand over her smooth cheek, tracing her jaw with his thumb, feathering a light touch down her long, graceful neck. Her pulse pounded beneath his fingers, and his own veins ran hot with lust. His fangs began to stretch in anticipation, but he couldn't bite her, and he willed himself to calm down. She might have a vampire fetish, but he seriously doubted she would react well to the real thing.

Still, he couldn't resist putting his lips to her throat. A sigh escaped her, and she arched into him, her breasts rubbing against his chest. Gods, she felt good against him. This was so wrong. So right.

She dragged her hands up his back to knead the muscles that had begun to knot at his line of thinking. The intimacy of the innocent act was shocking; females touched him to get sex, not for the simple pleasure of comfort. The sensation ripped through him, leaving him stunned and warm . . . and really goddamned annoyed.

Enough of the touchy-feely crap. They needed to get down and dirty. Especially after the true-confessions session in the dining car, when he'd rattled on about his childhood trauma like a dumbass.

He dropped his hand to her ass and tugged her hard into his erection. Then he spread her thighs with one of his and curled his fingers into the seam between her butt cheeks. She stiffened, but she didn't resist when he rocked his leg upward and began a slow, circular grind.

'Oh, God,' she breathed. 'This is ... you know I can't—'

'Shh.' He captured her mouth with his and kissed her hungrily, careful, as always, to be the aggressor so her tongue didn't catch on the sharp tips of his fangs. 'Let me make you feel good.'

She arched beneath him. 'Good ... yes.'

He let his fingers stray lower, so they brushed her cleft through the thin fabric of her skirt. 'I'll be a perfect gentleman. I swear to you, nothing but my hands and mouth will touch you.' He reared back to peg her with another promise that came out in a low, harsh growl. 'I also swear that there will be nothing gentlemanly about what I do with my hands and mouth.'

Her sharp intake of breath accompanied a blast of lust that made his head swim.

'Well,' she said, in a deep, seductive drawl, 'I should hope not.' And then she kissed him.

ᘓ

Serena felt Josh's surprise in the tautness of his body, but when she flicked her tongue over his bottom lip, he relaxed and drew her even harder against him.

He made an erotic noise of approval when she tugged her skirt up so she could hook her leg over his, putting her core in contact with the large bulge behind the fly of his jeans. Her senses flamed, and she shivered with pleasure.

She'd made out with men before, experimenting, testing her will, each time going a little further. But she wanted so much more than she could have, and heavy petting only frustrated her.

This could end in orgasms for them both, but ultimately, she knew it wouldn't be enough. It could never be enough with a man like Josh. With him, she knew she'd want it all.

As good as it felt to have Josh's hand stroking her between her legs like this, so deftly that she was nearly panting, this was a dangerous game. One she couldn't play.

'No,' she croaked. 'No!' She shoved hard at his chest and scrambled away. Too close to the edge of the mattress, she fell over the side and dropped heavily to the floor. Panic weighed her down and she couldn't get to her feet, so she crawled in a mad bid to get to the door, her skirt tangling in her legs.

'Serena.' Josh's hand closed on her ankle, and she cried out in surprise and panic and fear. Not *of* him, but of what she might do *with* him.

'Leave me alone!' She kicked, clipped him in the chin with her heel. Her fingers brushed the door—

Josh's heavy body came down on top of hers, pinning her to the floor. She forced herself to breathe at the realization that her charm hadn't protected her from being caught ... and it wasn't because her charm had failed. She'd *wanted* to get caught.

She was in a lot of trouble.

'Serena,' he repeated, his voice a sensual purr that rumbled through the weakest parts of her. The parts that were aching for his touch. 'You don't need to fear me.'

She swallowed, going lax in his arms as he rolled so they were both on their sides, his chest to her back, his arms caging her sweetly against him. 'It's not you I'm afraid of.'

His lips skimmed her cheek, his hot breath leaving a pleasant tingle on her skin as he spoke. 'Then what?' He slid one hand to her belly to twine his fingers with hers. 'Tell me.'

Wetness stung her eyes. 'I'm afraid of what I want.'

'And what do you want?' When she said nothing, because her throat had closed up, he squeezed her hand. 'What do you want, Serena? Show me.'

Desire swirled, collided with caution and consumed it. Fighting against the force of Josh's sensuality and her own hunger was a losing effort, and for now, just this once, she'd cede the battle. Slowly, she dragged his hand down. When she reached the juncture between her legs, she arched, involuntarily, into his palm.

'Good girl,' he whispered, and kissed her cheek even as he fisted her skirt and dragged it up her legs. His other arm was pinned beneath her ribs, but his hand was free enough to slip beneath her gauzy blouse. His fingertips tickled her skin as they pushed aside her bra. When he cupped her breast and circled her nipple with his thumb, she heaved a breath she hadn't known she'd held.

'Oh, yeah.' His other thumb stroked the silk fabric covering her core. 'I want to do this with my tongue. I *will* do that with my tongue. Later.'

There wouldn't be a later. This had to be a one-time deal.

The sensation of his warm breath on the cool skin of her neck drew her out of the depressing thoughts and back to where her body tingled and her lungs pushed and pulled air that had grown thick with the desire arcing between them. His fingers found the lacy edge of her underwear, and behind her, prodding her rear, was his erection, a massive, brutal presence. Even as he tunneled his hand beneath the fabric of her panties, he ground that male organ against her. Would he come like that? Maybe she should take him in her hand and give him some relief. . . . She tried to roll over but he restrained her with his strong arms.

'Stop,' he murmured, going up on his elbow to lean over her and kiss her lips. 'Just relax and let me pleasure you.'

Her head fell back, her lips parting, and Josh took advantage, sinking his tongue into her mouth with a thrust while at the same time penetrating her with his finger.

She moaned, rocked against his hand where his palm created a delicious pressure against her clit. He stroked her, inside and out, between her legs and in her mouth. The friction built, creating a hot burst of pleasure that streaked from her core to her breasts. Her body liquefied, the blood in her veins approaching the boiling point, and still Josh plundered her mouth and her sex, adding another finger, stretching and filling her.

Her explosion grew imminent. She perched on the edge of orgasm, a blissful, amazing place where only she and Josh existed.

He ceased the delicious thrusts and dragged his slick fingers through her slit, easing her just off the ledge. She whimpered in protest, felt his smile against her lips.

'I love the sounds you make,' he said, speeding up the long, firm strokes that only grazed the place she needed his skilled touch. 'But you're so quiet. Make some noise for me. Say my name when you come.' He skimmed his finger over her nub so lightly she nearly shattered, but the contact was fleeting, and she cried out in frustration when he denied her the release she so needed. 'Say it. Say it now.'

'Yes ... oh, yes ... Josh ... *Josh!*' She thought she heard him utter a raw curse, but then she went deaf and blind as the mind-blowing orgasm brought her off the floor with such force that he had to throw a leg over hers and tug her tight against him as he brought her down with the gentle strum of his fingers over her core.

When it was over, she dissolved into a quivering puddle, but behind her, Josh remained tense, his shaft throbbing against her. Wriggling around to face him, she saw that he'd closed his eyes as though in pain. She palmed him, but with a hiss, he grasped her wrist.

'No.' His jaw was a straight, grim line, and his cheek pulsed against the grind of teeth. 'I can't ... can't get off that way.'

'Ah, you mean, with a hand?'

'Yeah.' He swallowed. 'Weird sexual hang-up.' He let out a long, ragged breath. 'I did this for you. Not me.'

Closing her eyes, Serena rested her forehead against his chest. 'Why?'

'Because you needed it.'

'I could have given myself an orgasm if I needed it that badly.'

'Not one like that,' he said, with more than a little satisfaction, and she wrenched her arm from beneath him just enough to punch him in the shoulder.

'Seriously.'

'I was serious.' When she punched him again, he heaved a sigh. 'You needed the connection between two people.' He snorted out a laugh. 'My brother Shade says that if you pay attention, really listen, you will know what a female needs. I always thought he was full of it.'

'Shade?'

'Nickname.'

She nuzzled his neck, taking in his musky male scent. 'Like Wraith?'

'Kind of.'

She braced a palm against his breastbone and pushed back a little. 'How are you feeling?'

His hand curled around hers, and he brought it up to kiss her knuckles. 'Better, thanks to you.'

'You said you'd been ill like that before. What was it? Are you sick?'

'Nothing to worry about.' He pulled away, and the temperature in the room seemed to drop.

'I *am* worried.'

'Why?' Josh sat back against the bed, feet flat on the floor and forearms braced on his spread knees. His heavy-lidded gaze was wary. 'Why would you worry about a complete stranger?'

'We're hardly strangers now.'

He stared at her. 'You know what I mean.'

'No, I really don't.' She shifted onto one hip and smoothed her skirt out, more for something to do with her hands than because she was worried about wrinkles. 'We haven't known each other long, but we've been through some pretty intense stuff. More than most people go through together in a lifetime. I like you, Josh. A lot more than I probably should.'

He cursed, which confused the hell out of her.

'What is wrong with liking you? Would you rather I hated you?'

'No. I need you to like me—' He cursed again. 'I mean, shit. Just, shit.' He threw his head back and stared at the ceiling. 'Just stop worrying about me, okay?'

'Why wouldn't I worry about you?'

'Because it's stupid,' he snapped. 'I don't need your concern. I get enough shit from my brothers.'

'Stupid? *Shit?* I'm giving you shit by taking care of you?' He didn't answer, and anger roared through her. 'I get that you had a horrific childhood, but you have people who care about you now, and you should be grateful.'

'You don't know anything about my life, and you don't want to.'

'How dare you?' She scrambled to her feet. 'How dare you dismiss what I feel, as though it's nothing?'

He let out a long-suffering sigh, as though this was all just so much inconvenience for him. 'I didn't ask you to feel anything for me.'

'Well, excuse me for being human.' She whipped open the door. 'I'll just go, since I'm stupid and my worry is such a bother to you.'

Josh cursed. 'Serena, wait—'

But she didn't hear the rest, partly because she'd slammed the door, and partly because her pulse was pounding so hard in her ears that it blocked out everything else.

Everything but the hurt.

ELEVEN

The knock at Gem's apartment door came right on time. The table was set, the rosemary pork loin and oven-roasted potatoes were almost done, and dessert, a homemade pineapple upside-down cake, sat on the counter, looking all glazy and perfect. Kynan wouldn't know what had hit him.

Nerves made her palms sweat as she walked to the front door. She'd put on her most conservative but sexy clothes – a flared, above-the-knee black skirt with a subdued skull-and-bones design at the top of the slit in the back, a creamy, sheer lace top, and chunky-heeled, ankle-high boots.

She was going to make him eat his rejection.

Her resolve almost flew out the window when she saw him. He looked hot, as usual, dressed in worn jeans, a blue sweater, and the leather bomber. His spiky hair was wet and he smelled like outdoorsy soap.

God, she wanted to jump on him, take him down to the floor, and ride him twice before dinner. Resisting the urge to fan herself, she ushered him in.

'Wow,' he said, as he stepped into the entryway. 'You look nice.' He sniffed the air. 'Something smells good.'

'Pork loin.' She led him to the kitchen. 'Something to drink? Beer? Wine?'

'I don't drink anymore.'

She drew up short as she reached for the fridge door. 'Oh. Okay.' She didn't drink, either. Not much, anyway, and she figured he was thinking that as he eyed the tattoos that circled her wrists, ankles, and neck. The magically enchanted designs prevented her demon half from rearing its evil head when she was angry or upset, but alcohol reduced her ability to control the demon inside and negated the power of the tattoos.

She turned around slowly, drew an appreciative breath as Kynan braced a hip on the counter and crossed his feet at the ankles. She let her eyes drop for just a second, to his slim hips and long, muscular legs, and then, with a shake of the head to bring her back into focus, she said coolly, 'So, are you going to tell me why you left with the Army that day?'

'No small talk, huh?'

'No point in it.'

He blew out a long breath and looked up at the ceiling. 'Remember how I told you I needed to find myself again?'

She nodded. 'Before your Army buddies broke in, you said you were going back to The Aegis.'

'That was the plan, but the Army wanted me back. They told me they thought I was part of some prophecy.'

'Tayla mentioned something about that,' she snorted. 'Do you know how cryptic prophecies are? And how often they don't come true?'

'Yeah. I know. But I needed to find out why they thought I was involved, and if the fallen angel thing was true.'

'"Fallen angel thing"?'

He met her gaze. 'Apparently I have a fallen angel perched in my family tree. From way back. Probably Biblical times.'

Well, that was kind of cool. 'So the Army thinks this is important?'

'That's why they wanted me back. They didn't really give me a choice.'

'Oh, come on,' she scoffed. 'You'd have gone anyway. You and your hero complex.' It was a bitchy thing to say, but he just shoved his hands into his jeans pockets and nodded.

'I deserved that.'

'You more than deserved it.' So much for keeping her temper in check. 'How could you do that to me? I mean, I get why you left, but how could you tell me you want me and then turn around and send a kiss-off message through Runa? You couldn't do it yourself? What kind of chickenshit move was that?'

'The kind of move that sends you straight to some other guy,' he snapped.

'And you wanted that . . . why?'

Suddenly he was in front of her, his hands clamping down on the kitchen island behind her, penning her between his body, his arms, and the counter.

'I was in a really bad place. I missed the hell out of you, and I figured that if you moved on, I could concentrate on what I needed to do. But I should have known better, because I couldn't think about anything but you.' He emphasized his words with a slow grind of his pelvis against her belly. 'The idea that another man might have been making love to you killed me.'

'Good.' She tilted her head to look at him. 'You hurt me.'

He lowered his mouth to hers. 'I'm sorry,' he said against her lips, and a shock of heat sizzled all the way to her core. 'I'm so sorry.'

Tentatively, he kissed her, but she didn't kiss him back. At least, not until he swiped his tongue over her bottom lip while pushing his hips into hers, making her gasp and open up to him. Instantly, he penetrated her mouth, the hot, wet slide of his tongue against hers forcing her participation.

A slow burn heated the blood in her veins, loosened her up so that when he dragged his mouth along her jawbone and down her neck, she threw her head back and thawed completely.

'More?' he murmured against her skin.

All she could manage was a soft, 'Mmm-hmm.'

Her breath caught as he swept her up and spun around to plant her butt on the table between the plates and the candlesticks.

Roughly, he shoved her skirt up around her waist and then unbuttoned his jeans. He didn't release himself, instead turning his attention to yanking off her panties. They tore when they caught on one of her boots, but she didn't care. He did that to her, made her forget everything except how she felt when he was touching her.

Needing closer contact, she gripped his shoulders, but he caught her wrists in one of his large hands and stretched her arms over her head. He hooked his other arm behind her waist and bent her back, dragged his tongue from her throat to where her shirt gaped open between her breasts as he lowered her to the table.

He looked at her, the raw hunger and flickering candlelight making his eyes flash. 'I'm going to do you right here on the table, Gem. Can you handle that?'

'Yes,' she moaned, and tightened her thighs around his hips so her core fit tight against his cock, which had been freed from its denim prison. She could handle anything he dished out. She'd have sex with him anytime, anywhere, in any way he wanted to do it.

Later, she'd chastise herself for being such a pathetic doormat, but right now she just wanted to revel in how he made her feel. And right now, he was feeling her arms, sliding his fingers down the sensitive insides until he reached her rib cage. Tingles shivered over her skin, and they only intensified when he unbuttoned her shirt to expose her braless breasts to his gaze and his hands.

She bit her lip to keep from crying out when he rubbed slow circles around her nipples and then lowered his head to flick his tongue over the tightly pebbled tips.

'You like that,' he growled. 'Say it. Tell me what you want.'

'Bite them,' she breathed. 'And fill me. I need you inside me.'

A shudder shook his body, as though he was relieved to have been given the go-ahead. A stab of pain sliced through her as his teeth closed on one nipple, not hard, but with just enough pressure to enhance the pleasure of his shaft stretching her entrance as he slid home.

She tightened her thighs around his waist and arched up, taking all of him as deep as he could go. For a moment he remained still, using his teeth, tongue, and hands to create the most exquisite sensations in her breasts. But too soon, yet not soon enough, he stood straight, grasped her hips, and tugged her firmly against him. Her legs dangled over the side of the table, her butt just barely on the edge.

The vulnerability of this position was breathtaking, her skirt bunched around her waist, her breasts exposed, her arms still over her head because she dare not move them. Not while he watched her with a commanding expression on his face, the orders issued through his gaze alone.

Heat from the candle flames licked her skin, tiny flicks of warmth. She longed to feel Kynan's tongue licking her like that, swirling around her navel piercing, tracing the long-stemmed rose tattoo on her leg, stroking between her legs.

But she didn't think she could ever ask for that. She might possess self-confidence when it came to her job, but her sexual inexperience made her too shy in the bedroom.

Closing her eyes, she rolled her hips, smiling at the sudden hiss of air between his teeth. 'You're wanting to come already?' His thumb spread her folds and found that sweet spot that made her cry out. 'Can't wait, huh?' His hips pumped once, twice, bringing her to the edge.

'God, yes,' she gasped.

'I want to make you come over and over. Every day.' His voice was husky, smoky, and she wondered what it would feel like if he spoke against her aching core.

'Oh, yes . . . Kynan . . . now.'

As though a dam had broken, he began to pound into her, at the same time he slid her back and forth on the polished tabletop. The friction burned her back, candle wax sprinkled onto her belly and breasts, and lust blazed between her legs.

His pace became furious, and the wet sound of their bodies colliding became a trigger for that most primitive response for any human or demon. Release blasted through her, rocking her so hard that one of the candles tipped over, splashing hot wax across her ribs even as Kynan's hot semen splashed inside her.

It struck her then that he'd not used a condom.

She was on the Pill, thank God. She wasn't worried about disease. She was much more worried about accidental pregnancy. Any child born to her and a human would be three-quarters human, one-quarter demon, and, to many, an abomination.

Though she could scarcely breathe, she managed to lift her upper body enough to prop herself on her elbows. She and Kynan were still locked together. He stood between her legs, head hanging, chest heaving with the force of his breaths. His sweater had ridden up, revealing a holster beneath. He was armed, ready for a fight.

'Shit,' he breathed. 'Condom.'

'I'm on the Pill.'

'I'm sorry. I couldn't wait. The thought of that ... guy ... touching you—'

'What guy?'

'Last night. I saw you with someone in the hospital parking lot.'

Bitterness welled up, ruining her postcoital glow. 'Lore? So that was what this was about? You were jealous?'

In the dim light cast by the candles, she saw his expression turn savage. 'What were you thinking? The guy is a demon—'

'And that's none of your business.' She shoved at his chest hard enough to make him step back, and she nearly cried out at the loss, the emptiness. 'You gave up the right to be jealous when you dumped me.'

'That's not how it was.' His voice was hard and his jaw was tight as he tucked himself back into his pants so quickly that in seconds she never would have known they'd just had incredible sex.

Except she was still exposed, half-naked. Awkwardly, she yanked down her skirt and tugged her shirt together to cover her breasts. 'No? That's how it was to me. And this?' She gestured between them. 'This wasn't making love. This was a jealousy fuck. A year ago, that would have been enough for me, but not anymore. So get out.'

'Gem—'

'*Get. Out!*'

He regarded her with shuttered eyes, his frustration obvious in the taut lines of his body. For a second she thought he'd argue, but then he stalked to the door and whipped it open. She hadn't thought he could hurt her more than when he'd given her the kiss-off through Runa, but as he closed the door behind him, she realized she was wrong.

So very wrong.

ൟ

That could have gone better, Kynan thought, as he walked down the hallway of Gem's apartment building.

He scrubbed his hand over his face and tried to tell himself that he wasn't the world's biggest bastard.

Liar.

He'd come over here to talk, to be seductive and romantic . . . and instead he'd treated Gem like she was a sex toy. He'd wanted her, he'd been jealous, and selfishly, he'd acted on impulse.

He turned around and stared at her door, tempted to go back and explain. Apologize. Except she was seriously worked up, and he doubted he'd get far.

He was such an asshole.

Asshole doesn't cover it, asshole.

Cursing, he spun around and headed for the elevator. He was staying with Eidolon and Tayla, because although he'd prefer a hotel room, Tay had insisted. Besides, staying with them gave all of them an opportunity to catch up and compare notes on the recent happenings on Earth and in Sheoul.

He wondered if Gem knew he was staying with her sister.

Him and his *hero complex.*

Okay, that was a fair assessment. But his complex wasn't about accolades or the happy-happy feeling that came from rescuing kittens in trees or parachuting into war zones to save downed soldiers. He didn't care if anyone knew the good he'd done. He just needed to do it. To make a difference.

Sure, he could make a difference on the streets as a paramedic or a cop. He could re-enlist and make a difference by patching up injured troops. But deep down, he'd always wanted to do things on a grander scale. Which meant saving not a few men, but mankind as a race.

That was a big fucking joke, because he couldn't save himself, let alone mankind.

He made it to the elevator, punched the Down button, and a moment later the doors slid open. The bastard Gem had been with last night stepped out.

Territorial rage spun up faster than a spring storm, and Kynan moved to block the guy. 'Lore, right?'

The male narrowed his dark eyes. 'Who are you?'

I'm the man who is going to sever your head from your body, demon.

Kynan reached automatically for the dagger tucked inside his jacket pocket, but fumbled the hilt as Gem's voice tripped through his head. *You gave up the right to be jealous when you dumped me. This wasn't making love. This was a jealousy fuck.*

And wouldn't killing her lover prove exactly what she'd said.

Though every instinct screamed at him to kill the demon in front of him, he drew his hand away from the weapon. 'Who am I?' he asked calmly. 'I'm your competition.'

൏

Red rotating lights on the emergency room walls announced the arrival of Underworld General's only working ambulance. The other had blown an engine this morning. Perfect. On top of the hospital's woes, Eidolon had been sick with some sort of demon bug, and Shade seemed to have caught it as well.

Wincing at his muscle aches, Eidolon donned a paper gown and finished gloving up as Shade and Luc rolled a stretcher laden with two hundred pounds of pregnant Suresh demon into the first trauma room. The female moaned and tossed her head, her black dreads smacking against equipment that threatened to topple.

'No progression of labor since we picked her up,' Shade said. 'I can make the womb contract, but there seems to be a blockage.'

'Page Shakvhan.' Normally Eidolon wouldn't require a female physician to handle a birth, but Sureshi females were notorious male-haters, and they responded much better to the same sex. How they ever managed to get pregnant was a mystery.

'I'll clean up the rig,' Luc said, and slipped out of the room. The warg was a great paramedic in the field, but once he brought in a patient, he wanted nothing more to do with them.

The Suresh lifted her head and screamed, and blood gushed from between her muscular legs. Shade gripped her hand, his *dermoire* glowing as he channeled power into her. 'It's coming.'

'Hurts,' she moaned through clenched teeth.

'Guess we're not waiting for Shakvhan.' Eidolon would have to take his chances with the female and hope she didn't bite his arm off.

Quickly, he set up a sterile field. Shade assisted with towels as the female pushed, her contractions coming one on top of the other.

'There we go,' Eidolon breathed, as the infant's head began to crown. It was big. Bigger than it should have been ... and smoother. 'Shade, contract the uterus.'

Shade moved his hand down the Suresh's swollen stomach and closed his eyes. The female cried out and bore down.

The infant's head emerged. Eidolon swore silently. This wasn't a Sureshi baby, and he had a moment of both dread and joy at his sudden suspicion.

'You're doing good, female,' he said. 'Shade, one more.'

Another contraction rocked her, and the infant slid fully out, covered in blood and birth fluids, but the *dermoire* on the infant's right arm confirmed his suspicions. Seminus demon. The mother was not going to be happy.

'Shade, I need you to take the infant.'

Surprise flickered in his brother's dark eyes. This was only the second Seminus born at UG. The first, over ten years ago, had possessed the markings of one of the Seminus Council members, and the mother had wanted the infant. Eidolon had a feeling the Suresh would not. At least, she wouldn't want to raise it. Eat it, maybe. Kill it, definitely.

'Where is it?' The female writhed on the table, trying to see her child.

Shade wrapped the squalling infant in a blanket and brought it around.

'*That?*' she roared. 'That is what grew inside me? That *parasite?*' She snarled and swiped for it, but Shade stepped out of the way. The writing on the walls pulsed violently, and she yelped at the activation of the Haven spell. She held her head and panted through the pain, but she never stopped glaring at the baby. 'Give it to me. I will take it outside and crush it.'

A low growl emanated from deep in Shade's throat. 'We will dispose of the infant.' He stalked off before the female could argue, but she cursed in a dozen different languages as Eidolon completed post-birth procedures.

When he was done, he found Shade with the baby in the nursery. He didn't look up as Eidolon entered. 'Congratulations, bro. You're an uncle again.'

'What did you say?'

Shade fastened a diaper like a pro and turned to him, keeping one hand protectively on the baby's belly. Shade had always been good with the young of any species, had practiced a lot with his sisters, but since becoming a father, he had developed an even stronger paternal instinct.

'This is Wraith's offspring,' he said, and Eidolon missed a step as he approached the changing table.

'Interesting.' Eidolon ran his finger over the infant's *dermoire*, pausing over the top mark, an hourglass at the base of his neck, the one that identified the father as Wraith.

'I've already called Runa. We'll raise it as our own.'

'You plan to tell Wraith? Because for all his faults, he *can* count, and eventually he'll figure out that you have four babies instead of three.'

Shade bundled the squirming infant in a blanket. 'Yeah, he needs to know. And he should be the one to name it.'

Eidolon shook his head. 'This is weird.'

Shade lifted the infant gently into his arms. 'It's never going to end, is it?' His gaze locked with Eidolon's. 'We're never going to be done cleaning up Wraith's messes.'

'He's doing what our breed does after *s'genesis.*'

'I'm not talking about populating the world with Seminus young.'

'I know.' Wraith had always been a troublemaker, and at one point, he'd nearly started a war between their species and vampires. Wreaking havoc was what he did best. 'And it's going to be even worse once he gets that charm.'

Shade looked down at the newborn. 'Sometimes I think the only thing that keeps Wraith going is the idea that, eventually, someone or something is going to kill him. If he gets the charm, he won't have that anymore. I don't want to see him lose his mind like our father did. Like Roag did.'

'Like I almost did,' Eidolon said quietly. If not for Tayla, he'd have turned into a beast his brothers would have been forced to put down.

'We can't give up hope.' Shade made some cooing noises at the baby and then looked up. 'Wraith is full of surprises.'

'Yeah, but they usually aren't good ones.' Eidolon rubbed the bridge of his nose as his persistent headache worsened. 'Hey, you feeling any better?'

'I wish,' Shade said. 'This morning my gut cramped so hard I think my spine cracked.'

'Are Runa and the kids okay?'

'They're great. In fact, I haven't seen anyone else who's sick. Maybe this is a breed-specific bug?'

'Maybe.' But something about that wasn't sitting right. Namely, they hadn't been in contact with any other Sems. Wraith was getting worse, but that was because of the poison ... 'Oh ... oh, fuck.'

'What?'

'I need to check on something. I'll page you when I get a definitive answer.'

'E—'

Eidolon ignored Shade and jogged toward his office. He had a sinking feeling this wasn't a bug. This was a cancer.

TWELVE

Wraith spent a fitful night after Serena left his cabin. He'd been aroused to the point of pain, requiring an injection of Eidolon's anti-libido drug, but that had only been a minor part of Wraith's sleeplessness.

He hadn't been able to get Serena out of his mind. Her voice, her scent, the sounds she made when she came. Gods, the feel of her slick honey on his fingers . . . he'd wanted to taste her and then bury himself so deep inside her she'd feel him there for weeks.

Except, would she have weeks to live afterward? To think about him and regret what she'd let him take from her?

He'd warred with himself over whether or not he should go after her and apologize, but in the end he'd decided to give her some space. Besides, his failure to take her virginity when he'd had a couple of prime opportunities was eating at him. Why the hell was he stalling? He told himself that he was playing with his prey the way he often did, but was he? Or was he holding off the grand finale because for the first time in his life, he was enjoying being with a female for something other than sex?

He'd lain awake for hours thinking about it, and when he finally had fallen asleep, he'd succumbed to nightmares again. He'd been transported back to that dark basement, the dungeon where he'd spent his childhood, locked in a cage with nothing but a scratchy wool blanket on the dirt floor to sleep on and a metal pail in the corner that functioned as a toilet.

He shook his head free of the memories and nightmares as he exited the dining car and headed to Serena's cabin. She hadn't shown up for breakfast, and now he was concerned that she'd been spooked by what had happened between them last night and had gotten off the train at Luxor or Cairo, the two stops before Aswan. If she had, he'd be screwed, right to the wall and right into his grave.

Shit.

He increased his pace from a walk to a jog as he approached her sleeping car. When he reached her cabin door, he knocked. Waited. His lungs ached, and he realized he'd been holding his breath.

She didn't answer. He knocked again and was about to kick the door in when she finally opened up. She wore khaki cargo pants and a long-sleeved, olive button-down, but her feet were bare and her hair was a fluffy tangle of gold around her shoulders, and he got the distinct impression he'd woken her up.

'Hey,' she said. 'I must have fallen asleep after I got dressed this morning. Did you already eat breakfast?'

He nodded and held out the box in his hand. 'I figured you'd slept in, so I brought you something.'

'You didn't have to do that,' she said, even as she snatched the box out of his hand. 'But thank you. Are you feeling better? How's your stomach?'

'Fine.' He stood there like a dolt, feeling awkward and stupid, and she wasn't making things easier by staring at him as if she expected something. Like, maybe, an apology. Fuck. He wasn't good at those. He rubbed the back of his neck, which did nothing to ease the tension there. 'Ah . . . could I come in?'

She backed up in the narrow space. 'Suit yourself.'

He stepped inside. 'I owe you an apology,' he blurted. Man, that hurt.

'I agree.'

Okay, what now? He shoved his hand in his pocket and felt up his switchblade, which always comforted him. 'So . . . I'm sorry.'

'Boy, you suck at apologies.'

'What do you want me to do? Fall at your feet and beg for forgiveness?' He snapped his mouth shut, because talking to her this way was definitely not going to score him points.

He seemed to be losing ground with her a lot faster than he was gaining it, and he needed to get back on track and fast. He'd called E this morning, and his brother had sounded like hell as he talked about all the shit that had gone down. Apparently, the hospital's entire third wing had collapsed. Six staff members had died and it had taken some seriously powerful magic to keep the New York City streets above the underground hospital from caving in.

Suck up. Just suck up. 'Serena, I'm sorry. I really am. I'm not good at apologies. Obviously.'

'It's okay,' she sighed. 'It's not all your fault. I overreacted to something that shouldn't have been a big deal.'

'No.' He took the box away from her, tossed it onto the bed behind her, and framed her face in his hands. 'I'm the one who overreacted. I'm not used to anyone worrying about me. No one except my brothers, anyway.' Hey, that wasn't so hard. Probably because it was the truth. Novel idea, telling the truth. . . .

'And your brothers worrying is a bad thing?'

'It's like they think I need a babysitter.'

She covered one of his hands with hers, stroked his fingers with her thumb. 'So, are they overprotective, or have you done something to deserve their concern?'

He blinked, taken aback by her blunt question. 'You speak your mind, don't you?'

'I've found that beating around the bush takes too much time to get to the same place.'

Man, he liked her. He really, *really* liked her. 'Baby, you're speaking my language.'

'So . . . about your brothers?'

'It's a little of both with them,' he said, running with the honesty thing. 'E's a doctor, so he's naturally a worrywart, and Shade's always been the nurturing kind, but he's gone overboard since he became a dad.'

'And what about you? What have you done to make them worry?'

'There isn't enough time in this day to list it all,' he admitted. 'Let's just say that I've been a very bad boy.'

Something sparked in her eyes. Excitement, as if she was picturing him doing naughty things. Maybe to her. 'Girls like that, you know.'

'Like what?'

She hooked a finger under the collar of his T-shirt and tugged playfully. 'Bad boys.'

'Oh, yeah?' His voice was low and rough, and he liked it. 'What about you? Do you like bad boys?'

'There's definitely appeal,' she breathed.

'Good.' He bent and clipped her earlobe with his teeth. The scent of her desire filled the air, and his nostrils flared, taking it in. 'Because they don't come badder than me.'

'I don't know . . . ' Her tone was flirty, yet husky, made more tantalizing by the way she dragged the ball of her foot up his calf. 'I'm hearing a lot of talk and no action.'

'You know what happens when you stir up a hornets' nest, right?' He nuzzled her neck, enjoying the sound of her soft moan.

'Good thing I'm not allergic to bee stings.'

He opened his mouth over her jugular and allowed his vampire canines to just brush her skin. 'My sting is a lot more potent.'

She sagged against him, and he'd have been content to play this scene out, but they'd be pulling into Aswan in a few minutes. 'I'm going to go grab my bags. I want you to have eaten everything in the box by the time I get back.'

She stepped out of his arms and jammed her fists on her hips in annoyance, which might have been more effective if she hadn't whacked her elbow on the wall. 'You sure are bossy.'

He shrugged. 'Part of the bad boy thing. Now eat. I don't want you passing out before we even get to the hotel.'

'I'm not going to pass out—'

He cut her off with a kiss. 'If you did, I'd catch you.' Gods, he'd laugh at either of his brothers if they said that to their mates, the pussywhipped idiots. So he tried to tell himself this was all part of the seduction. That it was all part of his dastardly scheme to take Serena's virginity and her charm.

That it was anything but the truth, because the truth was that Serena was turning out to be so much more than a mission.

❧

They don't come badder than me.

Josh's words rang through Serena's head as they approached the hotel on foot. She didn't believe him. Oh, he walked the walk, talked the talk, and all those other clichés, but she sensed vulnerability beneath the handsome, tough exterior. Like when he'd talked about his childhood. That had been a knife to the heart.

His mother had kept him in a *cage*? And her family had killed his father? How had he gotten away from that situation? And what had happened to his mother?

Serena prayed she was rotting in jail somewhere. Josh had lived a hellish life, but the fact that he'd survived – with a sense of humor, even – said a lot about his strength.

He walked beside her, sunglasses on, clearing a path through the crowds with nothing more than his size and presence. The cool breeze coming off the Nile ruffled his hair, and every once in a while he'd rake it back from his face to reveal the angular profile she'd never tire of admiring.

Pathetic, really.

He slowed to pet a cat hanging out in front of a meat market. The mangy tom eyed her warily, but it rubbed against Josh like an old friend.

She just shook her head in amazement that someone so strong, so powerful, could be so gentle with a little animal. Then again, his touch with her last night had been skilled and nimble, and she heated up just thinking about it.

'I wouldn't have taken you for an animal person,' she said, when the cat ran to some scraps tossed into a dish near the shop's side door.

He shrugged. 'For some reason, they like me. My brother's ... wife ... has this weasel that won't leave me alone. She says he's a traitor.'

'Your brother?'

'The weasel.'

'Well, the weasel has good taste.' His faced colored, and she couldn't help but smile. 'My mom used to say that a man who hates cats is insecure, but a man who likes them is one worth keeping. If he can appreciate a cat, he can appreciate a strong, independent woman.'

He snorted. 'Sweetheart, I can appreciate any woman.'

'But the strong, independent ones are the best, right?'

At her teasing – okay, fishing for compliments – tone, he grinned. 'I'm starting to see the benefits.' He adjusted the bags he carried on his shoulder. 'So, where are we going?'

She crowded next to him to avoid getting run over by a man on a bike who had swerved to avoid a vehicle popping up on the curb. She loved Egypt, but seriously, no one in this country knew how to drive.

'Philae,' she said. 'The Temple of Hathor. I believe that hidden inside one of the pillars is a stone tablet with writings that are supposed to work in conjunction with the coin I found in Alexandria.'

He ground to a halt, jerking her to a stop with him. 'What is it you plan to do with these artifacts?'

'Why do you ask?'

'Curiosity.'

'When I'm merely curious, I don't squeeze anyone's hand into a pulp.'

Josh cursed and loosened his grip. 'Did I hurt you?'

'I'm tougher than that. But why are you so *curious*?'

'Ancient magic isn't something to fuck around with.'

She rolled her eyes. 'I'm not going to perform a ceremony myself. The items are for Val. You know there's something going on. Something bad, or demons wouldn't be after me and the artifacts, right?' Speaking of which, she needed an Internet connection as soon as possible. She had to find out what might have affected her charm, and Val's Aegis research site seemed the best place to start digging.

Josh rubbed the back of his neck, the movement making the muscles in his arm flex and roll beneath his tanned skin. 'I guess. We going to go, or what?'

She glanced at her watch. 'I suppose we should check into our hotel.'

'Yeah. But here's the thing.' He stepped into her, so close she took a step back, but he moved with her. 'You've got something after you. I can protect you. We share a room.'

'I can protect myself.' From everything except Byzamoth. And maybe other demons. And Josh.

'I can do it better. I can do a lot of things better,' he said, and the husky, wicked tone told her he was thinking of the orgasm he'd given her. 'You need me.'

From somewhere deep inside, she felt like she wanted to protest, but he was right. And the way he was looking at her, his gaze heated and hypnotic, seduced everything that made her female.

'We get a suite, and you can have the couch,' she managed, even though she knew he'd end up in her bed.

His cocky smile said he knew it, too. But he had the grace to not say anything. Instead, he dipped his head. She thought he was going to kiss her, but he didn't. Not on the mouth. No, he tipped her chin back with his hand and opened his mouth right over her jugular. Right in the place he'd bitten her in her dreams.

She swayed, her knees going weak. His teeth scraped her skin and for a crazy moment she thought he truly would bite her, like this was some sort of fantasy come to life. She moaned and clutched at his shirt, holding him there, encouraging him, wishing they were in private, because a deep ache had taken root between her legs, and screw the one-time deal thing she'd told herself last night.

She was so going to do some of those *other things* tonight.

THIRTEEN

There was a Harrowgate on the island of Philae. Wraith knew because he could sense it. And because he'd used it twenty years ago when he'd come here in search of a statue of Isis.

The fact that the island hosted a Harrowgate was bad enough, given that demons were after Serena, but worse, it had recently been activated.

Something was very, very wrong. Whatever had come out of the Harrowgate was still here. In fact, Wraith could sense multiple evil presences. It wasn't unusual for demons to be on the island – it was, after all, a hot spot for demon rituals. But not during the daytime, and certainly not in the number Wraith sensed.

He and Serena had come by boat after checking into the hotel. He'd been annoyed, at first, by her insistence on a suite, but the extra room had given her the space she'd needed to feel comfortable, and anything that made her comfortable worked to his advantage.

He'd done the medication thing while she showered, giving him a chance to head off the nausea that had taken hold right after they'd checked in. He didn't need to deal with getting sick again.

Hell, he didn't want to deal with any of this. He'd kept himself awake last night wondering why he hadn't taken her virginity yet, but this morning, another horrifying thought had come to him. Was he dragging this out because he wanted to get to know her? Was he hoping she'd get to know him, learn to love him, and want to show him by making love to him?

He almost laughed out loud. Who the hell would love someone enough to give up their life for a night of sex?

No one. Which meant he might as well give up. He could stay with her, protect her until she got home, and then he could go out in a blaze of glory, killing vamps or something.

He'd had worse plans.

So ... that was it, then. He was going to die, and Serena was going to live.

He waited for panic to set in, or at least, a change of heart. But nothing happened. If anything, he felt ... lighter. Was this what it felt like to do something unselfish?

The sensation was weird. Uncomfortable, yet ... not awful. Like liquor that tasted like shit but went down smooth.

Wraith watched Serena standing in the sun, her delicate profile a stark contrast to the harsh landscape. She wore no makeup, but her bronze skin glowed with vitality, and the toned lines of her body spoke of strength and stamina.

Gods, she was magnificent.

And he was a dumbass for admiring her when he should be guarding her. He forced himself into battle mode, staying alert as Serena wandered through the ruins, completely oblivious to the danger surrounding them. When a stick snapped beneath her foot, he whirled, fists clenched and ready to strike.

'Geez, you're jumpy,' Serena said. She gestured to the multitude of visitors swarming the island. 'Are you worried we'll get caught?'

He stared off in the direction of the Harrowgate. 'It's not that. Something else. Bad vibes. Maybe we should go. Come back later.'

'Does this have something to do with Byzamoth?' The way she

asked, with a slight hesitation in her voice, surprised him. Up until now, she'd been incredibly nonchalant when it came to the demons they'd encountered.

'Maybe.'

She appeared to consider his suggestion to come back later, but after a moment shook her head. 'We'll be fine. This is too important to wait.' She started for the Temple of Hathor, and he had no choice but to follow. He kept his eyes peeled, scanning the landscape for anything out of place or unusual. The hair standing up on the back of his neck told him something was watching. Waiting.

They worked their way across the hot, dusty land to the temple, which rose up out of the island, a broken shell of the great building it once had been. Its small courtyard was empty of visitors, but then, the courtyard was pretty much an uninteresting pile of old rocks.

She stopped at the enclosure wall. A breeze, cooled slightly by the surrounding water, blew her hair into her face, but she didn't seem to notice. She'd gone statue-still, her eyes twinkling like amber caught in the sun.

'Can you feel the history?' She finally brushed the hair off her cheeks. 'I love the places I get to visit. I love the way they come alive. The vibes here are almost overwhelming.'

'You can say that again,' he muttered, but he wasn't talking about the same vibes. He was still picking up demons on his radar. But he knew what she meant. Back when E had first asked him to be UG's artifact hunter – a job created solely to keep Wraith out of trouble – Wraith had been game because he liked the chase. The danger.

But gradually, thanks to all the research and travel he'd done, he'd come to appreciate the history – both human and demon – bound to the places that turned up the treasures. They all possessed a different feel, some good, some bad ... most somewhere in between. But always there was a palpable imprint of past activity that energized him.

She moved off, working her way carefully over the stone slabs, a hand-drawn map in her hand. The sense of malevolence grew stronger, almost with every step she took, and he was seriously ready to get the fuck out of there.

'We need to hurry. How can I help?'

She held up her hand, her concentration so fierce she obviously didn't want to be interrupted. Frustrated, he kept an eye on their surroundings as she muttered to herself, checked each pillar with methodical precision, poked around the rubble at the bases.

'Oh, crap.' She kneeled next to a broken pillar lying on its side.

'What is it?'

'The pillar. It's been destroyed. It either fell over or was pushed.'

He crouched beside her. The broken edges were sharp. This was fresh. 'Serena? What is this tablet you're looking for? Straight up. What's it do?'

She rubbed her eyes with the heels of her palms. 'Val – and the Elders – believe there's some sort of demon invasion coming. The Tablet of Mons Silpius is supposed to work with the coin to provide some sort of protection. I think ... I think it's supposed to render the Harrowgates useless.'

That was some damned powerful magic. And any demon in his right mind would do whatever it took to prevent The Aegis from carrying out their plan. Maybe that was why he was sensing the evil presences – demons had taken the tablet already, and they were either on their way off the island with their treasure ... or they were waiting around for the person who carried the other half of the equation.

He grabbed her wrist. 'We're out of here.'

'Absolutely not.' She tried to jerk free, but when that didn't work, she started peeling his fingers off her arm. 'I can search the broken stone and see if the tablet is still there. And intact.'

A tingle shot up his spine and spiked through his brain. This was bad. Very bad. Inside he was chafing, all his instincts spinning like blades in his chest, telling him to grab Serena and run.

And goddammit ... his stomach had chosen now to act up with poison reflux. 'No—'

A foul wind spun up, swirled around them like a dust devil. Still crouching, he whirled around with a hiss.

'Josh?'

'We gotta go, Serena.' He leaped to his feet, but it was too late.

They came at them from all sides. Silas demons, the mercenaries of the underworld. Wraith had always hated the fishbelly white, eyeless bastards, sellouts who could be bought for any job for the right pay.

'Oh, boy,' she breathed. 'Cue the *Raiders of the Lost Ark* music.'

'These aren't Nazis, babe.'

Wraith shoved Serena to the ground. Silas demons were tall, and while their long limbs and extended reach gave them fighting advantages, they couldn't bend easily, and if Serena remained flat—

She came to her feet and threw a punch at the Silas nearest her, knocking him to the ground. Blood flowed from his broken nose. Smoothly, she moved on to the next one, each action elegant and efficient, and damn, the woman could handle herself. He was relieved to see that her charm was in effect. It prevented her from taking blows, but she delivered them with brutal efficiency, dancing on the balls of her feet like a beautiful, untouchable Valkyrie. He'd like to get her in a gym, where they could spar until he took her down to the mat and—

A kick to the kidney leveled Wraith. He rolled and came to his feet. He'd been caught off guard, had been so busy admiring Serena that he'd let himself get taken. That wouldn't happen again.

He leaped into the air, spun, took out two Silases with combination kicks to their heads. Still, they swarmed like ants. In the distance, he heard screams and the gruesome sound of tearing flesh. The human tourists were being slaughtered.

There were high prices to be paid for human massacres, so

whoever had hired these scum must either be extremely powerful or this was a precursor to something worse, like the demon invasion Serena had talked about.

Wraith took a crippling blow to the gut. His muscles turned watery, and oh, fuck, the damned poison was attacking him from the inside as the demons were attacking from the outside.

A Silas kicked him in the head as Wraith doubled over. Stars swam in his vision. He went to his knees, wobbled, and caught himself with his hand.

Suddenly, the Silas went flying backward and landed at an awkward angle, its head wrenched a hundred and eighty degrees. Serena stood there like a guardian angel, looking pretty damned proud of herself.

Wraith would be proud of her too, except he was smarting from the beating and by the fact that he'd been rescued by a human. A human *female*. *He* was the one who was supposed to do the hero shit.

She leaped into action to take out another one, giving him the break he needed to get back on his feet. Another Silas came at him, and somehow he managed to pummel it, until an agonized cry brought him around. Serena had been captured by a black-robed figure. A flash of the face beneath its hood told Wraith all he needed to know about the bastard's identity.

Byzamoth.

His arm was hooked around her neck as he dragged her backward. She clawed at the male's arm, her legs flailing wildly.

'Serena!' Wraith sprinted toward her, silently willing the demon to let her go. He didn't think about the fact that her charm wasn't working against the demon. Again. He didn't think about the fact that by turning his back on the Silas horde he was opening himself up to attack. He had to save Serena.

He weaved through the masses, blocking strikes and dodging blows. He closed in on the demon, who had taken Serena to the ground, forced her to her hands and knees. Still, she fought, swiping at him with her nails, kicking out at his groin. Byzamoth snarled and punched her in the back of her head.

Serena sagged bonelessly to the ground.

Rage twisted into a vicious, gnarled knot in Wraith's chest. He dove for the other being, struck him in the back and knocked him into a boulder. 'You are so dead,' he snarled, slamming two rapid-fire kicks into the demon's face. Blood sprayed from his mashed nose, and then Byzamoth was on his feet, and Silas demons were swarming the Temple of Hathor.

'You are the one who is about to die,' Byzamoth said, and Wraith wanted to knock that sneer right off his too pretty face.

But now wasn't the time. Wraith might be the best fighter in the upper- and underworld, but he wasn't invincible, and he was beyond outnumbered.

In a quick series of moves, he lashed out with one foot, catching Byzamoth in the chest, at the same time twisting to chop a Silas in the jaw. As the two careened into other demons, Wraith swept up Serena without breaking stride. Their only hope was to reach the Harrowgate, and even that depended on Serena remaining unconscious.

Conscious humans died in Harrowgates.

He ran hard, leaping ancient stone carvings and dodging spears and knives thrown by Silas warriors. Serena's charm now seemed to keep her safe; twice, demons tripped and fell on their own weapons as they tried to impale her with blades, and once, two spears collided in mid-air and clattered harmlessly to the ground.

Ahead, the Harrowgate shimmered between two stone pillars of the Temple of Isis. Three demons, one Silas and two Cruenti, guarded the entrance. Behind Wraith, Byzamoth's shouts and threats grew louder. Shit.

He was going to have to plow straight through the sentries.

This was going to hurt.

Sucking in a deep breath, he held Serena tight to his chest and shot across the expanse of land. Head down, he rammed the Silas with his shoulder, knocking the male into a huge figure of Horus carved deep into a column. Wraith threw out one arm and jammed the heel of his hand into a Cruentus's nose. The thing howled in pain. The other one slashed at Wraith with his long claws, catching him across the back of the neck. Wraith stumbled and nearly fell.

The Harrowgate flashed, the shimmering curtain peeling back as another Silas emerged. Wraith punched it in the gut and dove into the Harrowgate. He tapped the map of the United States, which activated the gate and wouldn't allow anything else inside. For now, they were safe.

But as the blood trickled down his neck and back, he knew that their safety was only as good as the moment, because whatever Byzamoth was, he was powerful enough to not only negate the power of Serena's charm and command an army of demons, but to risk the wrath of both Heaven and Hell.

ᘓ

Wraith stepped through UG's Harrowgate with Serena still unconscious in his arms. Relief that she had remained out for the journey was tempered by worry that she was, in fact, still out.

'Get E and Shade,' he snapped to the nurse at the triage desk, and without slowing, he strode to the nearest exam room. Gently, he lay Serena on the bed. She didn't even stir. For a moment he stood there, petting her hair, wincing when his hand came away bloody. Dammit, where were his brothers?

The curtain swept open and Dr. Shakvhan entered. 'She's human?'

'Last time I checked. Where's E?'

'I'm on duty today.'

'I didn't ask if you were on duty,' Wraith said. 'I want my brothers.'

The curvy succubus sniffed haughtily, ignoring him as she began a vitals check. Even if it wasn't physically impossible for succubi and incubi to screw, he wouldn't touch her. In the dictionary, the word 'bitch' ran and hid from her.

'How long has she been unconscious?'

'Five minutes, maybe.'

'Her name?'

'Serena.'

Shakvhan peered into Serena's face. 'Serena? Can you hear me?'

Serena's lids fluttered, and she moaned. Not the greatest sign, but better than nothing.

'Wraith.' E moved inside, dressed in khakis and a black button-down shirt, which meant he'd been working in his office today. 'What happened?' He frowned and reached for Wraith's neck. 'You're bleeding.'

Wraith pushed E's hand away. 'We'll deal with me later. Serena needs help.'

'You know I don't like having humans here,' E said, moving to her.

'I don't give a fuck. Where's Shade?'

'On his way. The ambulance was just pulling into the parking garage when I got the triage nurse's page.'

The succubus rattled off vitals, ending with 'GCS of eight.'

Eight. Wraith had been on enough ambulance runs to know that eight and below on the Glasgow Coma Scale indicated a severe brain injury. His gut knotted with helplessness.

Eidolon started an IV. 'Thanks, I got it.'

Shakvhan shrugged and sauntered away, and Wraith yanked the curtain closed. 'We were attacked by demons on Philae. While I was fighting, she took a hit.'

E looked up from inspecting Serena's head wound, his expression one of relief. 'You slept with her.'

'No. That's the thing. Nothing should have been able to touch her, right?'

'Dammit,' E breathed. 'Someone else got to her.'

'That's impossible.'

'There's no other explanation, Wraith.'

The heavy strike of boots on the stone floor announced Shade's arrival, and the curtain swished open. 'What's going on?'

E's dark brows drew together. 'Head injury. I need you to do a system check and see how bad.'

'This is Wraith's charmed human?'

'Except for the charmed part.'

Wraith snarled. 'She's still charmed.'

E gave him a look edged with doubt and called out to the triage nurse to find Gem. He turned back to Shade, who had palmed Serena's forehead and closed his eyes. His *dermoire* glowed as his gift flowed from him to Serena, and it took every ounce of patience Wraith had to keep from interrupting with questions.

Finally, Shade opened his eyes. 'No skull fracture, but she's got a substantial subdural hematoma. I'm slowing the bleeding, but E, you're going to have to fix it.'

'It won't require surgery, will it?' Wraith asked. E could repair injuries, but only if he could touch them. If Serena had to go under the knife, she'd be in the hospital for an extended period of time, and explaining the situation would require some creative lies.

'Hope not. We keep losing power, and I'd hate to be in the middle of brain surgery and have it happen again. Not to mention the fact that brain surgery isn't my specialty.' E blew out a breath. 'I can summon a general healing wave, see if that works.'

'I'll monitor the injury and blood flow while you do it.' Shade closed his eyes again.

Wraith watched as E grasped Serena's arm, his *dermoire* glowing as bright as Shade's. He heard someone approach, sensed Gem before he saw her. She stood quietly next to him.

Gradually, both Shade's and Eidolon's *dermoires* stopped glowing.

'Well?'

Shade exchanged glances with Eidolon. 'I think you got it. We should get a CT scan though, just to make sure.'

'Josh?'

Everyone's heads whipped around to Serena, who watched Wraith through half-lidded, cloudy eyes.

Shit. Wraith clamped his hand down on her wrist and slammed his gift into her head, taking her consciousness to a beach. A skimpy swimsuit, clear ocean waters, and she was set. He didn't insert himself into the fantasy-dream – doing so would require too much concentration, and he needed to focus on what was going on around them in the hospital.

'Someone sedate her,' he said, his voice rough and low with the effort he was expending to talk while keeping the fantasy going. 'We can't let her see too much. And I need to get her back through the Harrowgate.'

Eidolon was already on it, was preparing to inject meds into her IV line. 'So . . . *Josh*?'

Heat scorched Wraith's cheeks. 'Long story.'

Once the sedative had been injected, Shade palmed her forehead again. 'She's out.'

Gratefully, Wraith pulled out of her mind. 'She's okay?'

'She's going to wake up with one hell of a headache, but she should be fine,' E said.

Gem gestured to Serena. 'So why am I here?'

E kept his gaze on Wraith as he talked to Gem. 'You're here to confirm Serena's virginity.'

'Or lack of,' Shade muttered.

'I told you . . . ' Wraith growled.

'Yeah, I know. But can you say with one hundred percent certainty that she didn't give it up to someone else? Or maybe some sort of incubus put a spell on her and took her while she was sleeping. We can't be sure. She got hurt, and that shouldn't have happened. Which probably means she's no longer a virgin. And if that's the case, you're wasting valuable time with her.'

'It hasn't been—' Wraith snapped his mouth shut before he said something stupid.

Fuck.

'Hasn't been what?' Shade's smirk said he knew exactly what Wraith had been about to say.

'Nothing.' Wraith's heart kicked in his chest as he looked at Serena, lying so still in the bed. 'I just don't want Gem poking around.'

'Would you rather I did it?' E asked.

'Hell no!' Wraith drew in a deep breath, which didn't do nearly enough to calm him. He seriously needed to get a grip. Maybe her virginity had been taken, but the charm only partially transferred. Clearly, Byzamoth had done *something* to Serena. 'Fine. But make it fast. And you two?' He gestured to his brothers. 'You wait outside.'

Shade strode past, and E clapped Wraith on the shoulder. 'Come with us. We need to talk.'

'Yeah, whatever.'

Outside the room, Wraith paced, unsure what he was more nervous about – Serena's possible lack of virginity, her health, or the fact that some mad demon was after her. Had hurt her. Man, he really wanted to cause Byzamoth a whole lot of hurt, because some weird possessive instinct had come over him, and fighting it was starting to feel like a waste of time and energy.

Both of which he was short on.

Eidolon crossed his arms over his chest and leaned against the wall. 'Tell us exactly what happened.'

'We were on the Island of Philae. Looking for some tablet that can be used to shut down the Harrowgates.'

'Ah, not cool,' Shade said.

'Duh.' Wraith reached up to rub the back of his neck, wincing when he discovered the gash there. Immediately, E replaced Wraith's hand with his own and channeled a healing wave into the wound.

Pain shot straight up Wraith's vertebrae and into his skull. E's healing gift often caused extreme discomfort, even as it healed. When it was done Eidolon backed off.

'Better?' When Wraith nodded, E propped himself against the wall again. 'Back to Philae,' he prompted.

'Right.' Wraith resumed pacing. 'I sensed demonic presences the moment we stepped onto the island. The Harrowgate had been used. A lot.'

'Philae is a place of worship for several species, right?'

'Yep, so I wasn't too concerned at first. Which should have been a fucking clue, because I'm always concerned.'

Shade looked up from checking his cell phone, probably making sure Runa hadn't tried to contact him. Those two were connected at the hip. If she didn't force him to go to work, he'd never leave their home. 'So was the attack directed at you?'

'Why would it be directed at me?'

Shade rolled his eyes. 'Like it's so out of the realm of possibility that someone would attack you. You know how you're always making friends.'

'You're a riot,' Wraith said. 'But the guy who hurt her was the same dude who was talking to Serena when I arrived in Alexandria the first night, and who later showed up at the Hall of Caracalla. This is definitely about her.' He shook his head. 'I thought it might be about the artifacts she was after, but it's too coincidental that she's being stalked by a guy who can hurt her.'

'If he'd already gotten her charm, then why would he want to hurt her?'

'I'm telling you, he didn't get it. No one did.'

Gem swept open the curtain. 'Wraith's right. This human is untouched.'

Wraith bit back an I-told-you-so. 'So how the hell could anything hurt her if she's still a virgin?'

'We'll work on that,' E said. 'In the meantime, you need to work on getting the charm. I'm surprised you aren't taking the opportunity while she's sedated to get her ready and willing . . . '

Wraith found himself in his brother's face, nose to nose. 'You think I'm so demented that I'd take her in her sleep?'

Eidolon's dark gaze narrowed on him, but he said nothing. Wraith ground his teeth, just waiting for his brother to say something stupid. Shade's hand came down on both Wraith's and Eidolon's shoulders.

'Now's not the time for this,' Shade said. 'But Wraith, you've got to do something. You're running out of time.'

'Gee, thanks for the news flash.'

E scrubbed a hand over his face, and then froze. 'Wait. If her charm isn't working ... '

'Then maybe it won't work for Wraith, either,' Shade finished.

'It's working,' Wraith said. 'None of the other demons on the island could touch her.'

'So why the one guy?'

Wraith shrugged. 'Sounds like a visit to our resident angel is in order. Can one of you take care of it?' Wraith stalked into Serena's room. Gently, he removed the tape holding the IV catheter in Serena's hand. 'I'm taking her to her hotel room.'

'I think you should wait,' E said. 'I'd like to run tests. Maybe there's a medical answer to why this one demon can get past the charm.'

'Is she healthy enough to go?'

'Yes, but—'

'Then I'm taking her.'

'Wraith—'

'Don't fuck with me on this.' He pulled the catheter free of her vein, stopped the bleeding with a gauze pad and direct pressure. 'She needs to be topside. She needs sunlight. Air. I don't want her waking up and seeing even more of the hospital. There's no way I can explain, and I'm not messing with her memories again.'

He could practically feel his brothers' stunned gazes, but they said nothing as E touched Serena's hand and healed the tiny spot where the IV had been, erasing all evidence of having been in a hospital.

Gently, Wraith gathered her in his arms, her weight so pitifully light. 'Let me know what you find out. I'm outta here.'

'Wraith.' E's stern voice brought him to a halt. 'You need to close the deal. Now.'

'Yeah, about that? I don't give a shit anymore. I'm not going to kill her.' He spun around and met their surprised gazes head on. 'Sucks to lose the hospital, but you two will survive. So stop with the urgency bullshit. It's getting old.'

Shade grabbed Wraith's biceps in a bruising hold. 'That's the thing … this isn't about just you or the hospital anymore, bro. Seems that all of our life forces are tied to the hospital. As you die, UG dies. And when the hospital goes …'

A chill sliced through Wraith, leaving behind raw grief and incapacitating pain. He couldn't breathe, couldn't speak, and when he finally could, all he could do was finish Shade's sentence.

'So do you and E.'

FOURTEEN

Eidolon and Shade swept through the hospital, both seeking out the one being who might possibly know something about what was going on with Serena.

Reaver.

Since the intercom was down, Shade checked out the dining hall and gym while E hit the patients' rooms. He found the fallen angel finishing up with a hyena shifter in the next room.

'I need to speak with you.'

Reaver nodded, his mane of golden hair swishing around his shoulders. He patted the teenaged hyena on the shoulder. 'Good as new. But stay away from lions from now on.'

The boy rolled his eyes. Like their counterparts in the animal world, hyena and lion shapeshifters hated each other with deadly ferocity. But the kid didn't argue, merely thanked Reaver and beat feet out of the room.

Reaver started cleaning up the area, dumping bloody bandages and wrappers in the biohazard bins. 'What's up?'

Eidolon cut right to the chase. 'We need more information about Serena Kelley.'

Reaver fumbled the shears in his hand, but recovered quickly. 'I've said more than enough.'

'Bullshit.'

For a moment, Reaver continued his clean-up, almost frantically, as though finishing would get him out of the conversation. Eidolon settled in for the long haul, braced one shoulder against the doorjamb and crossed his arms over his chest and his feet at the ankles, a silent message that said he wasn't going anywhere until he got what he'd come for.

'You're going to talk.'

Reaver snarled, his beautiful face twisted into as deadly an expression as Eidolon had ever seen from him. He hadn't known much about fallen angels until Reaver came to him, wanting a job and a place to stay, and though Reaver had been at UG for sixteen years, Eidolon still knew very little.

'Serena is not something I can discuss with demons.'

'You've already discussed her, and in case you hadn't noticed, you aren't exactly bound by heavenly law anymore.'

Pain flashed in Reaver's blue eyes. 'I am bound by no law, heavenly or otherwise, since I've not entered Sheoul. But that doesn't mean I don't follow any rules.'

Eidolon's Justice demon background gave him a sense of fair play, of law and order, and an appreciation for rules. But a lot of lives were at stake and his head fucking hurt and rules could take a flying fuck out the window.

'Here's the deal,' he said, pushing himself off the doorjamb. 'Wraith brought her in a little while ago. They were attacked by demons, and she was injured.'

Reaver looked so stricken Eidolon would have thought someone had died. 'He already has the charm.'

'No.'

'Then she gave it to someone else.' Reaver sank down on a rolling stool and buried his face in his hands.

'We confirmed her virginity,' Shade said from the doorway. 'It's not possible that she gave it to someone.'

'Neither is her getting hurt.' The fallen angel's voice was muffled by his palms.

Eidolon closed his eyes, thinking. 'So there is nothing, nothing at all, that can harm her?'

'What part of divine charm are you not understanding?'

'Okay, then what about someone else who is charmed? Could they hurt her?'

Reaver's head snapped up. 'I wouldn't think so, but . . . '

'But what?' Shade asked. 'Looks like maybe you heavenly geniuses didn't think of everything, huh?'

'I just don't know why another Sentinel would try to harm her. It makes no sense.'

Eidolon pondered that for a second. 'Could they turn evil?'

'Unlikely.'

Eidolon cocked an eyebrow. 'But you don't know for sure.' Reaver didn't reply, which was answer enough. 'Can you contact your angel buddies and see—'

'No!' Reaver came to his feet. 'I am not allowed contact with those who still serve.'

Eidolon got in the fallen angel's face. 'What *are* you allowed to do? You aren't allowed to talk. You aren't allowed to help. Seems like you are pretty damned useless to everyone.' E poked Reaver in the chest. 'I get that you aren't willing to help Wraith, but dammit, Reaver, don't you feel the unrest in the underworld? Serena is a part of it, and we've got to find out why. You need to open the fuck up.'

Reaver's lips peeled back to reveal two sharp canines Eidolon had never seen before. 'Never. You. Are. Demons.'

'Hate to break it to you, buddy, but so are you.'

Reaver's head rocked back with such force Eidolon expected to hear the crack of spine. And then Reaver's fist was in Eidolon's face, and Eidolon hit the wall so hard the plaster came down around him as he hit the floor.

'What the fuck?' Stunned, Shade looked between Reaver and E. 'The Haven spell—'

He was cut off by the blare of sirens and the sound of battle. Running footsteps turned into a skid, and Gem popped her head through the doorway. 'Haven spell has gone down. Hospital's in chaos. This isn't good, E. This isn't good.'

ᘓ

Lore stepped out of the Harrowgate into Underworld General's emergency room and came to an abrupt halt. What. The. Hell.

Sure, fighting, fucking, and general chaos were staples anywhere you went in the demon world, but he'd figured a hospital would at least have a few rules. A demon of unknown species came at him, but he sidestepped the snakelike creature, wheeled around as it skidded past, and shoved its head into the wall. It fell to the obsidian floor with a soft thump.

He eyed the thing, hoping he hadn't killed it. Not that he minded killing – it's just that he preferred to get paid for it.

And speaking of getting paid . . .

He made his way to the triage desk, where a vampire nurse was futilely yelling at the patients and staff to stop fighting.

'Yo.'

She turned to him with a sigh. 'Do you require medical assistance?'

'And if I did?' he asked as he eyed the insanity around him. She gave him an apologetic shrug, and he shook his head. 'I need to see Shade or Eidolon.'

'I'm sorry, but we're a little busy.' She ducked to avoid being brained by a pipe someone had thrown. 'I suggest you come back later—' She broke off as some long-clawed thing as large as Lore hit her across the face.

Lore leaped over the desk and wrenched the demon's head around. There was a satisfying crack, a twitch, and the thing slumped, dead, to the floor.

Satisfaction had been his payment for that one. He glanced at the nurse, who was holding her bleeding cheek. 'You okay?'

'I'll live. Thank you.' She looked down at the dead demon. 'I quit.' She stalked off in a huff.

Well, hell. He stood there, wondering if he should search for the two brothers or not. He'd heard that Wraith was off trying to save his life, but Lore knew damned good and well there was no cure for the poison his partner had dosed Wraith with. The guy was as good as dead.

But the other two . . . he needed to find them. The way Roag had set up the payment schedule had specified that all three must be dead in order for the money to be released.

And that burned-up Roag guy had been specific. He'd had one hell of a bug up his ass about these brothers. He'd never said why he wanted them dead, but then, Lore hadn't asked. Didn't care. He had a job to do. But really, in his thirty years of killing for money, he hadn't come across anyone so desperate to see someone dead that they'd make arrangements for it to happen even after they themselves died.

Lore and his partner, Zaw, had received a third of the money up front, but the rest wouldn't come until the brothers were verifiably deceased.

Zaw's death had thrown a kink in that plan. Lore had been helping out the Byzamoth loon while Zaw was taking out the brothers. They'd been in contact via radio earpieces, and Lore had known exactly when Zaw had been taken out.

It had sounded pretty gruesome. As far as Lore could tell, Zaw had been eaten by a werewolf.

Nasty.

Lore much preferred a clean, bloodless kill. He might be an assassin, but only because he was good at it. And because he couldn't do anything else. The demon world didn't want him, and neither did the human one. As a half-breed, he was trash in either place.

Oh, and because he was owned by a demon who pimped Lore's services out and demanded a cut of the money. Or else.

He looked down at his hand, covered by a leather glove to protect people from an accidental touch. He could kill even through the leather if he tried, but he didn't have his kill skill turned on right now, so no one here was in danger. No one but the brothers he was after.

Something screamed, and simultaneously, blood sprayed in a fine mist, catching him in the face. He wiped his eyes with the back of his gloved hand and turned to the Harrowgate.

'Lore!' Gem's voice rang out over the chaos. The smoking fine Goth chick jogged toward him, her stethoscope bouncing against her ample breasts.

What a stroke of luck it had been to run into her in the parking lot the other night. He'd stopped her to ask a few questions, but there'd been a spark there, a tangible one he hadn't felt with a female in a long time.

Mainly, because he avoided them. Accidentally killing a partner he liked during sex wasn't something he cared to repeat. Killing one during sex that he'd been paid to eliminate ... that was a little different.

But Gem had fascinated him, and besides, she knew a lot about the hospital – and about his targets. He'd had a prime opportunity to kill two demons with one stone; he'd gotten to hang out with the sexiest female he'd been around in a long time, and he'd gotten good intel.

Last night he'd gone to her apartment, but she'd been upset, obviously by the aggressive human at the elevator, and she hadn't wanted to talk.

Apparently, she hadn't done much talking with the human male, either, because they'd both smelled of sex, which had gotten Lore worked up and, at the same time, pissed off. He wanted Gem for himself, no matter how bad an idea that might be.

Hey, baby, yeah, that's right ... we can get down to it, but never mind that I have to stay covered up and keep my glove on. Oh, and I can't touch you at all with my right hand because when I come, I kill whoever I'm touching even through the glove. But yeah, just keep doing that thing with your mouth and I'll try not to put you in your grave ...

'Gem,' he said, pulling her out of the way of a thrown chair. 'You didn't mention your hospital is a war zone.'

She blew out an exasperated breath. 'It normally isn't. This is—' She broke off to yell at a horned demon in scrubs who was trading blows with a vampire in a hospital gown. 'This is insane.'

'Good to know this isn't the normal state of operations.'

'Not at all.' She frowned. 'I need to go, see if I can help get the Haven spell back up.'

'I'll see you later, then.'

She didn't answer, was distracted by a leopard shifter who was stalking an imp near a bathroom. This was one of the strangest scenes he'd ever witnessed, and he'd been around for over a hundred years, so he knew strange.

Speaking of which ... the human from last night was standing near the ambulance bay doors, his gaze full of murder. So it was with great pleasure that Lore grasped Gem by her upper arm, pulled her around, and kissed her.

With tongue.

He kept his gaze locked on the human, and as he stepped back from Gem, he flipped the guy off. Cold rage burned in the male's eyes, as well as an unspoken threat that promised pain.

Too bad he couldn't compete with what Lore promised.

Death. And the human male's was going to be on the house.

ɷ

Gem stood, stunned, as Lore wheeled around and disappeared into the Harrowgate. Her lips tingled from his kiss, and her mind reeled. He was fiendishly handsome, and had she met him even a few days earlier, she might have taken that kiss and run with it all the way to bed.

But no, Kynan had to show up and stir the pot.

'Gem.'

Speak of the human. Heart pounding, because it seemed to think she'd just been caught doing something wrong, she turned to him.

And drew a surprised breath. His expression was dark, his gaze seething as he stared at the Harrowgate Lore had disappeared into.

'Okay, stop the jealousy horseshit,' she snapped, even though a part of her was secretly pleased. 'You should be sucking up, not acting like a cave devil in a mating rut. And right now, there's more to worry about than my love life.'

A viper ghoul, a nasty, man-sized cobra-ish thing that looked like it had been dead for a month, slid from behind the triage desk, and before Gem could shout a warning it had wrapped itself around Kynan. Its fangs dripped venom from its open mouth, and its eyes focused on his throat.

Gem punched the thing as Ky struggled in its grip. His face turned red and his breath grew labored as the snake squeezed.

Helplessly she pounded the snake's face, but the viper barely flinched. It was going to make a meal of Kynan.

Tears of frustration burned her eyes. She had no choice. Like it or not, she shifted into her hybrid Soulshredder form. Her bones popped and contorted, her skin stretched and split, and in seconds she was twice as large, winged, and had nasty, serrated claws. The snake hissed.

She raked her claws down its side, and it struck at her, its fangs scraping her cheek. She swiped at it again, catching it in the eye. It screamed a god-awful noise and uncoiled its body from around Kynan. Ky leaped away from it . . . and from her.

Instantly, she shifted back, but the wariness still lingered in Kynan's eyes. It hurt more than she'd care to admit.

'What the hell is that thing doing in the hospital?' He panted, trying to catch the breath that had been squeezed from his lungs. 'Shouldn't it be at a vet's?'

'Yes,' she said, her voice gravelly from the shift. At least her scrubs were intact. 'Must be someone's pet. E really needs to get this fixed.' She waved her hand at the battling demons, but before Kynan could reply, shrieks of agony replaced the sounds of fighting. Several patients and staff members grabbed their heads, and others fell to the floor, writhing in pain. The Haven spell had kicked back in.

'It's about time.' Kynan rubbed his sternum. 'And thanks for saving me.'

'Big demon hunter like you? You'd have gotten out of it.'

He looked a little skeptical, but he didn't argue. He helped patch people up, along with all available medical personnel. When they were done, he took her hand, and though she knew she should resist, she didn't. She was too curious about what he was doing, leading her to one of the patient rooms.

Kynan opened the door. Inside, candles burned, and on the floor was a blanket laden with food, wine glasses, and a bucket of ice containing a bottle of what looked like sparkling grape juice. Around the blanket were IV poles, and from them hung saline bags full of something that glowed with green fluorescence.

'What . . . what is this?'

He smiled, that killer one that always made her heart do somersaults. 'It was partly Tayla's idea. I wanted to do something romantic, but she said your idea of romance was stitching up wounds . . . '

'Clever how you combined the two,' Gem murmured.

'Sometimes a guy has to play dirty.' He gestured to the blanket. 'Sit.'

This was stupid, and she knew it. She didn't have the willpower to resist him, and she had no doubt this picnic would end up on the bed he'd rolled to the back wall. Not that getting naked with him would be a bad thing, but her battered heart was tapping out warnings in Morse code against her rib cage.

'I'm not sure,' she said, still unable to erase from her memory the look of disgust on Kynan's face when he'd seen her in demon form. 'This is nice, but . . . '

'But what?'

'Honestly?' She tapped her tongue piercing against her teeth as she summoned the words she didn't want to admit. 'I'm scared.'

Kynan closed his eyes. When he opened them again, they'd gone dark with regret. 'I'm sorry I hurt you, Gem. I want to make it up to you. I know this won't do it, but it's a start.' He patted the blanket. 'Please.'

Her mind screamed that this was a mistake, but still, she sank down on the blanket next to him and kicked off her Crocs. God, she was easy.

He poured two glasses of sparkling juice and handed one to her. 'I don't want you kissing that guy.'

'That isn't your call.' She sipped from the glass, her tongue piercing making a little clink against the edge.

'I know.' Kynan pulled a tin from inside the basket. 'But that doesn't mean I'm not going to use every trick in the book to make sure it doesn't happen again.' He opened the tin, and she grinned.

'Chocolate-covered oranges. My favorite. How did you know?'

'Tayla.' He removed one from its gold foil cup and held it to Gem's lips. 'Bite.'

She did, nearly letting out a moan at the exquisite sweetness. He watched her, a slow smile curving his lips, his eyes darkening dangerously.

'That's good,' he murmured. 'Enjoy it.' He used the bitten end to trace her lips, the wet, cool stroke of the fruit a strangely erotic sensation over her suddenly hot flesh. 'Lick the juice.'

He drew the orange slice away and watched as she used her tongue to swipe the liquid from her lips. His gaze was focused, half-lidded, and blazing with heat. Wow. This was power. He might be giving the orders, but she was working him up too, and they hadn't even touched.

'Another bite,' he said, his voice lower and rougher than it had been a moment before.

Holding his gaze, she sank her teeth into the orange, noted the slight hitch in his breath as she sucked on the juicy bite. She chewed, swallowed, but didn't have time to lick her lips because his mouth was on hers and he was doing it for her.

Sighing, she opened up for him and hooked her hand around the back of his neck. His tongue penetrated, meeting hers, and just like that, the sensual teasing turned to erotic, demanding play.

As her body sparked to life, she dug her nails into his skin, drawing a hiss from him. 'You kill me, Gem,' he said against her lips. 'You have since that night. . . .'

She knew the night. It was burned into her memory, because he'd given her the first orgasm she'd ever had with a guy. And then he'd pretty much kicked her out of his apartment.

'You didn't want to be with me.'

'I didn't want to be with anyone. Not after what Lori did to me.' He gripped her hips and hauled her up against him. 'I was an idiot.'

'I won't argue that.' She scored his neck with her nails and enjoyed the way he bared his teeth. 'Now, make it up to me.'

He had her flat on her back in an instant, his thigh between hers, his mouth doing wicked things to the sensitive skin of her throat. 'You're so soft, Gem.' He slid his hands beneath her scrub top and up her rib cage. 'So gorgeous.'

Arching her back, she spread her legs to cradle him between them until she felt the hard ridge of his erection against her core. She nearly panted at the sensation, especially when he began a slow grind that caught her in exactly the right place. She could come like this, knew it for a fact, because the night he'd mentioned had been much like this, and she'd flown apart while he watched.

Shoving aside the bittersweet memory, she ran her hands down his back, reveling in the flex and roll of the muscles under her palms. His hands played lightly on her ribs and belly, but they didn't stray, remaining tamely centered. Totally rated PG when she wanted R. Or triple X.

A low, rumbling noise came from deep in his chest, the purr of a male in need, and her body responded instinctively, going utterly wet between her legs.

'Christ, you make me hot. So hot I can't think.' He shifted his weight and took her face in his hands, pressed his forehead to hers. 'I want to make love to you.'

Her breath left in a rush. 'I . . . oh, God, I want that, too.'

'But not here. Not now.'

She blinked. 'Say again?'

'I want to do it slow and right. With a bed, and I want to spend all night doing it.' He kissed her, just a light brush of the lips, and she wondered where he got his self-control, because she was ready to strip them both of their clothes and ride him hard. 'All the other times, I was drunk or angry or jealous. I don't want it to be like that again.'

It was the best, sweetest thing he could have said. But her body was too worked up, strung tight and aching. 'I'm on fire, Kynan,' she whispered, angling her pelvis to rub against him. 'I don't want to wait.'

His tongue was an erotic stroke over her bottom lip. 'I'll give you an orgasm, if you want. Hell, I want that. I want to taste you everywhere,' he said, and she nearly came from his words alone. 'But I'm not going to fuck you. This is a date, something we haven't had. We're working backward, and when we're done with the date, and you're done with your shift, we're going to your place and I'm making love to you until dawn. Got it?'

Oh, yeah, she got it. Got it so well that when he dropped his hand between her legs and began to stroke, she shouted with an explosive release so hot she expected flames to erupt from her skin.

She clung to him, knowing that the world outside had gone insane and soon she'd be back to worrying about the future. But for this brief moment, she'd finally found happiness.

FIFTEEN

Serena woke with a killer headache, knifelike stabs of pain shooting through her skull. The first thing she saw when she opened her eyes was Josh, sitting in the dark, in a chair near her bed, face buried in his hands.

'Josh?'

His head snapped up and then he was at her bedside, kneeling next to her. 'Serena. How do you feel?'

'What . . . what happened? Where am I?'

'The hotel room. I dimmed the lights so you could rest.' He carefully touched the backs of his fingers to her face. 'You okay? Does your head hurt?'

'Like someone took a sledgehammer to it. I haven't felt this way since . . . ' She let her voice trail off, not wanting to tell him about her childhood misery. But this was weird. What was going on with her charm?

Groaning, she sat up, but Josh pushed her back and fluffed the pillow before letting her head rest on it. 'You need to take it easy. You took a blow that would have brained a rhinobeast.'

'That's not possible,' she said, though it was a stupid thing to say, because clearly, something had happened.

'Why not?'

'I just don't remember, I guess.' It wasn't a lie; she truly had no idea how she'd been injured.

'You don't remember anything?' he asked, and she thought he sounded relieved.

Closing her eyes, she let herself drift to the last thing that stuck in her mind. 'We were at Philae. There were noises.' An ache started between her eyes as a screeching sound rattled through her memories. 'Demons attacked us.' Her heart pounded as though she were still there. Josh grasped her hand.

'I'm here. You're safe now.'

But when she opened her eyes and saw the glint of fury in his gaze, she knew that she wasn't safe at all. The memories flooded back, of Josh plowing through the creatures like a machete through tall grass, and how, of all of the dangerous things on the island, Josh had been the most deadly. She shivered and drew her hand away from his.

'Obviously, I'm not,' she snapped, unsure if she was talking about Josh or the fact that she'd been hurt twice now, and could be hurt again. Maybe even killed.

Crushing memories of her mother's broken body on a cold slab in a hospital morgue squeezed away her breath. She'd snuck away from Val to see her mother one last time, her nine-year-old brain unable to process what death truly meant.

Until she'd seen her mother's corpse.

Josh scrubbed a hand over his face, the hand that had just been holding her, caring for her. Abruptly, she felt bad for snapping at him when he was only trying to protect her.

'I'm sorry,' she murmured. 'I'm not used to being injured. Guess I'm not a very good patient.'

'Ditto.' His hand continued to make long, tired passes over his eyes.

'Are you okay? You seem a little off.'

'Got some bad news from my brothers earlier. Nothing you

should worry about.' He rose from the chair and started prowling around the room. 'So, what do you remember after you got hurt?'

She sat up, wincing at the stabs of pain in her brain. 'Not much. Everything went black.' She frowned. 'Did you take me to a hospital?'

Josh wheeled around to stare at her. His eyes seemed to glow in the dark with an eerie luminescence. 'No. Why?'

'I don't know . . . I had these weird dreams. I was at some sort of scary hospital. It was dark, and there was this strange writing on the walls.' She shuddered. 'And chains hanging from the ceiling.'

'That conk on the head messed with you,' he said. 'But I brought you straight here. No hospitals.'

She shuddered again. Too much time spent in hospitals as a child had given her an intense hatred of them.

The smells, the sounds . . . everything about hospitals made her skin crawl. Little wonder that her dream had turned a hospital into a place of torture and horror. 'It wasn't all bad though. Right after that, I dreamed I was on a beach. Which is weird, because I've never really been a beach person.'

'I'll have to remember that,' Josh muttered.

'Okay, so how did I get hurt?'

That dangerous light sparked in his eyes again, gold flints flashing in the dark. 'Byzamoth.'

A knot twisted her stomach. She'd known he was a threat, but she'd ignored it, had put Josh in danger of being seriously injured or killed, and all because of her arrogance.

'I'm so sorry, Josh.'

'Hey.' He sank down on the bed and drew her into his arms. 'It wasn't your fault.'

'You tried to warn me. You tried to get me out of there, but I didn't listen, even though I knew he was after me.' She swallowed hard and pushed away from him. 'Even though you've been right from the beginning.'

'Let that be a lesson,' he intoned, but his eyes glinted with mischief. 'I'm always right.'

God, he was perfect. He was a little moody, but with a past like his, who could blame him? He was also kind and smart and deadly.

He deserved better than what she'd given him, which was a whole bucketful of lies.

He'd been a Guardian, for heaven's sake. He could handle the truth. He fought for the side of good . . . and since he was protecting her, he should know.

'Josh . . . I need to tell you something. It's going to sound crazy—'

He put his finger to her lips. 'Trust me, I know crazy, and whatever you say won't fit into that category. I promise.'

'Yeah, well—'

'I'm always right, remember?'

'You're also pretty full of yourself,' she muttered, but she was teasing, and he knew it, and rewarded her with a smile that could stop the Earth from rotating.

'Lay it on me,' he said, sitting back on the bed and watching her expectantly.

'Remember our talk in Alexandria? About the humans charmed by angels?' She took a deep breath. 'Well . . . I'm one of them.'

'Seriously?' His expression didn't change, even when she nodded. He merely looked curious. 'So, shouldn't you be immortal and immune to injury?'

'Well, I can be hurt . . . but only if I want it or feel like I deserve it.' At his raised eyebrows, she said, 'Like, once I lied to a nun, and I felt bad about it, so I let her rap my knuckles with a ruler. That hurt. A lot.'

'I could think of more fun ways to get hurt,' he said with a wink. And then he sobered. 'But how do you explain Byzamoth?'

'That's the million-dollar question. I was hoping to do some research . . . guess it'll have to wait. Maybe you could feel around some of your Aegis contacts until I can get to a secure Internet connection?' When he nodded, it was her turn to narrow her eyes at him. 'You're accepting this pretty easily. Why?'

'I work in a hospital that uses magical cures.' He shrugged. 'And there's the Aegis thing.'

The tension poured out of her. It was such a relief to be able to confide in someone other than Val. Someone who cared about her on a different level than the man who hovered over her like she was a toddler learning to walk.

Josh's brow creased. 'I know about Marked Sentinels because of The Aegis, but the details are sketchy. Researching Byzamoth might be easier if you tell me the purpose of the charm. I mean, angels don't run around charming people for shits and grins.'

'No, they don't. Anyone who is charmed is in possession of something that needs to be kept out of the hands of evil.'

'Like the coin you found in Alexandria. That was what the charmed guy carried.' At her nod, he continued. 'So what are you protecting?'

Her hand automatically went to her necklace. 'This.'

'What is it?'

'Honestly, I'm not sure. It's called Heofon, Old English for Heaven. But that's all I know. The guardian of the coin we found was the last Sentinel to have a full understanding of what it was he was holding. According to Val, Sentinels were no longer allowed to know exactly what their object's purpose was, for fear that they'd reveal it to the wrong person, or that they would use it improperly, as the coin's guardian did.'

'But didn't he think he was helping souls cross over or something?'

'Yes, but by killing himself and leaving the coin unprotected, he risked allowing evil forces to retrieve the coin.' She now had to keep the coin with her until it could be given over to The Aegis. According to Val, once such an object was safely in the hands of Guardians, a new Sentinel would be chosen to guard it.

'So the Byzamoth guy . . . he's been after *you,* hasn't he? Not the tablet.'

'I think he definitely wanted the tablet to keep The Aegis from closing the Harrowgates, and I've no doubt he'd take the coin as a bonus, but yes, I think he's after me. I'm sure he wants the necklace and my charm.'

'How could he get them?' Josh's voice had gone deep and dangerous, and she shivered with both dread and feminine appreciation.

'Sex. That's why I'm celibate. That's also why Val is so protective.' She looked down at her lap and then back up again. 'That's not all. If Byzamoth takes the charm from me, I'll die.'

She couldn't read his expression. At all. With a curse, he got up and paced again, his hands in fists at his sides.

'Josh, look, I'm sorry I didn't tell you sooner—'

'It's not that,' he snapped. His fury was a storm in the room, an electric surge that stood her hair on end. 'Dammit. *Goddammit!* I hate this!'

She hugged herself, rubbed the goose bumps that pebbled her arms. 'I don't want to talk about this anymore, okay? We just need to get out of here.'

'Agreed,' he growled. 'I already booked us on the next train.'

'When is that?'

He looked at his watch. 'Tomorrow. Five p.m. Actually, today. It's after midnight.'

She'd been out of it for longer than she thought. Which would explain why her stomach was growling. She swung her legs over the edge of the bed. 'Where's my knapsack?'

'Uh-uh.' Josh held her in place with a palm splayed between her breasts. 'You need to rest. I'll get your bag. What do you need?'

'I need to not be babied,' she said, but she was only half serious. It felt good to be cared for like this. 'And I need a granola bar. I always keep a couple in my bag.'

'I figured you'd wake up hungry, so I had the kitchen prepare some grub for you.'

He went to the dresser, lifted the lid off a large plate sitting on a bed of ice. When he brought it to her, she practically drooled at the delicious sight of the meats, cheeses, and fruits. No matter what the circumstances, she'd always been able to eat.

And then, like a big baby, she began to tear up. 'That was so thoughtful.' She covered his hand with hers. 'You really don't need to take care of me like this, but I can't thank you enough. You've done so much. You're a good man, Josh.'

'There are so many reasons you're wrong,' he said quietly.

'I doubt that.'

'Yeah, well . . . you don't know me.'

She tightened her grip on his hand when he would have pulled away. 'I know you saved my life.'

'I did what any guy would do.'

'No, any guy wouldn't have done that. They would have run screaming from those demons. You fought them, and you saved me from Byzamoth. I can never repay you or thank you enough.'

He slid her a troubled glance she didn't understand. 'I should let you eat and get some rest. I'll be out in the front room.'

'Please,' she said. 'Stay. I don't want to be alone.'

Her fear was stupid and childish, a kid afraid of the dark, but after everything that had happened, she felt safe with him. And not so utterly alone, especially now that he knew the truth.

'Yeah. Okay. I'm just going to do a sweep of the hotel floor—' His entire body convulsed, and he stumbled backward before catching the back of the chair with one hand and the wall with the other.

'Josh?' She tossed the tray of food to the bed and leaped up, ignoring the spinning in her head. 'What's the matter?'

'Stood . . . too . . . fast.' He breathed deeply and braced his forehead against the wall.

'You got hurt in the fight, didn't you?' She ran her hands over his body, looking for injury, but he hissed – honest-to-God hissed – and spun away from her.

'Stop,' he croaked. 'I'm fine.'

She reached for him again, catching him by the wrist. His tattoos felt like they were on fire, and the one on his face stood out starkly against skin that had gone ashen. 'You are *not* fine.'

'I'll live.' His voice was gruff, but his touch gentle as he peeled her fingers off his arm. 'I just need to do a check for demons who might want to rape you, and then shower.'

Whoa. He was worked up. 'Be careful. Please. I don't want you to get hurt because of me.'

Letting out a long breath, he closed his eyes and bowed his head. 'Damn you,' he breathed. 'Can you stop worrying about me? Stop caring?'

'Can you stop being an ass?'

His head snapped up. 'What?'

'It's rude to ask someone to stop feeling something they have no control over. So get over yourself already. I care, and I'm not going to stop. Accept that, or leave. Your choice.'

He stared at her for so long her stomach began to churn. What if he truly decided to leave? She needed him, and for the first time, she realized that she needed him for more than protection.

Oh, God. She was falling for him, wasn't she?

Finally, he nodded. His expression was fierce, but his voice was quiet as he said, 'You're going to be the death of me, Serena. I really think you are.'

൭

Wraith was practically hyperventilating by the time he got to the bathroom. He closed the door behind him and collapsed against it as though doing so could hold back the demons chasing him.

The demons that had been with him all his life. In his head. His soul.

You're a good man, Josh.

If he wasn't having so much trouble breathing, he'd laugh. He wasn't good. He wasn't even a man.

No, he was a sex demon whose libido had been killed by a powerful toxin.

Except, his libido wasn't completely dead. Not around Serena.

When she had touched him just now, his body had erupted like a newly awakened volcano. That, combined with the sudden bout of poison sickness, had sent his nervous system into stimulation overload, and he'd had to get out of there. His body had felt pulled in several different directions, and he hadn't been sure how he'd react. He could easily have pounced on her for sex. Pounced on her for blood. Or thrown up in the middle of the room.

Fantastic choices, all of them. Kill her with sex, kill her by bleeding her out, or just really gross her out.

Shaking violently, he sank to the floor and took deep, calming breaths. When the room stopped spinning, he dug through his duffel and tossed a half-dozen items on the tile before grabbing a unit of O-negative from the cold pack. Gods, he hated cold blood, but he didn't trust himself to hunt right now. His bouts of illness were coming more often, and the last thing he needed would be to catch a meal and get sick while feeding, leaving himself vulnerable.

He supposed he could go to UG, where he could find a willing female to satisfy his nutritional and sexual needs, but at this point he didn't think he could get it up for anyone but Serena, and how humiliating to not be able to perform. He had a reputation to uphold, after all.

Besides, he couldn't handle seeing his brothers. The bomb they'd dropped on him had torn him open and apart. He'd been willing to give his own life to save Serena, had been okay with sacrificing UG. But how could he turn his back on his brothers after all they'd done for him?

He couldn't.

He shot up with the anti-libido medication, and immediately, the pump of arousal in his groin mellowed out, and his skin, which had felt too tight for his body, loosened. He tossed the syringe into the garbage. Puncturing the bag of blood with his teeth, he took a long, slow pull to swallow the pills.

He gave himself fifteen minutes to finish his meal, brush his teeth, and shower, and then he dressed in sweatshorts and a T-shirt, and carefully re-packed his bag so his blood packs and meds were buried beneath his clothes. A muffled beeping noise drew his attention to the phone in his pocket. Eidolon's callback number flashed on the screen, but Wraith wasn't in the mood.

Between his brothers' announcement and Serena's true confessions, he was hanging from his last thread of sanity.

He couldn't believe she'd confided in him like that. He should be thrilled that she trusted him enough, but guilt was starting to eat at him for the deception he was carrying out, and the more she trusted him, the more she cared about him . . . the more he hated himself.

And fuck if he was going to let Byzamoth near her again.

Anger flushed through his veins at the very thought. He'd suspected that the demon had been after her charm, but to hear confirmation from her had set him alight. If she was going to lose her charm, it would be to someone who gave her the most intense pleasure of her life.

It would be Wraith.

Except . . . even with his brothers' lives at stake, could he really do it now? The idea that she would die because of him hadn't thrilled him from the beginning, but now he'd gotten to know her. Care about her.

Man, he was a really sucky demon and a terrible excuse for an incubus.

Maybe . . . maybe he could save her. E might be wrong about his ability to cure her. If Wraith could take her virginity and make sure she survived, everyone would win. Hell, he'd done the impossible last year when he'd found the cure for Shade's curse. Okay, so he didn't find the cure, exactly, but he found the means to activate the cure. And the same demoness who had helped Wraith go through his *s'genesis* early could surely cure Serena.

Feeling better than he had since this whole thing began, he headed back to Serena's bedroom.

When he reached her closed door, he took a bracing breath and knocked, cursing the wild pounding of his heart. She opened the door, hair wet and wearing a *Family Guy* nightshirt that somehow covered too much and not nearly enough.

'I showered,' she blurted, her face taking on an adorable blush as she tugged down the nightshirt.

As if doing so would make him stop admiring her legs.

And ... adorable? Had he really thought that? Gods, he was going soft.

He needed to kill something.

'Are you feeling better?' she asked, and he nodded as he strode inside.

'Chronic headaches. Took some aspirin.' He glanced at the tray of food that was still too full. 'You need to eat more.'

'I will. I was just waiting for you to get back. You didn't find any demons lurking in the hotel, did you?'

Just one. 'Nope. We're demon free.' When she didn't answer, he cupped her freshly clean cheek with one hand. 'Hey, are you okay? Do you want me to go?' He really needed her to say yes.

She closed her eyes and nuzzled his hand in a gesture so affectionate, so tender, he felt something inside break a little. 'I want you to stay,' she said softly. 'I'm just not used to spending the night, you know, with a man.'

'Yeah, me either,' he teased, and she laughed, lightening the mood. 'So, *Family Guy*, huh?'

Her smile socked him right in the heart. 'It's a guilty pleasure. Stewie is so wicked. I love him.'

'He's the best.' He grinned. 'I figure if I ever had a kid, that's what he'd end up like.'

'I doubt that.' Serena climbed into the bed and pulled the covers up to her chin.

She was wrong, so wrong, but he couldn't tell her why, so it was pointless to argue. Instead, he eased onto his back next to her, careful to stay as close to the edge as he could, not wanting to spook or touch her. Well, he wanted to touch her, but the way she lay there, stiff and eyeing the door like she wanted to bolt, told him now wasn't the time.

'How's your head?' he asked, and she rolled to face him.

'Better. Thank you.'

He stared at the ceiling. 'You really shouldn't thank me for anything.'

'Remember that conversation about you being an ass?' Her fingers came down lightly, hesitantly, on his right arm, which lay across his abs. 'Just let me be grateful.'

He'd be grateful if she stopped touching him. Stopped using the pads of her fingers to trace his *dermoire*, the most sensitive part of his body. Well, the second most sensitive.

She used the backs of her nails to stroke one of the symbols on his wrist. 'What's the significance of your tattoos? They're extraordinary. Sometimes they seem to actually move.'

That was because they did. Usually during sex or while using his gift. They would glow or pulse, sometimes appearing to writhe. 'Trick of the light,' he said smoothly. 'They're sort of a history of my family. My dad's side.'

'Really? How? The designs are familiar.'

'Ancient Amorite,' he lied. They were actually Sheoulic, symbols and words in the demon language. 'My father's family is big on tradition.'

'I know you never knew him . . . '

'So why get the tats?' He couldn't very well tell her he was born with them, but lying to her was becoming harder to do. 'It's a family thing. I'm tight with my brothers, and we all wanted to do something together, so we got the tattoos. Corny, I know.'

'No, it's not. It's cool. It would be great to have family like that.'

'What about you? I know your parents aren't around, but brothers? Sisters?'

'Neither. My mom was pregnant when she died.'

Giving comfort wasn't something he was used to or good at, so he said simply, 'I'm sorry.'

‘Thank you.’ She wriggled closer, so her head was on his shoulder. ‘Do you mind?’

‘No,’ he croaked. ‘Feels good.’ Right down to his dark soul, it felt good. ‘So, what happened to you after she died?’

‘Her will specified that I be raised in a convent. So I grew up with nuns who were really disappointed that I didn’t become one myself.’

‘Yeah, I’ll bet.’ The idea that she’d grown up with nuns, well, it gave him the jeebies. The things she would have learned, about sin, about sex . . . a weight settled deep in his gut. Even if he got the sex, they wouldn’t be friends or have a relationship . . . and *good Gods*, what the hell was he thinking? Friendship? *Relationship?*

Motherfucking poison. Eidolon had said it would turn his organs to mush, but he hadn’t said anything about his brain.

She propped herself up on one elbow and watched him like he was some sort of mystery and she was fucking Sherlock Holmes. ‘You don’t like being touched, do you?’

He liked it when she touched him. Liked it too much, which was the problem.

‘I’m not used to it.’

‘Me either.’

‘I’ll bet, seeing how you’ll die if you have sex. That would suck.’

She laughed. ‘It doesn’t mean I can’t do *other things*.’ Her voice was husky and low, touched him in places her fingers couldn’t reach, and he couldn’t stop himself from turning to her. ‘Like the other night.’

‘What are you saying?’ He knew, but he wanted to hear her say it.

‘I’m saying I want to be with you. In whatever way we can.’

ର

Serena welcomed the firm pressure of Josh’s soft lips against hers. He took his time, first brushing his lips across hers and then flicking his tongue over her bottom lip before catching it in his teeth. The little pinpoints of his sharp canines made her gasp at the pinch of both pleasure and pain.

He licked where he'd bitten, a warm sweep of his tongue over her sensitive inner lip. Her mouth opened for him, and so did her legs as he settled his hips between them. She cocked her knees to allow for greater contact, and nearly groaned at how well they fit together, his erection cradled by her sex, with only the thin barriers of her underwear and his shorts between them.

'Don't worry,' he murmured against her mouth, 'I won't do anything you don't want me to do.'

'I know.'

He was so big, dominating, and possessive, yet his sensitive, gentle streak surrounded her like a satin ribbon, making her feel feminine, sexy, and wanted. And when he slid his tongue inside her mouth and began a penetrating, thrusting motion that mimicked something much more intimate, she was the one who wanted. Wanted so much more than she could ever have.

For now, though, she'd take what she could get.

He rocked against her as he made love to her mouth. She felt herself go wet, and as if he knew, he growled deep in his chest and dropped one hand between their bodies. His fingers found her core, and she nearly came from the light, sweeping contact.

'Oh, damn,' he rasped against her lips. 'I can smell your arousal, and it's killing me. I need to taste it. If you don't want it, you'd better tell me now.'

Her breath left her in a rush as his raw words sank in and the images, the fantasy, began to fill her thoughts.

'No objections, then,' he rumbled, sliding down her body to pull off her underwear. Slowly, like a great cat, he prowled from her feet back up her legs, his muscles bunching and shifting fluidly under his skin. Her breath came in labored spurts as he spread her thighs.

She wanted this so badly, but he was looking at her and she was nervous and afraid she'd made a terrible mistake, when he whispered, 'Gods, you're beautiful.' Gods? Gads, maybe. Didn't matter what strange word he'd used, because she went light-headed and at the same time, heavy with a deep-down ache.

Closing his eyes, he inhaled, and when he opened them again, she swore they glowed gold, but he dropped his gaze so quickly she couldn't be sure. 'Your scent is so sweet. I could spend all night between your legs.'

His hands slid up from her thighs to part her slick lips, and she held her breath as he lowered his head slowly, so slowly she wanted to scream. And then she did scream when his tongue made a tentative sweep from her core to her clit.

'*Josh.* Oh ... oh, wow,' she breathed.

A purring sound vibrated through her body, and his hot breath bathed her in sensation. 'If I hurt you or you don't like this, tell me.'

Not like it? Was he crazy? 'I don't think that's going to happen.'

'Don't want to get carried away ... you taste so good, and I've never done this before. ... '

Her jaw dropped, but she didn't have a chance to say anything before his mouth was on her again, kissing and sucking, bringing her hips off the bed. Nothing in her dreams or fantasies could have prepared her for this. Exquisite sensations broke across her body with every stroke of his tongue, which swirled and stabbed until she was grinding herself against it, pumping her hips wantonly. And when he caught her clit between his lips and suckled, she finally flew apart. Into a million pieces that shattered her mind.

Josh's voice floated somewhere above her, and dazed, she opened her eyes. 'That was ... oh, damn,' she sighed.

He watched her with awe and not a little cockiness in his expression. 'You're so sexy when you come. Let's do that again.'

Though she scarcely had the energy to breathe, she managed a laugh. 'As much as I'd like to—'

'Why not? Is it your head?' Now he was watching her with concern, his blue eyes bright. 'Serena? Are you okay?'

'Oh. Yes. I-I'm fine.' Which was a lie, because she wasn't fine at all. She was falling for this man, and that was definitely not fine. But she was light-headed, and she could use a nap.

'Shit. We shouldn't have done this. You're injured and you need to rest—'

'Shh.' She touched his face, shutting him up instantly. 'You sound like a doctor.'

'A side effect of working in a hospital and having one brother who is a paramedic and another who is a doctor.'

She smiled weakly, because she was still recovering from the mind-blowing climax. 'Must be nice to have medical people in the family.'

'Yeah, well, you haven't met my brothers.' He eased onto his side and stretched out against her. 'Go to sleep. We'll discuss why brothers are major pains in the asses tomorrow.'

She snuggled against him and didn't bother hiding her yawn. 'Tomorrow, then.'

'Tomorrow,' he said, and for some reason he sounded . . . sad.

SIXTEEN

Wraith and Serena slept until after noon. Well, Serena had slept. Wraith mainly kept guard, pacing the suite and the hotel floor. Nothing was going to get past him to Serena. Nothing.

He'd called his demoness contact to let her know he needed a cure for a Mara disease and that he'd pay any price, but hadn't heard back yet. He also knew what she'd require for payment. His body. For days.

For the first time in his life, screwing a beautiful demon nonstop didn't appeal to him.

He shifted his gaze to Serena, who was just finishing up a phone call with her boss.

She caught him staring at her as she hung up and made her way across the lobby. 'We need to take a detour on the way to the train. Val wants me to drop off the coin with the local Aegis Regent.'

Wraith broke out in a cold sweat. What if the Aegi knew what the real Josh looked like?

'Why?'

'Because if Byzamoth is after me, the coin is also in danger, and we can't let him get it.'

'We can't let him get *you*,' he growled. 'We need to get on the train and get the hell out of Aswan.'

'It'll only take a minute. The Regent lives just a few blocks from here. And if he has a computer, I might be able to do a little probing into Byzamoth.'

Well, shit. 'Fine. Let's go.'

They walked, Wraith scanned their surroundings. He'd also loaded up on meds before they left, and as they approached the Aegis dwelling, he wondered if he should up the dosage. He was tiring out more rapidly and severely now, and he needed to be on top of his game.

Eidolon had given him a month to live, but Wraith could feel his health deteriorating, and his gut told him he had a couple of days.

A bone-deep ache had settled into every cell in his body, but even though his mind fuzzed out sometimes, it didn't want to roll over in defeat. Which was strange, given that he'd pretty much lived his entire life nursing a death wish.

'It should be just ahead,' Serena said, studying her map.

The breeze picked up, bringing with it dust . . . and the scent of human blood. A lot of blood. Wraith jerked to a stop, slapped hard by a wall of evil. '*Serena.*'

'What is it?'

'Demons.'

Her head whipped around. 'Where?'

'I don't know. But something felt weird on Philae, and I'm getting that same vibe now. How close are we?' he asked, and she pointed to a house a dozen yards away. 'Okay, let's get out of the open, see if this passes.'

She didn't argue. She let him take her hand and lead her to the house, but as they drew closer, the coppery odor of blood grew stronger. It was coming from inside the Regent's place. The hair on his neck stood up, and though his mouth should be watering at the scent, it went dry.

'Serena,' he said, 'I need you to stay here on the porch while I check inside.'

'But—'

'This isn't up for debate. I have a really, really bad feeling, and my gut is always right.'

'Okay.' Her voice was firm, strong, but he picked up the sound of her heart rate doubling. 'Okay. I trust you.'

He wished she'd stop saying that. 'Just stay here, and yell if you need me.' He kissed her, and it felt like the most natural thing in the world to do.

Cursing to himself, he tried the door. Unlocked. It swung open with a creak, and the stench of death hit him so hard he took a step back. Not just death, but misery. Blood. Bowels. His stomach lurched as he moved cautiously inside. His senses didn't pick up the presence of others, but that didn't mean he was alone. Many creatures didn't have heartbeats or physical bodies. And some could conceal their life forces.

He cast a quick glance over his shoulder to make sure Serena had stayed put. She had, but the way she shifted her balance and worried her bottom lip told him she wasn't going to stay there for long.

He found the Regent in the bedroom. And the bathroom. And the kitchen.

He lost his lunch in a garbage can, and as he splashed water on his face and rinsed his mouth in the kitchen sink, he became aware of the fact that he wasn't alone. He whirled around and found himself face to face with Byzamoth.

'Humans are so … fragile.' Byzamoth smiled and licked the blood from his fingers. 'We'll see how Serena compares. I do hope she's intact. For both your sakes.'

Wraith smashed his fist into the male's face. Twice. He followed with a knee to the groin and an elbow to the throat. Byzamoth didn't have time to be surprised. He went down hard.

'That's what I'm talkin' about.' Wraith delivered a kick to the demon's privates. 'Oh, yeah – *oof!*'

Byzamoth had swung his legs out, catching Wraith in the knees. Wraith slammed into a cabinet, barely kept from hitting the floor. The demon hit him with a full-body slam, and Wraith's skull cracked hard on the wall, putting a dent in the plaster and putting his temper into orbit.

With a roar, he rammed Byzamoth into the counter, sending glasses and dishes crashing. The guy was stronger than most, and it didn't take long to realize that in his weakened condition, Wraith might, for the first time, not come out on top of this.

Byzamoth's hand closed around Wraith's throat and squeezed. A vise grip of pain tore all the way to Wraith's spine. He fumbled behind him with one hand, seeking the knife block he'd seen on the counter. Byzamoth's face was a mask of evil, his teeth bared, blood staining them red.

'She's mine,' he hissed, squeezing so hard Wraith's vision dimmed. 'No more games. It's time for you to die.'

Not yet, asshole.

Wraith closed his hand around the hilt of a knife and swung. It plunged into the male's neck, in the soft spot between his neck and shoulder. Blood spurted, and an unholy scream issued from the hellish depths of the demon's body. He released Wraith, but the knife didn't slow him down. His eyes glowed crimson, and shit, his entire body began to glow. And grow. And morph.

Fuck a motherfucking fuckduck. Byzamoth wasn't your average spawn of hell. He was a fallen fucking angel. Time to haul ass.

Wraith charged to the door, just as Serena rushed over the threshold. 'What's happening?'

'Go!' he yelled. 'Now!'

She dove back through the door, and he was right on her heels. An infuriated roar followed them, so powerful Wraith felt a blast of heat scorch his back. He grabbed his bags in one hand and Serena's wrist in the other and sprinted down the street. Ahead, a man was getting into his car. Wraith shoved the guy out of the way, took his keys, and pushed Serena into the vehicle.

The guy cursed at Wraith in Arabic as Serena scrambled into the passenger seat. Wraith ignored him, leaped into the driver's seat, and started the car.

In the rearview mirror, he saw the angel coming after them ... looking like a massive gargoyle with big fucking teeth and giant-ass wings ... scratch that: only one wing. He gunned the engine and peeled out of there, driving like a madman until they reached the train station.

'What was that thing?'

'Byzamoth. He's a fucking fallen angel.'

'Holy shit.'

'Pretty much.'

'Did it ... did he ... kill the Regent?'

'Yes.'

'Oh, God.' She fingered her necklace as she twisted around to peer through the rear window. 'Josh?'

'What?' Wraith screeched around a corner and slammed the car into a parking space.

'Why would Byzamoth have been there?'

'Because he knew you ...' Oh, *shit.*

'Yeah. He knew I was going to the Regent's place.'

They locked gazes, because he knew where this was headed. Only a few people in The Aegis would have known her plans. 'You weren't booked for this train, right? So no one knows we'll be on it?'

'No.' She shook her head. 'Only Val. I was supposed to be on tomorrow's.'

Wraith shouldered the backpacks and got out of the car, but for some reason, he didn't feel relieved.

൭

Reaver's blood ran freely from his wrists as he kneeled on Mount Megiddo – Har-megiddo, as he'd always known it. His blood was not the first to be spilled here, nor would it be the last. Battles had been fought at Megiddo since ancient times, and the valley below would, someday – maybe soon – become the gathering place for armies who would engage in the ultimate battle between good and evil.

Night was falling, but the sky was already dark with roiling clouds. He'd stirred up the Heavens with his presence – and his request.

He waited, his blood forming twin rivers that snaked along the hard-baked soil and around jagged chunks of stone. Spots formed in front of his eyes and nausea swirled in his stomach. If no one appeared before him, he could die, and this was not the way he wanted to go.

Any fallen angel willingly drained of his blood would know eternal torment at Satan's side. Worse, all hope for Reaver to return to Heaven would be lost.

'You dare to petition me?' The booming voice resonated through his head, ringing painfully in his ears.

Reaver didn't look up at the owner of the voice, the angel Gethel. He was no longer allowed to view any who still Served. Instead, he kept his gaze on the ground that grew damp with his blood.

'I deemed this to be worthy of your attention,' he answered carefully.

'I will be the judge of that.'

'Of course.' A wave of dizziness washed over him, and he wondered if she'd let him bleed out. 'The Sentinel, Serena, is in danger.'

'We are aware of that.'

'What is being done?'

'We cannot interfere.'

He knew there were restrictions on how much help angels could provide until the situation crossed out of the realm of human free will and into a true crisis of good and evil. But Serena needed help.

'I could go to her—'

Lightning flashed. Thunder ripped through Reaver's brain, shattering his eardrums. Pain screamed through his head and his wrists, as the blood that had been streaming turned to ropes that secured him to the parched earth.

'*You will not go near her.*'

'Something must be done!' Reaver lifted his head. He was done begging and cowering like a whipped dog.

Gethel stood before him, larger than life, terrible and beautiful as the wind whipped her gray robes and blond hair around her. 'You have done more than enough *for Serena*, Fallen.'

The reminder of what he'd done to cause his Fall became a crushing pressure in his chest. He'd committed a crime by breaking rules and interfering in the humans' lives, and even though he'd done it to save Serena, arguing his point with Gethel would get him nowhere. Once more, he bowed his head. He closed his eyes, but the memories played on the backs of his eyelids like a movie in high def.

There were only two ways out of the charm – suicide and sex. Patrice had been a treasure hunter, much like Serena. And in her travels and hunts, she'd found an object of major historical and religious significance.

She had found the true Spear of Destiny, the Holy Lance of Longinus, used to stab Jesus after his death. Though humans had speculated on the lance's powers for years, the truth, that it was capable of unspeakable evil in the hands of humans who would wield it for power, was something that must be kept secret until the Final Battle.

Patrice could have made herself rich and famous beyond belief, but she understood the power of the lance, and she returned it to its resting place, to be found again by one who would use it for the side of good in a time of need.

Her sacrifice had made her the perfect choice to be caretaker of the necklace, Heofon, after its previous keeper had killed himself two hundred years into his guardianship.

Patrice had worn Heofon with pride . . . until Serena was on her deathbed.

At that point, Patrice had begged whoever would listen to save Serena. When her prayers went unanswered, she'd pleaded for the charm to be transferred. It was something that had never before been done – wasn't allowed to be done.

But Reaver had done it.

And he'd earned himself a boot out of Heaven's door.

'I would do more for her if I could,' he said to Gethel.

'What you will do is think on your actions until I see fit to release you.'

With that, she was gone, and he was left staked out on the baking earth. He wouldn't bleed out now, but if he was still here at high noon tomorrow, he'd be transported to Heaven, to face one final judgment.

And he would fail.

SEVENTEEN

New York in the winter could be bone-chillingly cold, but the temperature didn't bother Gem as she and Kynan walked to Eidolon and Tayla's high-rise condo. Heck, nothing was bothering her now. Though she and Ky hadn't been able to make it back to her apartment, she still felt a buzz of promise after the romantic hour they'd spent in the hospital.

Then E had gone and ruined everything by insisting that everyone meet at his place. Whatever he was worked up about sounded bad.

E answered the door. 'Tay and Runa are in the living room with the babies. Shade and I are doing our best to not burn steaks in the kitchen.'

Kynan peeled out of his jacket, and Gem took a moment to admire how his black sweater molded to his toned body. 'I've cooked steaks on Humvee engines before. I'll help you out.'

'That's not a ringing endorsement, man,' E said, but he cocked his head toward the kitchen. 'Come on.'

Gem frowned. 'You said we were meeting to talk.'

'Bad news always seems better on a full stomach,' E said and disappeared down the hall, Kynan on his heels.

Gem hurried to the living room, which looked like a Toys 'Я' Us had exploded in it. Tay and Runa looked up from where they sat on the floor playing with the boys. It was impossible to tell any of them apart, except the newest addition, who was a little smaller than the others, pinker, and snuggled securely in Runa's arms.

Shade and Runa were thrilled to have the infant, especially now that Wraith's future was in question. Having a little piece of him seemed to be a comfort to everyone, and the little demon would be given all the love that Wraith had missed out on as a child.

God, Runa looked so happy, so content. Gem felt a tug in her abdomen.

Tayla patted the floor next to her. 'Cop a squat and grab a kid.'

'There are more than enough to choose from.' Gem eyed the three babies lying on blankets, their little hands clutching soft, colorful toys.

Tay dug a bottle out of a diaper bag. 'I don't know how you do it, Runa. I'd go crazy with just one.'

Runa smiled down at the infant in her arms. 'You'll change your mind when you're holding your own.'

'I doubt it,' Tay muttered. She and Eidolon wanted kids, but they were willing to wait. Like, thirty years, if Tayla had her way.

'So Wraith doesn't know about the baby yet?'

'No.' Runa stroked the infant's cheek. 'He's got so much to deal with right now. Even when things do calm down, it's going to be hard to tell him. Shade's afraid he'll short-circuit or something, if he thinks he has to be responsible for an innocent life in some way.'

'He doesn't. You'll make sure he knows that, right?' Tayla scrounged around in the bag again and pulled out Mickey. The ferret chattered indignantly, stole a pacifier, and scampered under the couch.

'Of course. We want to raise this little guy. But can you imagine how hard it'll be for Wraith to come to family functions and have to see his own son growing up without him? And what about when the baby starts asking questions? What do we tell him? That his father didn't want him?'

'I don't think you're being fair to Wraith,' Gem said quietly, and Tay and Runa stared like she'd just declared that Sheoul, with its dark, icy outer caverns and its molten lava core, was a primo vacation spot. 'Come on. We don't know how he'll react. He's always been unpredictable.'

'Yes, and that's what you want around children,' Tay said dryly.

Gem shrugged. 'I just think you need to give him a chance.'

Runa sighed. 'I know I'm being hard on him. He's got a protective streak a mile long, and he's been kind to me, but I don't know if any of that makes him good father material.'

'Speaking of father material,' Tay said, sliding Gem a curious look, 'how are you and Kynan doing?'

'Father material?' Runa leaned forward and lowered her voice. 'Are you and Kynan . . . expecting?'

Gem nearly choked on her own tongue. 'No way. Are you kidding?' She glanced over her shoulder, half afraid he'd walked up behind her.

'But you want kids someday, don't you?' Runa asked.

'Yes, but . . .' But what? She did want them, but what kind of world would she be bringing them up in? Demon or human?

A knot formed in her gut, tightening and squeezing until she could barely breathe. She'd grown up a product of two worlds, belonging to both and neither, and she swore she'd never put a child through that.

Heck, it was *dangerous* to put a child through that. Some demons, like Sensors, her adoptive parents' species, existed for the sole purpose of hunting down pregnant human women whose babies were of mixed species, and killing the infants. Other demon species made it their mission to destroy half breeds, just for sport.

Gem herself had been marked for death and would have been destroyed had her parents not been desperate for a child when it became obvious that they couldn't conceive. Tayla had been spared only because Gem's adoptive parents hadn't sensed demon in her and had left Tayla with their human mother.

She eyed Tayla and Runa, ashamed of the spike of jealousy she experienced at the knowledge that they didn't share her problem. Their children were – and would be – purebred Seminus demons.

'What's wrong?' Tayla asked. 'Do you think Kynan wouldn't want kids with you?'

'I think it's too early to even think about.' But no, she didn't think Kynan would want kids with her. It had taken him forever to have sex with a demon. Having children with one? He'd probably castrate himself before he allowed that to happen.

Runa thrust Wraith's son into Gem's arms. 'We'll have to let him see how great you are with them, then.'

Gem's eyes stung as she looked down into the tiny, scrunched face of the baby snuggled against her. His little fingers grabbed hers, and she felt that tug again, low in her womb. Heavy footsteps announced the arrival of one of the guys, and sure enough, Kynan crouched next to her, a glass of soda in his hand.

'I brought you a drink.' He set the glass on the end table. 'So that's Wraith's hellspawn, huh? He's cute – nothing like his father.'

A smile played on his lips, and Gem's breath caught at the longing in his eyes.

'He's a really good baby,' Runa said. 'So yeah, nothing like Wraith.'

Kynan's smile turned sad, and Gem knew he was thinking about Wraith's dire situation. 'Can I hold him?'

Gem handed the infant to him, and she choked up – actually choked up, when he cradled the little guy to his chest and began to rock him. He was father material, pure and simple. Someday he'd want them, and what then? What would happen when he realized that Gem couldn't bear him human children?

Nothing good, and it was time to face the facts.

She and Kynan could never have a future together.

ϭ

Dinner tasted like sawdust.

Kynan mostly pushed his food around his plate as Eidolon listed all the things that had gone wrong with the hospital, including the fact that the patch they'd slapped on the Haven spell was weakening. With the hospital running on minimal staff, E and Shade had decided that, should the Haven spell fail again, they were going to shut down.

But the worst of the news had come earlier, in private, when Shade and E had told him that their lives were also at stake, something they hadn't told their wives.

And still the bad news kept coming.

'Plans are solidifying in the underworld,' Shade said. 'There's been a call to arms.'

Ky's gut dropped to his feet. 'This is bigger than just an incursion, isn't it?'

E rubbed the bridge of his nose between his thumb and forefinger, looking exhausted and rougher than Ky had ever seen him. Now he understood why. He was dying. 'Armageddon for you, Reclamation for us.'

Shade took a swig of beer. He wasn't looking so great himself, and Ky had to wonder if Runa, Tayla, and Gem were really buying their 'Seminus flu' BS.

'Wraith called,' Shade said. 'The guy who attacked Serena is a fallen angel. He's after her charm and the necklace she's protecting.'

Kynan was sick of hearing about fallen angels. 'What kind of necklace?'

'Wraith didn't say. But everything happened at the same time – Serena's appearance on the scene and the underworld havoc. It's definitely connected.'

'Have you asked Reaver about him?'

'Tried. He's MIA.'

'Shit. Okay, where are the armies going to strike? I need to notify the Sigil, and the R-XR, if Runa hasn't.'

Not only did Runa's brother work for the R-XR, but she'd been employed by them as well, before she hooked up with Shade.

She shot Shade a none-for-you-tonight glare, which was actually a non-threat, seeing how he'd die without sex. 'I talked to Arik yesterday, but I'm hearing about all of this for the first time right now.'

Shade shrugged, though he sounded a little sheepish when he said, 'I didn't want to upset you. You've had enough on your plate as it is.' He turned to Kynan. 'I took a little trip to Sheoul this afternoon. Talked to people who know people . . . there's no word on an actual strike. Instead, armies are gathering in Israel.'

Whoa. Kynan put down his fork. 'Why would they be gathering aboveground? Couldn't they use the Harrowgates to get to the places they're going to strike?'

'There's fear that humans are going to cripple the Harrowgates,' E said. 'Besides, demons can't move in mass through them. They've got to gather near battle sites.'

'Makes sense.' This was good intel. The Aegis and military paranormal units could start putting their resources in place now. He stood. 'I'm going to get moving on this. And if Serena or her necklace is part of this, maybe The Aegis or the R-XR could grab her and keep her out of the fallen angel's hands.'

Shade and E looked troubled by that idea, which would, no doubt, end Wraith's plans to take her charm, but they didn't argue. More than their lives were at stake now.

'Tell them,' E said, his voice low and rough. 'Reclamation might sound like a good time to a lot of demonkind, but I like the world the way it is.' He gave Tayla and the babies a pointed look. 'Safe for my family.'

As Kynan took Gem's hand in his, he couldn't help but agree.

࿐

Gem had remained completely silent on the walk to her apartment. Kynan would have worried, except that he hadn't felt like talking much himself. The threat of friends dying and the world ending left him speechless.

Gem dug her apartment keys out of her purse and unlocked her door, but she didn't open it. Instead, she became very interested in her feet. The platform Mary-Janes added a good five inches to her height and made her long, bare legs into works of art. He'd never been one for Goth fashion, but he couldn't imagine her in anything else.

Anything but satin sheets, anyway.

He hooked a finger beneath her chin and forced her to look at him. 'What's wrong? Did I do something stupid again?'

A sad smile curved her lips, which were freshly painted with black lipstick. 'You didn't do anything.'

'Then tell me what's going on.'

'Besides a possible end of the world?'

'Besides that.'

'You . . . um . . . you know how I feel about you.'

Well, if that didn't just freeze the blood in his veins. No one started off a conversation like that unless they were going to say something bad. Like, 'I slept with your best friend.' Or, 'I slept with that leather-bound, tongue-pierced demon.'

'Gem—'

'Don't,' she said quickly. 'Don't say anything. I just want you to understand how hard this is for me.'

His heart dropped to his feet. 'What's hard?'

'Breaking up with you.'

After the time they'd spent in the hospital room today, this was the last thing he'd expected, and it took a good ten seconds for his brain to process. Even when it did, he had to repeat what she'd said. 'Break up with me?'

Her eyes filled with tears as she brought his hand to her lips and kissed his knuckles. 'I'm sorry. I'm so sorry.'

'Dammit, Gem.' His voice cracked, and he hated himself for it. 'Tell me what's going on.'

'You want children, don't you?'

He blinked, completely caught off guard. 'What's this about?'

'Kids. Babies. Little fruits of your loins. Do you want them?'

'Well, yeah . . . someday.'

Her chin quivered. 'That's what I thought.' She pulled her hand out of his and stepped back, putting a mile of distance in the three feet of space between them. 'There's no point in us dating, then.'

'What? Gem, you're talking crazy.'

'Oh, come on. Are you telling me you want to see where this goes, if it can get serious? Are you really thinking marriage? Kids? Because, Kynan, you know what I am. Have you considered the fact that if we had kids, they'd be a quarter demon? And not just demon. *Soulshredder.*'

Kynan's mouth opened, but nothing came out. He hadn't thought this far ahead, had been taking things day by day for so long.

'See? You can't even try to reassure me.' Her voice was soft, resigned, not angry like he thought she had every right to be.

'It's not that. It's just . . . can't we cross that bridge when we come to it?'

'No, we can't. God, Kynan, I feel so strongly about you now. I can't stand the thought that two years down the road, when I'm even more attached, you'd leave me because you want kids. And don't say the kid thing wouldn't be a big deal for you.'

'Gem. Listen to me. You know my stance on demons has changed. Some of my best friends are demons. And Tayla and you . . . the half-demon thing doesn't bother me.'

'It doesn't bother you now. But later?' She studied her shoes again. 'Even if you decided you could live without kids in order to be with me, you'd grow to resent me.'

'Thanks for the faith,' he snapped. 'While you were tagging me with unfair accusations, did you once sit back and think that maybe

I should decide how opposed I am to having kids with demon blood running through them?'

She glared at him. 'I'm just trying to save us both a lot of pain.'

'Bullshit. You're punishing me for all those months you wanted me but I didn't give you the time of day because you were a demon. I'm over that, Gem. I don't care. Why don't you get that?'

Her bitter laughter bounced off the walls in the narrow hallway, echoing darkly. 'You're the one who doesn't get it. Want proof?' She put her palm on his chest. 'I see your scars. It's what I am. Soulshredder, remember? I can see all your past damage, and I know instantly what it's about. And you know what? There's this huge gash running right here, over your heart. It's about Lori. And kids. And how you wanted them but she kept putting you off, and at some point before she betrayed you, you actually suspected, just for a minute, that maybe she was going to put you off forever. And then you'd be facing the hardest decision of your life. Keep her and not have kids, or leave her to find someone you could knock up. How close am I, Kynan? Because I gotta tell you, my demon half is really wanting to poke that wound and make it hurt.'

He felt the blood drain from his face, because he got it. He finally got it. She hid her inner demon well, but he needed to face the truth. Deep inside, she was a monster, a species of demon even other demons feared. He'd believed that just because he couldn't see it, it didn't matter. Didn't exist.

But it did. He'd seen her shift into her hybrid form at the hospital, but it had all happened so quickly he'd barely paid attention. But that wasn't true, was it? He'd shoved the image into the back of his mind, locked it up tight with all the other horrific memories he had. That was the only way a soldier or a medic could operate. If they dwelled on the things they'd seen, they'd end up eating the business end of a pistol.

He could keep that image stowed away, but was that fair to her? To him?

'So you're finally getting it,' she rasped. Her eyes had begun to glow, little red sparks lighting the green depths. 'As long as you don't see the demon, you can deal. I'm good enough to fuck, but not good enough to marry or bear your children.'

'Stop it!' he barked. 'Stop telling me what I think. What I feel. You have no idea.'

'Am I wrong?'

He no longer knew. His thoughts were so jumbled up with his emotions right now that he couldn't think straight.

'That's what I thought,' she said when he didn't answer. The red melted from her eyes, and she sighed. 'Look, let's not make this harder than it is. Let's end it while we still can. While we can be friends.'

God, his chest hurt. This couldn't be happening. Just hours ago, they were happy. And now . . . now it was all ruined.

'It doesn't have to be like this, Gem.'

'You know it does.' She put her key in the lock, but didn't turn it. 'What's so funny about this is that a year ago I'd have taken whatever scraps you were willing to throw my way. If you'd only come over once a week for a quickie and then left without a word, I'd have been grateful. But something happened to me while you were gone. I got stronger. And now I want it all. I won't settle. Not even for you.'

With that, she went up on her toes, brushed her lips across his, and disappeared into her apartment.

EIGHTEEN

For the first time ever, Serena wasn't sure she could eat, wasn't sure why she'd decided to even try. She felt strangely vulnerable here in the dining car, sitting by herself at a table. Everyone stared at her, or so it seemed.

Someone had betrayed her. Someone had been feeding Byzamoth information from the day she arrived in Egypt, and now everything made sense. Byzamoth approaching her in the street, finding her in the catacombs, and at Philae, and at the Regent's house.

God, she wanted to throw up.

She'd tried to call Val once she calmed down, but he hadn't answered, so now she was stuck waiting, and she kept obsessively checking for a text message or voice mail while she waited for Josh to finish checking the train for demon activity.

Thank God for him. How many times had he saved her life now? He'd given her so much in just a few short days – friendship, protection, out-of-this-world orgasms.

She just wished he'd hurry. She'd never been nervous, had always been supremely confident, thanks to the charm, but suddenly she felt exposed, and the only safe harbor was in Josh's arms.

The thought almost made her laugh, it sounded so cheesy. But it was true. Growing up, she'd felt secure with her mother despite the fact that for the first seven years of her life, death nipped at her heels. Her mother had kept her close, always, and even after she'd given up the charm to Serena, her protective, loving nature hadn't changed. Later, after her mother's death, Serena had been taken to the convent, where she'd felt as if nothing could touch her. The charm had given her an even more enhanced sense of security.

In a matter of days, a lifetime of security had been shattered.

Where was Josh?

She tucked her phone back into her pack and looked up to see him, finally, enter the dining car. Her heart pounded as he approached. He was so big, his presence so commanding that everyone stopped eating to stare. She knew from watching him for the past few days that if he looked at them, the men would avert their gazes. The women, however, admired him as though trying to decide what color bedsheets he'd look best tangled up in.

Personally, Serena thought he'd looked great in the hotel ones, his tanned skin contrasting beautifully with the crisp, white cotton.

His gaze held hers as he approached, his sapphire eyes targeting her like a sniper's scope. Her breath left her lungs in a rush, because right now, in this moment, for him there was no other woman in the room.

He wore jeans and a long-sleeved T-shirt that fit like a second skin and outlined every ropey muscle. His hair fell in a gorgeously messy curtain against his jaw and face, which seemed a little pale, his tattoo more prominent than before, and she wondered if he was feeling ill again.

'Hey,' he said, halting at the table.

'Hey.' She still couldn't drag her gaze away from his. The sensation was hypnotic, and she was perfectly happy to be in this blissful trance. 'Are you okay?'

'Motion sickness.' As he bent and planted a tender kiss on the top of her head, she inhaled, taking in that scent that was uniquely his, an earthy, burgundy musk that made her body bloom. He sank into the chair across from her. 'Train makes me queasy.'

He was lying. He'd been sick too often, and she knew more than she wanted to about serious illness. Still, she didn't think he'd appreciate her pressing the issue. But maybe later. After dinner. After they arrived in Alexandria. After they arrived back in the United States.

Because by now, she'd decided that she didn't want to let him go. He made her laugh, made her feel safe and cared for. They both loved adventure, and they worked well together. She didn't know how a relationship with him could possibly work without actual sex, but for the first time in her life, trying truly felt right.

Assuming he wanted the same thing.

'Are *you* okay?' he asked.

'Not really,' she admitted. 'The idea that someone could be betraying me like that . . . and to a demon. God, who could do that? And why? It makes me sick.'

Some odd emotion crossed his face, but then it was gone. 'Yeah.' He took a drink of the water the waiter had left. 'Did you get a hold of Val?'

'No.'

'Serena . . . is it possible that he's the one who—'

'No!' She lowered her voice. 'Absolutely not. He's watched over me for years, and my mom before that. He's been more than our personal guardian. He's a family friend. Besides, why would he send me to another country to get attacked? It makes no sense.'

'Evil rarely does.'

'He's not evil.'

Josh shrugged, as if he wasn't convinced, and her temper rose a notch. 'Your mother died under his care, didn't she?'

'I don't like what you're implying,' she bit out, because it was ridiculous to think he'd been responsible for her mother's death in a car accident. 'You don't know him. If you did, you'd see. I wouldn't have worked for him for so long if I'd had any doubts.'

'Okay.' Josh signaled the waiter and ordered two double whiskeys. 'Is that all you do? Work? You ever do anything for yourself?'

She recognized the manipulation for what it was, an attempt to calm her down, and she was grateful for it.

'Not really,' she said sharply, because she was still a little worked up. 'All the things I enjoy happen while I'm working. Looking for treasure, outsmarting traps, traveling . . . I love it. What about you?'

'You mean, do I do things for myself?' When she nodded, his mouth tightened into a grim slash. 'I've lived my entire life being a selfish asshole. It's always been about me. Only me.'

'I'm sure you're exaggerating.'

He snorted. 'Trust me, Serena. Pretty much everything I've ever done has been because I thought it would benefit me. Why do you think I haven't gone to see my nephews yet? I'll have to see how they took Shade away from me.' He cursed. 'See what a bastard I am? Jealous of three innocent babies.'

'It's understandable. You love your brothers. They're all you have.' She totally got that, because Val was all she had, and sometimes she found herself secretly jealous that David had a connection with him that she didn't.

He went darkly silent as the waiter arrived at their table to take their orders.

'You only ordered bread,' she said, when the waiter left.

'The motion sickness,' he muttered.

'Are you sure that's all it is?'

'Yeah.' He squeezed her hand, his tone saying he was through talking about it, so she just ran her thumb back and forth over his knuckles, loving how her hand felt so small in his.

'Oh, I almost forgot,' she said, as she reached into her backpack and fished out a toy. 'Here. I got it in the hotel gift shop.'

One tawny brow cocked. 'It's a top.'

Smiling, she placed the colorful wooden plaything in his hand. 'This is going to sound so stupid . . . but I just keep thinking about how you grew up, and … well, I can't imagine that you had many toys, and I kind of wanted you to have one.' She continued in a rush. Buying the toy had seemed like a good idea at the time, but now, the unreadable, flat expression on Josh's face told her she might have made a huge mistake. 'I'm sorry … I just thought maybe you should have something you didn't get as a child. It's dumb, I know—'

'You shouldn't have.' Josh's voice was a gruff whisper.

Serena took his hand in hers again. 'It's just a stupid toy.'

'Whatever.' Red splotches colored his cheeks, as if he was embarrassed to be pleased by a gift as small and silly as a child's plaything. 'Thanks.'

'Maybe next time I'll step it up and get you a jack-in-the-box.'

He grimaced, and that fast, the awkwardness vanished. 'No, thanks. Those things are creepy. I'll keep the top.'

His words were nonchalant, but the warmth in his gaze wrapped around her like a hug, and she wished she was sitting beside him instead of across from him so she could return the embrace. 'Good. I'd hate to have to call you an ass again.'

A passenger walked by, and Josh went taut … a very subtle stiffening of his spine, but she got the feeling he was checking out everyone in the dining car.

'Look,' he said, all commanding business. 'I've been thinking on how we can keep you safe. My brothers are researching Byzamoth, and I'm going to escort you all the way home.'

She smiled. 'Thank you. I appreciate the offer, and I'm not going to turn it down. Once I get back home, I'll have Val—'

'You'll also have me,' he said slowly, his voice a possessive drawl, and if she didn't know any better, she'd think he was jealous.

She paused while the waiter delivered their food, and once he was gone, she asked, 'What are you saying?'

'I'm saying that as long as you're in danger, I'm not leaving you unprotected. Either Byzamoth dies, or you have someone at your side.' He tore off a piece of bread. 'Someone besides Val.'

'Val is a Guardian. He's more than capable—'

'I don't trust him. Not with everything that's gone down.'

'You've made that quite clear, but I *do* trust him.'

'All the more reason for me to stay with you.'

'Now we're back to you being an ass,' she snapped, and he actually smiled.

They ate in silence. When they were finished, he walked her to her room, and although she didn't invite him in, he barged in anyway.

The door closed, something her mouth should have done, but instead she asked, 'I know it's crazy to ask this, but, well, where is this headed? Us, I mean. Where are we going?'

'Where do you want it to go?'

'In a perfect world?' When he nodded, she rubbed her belly, as if that would calm the fluttering. 'We'd both go back to the States, and we'd see where we could take this thing between us.'

He smiled, but it was a sad smile that did what her hand could not: quell the butterflies. Killed them, actually. 'I wish it were so simple.'

'It's the virginity thing, isn't it?'

In an instant, she was sandwiched between his body and the door, and his mouth was at her ear. 'Let's be clear on this,' he growled. 'You have no idea how badly I want to be inside you. Standing up, lying down, taking you from behind. All of it. Right now.'

Oh, God. Her knees wobbled, but he wrapped an arm around her and held her steady.

'Not being able to do any of that is killing me. Literally. But strangely enough, I like just being with you. Touching you however I can, whenever I can. So no. The virginity thing is not what will keep us apart.'

'T-then what?' He did something sinful with his tongue against the shell of her ear while rocking his massive erection into her belly.

'I'm dying.'

'Dying to what?' She reached down and brushed her hand over the bulge in his jeans, because the last two times they'd been together, she'd taken from him, and this time she was giving. 'Have me get down on my knees?'

'Yes, but . . .' His voice became strangled. 'I mean, I'm dying. Cancer.'

Her chest filled with ice. 'No.' She shook her head so hard her hair lashed her cheeks. 'No.'

He grasped her shoulders firmly but gently. 'Serena, listen to me. I'll keep you safe as long as I can—'

'You think I'm upset because I need you to *keep me safe*?' She stepped away from him, eyes stinging and her entire body trembling. 'You . . . you . . . ass!'

His gaze fell to the floor.

Now who's the ass?

'Oh, Josh, I'm sorry.' Still shaking, she wrapped her arms around him. 'Why didn't you tell me sooner?' She thought about the times he was sick, and now it all made sense. It made sense, too, why he'd wanted to hang out with her from the beginning.

I decided to make a vacation out of this trip. One of those one hundred and one things to do before you die.

'It wasn't important.' When she stiffened, because she was going to lay into him again, he added quickly, 'Not at first. But now . . . I just don't want you seeing a future that's not going to happen.'

Choking back a sob, she looked up at him. 'You should have told me.'

'Why? So you'd look at me with pity, like you're doing now? I shouldn't have told you at all.'

'You can't tell me something like that and expect me to not react,' she ground out, and she knew she shouldn't get angry, but dammit, this wasn't fair. They might not have had a shot at a normal life together, but now they didn't have a shot at any kind of life at all.

'Kiss me,' he said. 'Just kiss me and don't let this get in the way of the time we have left.' But he didn't give her time to kiss him. Instead, he dipped his head and kissed away her tears, his satin lips wiping away the traces of her pain.

He was right. They shouldn't be wasting what little time they had together. But how were they supposed to move forward? She wanted to bawl, the kind of sobbing you never wanted anyone to witness because it was messy and loud and left you with red, swollen eyes for a day.

'Hey. You're not with me, here.' His mouth found hers, and he kissed her so deeply she felt it to her soul.

His tongue stroked hers and his hand came up to her neck, kneading and caressing, making her forget . . . and how damned selfish was she to let *him* make *her* feel better? He was the one who needed to feel good, and here he was, putting aside the fact that he was *dying* to comfort her.

She was a seriously selfish bitch.

'Josh,' she murmured against his mouth, 'you've been so generous with me. I want to give you something back.' Though her hands shook, she drew them down his chest and abs. When she reached his jeans waistband, she plucked at the top button.

He closed his fingers around her wrist. 'I can't.'

'I know.' She stroked the back of his hand until he loosened his grip. 'But what if I kiss my way down? Slowly. Would you let me take you in my mouth?'

He made a strangled noise and stood still – frozen, in fact, as she stripped him of his shirt. But when she kissed his left pec, lightly, gently, his head fell back and his hands grasped her shoulders. He held her as though he'd fall over if he let go. As though he didn't *want* to let go.

She kissed her way lower, reveling in the taste of his skin, his masculine flavor, something she'd never truly tasted before. Not like this. She sank to her knees and used her tongue to trace his navel.

'Serena—' He tried to step back, but he was backed against the wall. Beneath the surface of his skin, he quivered.

'Shh.' She gripped his hips with firm but gentle pressure. 'Please. Let me do this for you.' She looked up at him, and her heart skipped a beat at the uncertainty in his eyes.

For a long moment, they remained still, until he nodded slowly. He didn't relax, though, tensed even harder as she unbuttoned his pants. At his sides, his hands clenched into fists, and though he rose full and thick from the opening in his jeans, she somehow felt like this was torture for him rather than pleasure.

How odd that here she was, the virgin, and yet she was having to gentle him, to ease him into this most intimate of encounters.

Her gaze dropped back down to that male part of him, and she couldn't contain a quick, appreciative noise of admiration. Oh . . . my. She'd seen and touched guys before, but none had been so beautiful.

Tentatively, she dragged a finger down his shaft, following a pulsing vein that ran the dusky length to where the base flared wide. His entire body jerked, and she heard the click of teeth as he snapped them together. Feeling a little breathless, she closed her fist around him and stroked, her palm moving slowly from tip to base and back.

'I like how you feel,' she whispered, and his moan drifted down to her, a soft sound of approval that flowed over her like syrup. 'You're like satin over marble.'

She added her other hand now, using one to concentrate motion at the tip, and the other to stroke the length of his shaft. He sucked air through his teeth, but as she worked him, he relaxed, began rolling his hips toward her, subtle thrusts into her hands.

A milky bead formed at the tip. Mouth watering, she leaned in, but his body went two-by-four stiff, so she dropped her head to kiss his inner thigh. Slowly, she worked her way up, still stroking, still holding him with the reverence he deserved.

'Serena,' he rasped, his hands closing on her shoulders once more. 'This . . . I don't know . . . '

Before he could protest further, she took him into her mouth.

His entire body surged forward. She gripped his hips, holding him steady. He tasted rich and earthy, the dramatic, luxurious notes much like fine Black Sea salt. Cupping his heavy sac, she licked the head of him, flicking her tongue back and forth over the little slit.

'Oh . . . man,' he breathed, and then he held his breath when she took him so deep he scraped the back of her throat.

His shaft was thick, hot, and it pulsed when she applied simultaneous suction and tongue action. His groans accompanied deep arches of his back as he began to get into it, and she wished she'd done this sooner, could have given him more moments of pleasure to take him away from his tragic future.

But no, she couldn't think on that. Not now. This was about him, and she wasn't going to be sad right this second. There was time for that later.

Gently, she squeezed his sac, and he shouted with pleasure. Though she didn't have experience with this, she knew instinctively to suck, to stroke, to lick . . . and she learned quickly where he was the most sensitive.

His hands came down to pet her hair, his fingers tender, his touch firm. It struck her then that she'd felt guilty about taking pleasure from him and giving none back . . . but as she measured his responses, listened, touched, tasted, she realized that giving pleasure was as much a gift as taking.

NINETEEN

Wraith's heart pounded so hard he was pretty sure it was going to explode. Hell, *he* was going to explode. He had never allowed a female go down on him. Too intimate, too dangerous, especially when most of your sex partners had teeth like needles.

But what Serena was doing was . . . extraordinary.

The warm, wet depths of her mouth took all of him, and though he knew she was unskilled, he couldn't imagine anything better than this. He could feel the care in her touch, could see it in the way she watched him for every reaction.

The sight of her pink tongue slipping out to swirl around the head of his cock had him clenching his hands into fists.

Serena did something amazing with her teeth, and he hissed with pleasure. His cock pulsed, dangerously close to release. His vision grew sharp and his fangs began to descend, and he knew his eyes had gone gold. Closing them, he kicked his head back against the wall and concentrated on the slow sweeps of her tongue back and forth on the sensitive ridge of his glans and on the twisting action she'd added to each stroke of her fist from his balls to where her mouth capped the head.

Oh, yeah, he was close. . . .

She moaned, a low purr that vibrated her lips and made him cry out. He pulled in a ragged breath and palmed the wall behind him, partly to keep himself upright and partly to keep from grabbing her head and thrusting as the last of his control slipped away.

'Serena,' he gasped. 'Gods, that feels good ... oh, yeah ... just like that.' He panted, hips jerking so hard he couldn't control it anymore. 'I'm going to come ... *fuck.*'

His orgasm blasted through him, more powerful than any he'd ever experienced. It shot up his spine and blasted fireworks in his brain. Serena kept licking and sucking and dragging her thumb along the seam between his balls, adding layers to his climax and keeping it going in sharp, pulsing bursts.

Gradually he came back down to earth, his muscles twitching as they unlocked. He willed his fangs to retreat back into his gums, and as his vision and hearing came back online, he heard what sounded like panting.

Oh, shit.

'Don't swallow,' he barked, but it was too late. Serena was still on her knees, her fingers digging into his thighs, her eyes glazed over and her face flushed. The scent of lust billowed up like a cloud from her, slamming into him and revving his libido all over again.

'Josh,' she whispered, throwing her head back in ecstasy as she ran her hands up and down his legs. 'What ... what's happening?'

Shit, shit, shit. Seminus demon ejaculate was a powerful aphrodisiac. His brothers had talked endlessly about the effects, but he hadn't paid much attention.

Now he wished he had.

Serena dragged her hand down her chest, hissing a little when her thumb brushed one breast. 'This is good ... so good ... '

'Ah ... someone must have slipped something in your drink at dinner. Just relax.' Relax. Great freaking idea, given how she was peeling out of her clothes and touching herself.

In less time than it took to leap through a Harrowgate, she was naked and rubbing against Wraith like a Trillah demon in heat, practically purring, and all the while nipping at the skin of his shoulders and neck. He'd never let any female bite him. Ever.

But when she took his flesh between her teeth, pain popped along his nerve endings, along with a rush of pleasure so intense he wished she'd bite harder. Draw blood. Take nourishment from him so she could thrive.

Except she wasn't a vampire, and if she were, he sure as hell wouldn't be here with her.

'Touch me, Josh,' she said against his throat. She laid her hand over his and pushed it between their bodies, between her legs. 'There ... yes, oh, yes.'

Man, he felt like a virgin himself, all nervous and freaked out, and he had no idea why.

'Jesus, you're wet,' he rasped. His fingers delved into her cream, and that was all it took. She cried out, her body undulating wildly as she crested.

'M-more,' she whispered, even before she'd come down, and he dragged his fingers up through her slit, barely skimming her swollen knot of nerves. Again she cried out, bucking and riding his hand, over and over until he lost count of her orgasms.

And then she was climbing him, so fast he barely had time to grab her butt to support her as she locked her legs around his waist.

'Make love to me.' She pinched his earlobe between her teeth and rocked her sex against his. 'I want to feel you inside me.'

The slide of his shaft through her slick slit made him groan. Seminus demons could, technically, only release inside a female, but he could dip just the head of his penis inside her, being careful not to break her hymen, and then he could pull out and—

What the fuck? The point of all of this was to break her damned hymen and take the fucking charm.

Serena writhed against him, growling and nipping, irritated at not getting what her body wanted. The friction brought her off again, though, which eased her lust temporarily. Like, for a couple of seconds. But it was long enough for him to get her on her back on the bed.

She wrapped her legs around him and arched her spine, tilting her hips so he damned near slipped inside her.

'Hold on, baby. Just hold on.' Somehow he managed to shed his jeans, even with her clawing at him. When he mounted her once more, settling between her legs, she sighed and pulled him down on top of her.

'You feel so good.' She brushed her lips across his. 'So right.'

He moved against her, loving how they fit together. 'What about the consequences?' He couldn't believe he was asking that when he should just dive inside, but for some reason, he wanted to know where her head was, that she was going to be at least a little okay with this later.

As she lay dying.

Pain stabbed him like a stake through the heart. And it had nothing to do with the poison.

'Don't care.' Her moan rattled through him as she wrapped her hand around his cock and guided him to her entrance. 'All that matters . . . is you. Being with you.' She kissed him, hard and deep.

When she let him go, they were both panting and the tip of his shaft was rubbing in her honey. One punch of his hips and he'd be home.

'I think . . . I think I love you.'

Wraith groaned. 'It's the aphrodisiac talking, Serena.'

'Shh.' She pressed a finger to his lips. 'Just make love to me. Do you want that?'

'Gods, yes,' he murmured, because at this moment, he'd never wanted anything more, charm or no. 'This might hurt a little.'

'It's okay. I trust you.'

He slipped his hand beneath her to tilt her hips. Instinct guided her, had her clamping her thighs around his hips even tighter. The head of him started to ease inside . . .

I think I love you.

Her words clanged around in his skull so hard it hurt. Sweat popped out on his brow.

I trust you.

Emotion clogged his throat and cut off his breath. Only Shade had ever really trusted him and even then, the trust had limits.

'Please, Josh.'

I trust you.

Serena was flame against him, her body scorching him on the outside, her trust and love warming him on the inside, a place that had been a dark, cold cavern for as long as he could remember. She was beautiful inside and out, and she didn't deserve what he was about to do to her. Not without a guarantee that she would survive afterward.

His brothers would never forgive him, but he couldn't take her life.

'I can't,' he panted, rearing back. 'No.'

'But—'

'I can't give you what you want, Serena. I'll never be able to. Not like that.' Gods, he was a fool, a fool who had just signed three death warrants. 'I'll make you feel good, though. I promise you that.'

He kissed his way down her body and dove between her legs, used his mouth to punish her for making him burn like this. His punishment made her come over and over, until she couldn't move, lay limp on the bed.

Shaking with a combination of extreme arousal, exhaustion, and not a little fear, he crawled up beside her and pulled her into his arms until her breathing eased into sleep. He thanked his lucky stars he'd shot up with the anti-libido drug before dinner, because although he was experiencing some serious blue balls despite the earlier release, he wasn't in crippling pain. This would ease off eventually. He winced as he adjusted himself. Hopefully, it would ease off soon.

He didn't know how long they lay like that, her sleeping

peacefully and him feeling the chill of death take hold, but when she began to stir, the sky outside the window had lightened. A muffled beeping came from his pants on the floor. He stifled a groan and dug his phone out of the pocket.

No cure.

The text on the screen from the demoness sat like a hot coal in his gut. There truly was no hope now. He lifted his other wrist, which felt way too heavy, checked his watch.

And knew what he had to do.

Carefully, he eased out of the tangle of their naked bodies and dressed. Every joint, every muscle screamed in agony, and he had a feeling that, this time, no amount of medication was going to help.

'Hey,' she mumbled. 'What are you doing?'

He jammed his foot into a boot, and when he didn't answer, because he didn't know what to say, she sat up and brought her hand down on his shoulder. He jerked away.

'The train will be pulling into Cairo in half an hour. I'm getting off. Going home.'

She blinked, her groggy gaze unfocused. 'I don't understand. Why?'

'We almost had sex.'

'No, we didn't.'

She didn't remember. He wasn't sure if that was a blessing or not.

'Yeah, we did.'

She rubbed her eyes. 'Even if we almost did . . . we didn't. So . . . why are you leaving?'

A shudder wracked his body as he exhaled. He bent to pick up the wooden top that had fallen to the floor. 'I'm leaving because I'm afraid that eventually, we will, and I can't be responsible for killing you.'

'*What?*' She came to her feet, tugged the bed sheet to her chest, as if that would hide anything. Her body, her curves, every freaking detail was imprinted on his brain. 'You think I'm not strong enough to resist you? You think you have to play martyr and keep yourself away from me so I won't weaken in your presence and force you to have sex with me or something?'

'Ah . . . no. I'm not exactly the martyr type—'

'So you just don't *want* to have sex with me?'

He opened his mouth, but before he could deny *that* particular question, she slammed her palm into his chest. Hard.

'Answer me!' she shouted. She was coming down from the effects of the aphrodisiac. He recognized the signs of a drug crash, had lived them himself.

'I can't risk your life, Serena. I won't. And I'm not strong enough to promise that I can be near you and not want you.'

'*Get out!*' She was coming down hard, practically spitting fire and completely irrational. She pointed at the door. 'Get out and . . . and go to hell!'

'That,' he croaked, 'is only a matter of time.' He opened the door and paused at the threshold. 'I'll make sure someone will get on in Cairo to take you the rest of the way home.'

He fled, steeling himself against her voice, calling out his name. He tore through so many cars he lost count, elbowing people aside, until he reached the cargo car.

Weak from the poison, shaken by what had just happened, and battling the intense desire to return to Serena, he collapsed onto a crate. An ache in his chest tugged at him, and he knew that if he gave into it, it would take him straight back to Serena.

Maybe he didn't have to leave. Maybe he could stay with her until the last possible minute, spend his final days – *hours*, probably – with someone who gave him a reason to live.

Right, because she'd no doubt love to care for him as he lay dying.

He wanted to stay with her, but for the first time in his life, he was going to do the right thing, not the selfish thing. He wouldn't make her watch him die. He'd go home, and she'd remember him as he was, not as some frail, failing shell.

He glanced at his watch again. Half an hour. He'd call Tayla, have her meet the train in Cairo and take care of Serena. Then he'd find a Harrowgate and be back at the hospital before things got really bad.

His brothers would take care of him like they always had, if they forgave him for signing their death warrants, that is.

TWENTY

Serena sat in her compartment, wondering what had just happened. Josh had left her *because* she might have sex with him? Why would he think that?

Last night she'd wanted to pleasure him as he'd done to her, and then . . . then . . . what? She blinked against the flood of fuzzy memories.

Make love to me.

Oh, God. She'd said that. *She'd really said that.* She'd been all over him, begging him for sex. Humiliation made her skin crawl and her face burn. What had he said, that someone must have slipped a Mickey into her drink at dinner?

Her clothes from last night lay scattered all over the tiny room, evidence of her lapse of control. Stomach turning over, she got dressed, cursed the wrinkles in her olive skirt and cream blouse. She looked like she'd been pulled out of a suitcase.

I want to feel you inside me.

Mortified, she groaned and sank down on the bed again. Everything came back to her, clear as crystal. She remembered how Josh had taken care of her but hadn't taken advantage of her hyper-horny state. He could have, but he didn't.

He'd wanted to save her life.

And how had she thanked him? By going into a rage, yelling at a dying man when he said he was leaving.

Leaving. Fear flickered in her chest. He'd said he was dying, but she wouldn't lose a single minute with him. And maybe . . . maybe The Aegis could help. Maybe Val knew of some curative magic or artifacts.

She could *not* lose him.

Someone tapped at the door. Oh, please, please, let it be Josh. . . . She leaped up and whipped open the door. 'Jo—' She cut off with a gasp.

Leaping backward, she tried to slam the door shut, but Byzamoth, looking as he had the first time she'd seen him – angelic and beautiful – blocked her effort, moving inside as sinuously as a snake. He closed the door behind him.

She opened her mouth to scream, but he crushed her to the wall, his hard, muscular body against hers. 'If you keep your mouth shut, I won't hurt you.' He dragged his tongue up her cheek, and she shuddered. 'Not much.' Terror turned her legs to jelly. He laughed, the sugary sound tangled with a thread of sinister darkness. 'But I am going to rob you. Of both your charms.'

His fist closed around her necklace, and she almost smiled, because that sucker wasn't going anywhere. Then, to her horror, it broke free of her neck and dangled from his hand.

He slipped the necklace into his dishdasha and hiked up her skirt. 'Now, the other one.'

He tore open his robes. His form morphed and, like a shapeshifting sequence in a horror movie, he went from being beautiful to the hairless gray thing with a batlike, veiny wing she'd seen at the Regent's place. Between his legs, his huge penis jutted obscenely upward, oozing a dark substance from the tip.

Sweet Jesus, he was going to impale her with that hideous thing. Her blood congealed. Petrified, shaking, she tried to scream, but nothing came out. Not even her breath made it past the lump of terror in her throat.

'What's the matter, love? Say something. Your fear arouses me.' He inhaled. 'The scent of your fear is intoxicating, but even more so is the sound of your voice. The tremor. The pitch. Say something.'

'Fuck you,' she croaked. 'That's something.'

He backhanded her so hard she saw stars. 'Bitch. I'm going to fuck you until you're dead.' He smiled cruelly, trailed his fingers over her cheek. 'You're afraid to die, aren't you? The smell of your terror is spiking. So arousing. . . . now, ask me why. Why I'm doing this.'

She didn't want to, but at this point, humoring him seemed like a better idea than mouthing off. 'Why are you doing this?'

He hit her again. 'Don't ask me stupid questions.'

Fury and pain overrode her fear. She was tired of being hit, and she wasn't going down without a fight. Snarling, she shoved him as hard as she could and kneed him between the legs. He didn't flinch, but he did slam his forearm into her throat, cutting off her breath.

'That was stupid.' His voice cracked like a whip.

She clawed at his arm and kicked at him as her lungs struggled for air.

He dangled her necklace in front of her face. 'Do you know what this is? What it does?' He let up on the pressure on her neck just enough for her to gulp air and shake her head. 'Of course not. Because that would be against the rules. And the rules must always be followed.'

There was a note of sarcasm in his voice she didn't understand and wasn't sure she wanted to. Pretty much, she just wanted oxygen.

'This is a key to the end of days. You, my dear, are also a key. And once I take your virginity, *I* will become the most powerful key of all.' He put his forehead to hers and looked into her eyes with his flat, soulless ones. 'I look forward to ridding the human infestation upon this earth. Starting with you.'

ʚ

Cairo. The Triumphant City. A sprawling urban rat race that came alive – and, in Wraith's opinion, looked best – at night. As a hunting ground, Wraith had always found Cairo to be adequate, but for the most part, he wasn't fond of it. The mix of modern and ancient, extreme wealth and extreme poverty, gave the city a mixed-up vibe, as if it couldn't settle on any particular mood. Its history fascinated him though, and sometimes he wondered what life would have been like back in the days of the pharaohs.

Not life for humans – that would have sucked. But being a demon back then would have been sweet. They'd been called gods – Ma'at, Ra, Osiris, Khepri, scores more – and had been worshipped as such.

Demons had long memories – many were immortal or damn near so, and they wanted that power and worship again.

If the shit going down in the underworld was any indication, it looked like things were looking up for those demons.

As the train pulled out of Cairo station, Wraith watched through a window, its reflection revealing that the sand in his hourglass glyph was down to the last grains.

He wondered if he'd made the right decision.

Even though Tayla was an incredible warrior, especially when she tapped into her inner demon, she wasn't strong enough to protect Serena. On the other hand, he wasn't at his strongest either.

Gods, Serena must think he was such an ass after he took off on her like that. She'd told him to go, but after watching Shade and Eidolon deal with their mates, he now understood that sometimes females wanted you to fight for them. Then again, sometimes they didn't.

As he fingered the top Serena had given him, he realized he'd never understand the opposite sex.

He came to his feet, knowing Serena wasn't going to be happy to see him again. Still, he was going to stick by her side until she was back in the States and he could get her someplace safe, because Val wasn't an option.

With a growl, he tore open the door to the cargo hold. Halfway to her cabin, a sense of wrongness slammed into him hard enough to make him stumble. The hairs on the back of his neck stood at attention, acknowledging the familiar evil.

Byzamoth.

Wraith hit the first sleeping-car door at a run. Slammed one of the passengers out of the way and went through the second door almost without opening it. The dark, oily sense of malevolence grew as he ran.

He skidded to a stop, nearly overshooting her door. A black cloud of evil pulsed all around the doorway, and he slammed his shoulder into the thin door, caving it in with a crash and explosion of twisted metal.

'Josh!' Serena's scream penetrated all the way to his heart.

The sight of her, pinned beneath Byzamoth's hideously transformed body, sent him into kill mode. All his aches, pains, and nausea disappeared as a veil of crimson sliced down over his vision and thoughts.

Wraith threw himself at Byzamoth, seized his leathery wing, and yanked him off of Serena. He slammed the angel into the narrow space between the door and the seats. A crack of bone accompanied Byzamoth's high-pitched yelp, and his wing drooped.

'Semin—'

Wraith popped him in the mouth. Lifting his knee, Wraith nailed the bastard in the junk. Very large, exaggerated junk. The knowledge that he'd planned to use that monstrous thing on Serena burned to ash what little remained of Wraith's control.

'You're so dead,' he snarled, and pulled Byzamoth's head down to meet his knee. Blood splashed on the floor, but not nearly enough. He threw the angel into the hall, slamming him into the door of another compartment.

The screams of passengers who heard the commotion pierced the air, mixing with Serena's bellow of fury as she came at Byzamoth, drilling a quick double-tap to his mouth, followed by a hard jab to his throat. Fierce admiration and pride lit Wraith up from the inside. *Good girl.*

The angel lunged for her, but she swung her elbow into his gut as Wraith put the heel of his hand into Byzamoth's nose.

'My necklace,' Serena yelled. 'Get it!'

'Mine.' Byzamoth spun away, his grayish lips pulling back from sharp, yellowed teeth. '*And so is she.*' He spun with a lot more grace than he should have had, given that his wing was broken and the passage was so narrow, but in an instant, he was sprinting down the aisle.

Wraith gave chase. At the end of the car, Byzamoth collided with a passenger. With a furious snarl, he hurled the male human at Wraith. They both went down in a heap. *Son of a bitch.* Wraith untangled himself from the human, who was whimpering, his dark skin turned ashen, his eyes haunted by what he'd seen.

Welcome to my world, buddy. Wraith jumped to his feet and tore off after Byzamoth, though the sense of evil had dissipated. He wasn't sure what powers the angel had, but he was pretty sure the bastard couldn't fly off with one wing, and a broken one at that.

Ahead, he found a group of humans gathered around an open door on the side of the train, their excited chatter telling him all he needed to know. They'd seen a guy leap from the train, though apparently Byzamoth had taken human form, because these people weren't nearly as freaked out as they should have been. But where had he gone?

Wraith sped back to Serena, taking no special care to go around passengers. Their indignant curses followed him, but all that mattered was getting to Serena.

The moment he blew through the twisted door frame, she flew into his arms. 'Thank God, you're okay. Oh, my God, thank you. Thank you.' She was babbling and sobbing, and only a colossal effort kept him from doing the same.

'It's okay. He's gone.'

'My necklace—'

'Gone, too.'

She cursed, the first really dirty word he'd heard from her.

'I'm sorry I left,' he said into her hair. 'I should have been here.'

She tore out of his arms, and he lurched, had to catch himself on the wall. She'd been holding him up, and a sense of dizziness nearly knocked him over. 'Don't you dare be sorry. I'm the one who should be sorry. I had no right to get mad at you. Or chase you away. God, I'm a fool.' She looked at him through watery eyes. 'Josh, are you okay?'

Pain tore through his gut, doubling him over. 'No.'

'Are you hurt? Did he do something to you?'

'Need . . . my . . . room.' He stumbled toward his cabin, doing his best to hold in the contents of his stomach. Though his room was next door, it felt as though it took about six months to get there, and when he did, he couldn't open the door. Instead, he sank to the floor, his muscles convulsing and his stomach heaving.

'I'm going to see if there's a doctor on board,' Serena said.

'No. Need . . . meds. Inside.'

Her soft curse made him smile despite his misery. Second use of profanity in as many minutes. 'Fine, but if it doesn't help—'

He grabbed her wrist, and when she winced, he kicked himself for being such a brute, and loosened his hold. 'No doctors. Promise.'

'I don't like it . . . but I promise.'

She opened the door. Gathering what remained of his strength, he dragged himself inside and crawled up on the bed. Soft. Cool. Fuck, he was going to die here, wasn't he?

'You're not going to die,' Serena said, and he realized he must have been talking out loud. 'Now, what meds do you need? Where are they?'

'Bag. Under bed.'

He heard her rummaging around, but then all sounds faded and the world went black.

TWENTY-ONE

Serena tried to control her fear as she pulled medicine bottles and some ketchup-sized packets filled with a dark red substance from Josh's bag. But panic had taken root and was growing into something unmanageable. He'd said he was dying, but she'd assumed he had time. This ... was looking bad.

A river of tears streamed down her face. She hadn't cried – truly cried – in years. There had been way too much of that when she'd been sick, and then even more when her mom had died. But this ... God, so much had happened since she'd met Josh, both good and bad. On top of losing the necklace, how could she deal with losing Josh, too?

Her hand shook as she gathered the bottles and one of the packets of the red liquid. Josh lay facing her, his breathing labored, sweat beading on his brow.

'Josh.' She smoothed her hand over his cheek. 'Josh? Can you hear me?'

No response. She patted his cheek, gently at first, and then with more urgency. '*Josh.*'

'Mmm?'

Her relief was cut short as he began to convulse, his eyes rolling back in his head. Helplessness made her tears fall faster, and by the time he'd settled down, she was sobbing.

'Josh, I have your medicine.'

His head lolled forward, and he groaned. 'T-the packet . . . pills.'

'Same time?'

'Mmm-hmm.'

She took one pill from each of the two bottles, tore open a packet, and placed the pills in his mouth. With one hand she held his head up, and with the other, she tipped the liquid into his mouth. He swallowed. When he finished, she covered him with a blanket. His hand caught hers, weakly.

'Dying. But . . . thank you.'

'You're going to be okay,' she whispered. 'Just fight, all right?'

He sucked in a rattling breath, the sound sending a shudder through her. Helplessly, she sank down on the floor, her back against the bed, and reached for her necklace out of habit, only to find that it wasn't there.

This was bad. So bad. She needed to call Val. He could help Josh. She knew he could. She dug into her skirt pocket for her phone. No signal.

Dammit!

Someone tapped on the door, and she jumped, her pulse kicking into high gear. 'Security. Open up.'

She pushed to her feet and confronted the two Egyptian men standing in the hall. One was inspecting her destroyed door.

'Ma'am,' the other said, gesturing to the room next to Josh's, 'this is your room?'

'Yes. Someone broke in.'

'Some passengers are reporting that it was a . . . monster?'

She smiled, hoped they didn't notice her mouth trembling. 'He was just a man.'

The men took her statement – she explained that someone had tried to rob her and then escaped – and when she was finished, they left her alone to question witnesses.

She closed the door and returned to Josh, wondering when – when, not if – Byzamoth would return.

He wasn't done with her. He'd come back for her, wouldn't stop until he'd taken her virginity. She shuddered, imagining the horror.

Armed with her charm, he said he'd bring about the end of days.

'I'm sorry, mom,' she murmured. Her mother had trusted Serena to keep the necklace safe, and Serena had failed. Somehow she had to get that necklace back, but she was defenseless against Byzamoth, and coming face to face with him again would be akin to offering her virginity up on a platter.

Again, the vision of the fallen angel attacking her, tearing her clothes away, assaulted her brain. She'd never forget his disgusting words, nor the smell of brimstone and feces on his breath.

Josh had saved her this time, had somehow been skilled and dangerous enough to take on Byzamoth and come out victorious. But he was dying, and he wouldn't have the strength to protect her again. Byzamoth was going to take her virginity and carry through with his diabolical plan.

Unless she could get the necklace back. Unless *someone* could get the necklace back. Someone like Josh.

She closed her eyes, knowing what had to be done.

௵

Serena's hands felt so good on him. Like nothing Wraith had ever felt before. They worshipped him, kneading his flesh and sizzling his skin as they glided down his stomach. Her lips tickled his chest, and tiny licks of her tongue made him hiss with pleasure.

Lower. *Oh, yeah, that's it.*

He kept his hands at his sides and let her play, let her unbutton his jeans and release his swollen cock. He thought she'd take him into her mouth, but instead, she straddled him. Her wet heat surrounded him as she began to move, rubbing his shaft between her slick folds.

Damn, this was a great dream. He'd been dying to make love to her, and here, in his sleep, he could. He nearly groaned when she angled her hips to guide the head of his penis to her entrance.

'I love you, Josh.'

Josh. Even in his dreams she couldn't call him by his name. He fisted the sheets, let the vibration of the train lull him when all he wanted to do was punch his hips upward and take her.

Train . . . *train?* Josh. *Not a dream!*

His eyes shot open, and oh, holy hell. Serena was braced above him, poised to take *him.*

'No!' Frantically, he grabbed her waist, but he was too weak to stop her. She sank down, burying his shaft deep. Her barrier broke, and she cried out before stifling the sound with her fist jammed in her mouth.

Instantly, a strange, wonderful energy permeated his body, coursing through his veins and kicking his heart into overdrive. The weakness that had been dragging him down was replaced by power and strength that howled through him in a mighty roar.

'Oh, babe,' he breathed. 'Oh . . . fuck, what have you done?'

She had to know she'd started a countdown to her death.

'I couldn't let you die.' She looked down at him, her gaze warm and liquid. She smiled, and then winced as she shifted. 'I know you said you can't give me what I want, but you already have.'

He wanted to argue, to rail against what she said, what she believed, but he couldn't. His feelings for her went too deep. 'I shouldn't have told you—'

'Don't.' She dug her nails into his chest. The pleasure-pain was exquisite. 'I've been waiting too long for this to ruin it with regrets.'

He didn't think he could feel anything *but* regret until she dragged the backs of her fingers up his pecs and brushed them over his nipples. Back arched, she rolled her hips in a fluid surge. He pulsed inside her, his desire growing more encompassing by the second.

There would be an eternity for regrets; right now he needed to make sure this first time would be something special for her. For them both.

He palmed the back of her head and pulled her down until her lips met his. Kissing her was the greatest pleasure he'd ever known. Her lips parted, and he slipped his tongue between them to meet hers. He hated that he had to be careful, to ensure she wouldn't get too up-close and personal with his canines, but right now careful was a good thing. This was her first time, and he wasn't going to behave like an animal.

Still, no matter how civilized he tried to be, some instincts couldn't be overridden. He cocked one leg up and gripped her hips, holding her as his thrusts grew faster, harder. He needed to go deeper. To go so far inside that he'd never come out again, but her whimper made him freeze. She still hurt. Gods, he was a brutal ass-hole.

'I'm sorry.' He kissed her tears away. 'You just feel ... so ... good.'

Her fingers stroked his neck, right over his jugular, and he had a crazy desire to ask her to bite him there. 'It's okay. I knew it would hurt.' She winced. 'But maybe not as much as it does.'

'I want to make it better, *lirsha*.'

'*Lirsha?*'

Shit. Well, he couldn't very well explain that it loosely translated to 'lover' in Seminus-speak, and to hell with it, he didn't want to explain at all.

'Shh.' He lifted her off him, the silky friction as his cock dragged through her wet channel nearly making him come. 'Trust me.'

She bit her lip, her expression softening, and she nodded. Wriggling down her body, he urged her up at the same time, until his mouth met her core. The bed was short and his legs were crammed up against the wall, but he was exactly where he wanted to be.

Serena moaned as he kissed her deeply, rolling her swollen bud between his lips. Hungrily, he ran his tongue up her center in a gentle, wet stroke. When he pushed inside her with a healing swipe of his tongue, she cried out in a sharp release, coming so hard he had to steady her with a firm grip on her thighs.

When it was over, she went limp, and he easily tucked her beneath him. 'Are you okay?'

'Oh, yes,' she murmured, her voice a husky trill. 'Wow.'

'It's only going to get better.'

Excitement sparked in her eyes. 'Really?'

'Yeah. Really.'

He shifted so her hips were cradling his and his cock was poised at her entrance. Bracing himself on his elbows, he kissed her until they were both breathless and rocking wildly against each other. Her undulating, grinding motion had him sucking air, and when she lifted her legs around his waist, he couldn't wait any longer. He tried to be gentle, but he was so worked up, and she was so wet . . .

He entered her in one smooth stroke.

'You okay?' he asked, though it would be a wonder if she understood him, the way the words had come out on a groan of ecstasy.

'Stop asking me that.' She tightened her thighs around him and arched up. 'Keep going. Please.' She pumped her hips and locked her arms around his neck for leverage, and damn, he was just going to have to hang on for the ride.

He couldn't believe he was doing this . . . with a human, with a virgin, with someone he cared about. But he didn't want to think about all of that. He wanted to give her a first time she'd remember forever.

Except, she didn't have forever anymore.

A nasty snarl came out of his mouth. He didn't care that her disease had no cure. There had to be another way. He would save her. He would. And then, she would be his. 'Mine.'

'Yours,' she agreed, tugging his head down to her throat. 'Kiss me there. Like in the dream.'

The vampire dream. The idea of biting her made him so hot he surged inside her as his fangs shot out of his gums. Willing his fangs to retreat, he latched onto her neck with his lips and sucked, knowing he was going to leave a mark and not caring. He wanted to mark her in every way he could.

He also wanted to be gentle, but she drove him to amazing heights that destroyed his self-control, and suddenly he was sweating and pumping and growling, his release building like trapped steam.

She scored his shoulders with her nails and cried out, but he recognized the sound – pleasure, not pain. Her tight sheath clenched around him, dragging him deeper, her hips thrusting upward to create a wild, violent tempo that must have rocked the train.

Ripples of pleasure hummed through his balls, up his shaft, as his come heated and gathered until he couldn't take it anymore. He came in a blinding, white-hot tide that crashed over him once, twice, oh, fuck ... his third orgasm roared through him.

Satin walls milked him as Serena matched him climax for climax. He was used to multiple orgasms – it rocked to be an incubus – but he knew they were a rarity for the females of most species. The guaranteed ability to climax over and over with a Seminus demon was the draw for many females, and as he came down from his fifth, he settled in to watch Serena have a couple more.

Panting, he eased to the side to keep from squishing her, but he held her close, turning her into him so he was still inside her, could still feel the clench of her inner walls as she came again. Her head fell back, her eyes closed, and she let out little gasps of pleasure.

'Josh, oh ... ah ... *yes.*' She convulsed, and he dropped his hands to her butt to press her closer.

Normally, he immediately pulled out and away, left the female to writhe in pleasure while he made his escape. But this was Serena. They'd talked about the rush, the *burn* of the hunts they enjoyed, but he'd never felt those things with any female ... any female but Serena. Sex with her was the ultimate rush, the ultimate burn, and he was going to be here to enjoy every single moan, gasp, and shudder.

'Wraith.' His voice was a guttural whisper against her ear. 'Call me Wraith when you come.'

'Now,' she moaned. 'I'm coming now . . . *Wraith.*'

He fucking came again when he heard her call out his name in her release. Afterward, they collapsed together, their skin slick with perspiration, their lungs sucking oxygen like there wasn't enough on the train.

'Thank you,' she said, taking a ragged breath. 'God, thank you.'

She was thanking *him*? She'd given him a miracle, had sacrificed her own life to give him something he didn't deserve.

So no, he didn't deserve thanks, and he wasn't sure he should thank her, either.

Because Serena had saved his life, but in a way, she'd killed him a little, too.

TWENTY-TWO

Eidolon experienced a strange mix of relief and anxiety as he hung up the phone after speaking with Wraith. Shade sat across from him in E's office, jaw working overtime on a piece of gum, waiting for the news.

Wraith had retrieved the charm, which explained why Eidolon suddenly felt like running a marathon, but it sounded like his brother had fallen for the human, and that was only going to end in disaster. Especially because he'd all but ordered E to find a way to save her at all costs, and nothing Eidolon said could convince Wraith otherwise.

'Shade, he got the charm, but it's not all good news—'

Reaver walked – or, more accurately, stumbled – through the door. The angel's hair, normally blindingly shiny and perfect, was tangled and dull, falling around sunken, bloodshot eyes. His hands were black with dried blood, his skin so white his veins beneath it read like a road map of misery.

'What the fuck?' Shade asked, coming to his feet as if to catch Reaver.

'Forget me,' Reaver croaked. 'Serena. Need to protect her.'

'Oh, now you're ready to help?' E asked, and Reaver bowed his head in a nod. 'Good. What's special about the necklace?'

'There are things I can't say.' Reaver met E's gaze, his cracked lips set in a stubborn line.

'Dammit, Reaver, it's been stolen, and it sounds like it's a pretty damned big deal.'

The very last drop of color drained from Reaver's face. He began to sway, and Eidolon shot to his feet to catch the angel before he keeled over. Fortunately, Reaver caught himself on the wall.

Good. Eidolon hated to admit it, even to himself, but the idea of touching someone of divine origins gave him the willies.

'It can't be,' Reaver said. 'What you're saying is impossible.'

'I'm telling you, it's not. I need to know about the necklace. Right now.'

Reaver's pale blue eyes were diamond sharp but haunted when he locked them with Eidolon's. 'The pendant,' he said, in a clipped voice that made every syllable vibrate, 'is Armageddon on a chain.'

Shade stopped chewing his gum. 'Come again?'

'The amulet. It's a piece of Heaven.'

'Ah . . . Heaven? Literally?'

'Yes.'

E exchanged looks with Shade, because this was big. Beyond big. 'Reaver, we need to know more.'

Reaver raked his fingers through his hair. Eidolon gave the angel a minute to compose himself, because he still looked like he was on the verge of coming out of his skin. Finally, Reaver stopped messing with his mane but started pacing – slowly and with a limp, but pacing.

'In the *Daemonica*, there is mention of a celestial lock and key.'

E nodded, because he knew the passage in the demon bible, but it was vague. Demon scholars had been trying to decipher it for centuries. 'Go on.'

'It is said,' Reaver continued, 'that when Satan was booted from Heaven, he took a piece of it with him in hopes that it would allow him to return someday. He kept it hidden, and then, during a skirmish battle between good and evil, the angel Hizkiel took it back. But thousands of years of corruption had altered it. It could not be allowed back in Heaven for fear of taint. But neither could it be left on earth for demons to use as a way to open the celestial gate between Heaven and Hell. So it was decided that it should be put into the keeping of humans, since ultimately, the power struggle between good and evil has always been about mankind. Should they fail to safeguard it, their downfall will be their own doing.'

Eidolon had a bad feeling about this, especially with Wraith landing smack in the middle of a conflict between good and evil. 'So it's been left in the keeping of a human who has been charmed?'

'Yes. Many humans. Serena was the most recent. Theoretically, it should always be safe.' Reaver shook his head. 'I don't think even another Marked Sentinel could bypass the charm. Sentinels have come up against each other in battle, and their charms made them both untouchable even to each other.'

'It wasn't another charmed human who took it,' Eidolon said. 'It was a fallen angel. Name of Byzamoth.'

'*Byzamoth?*' A concussion wave shattered the windows in the office area, and the hospital shook with such force that Eidolon wondered if humans would register the rumbling on their Richter scale.

Shade moved toward the angel. 'Hey, man, check up. We kinda like having a roof over our heads. One that isn't crumbling.'

'It's a little late for that,' Eidolon muttered, but now that Wraith was no longer dying, the hospital should get back to normal. Too bad the lack of staff couldn't be so easily fixed.

'Byzamoth.' Reaver's eyes flashed blue fire. 'Is Wraith sure?'

'That's what he said. Why? Who is this guy?'

Reaver shoved a chair aside so hard it flew into the wall and impaled itself in the plaster. Eidolon had never seen him so riled. Hell, he'd rarely seen him even mildly annoyed. 'He was an angel of Destruction. Now a demon of Destruction. He fell during the first war in Heaven. If he has the necklace and the charm—'

'He doesn't. Wraith has the charm.'

Reaver barked out a bitter laugh. 'It's a sad day when I'm relieved that *Wraith* is the one who took the charm.'

Shade scrubbed his hand over his face. 'Okay, so what does Byzamoth want with this stuff? If he's a fallen angel, he doesn't need an invincibility charm.'

'No, but he needs the blood of a charmed one to work the amulet and open the gate between Heaven and Hell. If he had possession of the necklace *and* the charm, he could use his own blood at his convenience. Since he's not charmed, he needs the blood of the Sentinel who guarded the amulet.'

'But Serena is no longer charmed.'

'Exactly. So once he knows that, he'll need the blood of the one she passed it to.' Reaver finally stopped pacing. 'The good news is that if anyone can take care of himself, it's Wraith.'

'And obviously, the charm won't work against Byzamoth.'

Reaver nodded. 'I don't think anyone anticipated the loophole.'

'That loophole being that an angel could bypass the charm ... even a fallen one.'

'Obviously.'

'So what, exactly, will Byzamoth do with the amulet?'

'He'll open Heaven to the forces of evil. Demons will swarm inside.' Reaver wobbled as he sank down on an office chair. 'Humans have always been focused on the Apocalypse. They see it as the end of days, but for believers, it's not such a bad thing. They know that after the battle of good and evil, the righteous will go to Heaven.' Reaver's voice went as thin as the air in the darkest reaches of Sheoul. 'Humans think the Apocalypse will be the battle of battles. Hell on earth. But with that pendant, Byzamoth will open the gate between Heaven and Sheoul, and the resulting battle will take place on many realms, on an unimaginable scale. Heaven could ... cease to exist, souls will default to Satan, and humans would be trapped in a hell so terrible it can't be conceived of.'

Reaver's eyes grew haunted. 'Boys, this is much bigger than an apocalypse. This is the end of existence for all but the victor.'

൭

Shade, Eidolon, and Reaver spent the next hour arguing about what to do, but it always came back to Wraith.

'He needs to get that necklace,' Shade said, as he popped the top of the Fresca he'd fetched from the break room. He'd also called Runa to let her know he was running late. She'd sounded as exhausted as he was, but with four babies at home, it was no wonder.

'No!' Reaver slammed his fist on Eidolon's desk. 'If Wraith defeats Byzamoth and gets the talisman, that leaves Wraith in possession of the most powerful artifact in the universe. I don't think any of us wants that. The Aegis must retrieve it.'

Shade snorted. 'Those bunch of ignorant—'

Eidolon beaned him in the shoulder with a stapler. 'You're talking about my mate, you know.'

'And like it or not, they *are* the human Guardians of the earthly realm,' Reaver said.

Eidolon looked up from his computer, where he'd been researching Biblical and demonic prophecies. 'Whatever happens, it needs to happen fast. Tayla said that within the last twelve hours, demons have come aboveground and taken over three holy sites in Israel. The local Aegi have their hands full. Coincides with Byzamoth taking the necklace.'

'Hell's fires,' Shade muttered. 'Leave it to Wraith to start Armageddon.' Shade thought about his sons, so small and helpless, and about Runa, who he loved so much it hurt. He couldn't bear the thought that they could be caught up in this war.

'This is far worse than Armageddon,' Reaver added, as if Shade needed the reminder.

'Why now?' Eidolon asked. 'This Byzamoth asshole is obviously old, so why didn't he grab the necklace and charm centuries ago?'

'Fallen angels can't sense Marked Sentinels.' Reaver shook his head. 'I don't know how he could have found her.'

Eidolon tapped his fingers on his desk, and just as Shade was about to break his fingers, E froze, mid-tap. 'Wraith said Byzamoth only has one wing. Has that always been the case?'

'Not that I know of.'

Shade frowned. 'What are you getting at?'

'Roag's dungeon. Runa ripped off the wing of a fallen angel. I wondered why Roag would have a fallen angel working for him.'

Reaver snorted. 'He wouldn't. No angel would serve a demon.'

'Exactly. But what if he was there to get something from Roag?'

'Eth's Eye,' Shade said on a long, drawn-out breath.

Reaver stilled. 'What about it?'

'Roag stole it from my collection when he took the mordlair necrotoxin,' Eidolon said, going back to the tapping.

'You were in possession of Eth's Eye?'

'Yes,' E said, 'but it was impossible for us to use.'

'That's because only angels can use it for the purposes of scrying. If Byzamoth had it, he could have used it to locate the amulet.' Reaver cursed. 'Which explains why I felt her cloak shatter – a side effect of being discovered.'

'We need to involve The Aegis,' Reaver repeated, like a damned broken record.

'I agree.' Eidolon stood and walked around his desk. 'Tayla and Kynan are going to have to tell the Sigil what's going on. All of it. This is too big for us alone. And they're trained to hunt down beings like fallen angels.' He turned to Reaver. 'When will he try to open the gate?'

'The second dawn after the Sentinel's blood is shed. If he doesn't use the blood then, he'll have missed his opportunity. If he'd gotten Serena's charm himself he'd have more control of the timing. Now he's at the mercy of finding Wraith, and bleeding him.'

'Where will Byzamoth take the amulet and the blood?' Eidolon asked.

'Jerusalem. The Temple Mount. But he'll need to get the blood first. Where is Wraith?'

'Egypt.'

'Get him home,' Reaver said. 'We can protect him in the hospital.'

'That'll work.' Eidolon didn't sound too confident, though, probably because getting Wraith to sit still and do nothing would be like trying to chain a phantom. 'In the meantime, Tayla can contact the Sigil and Aegis cells within striking distance of Jerusalem. Kynan can deal with R-XR. Let them know what's up and get them ready for a battle.'

Shade cursed. Demon and human prophets had been saying for centuries that the end was near, and finally, it seemed as though they were right.

TWENTY-THREE

Serena dreaded this call, but now that she had a signal she had to make it.

'Serena?' Val sounded as worried as she'd ever heard him, and she answered quickly.

'It's me, Val. Everything's fine.' If fine included losing her necklace, her virginity, and her charm in a matter of hours.

'Thank God.' She heard the squeak of leather, knew he'd just sank into a chair. 'Where are you?'

'The train will be pulling into Alexandria in fifteen minutes.'

'And you'll be heading home immediately?'

Her heart started pounding. 'Not exactly. There's a problem.'

The chair squeaked again. 'What?' She didn't answer, and his voice dropped to a low, dangerous whisper. She'd seen him truly angry only once, and it was something she never wanted to experience again. 'What happened?'

'It's Byzamoth.'

'The demon?'

She swallowed dryly. 'He's more than a demon. He's a fallen angel.'

'Tell me everything, and tell me now.'

He was using his don't-argue-with-me-or-else voice, and she knew better than to push. She started at the beginning and ended with, 'He killed the Regent. And . . . and he attacked me.'

'Did he get the necklace?'

'Yes.'

'And the charm?'

'It's gone, too.'

His harsh curse was followed by a long, ragged breath. When he spoke, his words were broken, distorted. 'I should have known. There have been demon attacks all over the globe.' The sound of his breathing joined the frantic click of his fingers on computer keys. 'Are you . . . okay?'

'Josh is taking care of me.'

'Not well enough! Where was he when Byzamoth was attacking you?'

'He fought him, Val. Things could have turned out a lot worse than they did.'

Val muttered something she couldn't hear. 'When you get off the train, head straight to an address I'm having David text to you. He'll include instructions to get in. Wait until I arrive.'

'Will do. Where are you?'

'I'm still in Berlin. It's a zoo here . . . hold on.'

She heard commotion in the background, a lot of voices, some raised. David was shouting. The names Tayla and Kynan came with some curses, and then, finally, Val was back on the phone.

'Serena?' His guttural rasp told her she was in trouble. 'Byzamoth has the necklace, yes? But does *he* have the charm?'

Oh, God.

'*Serena!*'

'No,' she whispered. 'Josh has it.'

There was a curse and then a tense moment of silence before he said, 'As furious as I am with you, this might actually be good news. . . . Look, I need to go. There's some sort of emergency meeting going on, and it seems to have something to do with you.

I'll call as soon as I can. Just get to the address I send you. The Aegis will have people there as soon as possible.'

'They aren't there now?'

'All cells within the region have been sent to Israel. It'll take time to get help to you. In the meantime, stay alert.'

'Okay.'

Val cursed again, long and hard. Finally, she heard the chair squeak again, heard his forceful exhale. Knew he was stroking his tidy beard. 'How are you feeling?'

'Fine, right now.' She was a little nauseous, but there was no point in worrying Val even more than he already was. 'How long do you think? Before, you know . . . '

'I don't . . . ' His voice hitched. 'I'm not sure. The disease should progress rapidly now.'

'Bottom line?'

He drew in a ragged breath. 'I'd say you're down to days, maybe hours.'

Wraith was not onboard with this plan. When Serena said they were going somewhere Val had told her to go, every one of his warning bells had rung, and now as they drew closer to the place, on the outskirts of Alexandria's Greek quarter, the clanging in his head could have been coming from Hell's marching band.

They were on foot, having gotten out of the taxi several blocks back. He'd wanted to approach from the rear, come in as inconspicuously as possible, in case they were being watched. Byzamoth still wanted her, couldn't know that Wraith already had her charm.

Mine. And so is she.

Man, every time he thought about what could have happened, what the fallen angel still wanted, it made Wraith's killer instinct shove its way to the front of the line ahead the rest of his baser instincts. Weird, because usually *nothing* got ahead of sex.

And he definitely wanted to know who was tipping off Byzamoth about Serena's location. Wraith was going to gut the bastard and strangle him with his own intestines.

They were nearly there when Serena began to wheeze badly enough for Wraith to step off the sidewalk and draw her into the shade of a lush palm. Pink splotches colored her cheeks and shadows had tinted the crescents beneath her eyes, but still, she smiled.

'Do you need to rest?'

'It's the dust in the air. It's nothing.'

Her lie irked him. He wanted her to be able to lean on him, accept his help. And he needed to get her somewhere safe, where they were less exposed and she could rest.

They arrived at a nondescript house set between other, equally nondescript houses. But right away it became clear that there was nothing average about this place. No one who wasn't military special forces, a thief, or Wraith would notice the well-concealed alarm trip wire that had been set into the door and window frames. The extra-thick walls that Wraith would bet had been reinforced. The flame retardant coating that had been sprayed on the walls and roof. Or the 'decorative' slits that had been cut into the plaster below the roof overhang and that were the perfect size to cradle the barrel of a rifle.

When he crouched next to an ornamental rock at one corner of the property line, he noticed tiny protective symbols carved into it.

'I don't like this,' he said as he straightened to his full height. 'Something's off.'

'Val wouldn't send me someplace unsafe.'

It definitely wasn't unsafe. Too safe, was more like it. Serena wheezed again, and he set aside his paranoia. Nothing was too safe for Serena. Still, he kept a watchful eye on their surroundings, taking note of the vehicles, the houses, even the fucking birds, as he spoke. 'You're sick. We need to get you inside.'

'My throat is dry. That's all.'

Wraith swung around, stared at her through the amber filter of his sunglasses. 'Don't BS me. We've been through too much.' Enough that he wanted to bundle her up and take her to UG, where he knew he could keep her safe. From Byzamoth, at least. Her illness was a beast he didn't know how to fight.

'I know.' She hugged herself. Shifted her weight. He hated that he'd made her uncomfortable, but the time for making love and pretending she hadn't committed suicide was over. He was a fighter, and he was in kill-the-threat mode.

Especially since the threat was now to Serena.

He eyed the building. 'What did he say about this house?'

She pulled back a decorative shutter. Behind the wooden flap was a metal box mounted on the side of the building. She pushed some numbers on the keypad and retrieved a key. 'He said it's warded against vampires.'

'Vampires?' He hoped she didn't notice the way he'd choked.

Her hand fluttered to her throat, dropped again. 'I asked him why the house wasn't warded against demons, too, and he said that spells to repel vampires are narrow in scope and long-lasting. But with demons, it's different. Unless you ward against specific species of demons—'

'You'd need a very general anti-evil spell, and those don't last long.'

She nodded. 'Exactly.'

She stepped inside, but he hung back, unsure how the anti-vampire spell would affect him. He wasn't a true vampire, but he didn't want to take chances. The ward might work only on the undead – which would be smart, given that they were sitting in the middle of mummy land – or it could be some tweaked version that worked against any blood-drinking creature.

'You coming in?'

He cocked an eyebrow. 'That an invite?'

'You a vampire?'

'Yep.'

'Good.' Her sultry tone hit him in the groin. 'Come on in.'

'Your vampire fetish is going to get you bitten someday,' he warned, only half playing, because he really, really wanted to be the one biting her.

'I can only hope.' She opened the door wider.

'You're hope*less.*' He didn't need invites to get into houses, but if the place was warded . . . an invite couldn't hurt. 'I'm going to do a perimeter check first,' he said. 'Can't be too careful.' That, and he wanted to see what other security tricks had been built into this house.

'I'll see what kinds of supplies we have here. We're probably going to need to go shopping.' She stood in the doorway, her hair blowing in the breeze and glinting in the sun, and he wanted her. Right then, right there.

He shot to her like he'd come out of a cannon. Her soft sound of surprise was muffled by his mouth, easing into a contented sigh as she melted against him. Now wasn't the time or place to do everything he wanted to do, but he made his message clear.

He would take her ten ways from Sunday when she was cured, because he refused to believe it wouldn't happen.

And then he'd find a way to make her his. Humans couldn't bond with Seminus demons, but there had to be a way. Somehow, it could happen.

Right. As soon as she forgave him for lying to her, seducing her, oh, and being a demon.

Shit. He was living in fantasyland. All he needed now were mouse ears and fairy fucking dust.

Cursing silently, he broke away from her and made the circuit around the house. Nothing was out of place, but he discovered more subtle signs that told him this house was more than what it seemed. The entire property line had been carved out with a very narrow, shallow ditch almost invisible to anyone not looking for it. This would be where someone might put out a protective circle of salt, ash, holy water – any substance meant to guard against evil.

His inspection turned up several more curious features, including a number of tiny silver stakes in the ground, set out in the shape of a giant pentagram that spanned the entire property.

He headed for the front door, pausing at the threshold. He heard

Serena coughing somewhere in the house, but she was nowhere she'd see if the ward worked on him. Taking a deep breath, he stepped through the doorway.

Nothing happened. Cool. He wondered if the ward *should* have affected him, or if the charm was doing its thing.

Serena was drinking a glass of water in the kitchen, so he poked around the other rooms. In one of the back rooms he found a wooden chest. When he opened it, his blood ran cold.

It was full of weapons – swords, stakes, bottles of holy water, ropes, blades, and stangs. The double-ended blades of the stangs were each coated in a different metal to kill different types of demons. These were Aegis weapons.

Suspicion confirmed: Wraith had walked right into the middle of a fucking Aegis stronghold.

He slammed the lid shut and stalked into the kitchen, where Serena had set two colas out on the small dining table.

'I found drinks and canned goods. Some pasta—'

He slapped his hands down on the counter on either side of her hard enough to make her jump. 'When is the rest of the crew showing up?'

Caged in, she looked up at him in surprise. 'Crew? I don't know what you're talking about.'

'I think you do.'

She ducked beneath his arms and jammed her hands on her hips. 'I don't like your tone.'

'I don't like being lied to.'

'And I still don't know what you're talking about,' she shot back.

He believed her, but by now his nerves were frayed and he was juiced. He was a freaking demon standing in the middle of Demon Slayer Central. 'I thought only Val was coming.' Which was going to be a difficult situation as it was. He'd have to get into the guy's head again and do some creative memory reconstruction when it came to the real Josh.

'Well, gee. I'm so sorry I forgot to mention we'd be joined by people who can help us. Why does it matter?' She put her palm on his forehead. 'Are you okay? You're acting strange.'

Oh, hell. He was making her suspicious by flying off the handle like this. 'I'm fine.'

'You owe me more than that, Josh. We've shared too much for you to shut down now,' she said, throwing his words from earlier right back at him.

Fuck. She was right, and it only pissed him off. Mainly because his lies were sitting on him like a two-ton lava beast, and guilt was practically leaking out of him. Maybe he should tell her the truth. If she knew what he was ... what? She'd only hate him sooner.

Gods, this was fucked up.

He didn't answer her because his tongue felt glued to the roof of his mouth, and eventually she rubbed her temples and shook her head.

'Serena? What's wrong?'

'Headache,' she muttered. 'I need to lie down. Do you mind?'

Yes, he minded. He minded so much his heart was ripping in half. Because somehow, he knew that once she was down, she wasn't getting back up.

൭

Serena had just put on a tank top and shorts and was looking at the bed like a lover when her cell phone rang. Feeling unreasonably weak, she dug it out of her backpack and flipped it open.

'Val?'

'Where are you?' he barked.

She sighed. 'Hello to you, too.'

'*Where are you?*'

A sudden spike of dread made her legs wobble, and she sank onto the bed. 'I'm at the house you sent us to. Why?'

'Us. So you aren't alone?'

'Josh is with me.'

There was a moment of tense silence, broken by the sound of

someone near him whispering. David. 'Serena, listen to me very carefully.'

'You're starting to scare me.'

'Good. Are you somewhere private? Where you can't be heard?'

She glanced at the closed door. 'Yes, but what is this about?'

'In the smallest room at the back of the house, there's a chest full of weapons. As quietly as you can, I need you to arm up, and then lock yourself in the bedroom and wait. We should be there in a matter of hours.'

Goose bumps crawled over her skin. 'Val?' Her voice was trembling as hard as she was. 'What's going on?'

'I just spoke with Josh,' he said, the chill in his tone sending her into an emotional tailspin, 'and the man you're with isn't him.'

TWENTY-FOUR

Wraith turned off the stove burner and searched the cupboards for a bowl. He'd made Serena soup, and he wanted to get it down her before she fell asleep.

His pocket vibrated, and he checked his phone. E. 'What?' he said, as he poured soup into the bowl.

'You need to come home. Get to the nearest Harrowgate.'

'Not happening.'

'Wraith, listen to me. You're in danger. Byzamoth is going to come after you.'

Wraith went taut. 'I thought you said the charm can only be transferred through sex. If he thinks he can take it from me that way . . . ah, well, I don't play for that team, and even if I did, man, you should see him when he morphs—'

'He doesn't want to have sex with you.'

Wraith dug a spoon out of a drawer. 'I'm oddly crushed and relieved.'

Eidolon's voice sounded frayed with annoyance, as usual. 'He needs charmed blood. Once he figures out that Serena is no longer charmed, he'll want yours.'

'He's not getting that, either.'

'Dammit, Wraith, you need to come to the hospital where he wouldn't dare try to get to you.'

Wraith peeked down the hall to make sure Serena was still in her room. 'I'm at full strength now, bro. I can take him.'

'He's immortal.'

'He can still be hurt.'

'It's not worth the risk. We spoke with Reaver. The charm is ineffective against fallen angels. Come to the hospital.'

'I'm not leaving Serena.'

'Get your ass in a Harrowgate. Now.'

'You know what?' Wraith dropped the pan onto the stove, splashing soup all over the wall. 'Fuck you, E.'

'We're coming to get you.'

Wraith took a deep, soothing breath, in what was probably his first attempt to be calm. Ever. 'Eidolon, this isn't one of my rebellious, death-wish, stubborn-for-no-reason moves. For once in my life, I'm doing something for someone else. I'm going to keep Serena safe, and I'm going to find a cure for her.'

'Really?' Serena's cold voice came from behind him. He spun to find her standing in the hallway. Fire sparked in her eyes . . . and she was holding a stang. 'What do you plan to do, *Josh*?'

'Ah . . . hey. What are you—'

She launched the S-shaped blade at him, and though he was certain she had deadly aim, the weapon veered to the left and took out the bowl of soup. 'I knew it wouldn't hit you, seeing how you're charmed and all, but it felt good to throw it.'

Whoa, she was *lit up.* Wraith threw down the phone and moved toward her. 'What's going on, Serena?'

She took a few steps back, until she was at the bedroom doorway. 'Who are you? Who are you, really?'

Oh, shit.

She shook with fury. 'And don't you *dare* tell me your name is Josh.'

'It's Wraith. I told you, my name is Wraith.'

'Why should I believe that, when everything else you've told me was a lie?' Her voice sounded empty, as though she'd been carved out by pain.

Guilt made his chest hurt, because for the first time in his life, he understood how it felt to inflict pain on someone who didn't deserve it.

'Not . . . everything has been a lie,' he said lamely, because the important things had been.

'Uh-huh. Why did you do it? I mean, I can guess, but I want to hear it from your filthy, lying mouth.'

'I was dying, Serena. I needed the charm to live.' He inched toward her. 'It's not as bad as it seems.' It was far *worse* than what it seemed.

'Did you know I would die? Before I told you?'

He averted his gaze, but dragged it back to meet hers once more. She deserved that, at least. 'Yes.'

She blanched and stumbled back. 'Oh, my God. You disgusting, murdering, *bastard*!'

'Serena, listen to me—'

She slammed the door in his face. And locked it. She had to know it wouldn't keep him out, but he gave her credit for trying. He kicked it in.

'We aren't through yet.'

Tears shimmered in her eyes. 'Oh, we're through. We're so through. I want you gone,' she screamed. 'Get out! Get out and let me die in peace.'

'That's not going to happen. I can't leave you unprotected.'

'*Unprotected?* Are you kidding me? *You killed me!*'

Agony wracked his insides, far worse than anything the poison had done to him. 'I didn't mean for it to happen,' he said hoarsely. 'I couldn't carry through with it. Not once I got to know you. That's why I was going to get off the train in Cairo.'

'How noble,' she spat. 'How you must have suffered when I forced myself on you.'

'That,' he said slowly, deliberately, so she would never doubt this, 'was the best night of my life.'

'I actually believe that.' She snorted. 'It was the best night of your life because you weren't dying anymore.'

He got in her face so fast she blinked as though trying to figure out how he was suddenly inches away. 'No. It was because it was the first time I made love to anyone. You can call me a liar for anything else, but do *not* doubt me on this. And I swear to you that you were the first, and you will be the last.'

A cold ache drilled a hollow in his chest. He needed sex or he'd suffer, but he would never make love to a female again.

She swallowed hard, but in an instant the fury came back and she shoved hard at his shoulders. When he didn't budge, she scooted around him and put a good fifteen feet between them. It felt more like light years.

Sudden evil screamed through the air, increasing the pressure in the house with the violence of a spring storm. The window blew inward, and a swirling black cloud surrounded Serena. It solidified, and Byzamoth, grinning, was holding her, her back to his chest, his hand clamped over her mouth.

'Hello, *Josh*,' the fallen angel said, clearly aware of the truth. Serena's backstabber at work again. He looked between Serena and Wraith. 'Fucking tell me it isn't true. Tell me this little whore didn't give you her charm.'

'I'd tell you that,' Wraith growled, 'but it would be a lie.'

Serena made a noise of outrage, and Byzamoth shifted his hand, allowing her to fire off a shot. 'Oh, *now* you decide to tell the truth?'

Though her verbal slap smarted, he ignored her. If Byzamoth knew how much Serena meant to Wraith, he'd have a damned effective weapon to use against him. 'So, angel, what gave me away? Someone leak it to you? Or is the post-coital glow?'

Byzamoth hissed. 'Something like that, you fuck. You aren't cloaked.' He shoved Serena onto the bed. She bounced awkwardly and rolled into the headboard. Byzamoth drew a sword from his robes, a dull silver blade that glowed azure in a thin line down the length of the metal and at the hilt, where symbols pulsed. He pointed the sharp tip at Serena but never took his eyes off Wraith.

'No sudden moves, or I run her through. My specialty is destruction, Sem, so I know how to use this.'

Man, he was going to rip this guy's heart out and feed it to him.

'You've really fucked things up.' Byzamoth gestured to Serena with a flick of the blade. 'Fucked her all up, too. Pun intended.' He bared his teeth. 'No matter. I'll still get what I want. Destruction. Yours. Hers. The world as you know it. I think I'll start small and work my way up to mass chaos.'

Serena's glare promised pain if she ever got her hands on the fallen angel. 'You aren't going to get away with whatever it is you have planned, you know.'

Byzamoth laughed, carelessly lowering his blade. 'This is like a bad movie. The good guys all tied up with no hope of survival, but darn it, they're still plucky. "You'll never get away with this,"' he mocked.

Wraith charged Byzamoth. The angel spun and tipped up the sword. Serena cried out, and Wraith froze. A four-inch gash streaked her shoulder, its edges as smooth and clean as a scalpel's slash. The sword hadn't touched her, but it had somehow sliced her flesh open and was now aimed at her throat.

'Serena!'

'It's okay,' she said, slapping her hand over the bleeding wound. 'I'm okay.'

'Such bravery.' Byzamoth rolled his eyes. 'Does it really matter, Serena? Given your condition?'

Wraith's gaze cut sharply to the fallen angel. 'Go to hell, you sonofabitch.' He flexed his hands, dying to get them around Byzamoth's throat.

'Been there, done that. But then, so have you.' He made another tiny cut in Serena's arm to get her attention, and she didn't even flinch. 'You're going to pay for choosing him over me.'

'There was no choice.' She bared her teeth so viciously Wraith almost expected to see fangs. Under any other circumstances, that might have been hot. '*Josh* might be a lying scumbag, but at least he's human.'

Realization dawned, and Byzamoth turned to Wraith. Serena chose that moment to lunge at the fallen angel. Wraith leaped to catch her, but lightning fast, Byzamoth seized her, held her with an arm looped around her neck, her feet dangling off the ground.

'Idiot,' Byzamoth said into her ear. 'He's a demon. An incubus, a master of seduction. You gave it up for a demon as evil as I am, you stupid human slut.'

'Liar!' she spat, but when she looked to Wraith for support, her expression fell. 'Josh? Tell him.'

Wraith said nothing. What was there to say? She stopped struggling. Just stared at Wraith like she'd never seen him before.

'Was it worth it, Serena? Was having a demon between your legs worth your life, you foul whore?'

Wraith's body jerked with fury. Serena was good and pure and everything Wraith wasn't. 'Take your filthy hands off her!'

'Yes,' she snapped. 'Do. I'm going to kill him.'

Byzamoth laughed and released her. The moment her feet hit the ground, she launched herself at Wraith. She slapped him so hard his head snapped around. Her fists pounded against his chest. He did nothing. Closing his eyes, he took the strikes, wishing she'd hit harder, draw blood.

'You sonofabitch!' she screamed. 'You goddamned sonofabitch! *I hate you.*'

Her tears flowed in rivulets down her face. He could smell her fury, her fear, and it sliced at him like no physical weapon ever had.

She struck him over and over, each blow growing weaker. As her strength faded away, so did the color in her face. She swayed, blinking unfocused eyes, and then collapsed. He caught her before she hit the floor and swept her into his arms, feeling the fragility in her body, the delicate set of her bones that hadn't been there before. Or maybe he'd chosen not to notice.

The chickenshit bastard attacked while Wraith's arms were full. Byzamoth hauled the sword around, catching Wraith in the shins. The snap of bone rent the air, and a firestorm of misery swept his entire body.

Wraith's feet flew out from under him, but he twisted as he fell, took the brunt of the fall on his shoulder to protect Serena. His legs didn't work, crippling his ability to get back at Byzamoth, and the fallen angel didn't spare Wraith any mercy. His foot came down on the back of Wraith's skull, over and over, and as the kicks rained down, he could do little but roll on top of Serena, shielding her.

A searing, slicing pain ripped through his back and belly. Once, twice. The wet sound of a blade grating against bone screamed in his ears as, for the third time, a red-hot poker of agony gutted him. Through blurred vision, he looked between his body and Serena's, saw the bloody end of a sword buried in the floor.

Oh ... oh, Gods. He'd been stabbed through the back and impaled, the blade barely missing Serena.

Cranking his head around, he saw Byzamoth smile as he crouched to catch a stream of Wraith's blood in a vial he'd drawn from his robes. 'And the blood of the Charmed One shall open the Gates of Abyssos.'

'No.' Serena's voice was a weak whisper as she struggled to crawl from beneath Wraith.

'Now, you little whore, you can watch your demon lover die.' Byzamoth drew one finger across her cheek. 'I think, after I've taken my place as a god, that I'll make you *my* whore. See, I can keep you alive, and soon enough, you will beg for death.'

Byzamoth swirled in a dramatic circle, and in a poof of dark smoke, he was gone. Wraith groaned and fell onto his side, pain tearing through him as the blade wrenched through his gut.

'Josh? Josh!'

'Not. Josh. Wraith.' He spoke through clenched teeth and bubbling blood, struggling for every word. Every breath.

He was dying. All this shit he'd put her through, taking her virginity and her charm . . .

All for nothing.

ⓖ

Lore approached the hospital's ambulance bay doors with trepidation. He'd been researching the hospital, a little Q and A with demons who had been patients, and apparently, what Gem had told him was true. The fighting inside the hospital was unusual. Still, he didn't want to take that chance. He might be a killer, but he wasn't stupid, and he valued his own life above all others.

He'd also learned that Eidolon and Shade were something called Seminus demons. Sex demons. Cool. But Lore had no idea what made Seminus demons different from other breeds of incubi. Mainly because, although Lore was a demon himself, he'd been raised by humans and hadn't actually stepped foot in the demon realm until about thirty years ago.

Still, he'd remained on the outskirts of demon and human society, but at least he'd learned to use the Harrowgates. Those things were seriously weird. He used them only when he had to, hating the strange twinge he experienced every time he used one, as though each trip through the portals leached away a bit of his humanity.

He was an assassin, but he wasn't a monster. Well, he probably was, but if he could just hold on to his human roots, maybe he could deny the truth about himself.

Ruthlessly, he growled, dropped his hands, and entered the hospital. He had a job to do, and it was going to get done. Right now.

The hospital was strangely calm and quiet. He saw only Gem, sitting at the triage desk. She acknowledged him with a sad smile.

'Hey, Gem. You seem a little down.'

'It's nothing,' she said, and he wondered if her mood had

anything to do with the total tool she called Kynan. He'd have to see if maybe she wanted the tool dead, because Lore would be happy to give her a freebie on that one.

'Can I kill someone for you? Make it better?'

'That's the nicest offer anyone has made in a long time.' She smiled, and this one seemed genuine. His heart did a little flip. 'So what can I help you with?'

'I'm looking for Eidolon and Shade.'

'They're probably in E's office. If you want to hit them up for a job, now's a good time. We're seriously hurting for staff. Just head straight down the hall. Can't miss it.'

A little burst of guilt made him pause. He didn't give a shit about the brothers, but Gem might not be happy when she found out what he'd done.

He shook himself out of it, because he had a much more powerful demon to answer to than Gem. She'd get over it. The bastard holding his life in his hands wouldn't.

'Thanks,' he said. 'I'll catch up with you later.'

The hall was dark like everything else, with only caged red bulbs overhead giving off light. He passed cages and drains from which slithering noises drifted up, and dark liquid trickled in a gutter in the floor.

This was so fucked up.

He found them exactly where Gem said they'd be.

The demon Lore assumed was Eidolon was yelling into his phone, calling Wraith's name. As Lore watched from the open doorway, Shade doubled over, his curse barely a whisper.

'E ...' Shade sucked in a breath. 'Wraith's hurt ... fuck, it's bad.'

Now was the time to strike. Lore rushed in as Eidolon came around the desk. He'd forgotten to unsheathe his hand, but it was too late for that. He grabbed Eidolon's right arm just as the other demon lay his hand on Shade.

Nothing happened. What the fuck? Eidolon wheeled around, and

Lore slammed his fist into the male's face. Eidolon stumbled backward, and then Shade's fist was in Lore's jaw. Lore went down in a heap, his killing arm pinned beneath him. He barely had time for a muffled groan when Shade stomped him in the throat with his huge-ass boot.

'*What the fuck?*' Eidolon stood in the center of the office, eyes red, blood dripping down his chin.

Shade grunted and put pressure on Lore's neck. Lore would have a footprint embedded in his skin for a week. 'You are so dead, dude.'

'How the hell did this just happen?'

'Well, E,' Shade drawled, 'this fuck walked in and hit you, so I hit him—'

'Not that! The Haven spell. It's been repaired.'

Shade's head whipped around. 'Then how did he attack you?' He backed away from Lore, who sucked in a few gulps of air.

And that was when Lore saw it. Eidolon's arm. The tats. Oh, holy fuck.

'Good question, Lore,' came the female voice in the doorway. Gem. Fab. This just kept getting better and better. She glared at him. 'I'm guessing you're the asshole assassin? Way to use me to get inside the hospital. Boys, I say kill him.'

Wow, she was bloodthirsty. Lore liked that in a woman.

'Gladly,' Shade growled. 'As much as I'd like to make it hurt, it'll have to be quick. We don't have time to play. Wraith needs us.' He came at Lore with murder in his eyes.

Lore rolled, whipping off his jacket as he did. 'Wait!' He sat up. 'My arm.' Eidolon reached for him, but Lore yanked his arm away. 'Don't. My touch kills.' Except, apparently not them.

'What the hell is going on?' Shade breathed, peeling off his own jacket.

Lore just stared. These guys sported identical markings, though theirs were darker, less diluted.

'Show me the top symbol,' Eidolon said, and Lore slowly tugged his collar down, exposing the base of his neck and the crooked arrow there.

'Hell's rings,' Shade muttered, cocking his head to reveal the same arrow ... only his sat just beneath an eye symbol. Eidolon's was positioned beneath a set of scales.

Lore blinked. 'What does this mean?'

Eidolon's expression shuttered. 'Unless this is some sort of trick, it means we're brothers. Somehow, we're fucking brothers.'

Gem tsked at Lore. 'Lu-cy ... you have some s'plainin' to do.'

'We don't have time,' Shade said. 'We've got to get to Wraith. Gem, get the Bracken Cuffs. Lore here is going to learn the meaning of brotherly love.'

TWENTY-FIVE

So much had happened that Serena wasn't sure what to do, think, or feel. All she knew was that the man she'd fallen in love with wasn't a man at all, and that he was now bleeding to death on the floor.

She didn't know what to do to help, but she did know that she shouldn't remove the sword that pinned him to the floor like an insect in an entomologist's display case. The sword protruded from his back, its hilt still glowing with a strange azure light that seemed to grow dimmer as Josh – Wraith – whatever his name was grew weaker.

Helpless, all she could do was sit there and try to not throw up.

'S-Serena . . . '

Her name came out in a gurgle of blood, and her gut clenched. She should hate him – she *did* hate him – but she couldn't stand this, didn't want to see him suffer.

'What can I do?' She sifted her hand through his thick hair, remembering how it had felt to do that when he'd been coming inside her. *Damn him.* 'Your brothers . . . I can call them, right? Are they really doctors?'

He didn't answer. Frantic, she felt for a pulse. It bounded weakly against her fingers, but at least he was still alive.

She had to find his cell phone. She'd call every number in his address book until she found help. Awkwardly, because her legs had gone numb, she stood, but she hadn't taken a step when she heard a pounding on the front door.

A weapon. She needed a weapon – the crack of wood rang out. Then, a rush of footsteps. Instinctively, she kneeled, crowding protectively close to Josh, but when she saw the two huge men ... or demons, she supposed ... barreling through the doorway, she nearly scrambled away.

Josh had told her he had two brothers, and with the exception of their dark hair these men resembled him so closely that they had to be related.

'Oh, fuck.' The one with long black hair, wearing head-to-toe black leather, froze, his dark gaze locked on the sword skewering Josh's body.

The other one, dressed in scrubs, charged into the room and dropped to his knees at Josh's side. 'Bro. It's Eidolon. Just hold on.' He turned to the doorway. 'Shade.'

The one called Shade shook himself out of it, strode into the room, and dropped the medic bag he was carrying. 'We need to get him to the hospital.'

'He won't make it.'

'We have to try!'

'And what do you suggest? Carrying him through the streets of Alexandria with a sword sticking out of him? A taxi? Transporting him could kill him.'

Palming the back of Josh's neck, Shade spewed out guttural, coarse words in a language she didn't know but understood nonetheless. 'Let me check the internal damage.'

Serena held still, hoping they'd forgotten she was there. Shade closed his eyes and concentrated. The tattoos on his hand, identical to Josh's, began to glow.

'Shit,' Shade whispered. 'Kidney, liver, stomach ... oh, man, he's fucked up. The blade severed his aorta. We move it, he bleeds out in seconds.'

Eidolon swung his fierce gaze, glinting with flares of gold and red, around to her. 'What happened?'

'He ... he's a demon.' Geez, that was a stupid thing to say, given his brothers were, too. But her mind seemed mired in fog. So much had happened in the last fifteen minutes, too much to process.

'Yes, we know that.' His voice was no-nonsense. Professional. Scary. 'How did he get impaled?'

Right. 'Byzamoth. Fallen angel. He ... he wanted Josh's blood.'

'Wraith,' Shade growled. 'His name is Wraith.'

Wraith moaned, his eyes fluttering open. 'Help ... '

'We're here,' Eidolon murmured. 'We'll help you.'

'No.' Wraith coughed, spraying blood. 'Serena. Help ... her.'

'She's okay, man. Right now, we need to take care of you.'

'Promise ... me.'

Shade's raw curses blistered the air, this time in plain English.

'*Promise.*'

'Yeah, yeah,' Shade muttered. 'Just relax. I need you to relax.'

Eidolon and Shade exchanged glances. 'I have to remove the blade,' Eidolon said.

'He'll bleed out.'

'I know. We need to get blood into him.'

'I'll start a central line.' Shade dug through the medical bag he'd brought with him and quickly inserted a catheter into Josh's neck. Eidolon hung up a bag of blood from the door handle, and Shade connected it via a long tube to the catheter. When he'd finished, he set up another bag of blood, connected a tube to it ... and held it out to Serena. 'I need you to feed this to him.'

She recoiled. 'What?'

'Just hold the tube to his mouth. He needs to drink.'

Oh, God, this was such a nightmare. 'I don't understand.' She still hadn't moved, and her reluctance earned a glare from both of the demons.

'He's a vampire,' Shade snapped. 'We need to get blood into him however we can. Now, do it or he dies.'

Vampire? But he'd warned her about them. And he was warm. Had a heartbeat. Walked in the sun. He couldn't be a vampire.

'*You a vampire?*'

'*Yep.*'

Okay, so he'd admitted to it, but ... she shook her head. This was crazy. Shade cursed. 'Never mind.' He propped the bag of blood against Josh's shoulder and inserted the tube into his mouth, but it kept falling out. The bag fell over.

'I'll do it,' she said finally, and held the tube between Josh's pallid, dry lips. He didn't suck, didn't move.

'Squeeze the bag.' Shade's deep voice was rough, his tattoo glowing.

She did as he said, and blood flooded the tube. She watched with morbid curiosity as it flowed into Josh's mouth ... and dripped out the other side. He wasn't swallowing.

'Dammit,' Eidolon breathed. 'Come on, Wraith. Fight. Damn you, I don't want to lose you now.'

Serena's eyes stung. She might hate Josh – she just couldn't think of him as Wraith – for what he'd done, but he'd asked his brothers to help her when *he* was facing more immediate danger, and she didn't want to watch him die. Some twisted part of her still loved him. Leaning close, she brushed her lips over his cheek.

'Please,' she whispered. 'Drink.' She stroked his lips, squeezing a little more blood between them. His mouth opened ever so slightly, just enough to encourage her. 'That's it. Take some.'

His brothers worked frantically, barking out status reports and commands to each other, and the squishy noises of surgical gloves working in blood and flesh made it all so horrific. Eidolon had somehow closed up one of the stab wounds, but now he was using a scalpel to open up the other one even more.

'Manage his pain, Shade.' Eidolon put down the scalpel. 'This is going to hurt.'

Shade's tattoo glowed even brighter as Eidolon pushed his hand inside the opening he'd made. Stomach rolling, Serena turned away. Still, the wet sounds kept her imagination working overtime. Their hushed medical-speak sounded so bad, so discouraging, almost as if they'd already resigned themselves to the fact that Josh wasn't going to come out of this.

He still hadn't drank. 'Swallow, Josh. Come on.' Gently, she stuck her finger in his mouth, unsure what she was doing, but needing to do something. He was a vampire, right? So he should have fangs ... she found a sharp point, remembered how they'd felt in her dreams. Had she had the dreams because she'd subconsciously known what he was?

It was a question for later. Right now she needed to get him to drink, and she knew those fangs were the key. In her dreams they were huge, much larger than what they felt like now. Carefully, she rubbed the tip of her finger along the length of one, from the tip to the gum ... and ... was it lengthening?

Josh moaned and opened his mouth. Yes, his canines were definitely descending, growing into monstrous daggers. God, how could she be feeling so many things at once – hatred, confusion, fear – and, at the same time, be a little ... turned on by this?

'That's it,' she murmured, as she squeezed some blood onto his tongue. 'Swallow. I need you to swallow, okay?'

The blood dribbled out of the corner of his mouth. Dammit. Sliding her finger down his tooth, she caressed the razor point ... and applied pressure. She tensed, felt the prick of his fang and the welling of blood on her fingertip.

'Take it,' she whispered, letting a drop fall to his tongue.

He jerked like he'd received an electric shock, and then, to her relief, he closed his mouth, drawing her finger inside. She remained still, and when he began to suckle, the world drifted away in a swirl of pleasure.

One of the brothers swore softly and said her name, but no one interfered. Somehow, she kept the presence of mind to squeeze more blood out of the bag and into his mouth. In a matter of seconds, he was sucking greedily, and she swore the heavy shroud of despair that had settled in the room lifted.

She fed Josh until the first bag of blood was gone, and then Shade showed her how to hook up another bag to the tube. She lost track of how much he drank, lost track of time. All she knew was that at some point, she fell over, and when she opened her eyes, dark spots swam in her vision. Eidolon was peering down at her, his expression a mask of concern.

'Josh,' she whispered. 'Is he – will he—'

'He's going to be fine. I've put him to sleep to finish healing. Now it's your turn. He didn't take much blood from you, but there's your other issue. . . . '

She struggled to sit up, realized someone had put her on the bed. 'I'm fine.' She shoved him away.

'I'm a doctor. I know you're not fine.' His voice was firm but soothing, and she let him push her back on the bed. 'I also know a lot has happened in the last few days, and I know you've been hurt. Wraith will never forgive himself for what he's done.'

'Good,' she muttered.

'You saved his life. And you knew you were sacrificing your own life to do it. We owe you. I'm going to do what I can for you, okay?'

She shook her head. 'I was bitten by a Mara that's now dead. My disease is terminal.'

'Yes.' So blunt, so like the doctors she'd remembered from years ago.

She studied Eidolon's scrubs, the strange medical symbol – a bat-winged dagger encircled by two serpents – he wore on a chain around his neck. 'You do have some sort of new age medical center, right? You said you'll do what you can . . . '

'I can make you comfortable, and I can give you a little more time, but . . . I'm sorry, Serena. You're going to die.'

࿐

Wraith was really freaking tired of waking up feeling like he'd gone a round with King Kong. He'd have thought the charm would have ended that—

Serena!

He sat up so fast his head nearly fell off. It took him a second to figure out where he was – in one of the rooms in the Aegis safe house. He swung his bare legs over the side of the cot, only to have hands push him back down.

Shade was right there in his face. 'Whoa. Just relax. You're going to fall on your ass if you don't take it easy.'

'Serena,' he croaked.

'Sleeping.'

'How . . . long?'

'You've been out a few hours. E and I have been taking turns staying with you. Tayla's here. And Gem. Luc. Kynan. Reaver. Our other brother, but he's in chains. He's also a total dick. You'll like him.'

Wraith shook his head, but that did little to clear it. 'Why? What's going on?' Wait, did he say, *other brother*?

Eidolon came in wearing his trademark gloomy expression, which meant bad news. Wraith vaguely remembered him in scrubs earlier, but now he was in tan cargoes and a plain black tee, which was as casual as he ever got. 'We have a situation.'

'Serena?'

'Not with her.'

'Then I don't care.' Wraith jackknifed upright again. 'She's sick. If you can't help her, I need to find someone who can.'

'It's not going to matter if we don't handle the Byzamoth problem.'

A low, rumbling growl erupted from Wraith before he could stop it. 'I'm going to rip his throat out with my teeth.'

'Good. It needs to happen now.' Eidolon ran a hand through his hair, which stuck up in wild tufts, as if he'd been doing that all day. 'He's going to use the amulet he took from Serena and your blood to open up a gate between Heaven and Sheoul.'

'Ah . . . that's bad.'

'You think?' Shade drawled.

Eidolon put his fingers to Wraith's wrist, checking his pulse. 'Reaver said he'll make his move at dawn.'

'Where?'

'Jerusalem,' Shade said. 'The Temple Mount.'

Made sense. If Byzamoth was going to pull off something like that, the Temple Mount was the place to do it. Many humans and demons alike believed the Foundation Stone, which was housed at the Temple Mount inside the Dome of the Rock, was where creation had begun and where Armageddon would kick off.

Wraith took his arm back from E. 'I'll go after him.'

'Not alone.' E tossed him a pair of jeans. 'The Aegis is mobilizing. Every cell that can arrive in Jerusalem by dawn will be there, as well as the R-XR and every sister paranormal military unit in the world.'

Wraith came to his feet and pulled on the pants. 'Sounds like you don't need me.'

'Byzamoth can't be defeated without you.' Tayla stood in the doorway, dressed for battle in leather – a dark red color that many demon species couldn't see, and hair pulled into a ponytail. 'Underground rumblings indicate that he's mobilized his own army. The Aegis might not be able to get through his horde to get to him.'

'But I'm charmed and they can't touch me.' Not unless the army was made up of fallen angels.

'Exactly. Kynan and I have been coordinating our attack plan with that of The Aegis and military units. We need you to at least keep him from performing the ritual until we can get to him.'

'And what are you going to do when you get there? News flash, slayer; he's immortal.'

'We're going to do the same thing you are. Hurt him. Keep him from performing the ritual and take the amulet back. According to Reaver, he's got only a few minutes to open the gate.' She grinned. 'Besides, The Aegis does have a few tricks up its sleeve. So keep him busy until we get there.'

'You won't need to get to him,' Wraith swore, 'because I'm taking his fucking head off. Even immortals have issues with decapitation.' He swung around to E. 'Now tell me about Serena.'

'Wraith—'

'Now.'

E and Shade exchanged glances, and Wraith braced himself for the worst. 'You know she's dying.'

'Yeah. Fix it.' Shade moved toward him, but Wraith backed up, unable to bear any touch but Serena's right now. And he knew damn good and well she wouldn't be touching him. She hated him. She had to. 'How . . . how is she?'

Eidolon gave a dismal shake of the head. 'Her disease is irreversible, and it's progressing fast.'

Wraith felt like he'd been stabbed in the gut. Again.

'I've given her something for the pain, and Shade's been getting inside and forcing her organs to work optimally, but the effects of both are temporary. It's only buying her time and making her more comfortable.'

'We traded places,' Wraith murmured, rubbing his chest where he could already feel the loss. 'What am I going to do without her?'

'I'm sorry, bro,' Shade said, but Wraith held up his hand, not wanting to hear it. Hearing it would make it real.

He brushed past Tayla and came to an abrupt halt at the sight of a dark-haired male sitting in the hallway, his arms and legs bound in Bracken Cuffs – chains used by the Judicia to negate a demon's abilities while in custody.

The dude was wearing leather pants and boots, but no shirt.

His *dermoire* appeared to be faded, but it was an exact replica of the markings Wraith and his brothers wore, minus their individual signs. And he had a strange, palm-shaped burn scar over his heart.

Wraith didn't know what the hell was up, but right now, he really didn't care.

Serena could have very little time left, and Wraith wasn't going to waste a single minute.

TWENTY-SIX

Serena was in the bathroom when she heard the bedroom door open. Her heart gave a great thump at the whisper of feet on the floor. Maybe it was Eidolon or Shade coming to do whatever they were doing to make her feel better when they touched her. It was about that time. She was growing weak again, and the pounding in her head was making her vision blur.

'Serena?'

Oh, God. Josh. Maybe if she didn't say anything, he'd go away.

'Serena. Come out.' There was a long pause. 'Please.'

She couldn't face him. She was still too angry, too hurt, too damned conflicted. She stood there at the sink, quietly studying her face, the dark circles under her glassy, red-rimmed eyes, her straw-like, mussed hair, her sallow complexion. God, she really was dying.

What an unbelievably stupid thing she'd done.

Closing her eyes, she bowed her head. No, not stupid – *if* Josh could retrieve the amulet and save the world. Except ... he was a demon. Why would he want to save the world? And if he did want to get the amulet, would he keep it for himself?

She banged her head on the mirror. *Stupid.* Bang. *Stupid.* Bang. *Stupid!*

She'd fallen hard for him. An incubus who had probably used his sex demon tricks on her. Thing was, he hadn't even seduced her with smooth lines and pretty talk. No, he'd done it by protecting her from danger, being nice to cats, and giving her out-of-this-world orgasms. He'd done it by being rough and tough, with a touch of sweet. But how much had been an act?

She heard a sigh, a shuffling of feet, and a door closing. She waited another minute. Cautiously opened the bathroom door.

Only to see Josh sitting on the floor, back against the wall, looking up at the ceiling. He was wearing jeans but nothing else. Even his feet were bare. His broad, thickly muscled chest heaved with the force of his breaths, and lower, his chiseled abs bore no signs of injury.

'You look pretty good for a guy who got run through with a magical sword and almost died.' The words were casual, but what she felt for him was not, and she prayed he didn't hear the emotion in her voice.

'You saved me.' He didn't look at her. 'I can still . . . taste you.'

'Because you're a vampire.' She snorted. 'And a demon. Let's not forget that minor detail.'

A shudder shook his body, and he closed his eyes. 'Yeah.'

'*Yeah?* That's all you have to say?' She cursed, a nasty, base word she'd never used. 'Was anything you told me about your life true?'

He finally looked at her. 'Too much of it, actually.'

'Tell me more.' She crossed her arms across her chest, wondering why the hell she was bothering, why she had this crazy need to understand him.

'Serena, you don't want to hear.'

Anger lit her like a match. 'I gave you my life, *Wraith*, so you can damned well tell me about yours.' He flinched, and she almost felt sorry for him. Almost. 'Give me all of it. Starting from the beginning.'

He rubbed his eyes, and when he was done, he looked at his lap, shoulders hunched. And there she went feeling sorry for him again.

'You're right. But don't say I didn't warn you.' He ran his hand up and down his chest, as though it hurt. It was a long time before he said, 'My dad had the same gift Shade has – he can manipulate bodily functions. He found a woman who was on the verge of being turned into a vampire . . . she'd done the blood exchange and was just about to die when he raped her. Used his gift to keep her in that in-between human and vamp state for nine months, raping her over and over while I grew inside her. He left when she gave birth to me and by then she'd gone insane.'

Wraith spoke rapidly, the words coming so fast Serena barely had time to be shocked. And still, he kept his head bowed, his hair falling forward so she couldn't see his expression.

'She gave me to a wet nurse until I was five, and then she put me in a cage and turned my nurse into a vampire while I watched. She spent the next fifteen years torturing me. Torturing humans and demons in front of me. When I turned twenty, I went through the first of two maturation cycles. I needed sex or I'd die. My mother shoved a prostitute into the cage . . . I was crazed with need . . . ' His voice cracked, but his head came up to fix her with a penetrating stare. 'I took her, and I didn't wait for her consent.'

'Oh, my God.'

'I warned you.'

He had. But she needed to hear more. 'Go on.' When he hesitated, she put her hand on his knee out of some crazy need to comfort him. 'What happened?'

'The prostitute was just doing her job, right?' His voice was hollow. Dead. 'That's how I've always justified what I did. Sometimes, the lie even works.' A flicker of emotion passed over his face, disgust, she thought, but then he looked down and she couldn't read him anymore. 'The next time my mother put a female in with me, I refused her, even though I knew it meant I could die. My mother tortured the girl in front of me for hours, until she finally bled out. The next time a woman was put in the cage, I did what I needed to do, but by then I had learned to use my gift. She thought she was doing her boyfriend on the beach.'

'What gift?'

'I can get inside the mind, read thoughts, trick people into thinking things that didn't happen. I can give them nightmares.' His head came up. There was a challenge in his eyes, as though he expected her to get violent with him. And wanted it. 'Or dreams.'

She inhaled sharply. 'The dreams I had. Of you ... it *was* you.'

'The first one. Any others were all yours.'

The urge to slap him made her hand tingle, but she wasn't going to give him the satisfaction. Instead, she said quietly, 'You're a bastard.'

He shoved both hands through his hair and left them there, bracing his elbows on his knees. 'I'm a demon, Serena. It's what I do.'

She supposed that was true enough. Didn't make her feel much better, though. Especially because it was also true that he was much more than just a demon to her, no matter how much she wanted to believe otherwise.

'So what happened? After you learned to use your gift?'

'My mother lost interest in me. One day she came into my cage to kill me. I killed her instead. Escaped. Ran until her clan caught up with me in Chicago. They strung me up in a warehouse and tortured the fuck out of me for two days. Maybe more. I don't know. After the first day, they gouged out my eyes.'

Oh ... Jesus. Sweet Jesus God Almighty. Black spots swam before Serena's eyes and she felt herself start to go over. Wraith caught her, and she was too weak to fight him. Plus, it felt good to be in his arms again. Her body was a traitor. So much so that when he lay her on the bed, she clung to him, pulled him down beside her.

'I don't think I want to hear any more,' she said in a voice so shaky she barely understood herself. 'But how ... how did you survive?'

'My brothers found me.' He petted her hair with loving, comforting strokes. 'They killed the vamps. Kept one alive to give me back my sight.'

She almost asked why they hadn't used a dead vamp as an eye donor, but duh, they had a tendency to flame to ash when they were killed.

'And then?'

'I went with them to New York, where I spent the next few decades wasting my life. I was worthless. Lived like a rat in sewers, eating junkies and drunks, losing myself in any way I could. Then E and Shade started the hospital. I didn't want to learn how to save lives, but they didn't give me a choice. Taught me to read and write. Got me straightened out. Mostly.'

'Dear . . . God.' His life had been a waking nightmare.

He snorted. 'God abandoned me a long time ago.' Gripping her hand, he squeezed gently. 'Look, Serena, by human standards, I'm a bastard. Hell, even by some demon standards I'm that. I've always been selfish, not giving a shit about anyone or anything but myself. I knew what losing the charm would do to you, and if I could give it back, I would. I know you don't believe this, but . . . I love you.'

Her eyes stung, and her stupid heart responded with several stuttered beats, because it believed him. 'You don't need to lie to me anymore.'

'I'm not. Never again.'

'Easy to say when I've only got hours left to live.'

He made a sound low in his throat. 'Don't say that.'

'It's time to stop denying it.' Strangely, it felt liberating to say it.

His hard swallow was audible, his voice strained. 'I know.'

She propped herself up on her elbow so she could see directly into his eyes. 'I hate you.'

'I know,' he whispered.

'Kiss me.'

He didn't hesitate. His mouth met hers in a bruising kiss. For the first time, he opened up and let her explore with her tongue, let her feel the sharp points of his teeth. Now she knew why he'd always led the way with his kisses, why he'd pulled away when she'd made aggressive moves. Even now, he reared back a little, but she grabbed the back of his head and forced him to stay still. This was for her, not him. He owed her, and she was going to take what she wanted.

His groan rolled through her, caressing all her erogenous zones and waking up nerve endings. Her lungs hurt and her gut cramped, but pleasure began to override the discomfort and pain.

Greedily, she reached between them and palmed his erection. She squeezed him through his pants, and he made a raw, male noise. 'Were you lying when you said you couldn't come like this?'

'No.' His tongue swept over her bottom lip. 'My kind can only achieve release inside a female.'

'Then get inside me.' God, she couldn't believe she wanted him this badly, but with such little time left, the insanity of all of this seemed so distant and unimportant.

His eyes shot open, and she drew in a startled breath at the beautiful gold color they'd gone. 'Are you sure?'

His concern pissed her off. He had no right to worry about her after what he'd done. 'Just do it,' she snapped. 'Now.'

Hurt flashed in his eyes, but then he was tearing open his jeans, shoving her shirt up, and ripping off her shorts, and in an instant, he was inside her. She cried out at the invasion, the incredible sensations that shot up her spine.

'Gods,' he growled into her ear, 'I can smell your need. It's taking me over the edge.' His tongue dragged over her throat, and for a moment she thought he was going to bite her. Some dark, wicked part of her *wanted* him to bite her. 'Mmm. You taste oddly . . . salty.'

'It's the disease,' she whispered. 'It causes salty skin.'

He stiffened, and a small sound of pain broke from his lips. 'I—'

'Stop.' She grasped his face, used her thumb to trace the markings on the right side of his face. 'Don't ruin this for me.' She was being selfish, but she shoved aside the tiny bit of guilt she felt.

A shudder wracked his body, but he closed his eyes and nodded. He began a slow, grinding pump with his hips, and little sparks popped all over her skin. She raked her nails across his back, and though he hissed, he hissed, 'Harder.'

Pleasure cascaded across her mind as he grew more aggressive, until he was hammering her into the mattress while whispering sexy, raw things into her ear. The things he wanted to do to her flipped like erotic pictures through her head, propelling her to a white-hot climax that wouldn't end.

She cried out, calling his name. His real name.

'No.' He nipped at her lobe. 'Call me Josh.'

'Yes . . . *Josh*!'

He roared in his own release, filling her with a hot splash that triggered another orgasm, and another. Her body felt out of control, a lightning strike of sensual energy that wrapped around them both and locked them into an electrifying series of climaxes.

Gradually, the storm of pleasure dissipated, and she'd never been so exhausted.

It was a long time before she had the strength to speak. When she did, her voice was raspy, her breathing wheezy. 'On the train . . . ' She had to pause, swallow, work some moisture into her mouth. 'You said someone slipped an aphrodisiac into my drink. It wasn't a stranger, was it?'

'No.' He rolled off her but kept his strong arms around her, gathering her close. His biceps bunched up hard, his skin was coated with a fine sheen of sweat. 'It was my semen. I didn't mean for it to happen.'

She wracked her brain to bring that night back to the surface of her hazy mind. She'd been crazed with lust, begging him to have sex with her. 'You could have taken my virginity then, but you didn't. Why not?'

'I couldn't.' He buried his face in her neck and breathed deeply, and a soft purring noise rumbled up from deep in his chest. 'That's why I was leaving. I changed my mind about everything, Serena.

Even though my decision would have killed my brothers, too … I couldn't betray you like that.'

'Your … *brothers*?'

'They were dying too. My illness and theirs were connected.'

Time slowed as she digested what he'd just said. She knew how much he loved his brothers, and yet, when it came down to a choice between their lives and hers, he'd chosen hers.

He'd just turned everything she'd ever learned about demons – from the nuns she'd grown up with and from Val and his monstrous library of books – upside down and inside out.

He checked his watch. 'I wish I could stay, but I don't have much time. Byzamoth plans to start the war of wars in a few hours.' He smoothed her hair away from her face, his touch light and tender. 'I'm going to get your necklace back. I'll stop him, Serena. If it's the last thing I do, I will stop him.'

'But … you're a demon.'

'So why would I want to stop him?' At her nod, he lifted one shoulder in a shrug. 'Most demons living among humans like things the way they are. Imagine your worst apocalyptic scenario, multiply it by a hundred, add a lot of chaos, gore, disease, and demons, and you've got Sheoul. The idea that everything could become like that? Freaks a lot of us out. There are going to be a lot of demons fighting on the side of good in this battle.'

'And you're fighting on the side of good.'

He flicked his tongue over a fang, one corner of his mouth turned up in just a hint of a cocky grin. 'Well, historically, good can't fight for shit. Really, they need me.'

Damn him for charming her and turning her on at the same time – while she was on her deathbed.

A commotion outside the door had Josh leaping out of the bed and yanking the covers up around her. The sounds of angry shouts, running footsteps, and flesh striking flesh came through the thin walls as if they were made of paper.

'Serena!'

'Val?'

Josh cursed as Val threw open the door, flanked by Eidolon. Shade was struggling with David and another man in the hallway, and if the more distant sounds were any indication, there was a battle going on elsewhere in the house.

'What the hell is going on?' Val looked between Serena and Josh, who was buttoning his pants. 'Jesus effing Christ, Serena! He's a demon!' He stalked into the room, glaring pure murder at Josh.

Serena sat up in bed, tugging the sheet up even though her top covered her. 'Calm down, Val. I know he's a demon—'

His hand clenched reflexively at his hip, and she wondered if he had a weapon concealed beneath his bulky shirt. 'Do not tell me this is the bastard you gave your charm to.'

'Then don't ask.'

He scrubbed his hand over his face. 'Oh, Serena. How could you have been so stu—'

'Finish that sentence,' Josh said flatly, 'and it'll be your last.'

Val turned purple with rage. For a moment, she thought he'd blow, but David laid a restraining hand on his shoulder. 'Let it go, Dad.'

Shade moved fully inside to stand near Josh, and suddenly the room filled with people. Total strangers. And here she was, wearing nothing but a tank top and in a bed where it was pretty obvious she'd just had sex. With a demon.

'Everyone needs to just calm down.' Eidolon crossed to Josh and Shade.

'Fuck you,' David said. 'We don't take orders from demons.'

Josh bared his fangs. 'Yeah, you do. Because right now, I'm your best hope to defeat Byzamoth. So if you don't want to spend eternity bent over and holding your ankles for him, you'll back the fuck off.'

Ky, Gem, Tay, Shade, and E all crammed into the bedroom, followed by six local Aegis Guardians and six members of the Sigil. Luc, Reaver, and several local Aegi made for a tense party in the other rooms of the house, and there were more agents patrolling outside.

And that asshole Lore was tied up in the hall. What the hell was up with that? Ky had no idea.

Kynan's hand hovered over his stang, fingers itching to draw down. The house was filled to the gills with mortal enemies, and the Guardians were loaded for werebear.

Powder. Keg. One spark and the place would blow.

Val reached for Serena, his Sigil ring glinting in the light from the overhead. 'I'm taking you home.'

And . . . that was the spark.

A god-awful roar vibrated the house. Wraith moved so fast Ky didn't track him until he followed the nasty growl to the bed, where Wraith was on all fours, crouched protectively over Serena.

Christ, his eyes burned the orange-gold of a jet's afterburners and his fangs had elongated into daggers. With his blond mane falling around his face, he looked like a fucking lion guarding his pride.

The familiar, ominous sound of weapons clearing their housings cut through the tension. The Guardians and Elders closed ranks at the same moment that E, Shade, and Gem stepped in front of the bed to stand with Wraith.

In a coordinated move that reminded Ky of how well he and Tay had fought together in the past, they placed themselves between the demons and the Guardians.

'I am taking Serena home, where she belongs,' Val repeated, his Romanian accent so thick Kynan barely understood him.

Wraith's voice scraped gravel. 'If you touch her, I'll drop all your buddies, and then I'll take you apart, piece by piece.'

'You,' Val bellowed, 'have no say in this. She's dying because of you!'

The Guardians shifted, bracing for battle, and Wraith's eyes went crimson. This was going to end very, very badly.

'Shade,' Ky said quietly, 'bring Wraith down.' He turned to Val, whose dark gaze promised as much blood as Wraith's. 'You'd best back off. We need him to get the amulet from Byzamoth. And you know you can't hurt him. Trying would be suicide.' Suicide, even if Wraith wasn't in possession of the charm.

Serena placed a restraining hand on Wraith's, and though he still looked like he was mentally fitting Val for a coffin, he'd stopped growling.

'Val, please,' she said calmly, as if she didn't have over two hundred pounds of enraged demon vampire crouched over her. 'The most important thing here is to stop Byzamoth. We all need to work together.'

'We agreed to work with the charmed one,' David said, 'but we didn't know he was a demon. We're not working with them. No way.'

'Then lube up and prepare to call Byzamoth daddy,' Wraith said, not helping the situation at all.

One of the Elders, Juan, cleared his throat. 'Kynan. Tayla. As Regent and former Regent, surely you recognize the problems inherent in Guardians working with demons?'

'I know firsthand.' Tayla morphed into her hybrid Soulshredder form, her veiny wings scraping the wall. Gasps filled the air. 'Because I'm half demon.' She shifted back, rolled her shoulders. 'Don't make me do that again. It stings and makes me very cranky.'

David turned on her, his glower twisting his handsome face into something hideous. 'You traitorous—'

'Be *very* careful what you say, human.' Eidolon's eyes had gone as red as Wraith's, and he now looked every inch the demon he was.

A long, tense silence had Kynan twitching. Finally, Val turned to him, though he shot wary glances at Tayla. 'Did you know about her? Did you know she was a demon when you recommended her for the Regent position?'

'Yes.'

'Jesus, Kynan. What the hell were you thinking?'

'I was thinking,' Kynan said, 'that she's a warrior with damned good instincts. She can think on her feet. She knows the difference between good demons and bad ones—'

'There are no good demons,' Val bit out.

'Right now none of that matters,' Kynan said, because they didn't have time to argue. 'What matters is stopping Byzamoth. And trust me, you need Wraith to do that.'

Muffled grumbles rose up in the Aegis ranks. Val held up his hand; everyone went silent. 'He's right. We need to concentrate on the situation at hand.'

Kynan swore the house breathed a sigh of relief. Still, the room was way too crowded with mortal enemies. And Serena didn't look comfortable in bed, where the state of the sheets and the discarded clothes on the floor told an X-rated story.

'Let's clear out,' Kynan said. 'We only need a few players in here.'

There was some discussion between the Elders and Guardians, and then most of them filed out, leaving only Val and his son, David. Gem and Tayla left to keep an eye on things outside. Reaver had come in, stood at the end of the bed, watching Serena with sad eyes.

Calmer now, Wraith sat on the edge of the bed, holding Serena's hand. Still, he locked gazes with Val, who cleared his throat imperiously.

'The city of Jerusalem is being evacuated. Hundreds of Aegis and military teams will be in place at the Temple Mount in a matter of hours,' Val said to Wraith. 'I assume you'll use a Harrowgate to make it on time?'

'Duh.'

Shade sighed, and Eidolon rubbed his temples.

'You will distract Byzamoth so The Aegis can retrieve the amulet. Should you gain possession of it, you will immediately hand it over to a Guardian.'

Kynan winced as Wraith came to his feet. 'Blow me. This isn't your show, and I don't take orders from slayers.'

'Josh. Val.' Serena's thin voice drew everyone's attention. The dark circles beneath her eyes seemed to have grown ten times worse in the last few minutes. 'Just … get the necklace. Don't fight.'

Wraith nodded and took her hand, and was it Ky's imagination, or did her arm look thinner, more fragile? 'Sorry.' He slid Val a covert glare, as if upsetting Serena had been entirely the human's fault.

The room fell silent except for the sound of her raspy breaths, until Reaver spoke up. 'I'm going with you.'

E cocked an eyebrow. 'I thought you couldn't help.'

'Fuck that.'

'How can you help, angel?' Wraith asked, and both Val and David gaped.

'Angel?' David echoed.

'Fallen. Don't get excited.' Reaver shook his head. 'I can fight him, but I can't do it alone. He's stronger than I am. He's drawing on the power of evil. I, on the other hand, can't claim the power of the Heavens or Hell.'

Wraith tucked Serena against him and ran his palm up and down her arm. 'So we tag team him.'

'We tag team him,' Reaver agreed.

E clapped Wraith on the back. 'I'm going with you. Tay, Luc, and Ky are coming with us. There'll be a lot of casualties.'

They'd decided not to send Shade, because his medical gift would be needed here to care for Serena, and Gem was staying behind to help. All of the Guardians would remain in what was now Central Command. They would be responsible for calling in reinforcements, providing situation reports to Aegis cells worldwide, and basically, acting as the second line of defense should Wraith fail.

Of course, should Wraith fail, a second line wouldn't make a drop of difference.

'Game on, then,' Wraith said. 'We leave together. But Shade? No one takes Serena anywhere.' Wraith glared at Val, his voice dripping with warning. 'No one.'

Shade crossed his arms over his broad chest, moved to the head of the bed, and nodded. 'No one.'

Wraith kissed Serena so tenderly that something lurched in Kynan's chest. He'd never in a million years have believed that Wraith could feel so strongly about anyone, especially a human. That the woman was dying only made the situation more unbelievable – and tragic.

Kynan thought of Gem and wondered what he'd do if he found out she was dying. God, he'd probably wither up and die with her.

Screw that. He wasn't going to lose her to death or to anything else. Not now, and since things here seemed to be under control, he slipped out of the room.

In the living room, he walked into a tension soup. Four Guardians stood on one side of the room, Luc on the other, and all were glaring. The Guardians couldn't know Luc was a werewolf, but they knew he was there with the Sem brothers, so they'd naturally assume he was some sort of baddie.

Ky pulled Luc aside. 'Have you seen Gem?'

'Not my day to watch her.' Luc growled when one of the Guardians not-so-casually drew his stang and tested the edge. 'But I saw her go into the kitchen a minute ago.'

Luc's gaze went right back to a female Guardian standing near a window, and strangely enough, her gaze was fixed just as intently on him.

'What's going on?' Kynan asked.

Luc smiled, which was little more than a baring of his teeth. 'She's a warg. She knows I know, but I'm guessing her human buddies *don't* know. She's afraid I'll tell.'

'Are you going to?'

'That depends.'

'On what?'

Luc's voice dropped an octave. 'Whether or not she gives me what I want.'

'And that is?'

'Fifteen minutes. Naked.'

'That's blackmail.'

Luc snorted. 'Wargs call it negotiation.'

'So you want fifteen minutes . . . what will she want?'

'With me?' Luc winked. 'Two hours.'

Kynan shook his head. *Wargs.*

He found Gem in the kitchen, staring into the fridge. He didn't bother asking her to come with him. He seized her hand and dragged her to the only room that was empty.

The bathroom. He shot Lore the bird on the way past.

'Kynan! What are you doing?'

He shut the door, spun, and kissed her. She made a small sound of outrage, but he pushed her up against the door, kept kissing her, and after a moment she relaxed against him.

'I don't care what you are, Gem. I want you. I love you. And if our kids are a quarter demon, I can live with that. If you can't, we'll adopt. Or we'll get a surrogate. It doesn't matter.'

Gem's mouth fell open. Closed. Fell open again. 'What . . . what brought this on?'

'The woman Wraith loves is dying. They might only have hours left together. I know you have hundreds of years to live, and I can only give you a fraction of that with me, but watching Wraith and Serena made me realize that I can't waste our time. Marry me, Gem. Be with me for as long as I have left.'

Her eyes filled with tears, and fear cut him wide open. He knew what she was going to say before she said it.

'I'm sorry, Ky . . . I can't. Maybe after the battle and things settle down, we can see, but right now, I think you're looking at the end and grasping at what you can.'

'Damn you,' he gritted out. 'Why do you keep telling me what I'm thinking and how I'm feeling?'

‘Because someone has to.’ She tore out of the bathroom, leaving him staring at the wall. Outside, he heard a commotion, the sound of weapons being prepared, of battle looming.

Good. He was going to take out his frustrations on a lot of demons, because the one he wanted . . . didn’t want him.

TWENTY-SEVEN

The thing that sucked about Jerusalem was that there were only a handful of Harrowgates. There was one just paces from the Dome of the Rock, a temple that housed the Foundation Stone Byzamoth would use to open the gate, but it would be under the enemy's control, and the next closest was on the outskirts of the city. Which meant that Wraith, Luc, Tay, E, Reaver, and Ky had to hoof it miles to the Temple Mount.

The city's atmosphere was bleak. The few people on the streets were silent, heads down as if they expected fire to fall from the sky – which was dark, the clouds roiling and edged in crimson. Lightning streaked to the ground and thunder cracked.

Wraith saw them in the distance. Two armies ... one massive, the other massively arrogant. Only The Aegis would think their righteousness would allow them to come out on the victorious end of battle when they were outnumbered twenty to one.

'Let's do this thing,' Wraith said, and Luc took off like a shot. No one liked a good fight more than a warg.

No one but Wraith.

Reaver pulled Kynan aside and Eidolon grabbed Wraith. 'Hold up, bro. Just a sec.' He turned to Tayla and framed her face in his hands so tenderly Wraith had a moment of longing for Serena. 'Don't shift into your Shredder form. I don't want any military idiot or Aegi mistaking you for the enemy.'

'And you stay back. You don't fight in this one. You heal. That's all.' Tayla took E's face in her hands and brought his mouth close to hers. 'I love you.'

Wraith turned away to give them a moment of privacy. He'd always made fun of their sappy relationship, had never understood how E could give so much of himself to Tayla. Now he got it. Got it so well it hurt.

He'd give anything and everything to Serena, if only she'd let him. If only she'd *live*.

He reached into his coat pocket, but instead of feeling up a weapon, which always soothed him, he fingered the top she'd given him. He'd grabbed it on the way out of the house, a good luck charm he wasn't going into battle without.

He felt two hands on his back – one belonging to E, and the other to Tayla. She gave him a tentative smile. 'Good luck, Wraith.'

With that, she took off.

'Ditto,' E said. 'I have faith in you.'

'Sorry, not buying it.' Wraith watched lightning streak across the sky, connecting the clouds in a celestial dot-to-dot. 'But I appreciate the sentiment.'

'I mean it. I've never given you enough credit. But I'm seeing something in you I've never noticed before.' Eidolon spared them both more mushiness by slugging him in the shoulder. 'Kick his ass, bro.' He set off after Tayla.

Wraith watched them go, took a deep breath, and moved out. Good thing he had broad shoulders, because the weight of the world . . . sucked.

Serena breathed deeply as Shade released her arm. She'd passed out right after Josh left, but Shade had done the glowy-arm thing that always made her feel better. He backed away and stood near the door like a sentry, his shrewd, sharp eyes shifting between Val and David, who both sat in chairs near her bed.

'You know,' Val said, taking her hand in his. 'I really would rather take you home, where you'll be more comfortable.'

She shook her head. 'I don't know if I could make the plane trip.' She also didn't want to go anywhere until she knew that the amulet had been retrieved.

And that Josh had survived.

She still wasn't sure how she felt about him, because his betrayal had been so huge, so ... awful. But she understood why he'd set out to seduce her, and how hard it had been not to go through with it when he knew he was dooming his brothers.

She wriggled into a sitting position, and Val fluffed the pillow behind her back. 'Shade?'

He looked at her.

'Josh – Wraith – said you and Eidolon were dying. But you weren't poisoned, right?'

Shade shook his head. 'Long story. He didn't even know about it until after the attack on Philae. He'd decided not to go through with the plan to seduce you. That's when we told him that we were dying, too.'

God, he'd backed off his plan even earlier than she'd thought.

'What difference does it make?' David asked. 'He's a demon.'

'He saved me from Byzamoth.'

'So he could have you for himself, you idiot! You actually believe this ... this creature?'

'David!' Val's hand tightened on Serena's almost painfully, though he didn't seem to realize it. 'That's enough.'

Shame colored David's face.

Serena coughed ... and couldn't stop. Immediately, Shade was at her side, his hand wrapped around her wrist, fingers to her pulse, tattoo glowing. In seconds, her lungs cleared, opened up so she could breathe better. Josh had said he was a paramedic, and no doubt, he was a good one. Attentive, efficient, and possessing an arrogant confidence that was justified. He knew what he was doing and he did it well. She'd bet he did *everything* well.

'You have a . . . mate, right?' she asked, and his incredibly long lashes flew up in surprise.

'Yes.'

'Did she know what you were when you met?'

He grunted. 'Not until she caught me in bed with a vampire and a Trillah demon.'

Her jaw dropped. 'And she still wanted you?'

'She wanted to kill me. Tell you what,' he said, giving her a sleepy, seductive grin that reminded her so much of Josh, 'I'll tell you the whole sordid story after Wraith defeats Byzamoth.'

She knew there were no guarantees that Wraith would survive the battle, but she appreciated Shade's efforts to calm her. He moved back to the doorway, and she tapped Val's hand to get his attention. He'd fixed his gaze out the window at the approaching dawn and had gone someplace far away.

'Val?' Her voice cracked as she spoke, and she couldn't believe the effort it took just to say his name.

'What is it?'

Nerves fluttered in her belly. 'Who all knew about my mission in Egypt?'

David spoke up. 'Everyone in the Sigil.'

'But who knew about the specifics? Where I was staying, where I was going to be at what times . . . things like that.'

Val's eyes narrowed. 'Why?'

She palmed the mattress to keep her hands from shaking. What if Josh was right about Val? 'Because Byzamoth was always one step ahead of me. He knew things he shouldn't know.'

David stiffened. 'What are you saying? How dare you accuse my father of betraying you.'

'I'm not accusing Val of anything. But someone was tipping off the fallen angel and trying to get me killed. He couldn't have known I was stopping by the Regent's house, and there's definitely no way he could have known what train I took from Aswan. Josh changed the reservations.'

'Well, there's your answer,' David shot back. 'And let's call him by his real name, shall we? Since he pretty much stole Josh's identity like he stole everything else.'

She slid a glance at Shade, who still watched in silence, but the way his chiseled jaw rolled gave her the impression that he was grinding his teeth.

'It wasn't him,' she insisted. It wouldn't have made sense for Josh to have been tipping off the competition.

David made a sound of disgust. 'It's so much easier for you to accuse us than to believe your demon lover could possibly have betrayed you, never mind the fact that it's all he's done since he met you.'

'You feeling a little guilty, human? Because she didn't accuse you.' Shade looked at Serena and shrugged. 'Just pointing that out.'

And he was right. 'Val, tell me. Who all knew about the Regent's house and the train?'

Val didn't say anything, but she knew the answer. He'd known . . . and so had David.

David shoved to his feet with such force that his chair tipped over. 'I'm not going to sit here and listen to this. Come on, Dad. We don't need this.'

Shade blocked the door. 'You don't have to sit, but you *will* stay.'

'I'm trained to kill your kind.'

Shade cracked his knuckles.

Wisely, David backed off, but his stung pride put him on the hot side of pissed. 'This is your fault, Serena.' He stalked to the end of the bed and nailed her to the wall with a hateful glare. 'Yours and your whore of a mother's.'

'Enough!' Val shouted, coming to his feet. 'You're out of line.'

'Really, Dad? *Really?* Because I'm thinking that your affair with Patrice was out of line.'

Serena's mouth dropped open. Val's snapped shut. Silence was an uncomfortable fourth party in the room until Shade drawled, 'Now things are getting interesting.'

'Tell Serena,' David said. 'Go ahead. Tell her how you cheated on mom for years. How every time Patrice snapped her fingers, you went running, leaving us alone. How, when she wanted to get pregnant, you couldn't jerk off into a cup fast enough.'

The air left Serena's lungs in a rush, leaving her woozy. 'Is this true?' she croaked.

Val spread his hands in a pleading gesture. 'I couldn't tell you. I didn't even know David knew.'

'How stupid do you think I am?' David snapped. 'You think mom didn't figure it out the first time she saw Serena? She was a carbon copy of you when she was little.' His voice vibrated with anger. 'It must have been such a relief for you when Patrice gave up her charm to Serena. You got the best of both worlds. Your precious daughter was protected and you could finally fuck Patrice—'

Val decked David so hard that it sent his son flying. David bounced off the wall, using the momentum to rush at Val, but then Shade was there between them, fisting David's shirt and easily holding him at arm's length.

'I don't care if you kill each other. But do it outside. Wraith will have my ass if the female gets caught in the cross fire.'

'She should be dead already,' David spat, and Serena went numb.

'Oh, my God,' Val whispered. '*You* did it. You betrayed her to Byzamoth.'

'So what? Mom is dead because of her! If you hadn't loved her and Patrice more than us . . . ' He jerked away from Shade and stumbled to the corner, where he put his head against the wall. 'Mom couldn't handle knowing you were cheating on her. All those years she put up with it, but when Patrice got pregnant again, it was the last straw. You drove her to it, Dad. You might as well have put the pills down her throat yourself.'

The truth of David's words put shadows in Val's eyes. He swallowed hard. 'I never meant for any of that to happen. I loved your mother. I love you.'

Dabbing blood away from his mouth with the back of his hand, David turned back to Val. 'But you loved Patrice and Serena more.'

Serena began to shake with fury. If she wasn't so weak, she'd hit him herself. 'You put the entire world at risk, betrayed the human race, just to get revenge?'

He recoiled as if she *had* struck him. 'I didn't know what Byzamoth was.' Tears swam in his eyes, and he dashed them away as he turned to Val. 'I swear to you, I didn't know. And I didn't know Serena would die, not until you got all freaked when she said someone was after her. I just wanted the necklace. *I* wanted to be special.'

Val shook his head as though trying to clear it, and Serena knew how he felt, because she was confused as hell. 'How did you find Byzamoth?'

'He came to the mansion after he discovered Serena's identity. He said he was a mage. I think he planned to take the charm then. But you'd already sent her to Egypt. I was pissed—'

'Because you wanted to go,' Val interrupted, and David gave him a petulant nod.

'Byzamoth made a deal with me. He said if I told him where she was, he'd take the charm and give me Heofon.'

'And you believed him?' Serena gaped at the man's stupidity.

'He acted like he didn't care about the necklace. I thought he just wanted the charm. Then he got interested in the artifacts, and decided to use you to get them, too.'

'So he *was* after the tablet and coin.'

Val laughed bitterly. 'Of course. Once David spilled the beans about those, Byzamoth would have realized that shutting down the Harrowgates would seriously disrupt his war. The gates between Heaven and Hell could still have been opened with Heofon, but demons wouldn't have been able to get to the Earth's surface to make war on humans. At least, not until they destroyed Heaven.' He made a sound of disgust as he rounded on his son. 'You idiot. You realize that even if you had gotten the necklace, you would not have been allowed to keep it.'

David's chin came up in defiance. 'The holder of Heofon is given the charm—'

'*If* angels deem that person worthy!' Val roared. '*You are not worthy.*'

'I never have been, in your eyes.' David stalked toward the door, and after a brief nod from Val, Shade let him go – but not before whispering something in David's ear that made his knees buckle. Once he caught himself, he couldn't get away fast enough.

Val sank heavily onto his chair, didn't look at Serena. 'I don't have the words to explain,' he began. 'So ask what you need to.'

Too in shock to speak, Serena said nothing. It was Shade who broke the ice.

'This is better than a soap. Not that I'd know.' He propped himself against the doorframe again. 'So, Aegi ... why didn't you ever tell Serena *you* whipped up her baby batter?'

Yes, she would like the answer to that oddly phrased question. Val buried his face in his hands, and she had to strain to hear him.

'How could I tell you when I couldn't even come clean with my own family? I honestly didn't think they knew. And after Patrice died, there was no point in saying anything. I knew that with the nuns, you'd be safe and well-cared for.' He lifted his head, watched her with bloodshot eyes. 'I was a coward. And because of that, my son hates me. Hates his own sister. I'm sorry. So sorry.'

'What will happen to David?' Shade asked, in a tone that said he'd handle things if Val's answer didn't satisfy him.

Val took a ragged breath that ended on a sob. 'It's a matter for The Aegis.' He came to his feet. 'I'll be back.'

Shade waited until Val was gone, and then muttered, 'Family sucks sometimes.'

God, he had that right. 'About family ... I think you should know the reason Wraith hasn't been to see your sons.' Shade opened his mouth, but Serena cut him off. 'He's afraid, Shade. He's afraid to share himself, like each piece he gives to someone is going to be a piece that goes missing when they turn on him. He feels like he's lost you and Eidolon to your mates and children, and you were all he had.'

'Why do you care?' he asked gruffly. 'After what Wraith did to you, you should hate him.'

'I also love him, and I can't turn that off.' She sighed and flopped back against her pillow, the day's events sapping what was left of her energy.

Shade crossed the room and sank down on the bed with her. Gently, he took her wrist, and his tattoo – *dermoire*, he'd said at one point – began to glow, and a pleasant tingling sensation spread through her veins.

'Funny things, humans,' he said under his breath. 'Just when you think they're all a bunch of morons, a smart one shows up and proves you wrong.'

She smiled drowsily. 'I do believe that was a compliment. From a demon. Go figure.'

'Yup. Just when you think we're all a bunch of morons . . .'

One shows up and makes you fall in love with him.

TWENTY-EIGHT

This charm thing was so cool.

Wraith and Reaver approached the Dome of the Rock with ease, practically untouched by the army of demons who swarmed around it. He could have shapeshifted into some heinous demon to make himself less conspicuous, but there was no fun in that.

No, he walked straight through the horde like a spear through flesh, his long leather trench coat flapping at his ankles, the comforting clank of his weapons ringing in his ears. Thoughtful of his brothers to bring his fighting gear.

Several demons attempted to assault him – not because they viewed Wraith or Reaver as enemies, but because demons were generally just assholes – but thanks to the charm, something always got in the way of their attacks. They'd stumble, strike another demon, miss him completely ... yeah, the charm thing was way cool.

Reaver pulled him to a halt at the top of the steps, just beneath the arched colonnade outside the golden-domed mosque. 'If this goes badly for me, you know what to do.'

Yeah, he knew. Reaver had told him that only an angel could kill an angel ... with one exception. If one drained an angel to death, they would temporarily inherit the ability to destroy another angel. The catch was that no one could drain an angel of blood – unless the angel volunteered.

Wraith hoped it didn't come down to that. He kinda liked Reaver.

'Got it,' Wraith said, and started walking, but Reaver stopped him again. 'Geez, what this time?'

'Kynan. You must give Kynan the amulet. Not anyone else in The Aegis. Understood?'

'No.'

Reaver made an exasperated noise. 'This is all fated,' he said, waving at the army around them. 'I don't know how this will end – the battle is fated, the outcome is not. But Kynan's fate is tied closely with these events.'

Wraith rolled his eyes. If there was anything he hated more than cryptic shit, it was fate shit. 'Whatever. Let's go kick Byzamoth's ugly, and I mean *ugly*, ass.'

They entered the Dome of the Rock, easily shoving away the burly, horned Ramreel guards. They didn't have to worry about the fallen angel's minions following; few demons would set hoof in so holy a building. They feared God more than they feared any fallen angel.

Even Wraith twitched uncomfortably in the mosque, where bright tiles and glass mosaics spelled out Qur'anic verses and religious depictions. Byzamoth stood near the center next to the giant Foundation Stone, his gaze fixed on the ceiling, an evil, ecstatic smile curving his mouth.

The sounds of battle erupted outside – Wraith's entrance had been the signal for The Aegis and militaries to launch their attack.

'Byzamoth.' Reaver moved next to Wraith, his skin glowing with a freakish white light.

Byzamoth's eyes flew wide open. 'Reaver?' He shifted his gaze to Wraith. '*You.* You live?'

'Nope. This is all in your imagination.' Wraith stalked toward him. ‘Hell of a way to get back into Heaven, don’t you think? When all you have to do is walk into the noon sun.’

‘Fool. That only works if an angel hasn’t yet entered Sheoul.’

‘My bad. I’m rusty on fallen angel rules. Don’t suppose they’ve got an Idiot’s Guide for that.’ Wraith studied his nails. ‘But one thing I know? If you die, you’re gone for good. Poof. No redemption, no reincarnation, no nothing. Buh-bye.’

He launched a morning star so fast Byzamoth didn’t have a chance to block it. The star caught him in the shoulder, went right through and buried itself in a pillar.

Byzamoth yelped in pain, but he recovered in an instant. ‘Did you think it would be so easy?’ He came at Wraith, feet not touching the ground.

Reaver met him head on, and they crashed together like two bulls. Light streaked with black voids swirled around them, encasing them in a supernatural funnel cloud as they grappled. Wraith hurled one of his daggers into the mix, aimed at the back of Byzamoth’s neck, but the weapon was caught up in the tornado and flung to the far side of the building.

Blood flew from the two angels, staining the vortex a gruesome red. The whirlwind imploded. Reaver flew through the air, coming down in a heap that slid across the floor, leaving a crimson trail.

Wraith attacked Byzamoth, ripping powerful punches into the male’s face. A knee to the groin earned a satisfying roar of pain. A bolt of energy slammed into Wraith’s chest, knocking him into the railing surrounding the Foundation Stone.

Wet tearing sounds filled the mosque as Byzamoth shifted into his grotesque gargoyle form. His one wing rose up high over his head, the clawed tip coming down to clamp on Wraith’s head.

Pain screamed through Wraith as sharp, serrated claws dug into his skull. Blood streamed down his face, and rage streamed through his veins. Snarling, he dropped to his knees and lunged sideways, breaking Byzamoth’s hold. He rolled, avoiding what would have been a bone-breaking stomp to the hip.

Wraith pivoted on his hand, sweeping his legs out for his own devastating kick. He caught the male in the knee, and though Byzamoth grunted, he didn't go down. Scrambling to his feet, Wraith dashed blood out of his eyes. In the distance, the air sang with the clank of weapons, the thud of fists striking flesh, and the screams of demons and humans in mortal pain.

'It's beautiful music, is it not?' Byzamoth edged sideways, keeping his body between the Foundation Stone and Wraith. Lightning flashed and thunder rocked the ground. Outside the dome, an evil storm spun up black twisters and blood-red rain. Through a single hole in the Heavens came a golden stream of light, but in a heartbeat, the roiling clouds extinguished it.

Byzamoth opened his fist to reveal Serena's necklace and a vial of blood. Wraith's blood. 'The sun has cast its first and last rays. It's time. Reconsider your fight, incubus. Stand with me, and you will reap unimaginable rewards.'

'As tempting as it sounds to be your bitch,' Wraith drawled, 'I'm going to have to turn down that offer.'

He launched himself at the angel. Byzamoth's wing caught him in the shoulder, knocking him off balance, but somehow, he stayed upright. They fought like fiends, with Wraith coming out on top every time they broke apart.

But Wraith was bleeding badly, one leg wasn't working right, and he was sucking air with a lot more effort than he'd like.

Byzamoth looked as if he'd gone for a pleasant jog. 'I can't be killed, filthy demon.'

'You're pretty judgmental with the demon thing,' Wraith said through panting breaths. 'Given that you *are* a demon.'

Evil laughter bounced off the walls of a place so holy that they seemed to writhe under the sound. 'I'm better than demon scum.'

'*Holier than thou* is kinda funny coming from a fallen angel.'

'I tire of your infantile humor.' Byzamoth popped open the vial of blood and whirled toward the Foundation Stone.

'No!' Wraith struck Byzamoth in the back, propelling him into a support column, but blood splashed from the vial and fell in thin streaks across the Foundation Stone.

Outside, the storm hushed. Inside, it had just begun.

The blood on the stone bubbled, releasing black steam into the air. Byzamoth struggled toward it, kicking at Wraith, who held onto his ankle. The fallen angel held the necklace stretched before him, trying to reach the blood.

'Damn you!' Byzamoth slammed his fist down on Wraith's skull like a hammer on a nail. Wraith crumpled to the ground, his legs not functioning. Byzamoth moved to the stone.

'Wraith . . .' Reaver's hand closed on his ankle. The angel had somehow crawled from where he'd fallen, his body a broken mess. 'Drain . . . me.'

Wraith brushed blood out of his eyes. Holy hell. If Reaver died like this, his soul would suffer eternal torment. 'Let me try—'

'There's no time!' Reaver rasped. 'You must slash Byzamoth's throat . . . and then fill the wound with your own blood after you drink mine. Hurry.'

Byzamoth was holding the necklace in the steam rising up from the blood on the stone, and the building had begun to rock. Reaver had exposed his throat. There was nothing to say. Nothing at all.

Wraith sank his fangs into the angel's jugular. The blood hit his tongue like an electric shock and began pouring down his throat.

'No!' Byzamoth flashed to Reaver, grabbed the other angel by the arm, and threw him like a Frisbee through the doorway. 'I want him dragged to the depths of Sheoul!' he screamed, and from nowhere, a horde of imps swallowed up Reaver and dragged him away.

Snarling, he turned on Wraith, crunching a foot into Wraith's chest. Wraith launched into the air and hit the far wall with a crack of ribs.

His vision swam. Byzamoth darted back to the stone. Hand shaking, Wraith fished in his weapons harness for something to throw – anything. Outside, the sounds of battle became a screaming roar, metal on metal and metal on flesh growing closer. And then Kynan was there by Wraith's side.

'Need Reaver,' Wraith gasped. 'His blood.'

'Take mine.'

Wraith shook his head, trying to make sense of what Ky had just said. 'I don't need to feed.'

'I know. You need to drain an angel. Angel blood runs through my veins. It won't be the same, but we're losing, Wraith. Either way, I'll die.'

'No.' Wraith grasped another throwing star and tugged it free of its housing. 'I'm not done—'

'Wraith!' Ky's voice was hushed but urgent as he grabbed Wraith's shoulders and shook him. 'Damn you, vampire. If you want to see Serena again, you have to do this.'

Byzamoth looked over at them, but he didn't view Kynan, a simple human, as a threat.

'Feeding won't help you, idiot.' Byzamoth turned back to the Foundation Stone, which was becoming lost in a giant, spinning black hole that extended upward to the cupola. It was growing, expanding, swallowing the ceiling.

Kynan tilted his head. 'Do it.' He swallowed, locked gazes with Wraith. 'Tell Gem . . . never mind.'

'Fuck,' Wraith whispered.

'Do it!'

Closing his eyes, Wraith latched onto Kynan's throat. The human stiffened, but after a moment he sagged so Wraith had to catch him.

He drank until Kynan's heart sped up to compensate for blood loss, and then he pulled harder as the human's veins collapsed, until his heart stuttered. Oh, shit, he was doing it . . . he was killing his friend.

His friend.

He'd never had one before, and the one he had, he was destroying.

Kynan stopped breathing.

Power ripped through Wraith, power and pain that felt as if his muscles were separating from the bones. He lowered Kynan gently to the ground and let the rage of what he'd done fuel him. Rage that Byzamoth was the cause of all of this.

The demon would pay with his life.

Wraith launched himself at Byzamoth with a vengeance. They knotted together, a vicious swirl of hand-to-hand, a form of combat at which Wraith excelled. He would not lose. He could not lose. Kynan's death would *not* be in vain.

Byzamoth's wing sideswiped Wraith and knocked him to his knees. The fallen angel kneeled beside him and wrapped his clawlike hand around Wraith's throat.

'I scarcely have time for this.' Byzamoth glanced at the horizon, where the clouds pushed against the sun's light.

Wraith opened his mouth, but nothing came out. Not even breath.

'I know who you are. A demon born to a vampire.' He licked the gash he'd made in Wraith's cheek. 'I found your dam. She's in Sheoul-gra.'

Sheoul-gra. The place where dead demons went until their souls could be reborn. But according to many, deceased evil humans, vampires, weres, and shapeshifters didn't go there, because they couldn't be reborn.

'You're wondering why she's there instead of suffering eternally in Sheoul?' Byzamoth dug his finger in the wound, and Wraith grit his teeth against the pain. 'She's serving there. Serving the demons who are waiting to be reborn. The things they make her do . . . '

Wraith could imagine. Didn't need to imagine, actually.

'She had a message for you, her darling boy.' Byzamoth punched his hand into Wraith's gut, and agony accompanied a wet, hideous rip. 'She can't wait to see you. And she'll make what she did to you as a child seem like, well, child's play.'

A shudder ran through Wraith, no matter how hard he tried to contain it. Even after all these years she could prey on his fears.

No. She was not going to win, and he was not going to be seeing her anytime soon. Because his mother no longer had control of his fears. Not when his greatest fear was losing Serena. He had to get to her. But Byzamoth's hand was deep inside his body, tunneling its way up to his heart.

'Now, I send you to see your mother.'

Wraith dug into his pocket for a weapon. His fingers, slippery with blood, found a blade, but he couldn't grasp it . . . but wait . . . he closed his fist around the wooden top. Byzamoth's fingers found his heart.

Byzamoth squeezed. Weakly, Wraith stabbed the pointed end of the top into Byzamoth's eye. The fallen angel reared back. Finally free, Wraith punched a dagger into the fallen angel's gut. It sank deep, and Byzamoth hit the deck.

'Mother,' Wraith rasped, 'is going to have to wait.' With a snarl, he slashed Byzamoth's throat. The fallen angel's neck opened up all the way to his spine. Blood flowed in a river, but the holy site seemed to be ready. Steam billowed up as the blood burned to ash. Quickly, Wraith slit his own wrist, let the blood drain into the wound.

Instantly, Byzamoth went up in smoke.

That was it? Wraith had thought an angel's death would somehow be more dramatic.

Outside, demons shrieked as they, too, began to flame. Wraith looked down at himself, made sure he wasn't on fire. So far, so good. Except for the fist-sized hole in his gut.

He seized the amulet from the floor where it had fallen when Byzamoth poofed, and staggered out of the Dome of the Rock. In the distance, Eidolon moved from human to human, healing where he could. Nearby, Tayla barked out orders to the less severely injured Guardians. Luc was rendering aid and looking a little worse for wear himself, but he appeared to have all his body parts. Near the Harrowgate, Reaver was spreadeagled on the ground, chains holding him down.

Wraith gathered Kynan's body in his arms and limped down steps that were tacky with burned demon remains and human blood. Eidolon looked up from healing a guy wearing what looked like a Spanish military uniform, his expression falling when he saw Kynan.

'Is he . . . '

'Yeah.'

Still, E's *dermoire* lit up as he lay his hand on Kynan. 'Ah, fuck.' His arm fell away.

'Yeah.' Wraith cocked his head toward Reaver as Eidolon channeled a healing wave into him. 'Someone needs to help the angel. I'm going to Serena.' He looked down at Kynan's limp body. 'And Gem.'

ᘓ

Lore had to take a leak. He had no idea how long he'd been sitting in the hall of what he'd figured out was an Aegis house, but he really could use an opportunity to stretch his legs and hit the bathroom. Why the fuck his brothers had brought him here instead of leaving him at the hospital was beyond his comprehension.

Being chained up there was just as good as being chained up here, and likely less hazardous to his health, given how the Guardians eyed him like they wanted to drag him outside and use him for target practice.

The door across from him opened, and Shade came out of the room.

'So.' Shade crossed the hall and stopped in front of Lore. 'What's your deal? We haven't had a chance to chat.'

'Too bad, too, because you seem like such a nice guy,' Lore drawled.

Shade thunked him in the forehead with his palm. 'Says the guy who tried to kill his own brothers.'

'Yeah, about that.' Lore glanced down at his arm, and then glanced at the matching set of markings that marched their way up

Shade's forearm. 'I know you and your brothers are a breed of incubi. So I'm guessing I am, too?'

'What did you think you were?'

'Dude, I didn't even know I was a demon until I was in my twenties.'

Shade gave him a you're-a-dumbass look. 'The fact that you were born with a *dermoire* wasn't a clue?'

'*Dermoire?* That's what it's called?' At Shade's nod, Lore shook his head. 'I wasn't born with it. It appeared when I was twenty.' He remembered the hell he'd gone through immediately prior to the appearance of the markings, the insane desire to have constant sex when, for twenty years, he'd not even gotten an erection.

'It *appeared* when you were twenty?' Shade frowned. 'What species was your mother?'

'Human.'

'Well, there's one piece of the puzzle. You're a cambion. Half-breed. Which is why we can't sense you.' He looked down the hall where two Aegis slayers weren't even attempting to be covert as they watched them. Shade flipped them off and turned back to Lore. 'So your human mother named you *Lore*?'

'Loren,' he mumbled.

Shade eyed him with sympathy. Because, yeah, *Shade* was such a great name. 'When were you born?'

'Eighteen-eighty.'

'Then you were one of our father's firsts. Idiot either didn't know any better than to impregnate a human, or he was already off his rocker.'

'You know, I'm not feeling the love here.' Lore shifted, wincing at the tingles shooting up his leg, which had fallen asleep.

'Our father got off on fucking things he shouldn't.'

Lore had no idea what that was supposed to mean, but Shade's tone didn't invite questions, and really, Lore had more to worry about than his deadbeat dad's choice of bedmates. Besides, Lore didn't have a lot of room to judge.

'Where is he?'

'Dead.' He gestured to Lore's *dermoire.* 'What's your gift?'

'Gift?' Lore laughed. 'Is that what you call it? Can you kill everything you touch, too?'

Shade cocked an eyebrow. 'I can kill with my gift, but I have to make an effort to use it that way. Its primary purpose is to force ovulation in females.'

Since Shade was an incubus, that made sense. 'Can all Seminus demons do that?'

'Wraith can get inside female heads and make them receptive to sex. Eidolon can ensure an egg is fertilized. You said you kill *everything* you touch?'

'Yeah. Except it didn't affect Eidolon.'

'Could be the brother thing ... or it could be because E had activated his own gift, and maybe they countered each other.'

It had to be the sibling thing. Lore had never hurt his sister with his touch, either. 'So why is my *gift* all fucked up?'

'Probably has something to do with the cambion thing. We're not meant to breed with humans. Stuff tends to go wrong with the offspring. Obviously.'

'Is there anything else I should know about? You know, that might *go wrong*?'

Shade appeared to consider that. 'Oh, hey, you're probably sterile. You know how when a donkey and a horse or a water sprite and a fire sprite—'

'I got the picture,' Lore snapped. For some reason, the sterile thing annoyed the shit out of him, but he had no idea why, since he couldn't fucking have sex without killing his partner. Having kids was a moot point.

Shade said something under his breath about him being high-strung. 'So why did you think killing me and Eidolon would be a good idea?'

'Some dude named Roag paid me.'

'And you didn't know who he was?' Shade threw back his head

and laughed, but the sound wasn't one of amusement. 'That sick sonofabitch.'

'Can I get in on the joke?'

'He was our brother.'

'Brother? As in, that sick fuck, too?'

'Yep. No doubt he knew who you were all along. I'll bet he had it arranged so that when you got the money for killing us, you'd learn the truth.'

Fun guy, his insane brother. Of course, the one in front of him didn't strike him as a load of laughs, either. 'I'm glad he's dead.'

'Well, he's not exactly dead. But he's suffering a fate worse than death. Trust me.'

A commotion in the front room brought Shade to his feet. The pounding of heavy footsteps and hushed curses heralded the arrival of something ... not good.

Wraith stalked into the hall, his arms cradling a body. The human male, Kynan. Oh, cool.

Gem's scream pierced the silence, and his feeling of satisfaction shattered.

'No ... no ... *no*!' She'd been in the room with the sick woman, and now she stood in the doorway, disbelief and horror etched on her face. She backed away, hand over her mouth, shaking her head, and as Lore watched, she stumbled and fell to the floor.

Wraith moved slowly down the hall toward the bedroom, his eyes closed, but his aim never wavering. Shade uttered a soft curse and moved aside as Wraith took the body to Gem and laid it before her.

'No, Wraith ... no!' She grabbed his hand, pleading with him to make Kynan not be dead.

Shade and Wraith both bowed their heads until Gem collapsed on top of Kynan, her sobs wracking her body.

Wraith seemed to weigh a thousand pounds as he went to Serena.

No one in the room seemed to know what to do, but Gem's cries lanced Lore's heart. He should use this opportunity to comfort her, to take advantage of her loss. Had he been the one to kill Kynan, that's what he would have done.

But seeing her suffer wasn't pleasant.

'Shade.' The guy didn't move. 'Shade!'

'*What?*' He was still standing, head bowed.

'Release me.'

'Fuck off.'

'Shade.' Lore swallowed, knowing this was crazy and that it might not work because he didn't know how Kynan had died, but he had to try. 'I might be able to help.' He kept his voice low, not wanting to give any false hope.

Shade turned, slowly, eyes bloodshot and narrowed. 'If this is a trick, know that I have no problem killing a sibling.'

Lore gave a single nod, and Shade crouched, released the chains holding him.

With Shade on his heels, he moved to Gem and Kynan. She was draped over him, her face buried in his throat.

Drawing a deep breath, Lore crouched at Kynan's feet. He grasped the human's still-warm ankle. He concentrated, let his 'gift' work its way down his shoulder to his fingers, until his markings glowed. A wave of energy spread up the human's leg, into his torso, his chest, his extremities.

The heart sparked. But the body was drained of blood, and it took several precious minutes for his marrow to start churning, creating new blood to fill his veins.

Gem turned to Lore, her eyes nearly swollen shut, but possessive anger shone through her misery. 'Get away from him!'

Shade knelt next to her and whispered something in her ear. She nodded and went back to sobbing.

There. The heart beat. Once. Twice. It shuddered as though unsure what to do next . . . and then it started up in a strong, steady beat. Kynan's chest rose, and his lips parted as he took in a giant, choking breath.

'Kynan?' Gem scrambled off him. '*Kynan?*'

'Yeah,' he rasped. 'Fuck. Yeah.'

Gem shrieked with joy and threw herself around him. Lore stood and backed away. A hand came down on his shoulder. Shade's.

'Thanks.'

'Don't mention it,' Lore said. '*Really.*'

Fuck, that was a stupid thing to do. Lore rubbed his hand across his chest, over the hand-shaped scar over his heart. These guys might have the answer to who he was, but really, did it matter? He could pretend to be his own man, could pretend to be a free agent. But the truth was that he was on a short leash connected to the fist of a demon who could – and did – call him to service at any time, on short notice, and for truly vile jobs.

He'd feel the life Lore brought back, and there would be punishment. On top of the punishment for not fulfilling the contract to kill the brothers. If there was one thing Detharu couldn't abide, it was reneging on a vow.

That, and being cheated out of his cut of the death money.

So Lore was in for a shitload of pain.

Good thing, then, that he liked it.

TWENTY-NINE

Wraith ignored the Guardians who gawked at the state of his clothes, at the blood dripping off him, and yeah, maybe at the sight of the little piece of Heaven in his hand. Only Val wasn't staring. He was sitting quietly in a chair next to Serena's bed, head bowed, holding her hand.

Relief that Kynan was alive was tempered by the fact that Serena lay deathly still on the bed, her chest rising and falling with shallow breaths. Shade gripped her wrist and channeled some of his gift into her.

'She's okay,' he said softly. 'I'm just keeping her asleep to slow down the . . . ' He didn't need to finish.

'Well, demon?' asked the Elder named Juan.

'Yeah, yeah. I got your precious amulet.' Wraith let the necklace slide through his fingers, totally getting off on how everyone – everyone except Val – was on their toes, holding their breath, waiting to see what he'd do.

'You need to hand that thing over, demon.' This from the one female Elder, Regan.

'To you?'

'Yes.' She held out her hand. 'The Aegis is the best qualified to keep it—'

Wraith laughed. 'Seriously, you people are so full of yourselves.' He stepped forward. 'I'll give it to Tayla then.'

'No!' Juan looked like he was going to stroke out. 'She's … she's … '

'Half demon?' Wraith offered. 'But she is a Guardian, and aren't they the best qualified to keep it?'

Serena's rattling breath reminded him that he needed to stop fucking around. Remembering what Reaver had said, he crouched next to the only human in the room besides Serena who was worthy of breathing the Earth's air.

Kynan was still sitting on the floor, sweat beaded on his pallid skin, being held up, as far as Wraith could tell, by Gem.

Kynan tensed. 'Wraith, no—'

Wraith looped the chain around Kynan's neck and stood. 'It's yours, man. The fate of all humankind is in your hands.' He winked. 'No pressure.'

While the humans gaped at Kynan, Wraith caught Lore by the shoulders. 'You. You can bring back the dead?'

The guy watched him calmly. 'Sometimes.'

Wraith shoved him into the wall. 'No half answers. I want to know that if something happens to her—' he pointed to Serena '— you can fix her.'

Lore's gaze was flat and black. 'What's killing her?'

'Demon infection.'

'Then no. Has to be a natural cause.'

Wraith gestured to Kynan. 'Having his blood drained by a vampire isn't exactly a natural fucking cause.'

'But bleeding out is.' Lore shrugged. 'Your female's problem is supernatural. Nothing I can do except make it happen faster.'

The casually spoken suggestion that Lore could put her down easily flash-seared Wraith's temper. But before he could rip the guy limb from limb, Shade put an arm around his chest and dragged him away.

'Not the time, bro,' Shade said. 'Not the time.'

Shade was right, but that didn't stop Wraith from shooting Lore a 'you're mine later' glare as he scooped up Serena. 'We're taking her to UG. Now.'

He'd wanted her to be around people she knew while he was battling Byzamoth, but now he wanted her to have the best medical care available in an environment he thought of as home.

Home. Actually, he'd never thought of it that way. Until now. Because he'd just realized that home was the place you returned to when things were bad.

And this was as bad as it could get.

ᘓ

Kynan sat there, unmoving and in shock as Shade and Wraith whisked Serena toward the door. Val tried to interfere, just once, but Wraith said something that froze him right to the floor.

As they were leaving, Reaver entered, looking like he'd been through a meat grinder, but at least he was alive. The last Kynan had seen of him, he'd looked about one breath away from his last. Then again, right after that, Kynan had taken his own last breath.

Wraith held Serena against his chest, but he paused long enough to give Reaver a respectful nod, which was returned, and then the two brothers were gone.

Gem still hadn't let go of Kynan, was wrapped around him like a blanket. Tears had left black streaks down her cheeks, but he'd never seen anything so beautiful. If he'd known he had to die to get her back, he'd have done it sooner.

And wait – how *had* he come back?

Juan turned on Kynan. 'This was a huge mistake. Hand over the necklace. The Sigil will guard it.'

Regan shook her head, making her long, dark ponytail swish around her thighs. 'Once the necklace is donned, it cannot be removed except by an angel.'

'Only if he's charmed,' Reaver said, 'which he's not. But if anyone tries to take it, they go through me.'

The Elders appeared less than thrilled about that prospect.

A curious warmth emanated from the cloudy crystal at the end of the chain, heating his skin. How could something so small – about the size of a marble – have caused so much trouble? It looked innocent enough, but it was a freaking piece of *Heaven.* He couldn't even wrap his mind around that, around the fact that he was *touching* it.

Wraith had obviously made a huge mistake by giving the thing to him. The Sigil would be the best guardians for it. He reached for it, prepared to hand it over.

A blinding flash caught them all off guard. When the light faded, Kynan nearly swallowed his tongue.

Standing in the middle of the room, bathed in a pale glow, was an angel. Female, with spun-gold hair and dressed in a white tunic that fell to the knee. She wore a sword in a scabbard at her hip, and in her hand was a golden scythe.

She looked at everyone in the room, and they pretty much gaped in awe right back. 'Aegi. Guardians of the human race. You humble me. I am Gethel. Greetings.'

She moved toward Kynan, her footsteps silent, her stride graceful, and he felt like a mouse caught in a cat's sights. He wanted to kneel or something, but he couldn't move even though his heart was hammering so hard he thought his rib cage might crack. She smiled as though she knew what he was thinking.

'You honor your race, human.' She touched him on the shoulder, and an odd, amazing energy shot through him. 'You are charmed.'

Stop gaping. 'Why?'

'You gave your life to save all that exists.' She smiled. 'And you hold the amulet.'

'You should give it to someone else.'

'Why is that?' There was a fierce intelligence in her eyes that told him she knew his answer.

'Because,' he said, bowing his head, 'I'm not worthy.'

'You feel you aren't worthy because you strayed from the path you were on?'

That about covered it. He'd lost himself for so long, and he wasn't a hundred percent sure he was back.

She touched him lightly on the face. 'You were tested. You fell and returned to your path. Only someone with extraordinary strength can set their lives right again. Those who have never fallen have not proved their resolve by finding their way back.'

'But . . . why me?'

'You are descended from Sariel.'

'Grigori,' Kynan breathed. 'A Watcher.' The Grigori were angels sent to Earth to watch over the human race, but they'd eventually succumbed to lust and mated with women. The Army was right.

And he born of man and angel shall die in the face of evil and may yet bear the burden of Heaven . . .

Heaven . . . he touched the amulet. Heofon. *My God.*

'Indeed.' She smiled at him. 'You will play a vital role in the Final Battle, as will your offspring. They will be born charmed – the first to have the charm passed on in such a way – and you will raise them as warriors. For someday, they will fight for all humankind.'

'Okay.' Okay? An angel had just told him that the future of mankind was in the hands of him and his offspring, and he says *okay*?

She laughed, a light, musical sound. 'Okay.'

Hand dropping to the hilt of her sword, she swung around to Reaver, who had propped himself against the wall. His hair hung in ropes around his face, he looked half-wild, but he pushed away from the wall and faced Gethel, shoulders back, pride in his eyes.

'Reaver.' She moved to him, halting a foot away. 'You interfered where you were forbidden. You associated with demons and revealed divine secrets to them.'

'I did.' Reaver bowed his head, and when he raised it, his eyes glowed with defiance. 'And I would not change a thing.'

Her fingers caressed her broadsword's ruby pommel, and

Kynan's pulse went tachy. Gem feared for Reaver as well, her fingers digging into Ky's chest as she tensed up.

'Strange, isn't it,' Gethel said, 'that alongside humans, demons and a fallen angel saved the world.' She leaned in and said softly, so softly that Kynan barely heard, 'You did well.'

A shell-shocked look glazed Reaver's eyes as she stepped back. Light enveloped the ex-angel, and suddenly, he appeared as he must have before he fell. He was . . . golden. No blood, no injuries.

A smile of ecstasy split his face as he tilted his head back and spread his arms wide. A sense of peace flooded the room, and then Reaver was gone in a fading shimmer.

'He is home,' Gethel said softly. 'He is home.'

Gem couldn't believe this was happening. An angel – a real divine being – was gliding around the room, speaking to every human for a moment before moving on to the next.

Gem figured she'd be ignored, but then Gethel was before her, smiling kindly, as if Gem wasn't a demon. Gem stood, because she couldn't very well speak to an angel from the floor.

You are not a demon, the angel said, though her lips hadn't moved. Gem heard her in her head.

But I am. My father—

Raped your mother. You were born of a human woman, by no choice of her own. Your soul is human.

Seriously?

The angel nodded. *Yes. How you treat that soul is up to you.*

But . . . Kynan. If he is to have charmed children, I can't . . . I mean, I couldn't . . .

Gethel's eyes seemed to blaze. *You can. And as long as you are with Kynan, you will share his immortality. You, too, have a role to play.*

Gem blinked, and then she was standing in the room that had been crowded with people, but she was alone with Kynan, who pulled her into his arms like he was never going to let her go. Not that she'd let him do that.

'So,' she murmured, 'you're some sort of immortal prophecy guy now, huh?'

'Looks like.' He looped a finger in a lock of her hair. 'I always wanted to save the world. Be careful what you wish for, I guess.'

She blinked back sudden tears that stung her eyes. 'God, you scared me. When Wraith brought you back—'

'Shh.' He held a finger to her lips. 'It's over.'

She punched him in the shoulder. 'Don't do that again.'

'I'm sort of immortal now,' he said, 'so I'm thinking it won't happen again.' He brushed her hair back from her face. 'But Gem, where do we stand?'

She opened herself up to her Shreddervision, and nearly gasped at what she saw.

Nothing.

He was as scar-free as a newborn baby.

'I believe you, Ky. I blamed you, but all along, the problem was mine. I've been a product of two worlds for so long, neither one fully accepting me, and it didn't seem possible that I could live with you in just one world.'

'So what changed your mind?'

'You died, Kynan. I had so many regrets. And I realized that what you did wasn't just for humans, it was for all species – human, animal, demon. I belong to two worlds ... but you know what? We also all share the same one. And our kids? They'll belong in one world. Ours.'

'That sounds really ... enlightened. And maybe a little sappy.'

'You're making fun of me.'

'Yup. Being raised from the dead puts me in a good mood.' He frowned. 'How did that happen, anyway?'

'Ah, trust me, you don't want to know.'

His gorgeous blue eyes glowed as his gaze intensified into something that took her breath away. 'I love you, Gem.'

The words she'd waited so long to hear settled in her heart, where Kynan had always been, and where he would always be. 'Good thing, because it seems that we both have roles to play.'

His lids grew heavy, and his voice went low and bedroom deep. 'Maybe we should get started on that roleplaying, then. . . .'

THIRTY

Serena wasn't sure how she ended up in a hospital – at least, she thought it was a hospital. Her vision was blurry and her head was pounding, but she could make out medical equipment. And other, less scary stuff, like chains and giant iron pincers. The steel-gray walls made the room seem cavernous, with dried-blood-colored writing and symbols marking them like cave drawings.

She closed her eyes and wondered if she was dreaming. Sucked to be dreaming about a hospital, though. And the beeping sounds were so real . . .

'Hey.'

Josh's voice drifted down to her, and she smiled, eyes still closed. 'Hey. Did we win?'

'We crushed them.'

'The amulet?'

'Couldn't be safer.'

She dragged in a relieved breath and tried to pretend she didn't hear death rattles in her lungs. 'Am I in a hospital?'

'Underworld General. The medical center I told you about. We treat a lot of nonhumans here.'

She was pretty sure he wasn't talking about a veterinary practice. 'Where's Val?'

'On a plane to New York. So, he's your father?'

'Apparently.'

He took her hand and massaged her palm, bringing circulation into her chilled fingers. 'As soon as his plane lands, I'll make sure you get to see him.'

That wasn't going to happen, and they both knew it. But it was nice of him to lie. 'I wish . . . I wish I could stay.'

'Don't go.' Josh's voice cracked, and she felt his forehead come down on her arm. 'Please . . . don't go.'

Needing to see him, blurry vision or not, she opened her eyes. 'I wouldn't change anything, you know. I would still have made love to you.'

A hot tear hit her arm. 'I would change everything,' he rasped. 'Anything for you to not be . . . not be . . . '

'Dying.' Ignoring the tug of the IV line, she sifted her fingers through his silky hair, remembering the way it had slid over her skin when he'd kissed his way down her body. The way it tickled her thighs when he'd pleasured her with his clever tongue. 'You can say it. It's okay. But there's one thing I'd change.' Her face heated when he looked up at her, his eyes red-rimmed and watery.

'What?'

'I would have – God, this is going to sound so stupid – asked you to bite me. You know, the vampire thing.'

One corner of his mouth tipped up. 'I wanted to. You can't know how much I wanted to.'

She drew in a sharp breath. 'Maybe you could . . . could you turn me into one?'

He looked down, as if he were ashamed. 'I can't. I'm not a true vampire.' He bit his lip, the tip of one sexy fang making a deep indent. 'But . . . would you really want to?'

'Become a vampire?' It sounded crazy when she said it out loud, no matter how fascinated she'd been by them. Then again, she was in a demon hospital. 'Are you serious? Is it even possible if I'm infected with a demon disease?'

'I don't know. Just ... hang on, okay?' He ran his palm up her arm to her neck to hold her jaw steady as he brushed his lips over hers. She barely felt the contact, but the emotion behind it came out strong, and it warmed her icy body. 'If this happens, I want you to bond with me.'

'Bond? Like marriage?'

'Sort of. But deeper. More permanent.'

She started to cry. She didn't know exactly what bonding entailed, but she sensed that for him to want it was a monumental step.

'It's okay,' he said quickly. 'You don't have to.'

'It's not that.' She sniffed and tried to swipe at her tears, but she could no longer lift her arm. Josh knew, and he caught them with his fingers as if they were precious diamonds. 'I always dreamed of having a family, but with the charm, it couldn't happen. And now ... now that it's within my grasp ... ' She was going to die.

'Fuck that.' Josh shouted for his brothers, who were there in an instant.

'What do you need?' Shade asked, as Eidolon checked her IV and the various machines hooked up to her.

'Keep her well until I get back. And while I'm gone, explain the bond to her.' He kissed her tenderly. 'I'll be back in a little while. Don't ... go anywhere.'

She opened her mouth to tell him she loved him, but nothing came out.

And now he'd never know.

൭

As Wraith stood in the antechamber to the Vampire Council's meeting room, he prayed to anyone who would listen that the assholes hurried. Gods, he couldn't believe he was doing this. Couldn't believe he was considering changing the female he loved into the one species that made his skin crawl.

He'd spent his life killing vampires when and where he could, and now he was not only going to get on his knees to beg them for a favor, but he was going to do it so he could spend eternity with one.

Obviously, being charmed didn't cure insanity, because this … this was crazy.

The iron-studded wood door to the main chamber creaked open, and a massive vamp wearing a black robe and a sword at his hip filled the doorway. 'The Council awaits,' he droned.

'I'll bet it does,' Wraith muttered, as he brushed past the male.

Inside, red and black candles burned in silver sconces and copper candelabras, lighting a room that could have been a B-movie set. From the crimson throw rugs shot with gold and the life-sized, gilded portraits of vampire heroes dating all the way back to ancient Rome, the place was a Hollywood cliché.

The Council members – seventeen of them – sat in a semi-circle in their high-backed thrones. The highest-ranking vampire in the world, the Key, motioned Wraith forward. It took every ounce of willpower Wraith possessed to obey Komir when what he wanted to do was stake them all.

'This is unexpected, incubus,' Komir said as Wraith halted in the center of a pentagram that had been set into the floor with white marble tiles. 'What brings you?'

'A request.'

A black-haired female to Komir's right laughed. 'You, who mocks vampire law and kills your own kind, want something from us?'

'That about sums it up.' As soon as the words were out of his mouth he regretted them, and offered a stiff, 'Apologies. I'm exhausted. You know, from saving the world.'

One of Komir's silver eyebrows shot up. 'Yes, we heard.' He tapped his fingers on the arm of his throne. 'So what do you want, oh, great hero?'

Sarcastic ass. Wraith respected that, though he hated to respect anything about these fuckwits. He could have asked one of UG's vampire staff members to turn Serena, but he couldn't risk the consequences. It went against vampire law to turn a human without permission from the Council. Those who broke the law were subject to a variety of punishments, including execution, a fate shared by their prodigies.

'The human I would take as my mate is dying. I, ah … humbly … beg that she be turned.' He'd rather be beaten than beg for anything. But this was for Serena, and for her, he'd plead until he turned blue.

A low rumble came from a red-haired male at the end of the semi-circle. 'You slaughtered my brother. I'd rather kill you than help you.'

Several others murmured in agreement with Red, and Wraith's gut did a slow slide to his feet. They were going to turn him down.

'Please,' Wraith said, bowing his head. 'I'll do anything.'

Komir sat there, all imperious. After a long, dramatic silence, he addressed the Council. 'Who objects to Wraith's request?'

Everyone raised their hand, and Wraith's knees went rubbery.

'Council aside, I'm inclined to grant you this favor,' Komir said, and Wraith's heart leaped. 'But it goes against everything we are. We must choose those we change very carefully. A vampire who sires another is responsible for introducing the changeling to vampire culture. We spend a year with them, teaching our ways, sharing everything from feeding to sex.'

Wraith went taut, couldn't prevent the low-pitched growl in his chest. No vampire would take Serena to bed. Ever. 'I will do that.'

'You? You've shunned vampire society and made a mockery of it. Murdered your own kind without mercy.'

'I was wrong.'

'You lie.'

Of course he did. Serena's life was on the line, and he'd never had a problem with lying. He was usually more convincing, however.

He stepped forward. 'See these eyes? They should be brown. But they're blue because vampires gouged out the ones I was born with. *Vampires.* Before they did it, they hung me from rafters and peeled off my skin. Burned the soles of my feet with blowtorches. Gutted me so my brothers had to shove everything back in and tack my intestines in place so they wouldn't slide down to my nail-less toes.' He stepped out of the circle he was supposed to be standing inside. 'So tell me, you bunch of dickless fucks, why I should have embraced my vampire half. *Tell me!*'

Several of them looked away.

'That's what I thought.'

Komir stood. 'Your brothers informed us of your past. Your greatest fear is torture, is it not?'

'It's my second greatest fear,' Wraith said, his voice strong and sure. 'My first is to lose Serena.'

'I almost believe you.'

'You'd better.'

'Perhaps you should prove it.' Komir walked from around the half-moon table and stopped beside a blood-stained platform. 'There has been much pain on both sides – yours and ours. But there will be more. If you wish to save your female, you will face your fear to do it.'

Oh, fuck.

'Are you willing?'

Wraith glanced at the platform, and flashbacks of being strung up in the warehouse blazed through his mind.

He fought to stay upright as he faced Komir. The charm couldn't protect him from this if he agreed to it. 'Yes.'

'Then bring her to me.'

Relief flooded Wraith, but dread followed on its heels when he glanced at the altar. No way was Serena coming here, to be laid out like a sacrifice on the stone slab. He knew how the ritual worked. The human would be stripped and laid out before the Council. The members would inspect the human, touch them in whatever manner they wished until the sire, also naked, mounted them. Sex wasn't required to make the change, but it went hand-in-hand, and often while sharing blood, the sire and victim fucked as the Council observed. Or participated.

'You'll go to her,' Wraith said.

Komir steepled his fingers in front of him. 'You don't truly want this, do you?'

'Serena is too sick to move.' To be safe, he added through gritted teeth, 'If it should please you.'

A draft of cold air circulated around the room, bringing with it the Key's displeasure. He flashed from where he was standing to directly behind Wraith, pressed his chest to Wraith's back as he leaned in and put his mouth to Wraith's ear.

'None of this pleases me,' he murmured. 'But that you would take a vampire as a mate after all you've suffered … perhaps it's time that the Council gives you a fresh start. But Serena will be mine to indoctrinate into vampire life.'

Wraith wanted to wail with grief, but if this was the only way to keep her from dying, he'd have to deal with it. Somehow.

But the second she was released from Komir's care, Wraith was bonding with her. She was *his* and he was going to make sure no male of any species touched her ever again.

'Yes,' he rasped. He cleared his throat and said louder, so everyone in the fucking room could hear. 'Yes.'

Komir bared his teeth. 'Then let's go kill your woman.'

THIRTY-ONE

Wraith rushed into Serena's room with Komir on his heels. Shade was sitting at Serena's bedside, head bowed, fingers wrapped so tightly around her wrist that her hand had turned white. Shade's *dermoire* was glowing fiercely, and Wraith knew he was burning a buttload of energy to keep her alive. Shade didn't even look up at him. Didn't say a word.

This was bad. Very, very bad.

Eidolon came in behind Wraith. He was in scrubs, his stethoscope looped around his neck, looking every bit the doctor he was – including his somber expression.

'I'm sorry, Wraith,' he said softly, 'but the moment Shade lets go—'

'Then don't let go.' Wraith turned to Komir. 'It'll still work, right?'

'Perhaps. If she is able to swallow blood.' Komir shook his head. 'There's always a risk – fully ten percent of turnings don't take. And with her being this far gone . . . '

'Ah . . . what's going on?' Eidolon eyed Komir. 'Is this what I think it is?'

'If you're thinking your brother wants me to turn this human into a vampire, then yes, it's what you think it is.'

'Hell's bells,' Shade muttered, still not looking up.

'I won't argue about this,' Wraith said. E held up his hands and took a step back.

Komir moved to Serena's side, and Wraith's heart rate jacked up. Nerves and jealousy were going to tear him apart. Though the elder vamp must have felt the waves of heat coming off Wraith, he ignored them. He walked around the head of the bed and braced Serena's face in his hands. Gently, he tilted her head to the side. His fangs extended, huge suckers that were, in a moment, going to be buried deep in Serena's neck.

'It would be better if I were lying with her—'

'No!' Wraith shouted, and E grabbed him before he could do something stupid, like lay out the vampire. The writing on the walls began to pulse as the threat of violence grew.

'Idle down, bro,' E said, and Wraith backed toward the door, a terrible, possessive ache centering in his chest. Maybe if he didn't watch . . .

Komir released Serena, and oh, fuck, Wraith had just ruined everything. The vampire brushed past him. 'Come with me.'

Wraith had no choice but to follow, and once they were outside the room, Komir turned to him. 'Strike me.'

The Haven spell prevented violence, but, like Serena's charm, if the person wanted the violence, that was different. 'Why?'

'Let your aggression out now, demon. The ritual cannot be interrupted.'

Wraith clenched his fists. 'We don't have time for this.'

'Then may I strike you?'

'Fine. Then let's get on with—' Komir's fist slammed into Wraith's mouth with the force of a wrecking ball, knocking him sideways and splashing blood onto the wall. Another blow came at him, but Wraith spun out of reach and smashed his fist into Komir's jaw.

The vampire crashed into a cart and slid ungracefully to the floor. He looked down at his bloodied knuckles and winced. 'You have a hard right hook *and* a hard face.' He shook his hand and shoved it into his mouth. His entire body tensed, and he jerked his hand from his lips. He stared at it. Then he stared at Wraith. 'You taste of . . . angel.'

'Ah, that. I sort of drank from one today—'

Komir came to his feet and touched his slicked-back silver hair, as though it might have gotten messed up during the scuffle. 'Then you don't need me.'

Hope soared through Wraith, followed immediately by confusion. 'What do you mean?'

'Our race . . . it was created by fallen angels. Their blood flows through our veins. It is the fallen angel blood that activates the turn.'

'So if Serena drinks my blood before Reaver's blood filters out . . .'

'Yes. Go.'

'I don't know how. The details.' The admission shamed him. He'd spent too many years mired in hate to learn anything about vampires besides how to hunt and kill them.

'It's instinct, Wraith,' Komir said. 'Feed beyond the point of no return, but not until the heart stops completely. Then give her your blood. As much as she'll take. The more, the better.'

'And after that?'

'You come to me. You have a promise to keep.'

So even though he was going to be the one turning Serena, they were still going to torture him. Bastards.

'Thank you.'

Komir bowed his head. 'What you did at Temple Mount has earned you the Council's gratitude.'

'You have a funny way of showing it,' he muttered, but he didn't hang around. He darted into Serena's room and dropped to his knees beside her bed. Wasting no time, he sank his teeth into her thin wrist as gently as possible.

Serena's blood hit his tongue, the rich flavor making him both moan and flinch. The tang of death tainted the sweet spice. It poured down his throat in a cascade of warm silk, and he wished like hell that he was drinking from her in a frenzy of passion instead of draining her in the hopes that she'd come back to him.

The flow began to thin and slow, even as her heart frantically tried to compensate for the blood loss. Her pulse tapped against his teeth as she hit the critical stage that tempted all vampires. At this point, they had a choice: stop and let their prey live or take a few more pulls and feel the high as the victim started to die.

Wraith needed her to die.

He took two more strong pulls. Her pulse was weak and thready, barely there. Quickly, he leaped to his feet and used his fangs to open a vein in his wrist. He held it to her lips. Blood ran in a thick stream down her chin.

'E? Why isn't she feeding?' Panic made his question into a shout.

'She's too far gone.' Eidolon cursed. 'We'll have to force it down.' He palmed her forehead with one hand and placed the other on her chin to open her mouth, CPR style. 'We may need to insert a feeding tube.'

Wraith fired up his gift and dove into her mind. It was all swirling light in there, no substance, no awareness except for a heart-shattering sadness.

'Oh, no, my *lirsha,*' he whispered. 'Come back. Come back to your dreams. I'm here. I'm waiting.' He inserted himself into the swirling light, forcing substance to form around him. He put himself in front of the Great Pyramid, with golden sands all around him.

And then she was there. Standing in front of him in a sheer, flowing white gown. 'Where have you been? I've been so lost.'

'I've been right here, baby. I'll always be right here.' He caught her by the shoulders and brought her to him. 'I'm going to have to let you go, but only for a little while.'

'But—'

'Do you trust me?'

Her liquid eyes beamed up at him. 'Yes.'

He struck, burying his fangs in her throat. She gasped before sighing and relaxing against him. She tasted good here, no taint of death. Just the pure, sweet nectar that only she could have running through her veins. He wanted to make love to her in the dream, but even now he felt her fading in his arms.

Reluctantly, he disengaged his fangs. Reaching up, he cut open his own throat with the blade he imagined in his hand.

'Josh!'

'Shh. It's okay. Drink. Drink now, and drink hard. Hurry, Serena!'

She latched on as if she'd been feeding for centuries. She was a hunter, with killer instincts whether she was seeking ancient relics or taking blood. So. Freaking. Hot.

Distantly, he heard Eidolon's voice. 'That's it, Serena. Swallow.'

It was working. She was drinking in the dream and in real life, and . . . she was gone. He was standing alone in the sand.

He snapped back into the hospital room, where she was swallowing weakly as his blood flowed onto her tongue.

The heart monitor beeped quietly. The blood pressure machine hissed as it released air from the cuff around her upper arm. An IV dripped saline incessantly into the tube connected to the back of one hand. And he stood there, feeling cold and empty.

Fuck that. This would not be a clinical operation. The woman he loved would take him the way this should happen. With him tangled up with her.

In one smooth move, he swung up on the narrow bed and stretched out beside her. As Serena swallowed, he nuzzled her throat and whispered to her. Soothing, comforting words he was surprised he knew. She was icy – too icy, and too still.

He didn't know how much time had passed when Eidolon peeled his arm away from her mouth and sent a healing wave into him to seal the wound.

'She's not drinking anymore,' E said. 'If this took, she'll wake tomorrow at dusk.'

'It will take,' Wraith said fiercely. 'It has to.' He spent a few more quiet moments with Serena before Eidolon shook his shoulder gently. 'It's time, bro.'

'No.'

'Wraith, Shade is about to collapse.'

Wraith glanced over at his brother, who was trembling so hard his teeth were chattering. His *dermoire*'s glow had faded and began to flicker.

'You've got to let her go.'

A sob welled up in Wraith's throat. The moment Shade let go of Serena, she'd die. And if the turning didn't take . . .

I'll lose her forever.

Eidolon gave Wraith's shoulder a little squeeze. *Oh, Gods* . . . Wraith closed his eyes and nodded. Instantly, Shade's power cut off, and Serena's chest stopped moving. Her heart thumped once. Twice.

And beat no more.

The only sound in the room after that was the sound of Wraith's scream.

THIRTY-TWO

Blackness swirled in an endless void. There was nothing there but a cold wind and a gnawing, relentless loneliness.

And hunger. Hunger . . . such as Serena had never experienced.

She felt like her stomach was caving in on itself with starvation. But the hunger went deeper than that. To the bone. To the soul.

She couldn't open her eyes, so she lay still and listened. She heard the thump-whoosh of a beating heart. Of whisper-light breaths. Another sense roared to life: smell.

She caught the scent of something smoky, maybe brimstone? Then there was the heady, musky odor of . . . Josh.

Warmth burned into her side, a heavy, satisfying heat that stretched from her shoulder to her toes. She peeled open her eyes, but closed them immediately against the intensity of the light above. After a moment, she tried again, driven by the insane hunger.

Squinting in what she now realized was very dim, reddish light, she looked up at the dark ceiling and the weird chains and pulleys she'd seen earlier. Josh was stretched out on the bed beside her, one leg over hers, one arm draped across her belly. His face was tucked against the crook of her neck and shoulder. He couldn't get any closer if he wanted to.

'Josh?' she said. Or tried to say. Her lips moved, but no sound came out. She licked her lips, her tongue catching on sharp points – *ouch.*

Were those . . . fangs?

The past few days rushed over her like an avalanche, cutting off her breath . . . breath? Wait . . . was she breathing? Sort of.

Vampire.

She'd talked to Josh about becoming a vampire, but that was all she remembered. Until now.

Hunger pangs sliced through her. With a yelp, she jackknifed into a sit.

Josh was right there in her face, eyes wide and mouth dropped open. 'Serena!'

'Hurts,' she moaned, clutching her belly. 'Hurts.'

Josh raised her upper lip with his thumb and let out a whoop of victory. 'Baby, it worked. Oh, man, it freaking worked!'

A veil of red came down over her vision and the sound of a beating heart drove her to the brink of madness. She wanted to attack him, to ravage his neck with her mouth, ravage his body with hers . . .

He seemed to know, and he tugged her to him, cocking his head aside to expose his throat. 'Take what you need,' he whispered. 'Take it now, and don't worry about hurting me – ow!'

She buried her new teeth in his neck, instinct guiding her beautifully. And nope, she wasn't worried about hurting him at all. She felt a moment of regret when he barked in pain, but then he moaned and pulled her down on top of him.

On some level, she thought she should be disgusted by the fact that she was drinking his blood, but the hunger had hijacked her body, and the need to just be with him had hijacked her heart and mind.

A deep, throbbing ache began between her thighs, and once again, he knew, because he dropped a hand and cupped her intimately. She'd been naked beneath the sheet. How handy.

His fingers were magic on her core, sliding through her slippery center and brushing her clit with just the right amount of pressure. His other hand fumbled with his jeans, and in seconds she felt his hard length rubbing where his fingers had been. He made a rough sound of need that matched hers. This would not be a long, leisurely encounter. Her desires roared through her on a primal level she couldn't understand.

He arched up as she gripped his rigid shaft and lowered herself onto it. The broad head stretched her sensitive opening, the velvet surface a bold contrast for the thick, textured shaft as it slid deep. The moment they locked together, she came in the most intense, longest-lasting orgasm of her life. Josh joined her, his shout of ecstasy ringing in her ears.

'Bond with me,' he panted as he came down. 'Be my mate.'

He took her left hand and threaded her fingers through his. The markings on his arm began to pulse. Feeling warm, a little drunk, and nicely sated, she lifted her head from his throat.

'Lick the punctures,' he rasped. 'Stops the bleeding.'

She did, and he groaned, pumped his hips so hard her knees came off the mattress. Another release roared through her, a full-body orgasm that hummed through her veins all the way to her skull.

Josh watched her with golden eyes. 'You're so beautiful.' His voice was like erotic thunder, and it rolled through her as yet another orgasm. He came, too, and before the last tremors had even quieted, he said again, 'Bond . . . with . . . me.'

Shade and Eidolon had explained the ritual, the benefits, and the consequences, though she'd faded in and out for a lot of the conversation. If what she remembered was true, the ritual involved the sharing of blood – which obviously wasn't a problem – and when it was over, she'd have markings on her arm to match Josh's. They'd be bonded for life, and neither could have sex with another.

She drew her finger down his chest. 'Explain to me the benefits.'

He gripped her hips and held her still, because every tiny movement made him hiss. 'Mindfuckingblowing orgasms. A mental connection. No more loneliness. Or empty sex. You'll have a protector. A partner. Someone who will love you forever.'

'Sweetheart, you sold me at the orgasms.'

'Gods, I love you.'

She smiled, and he reached up, stroked one of her fangs with his thumb. An incredible sensation shot to her core, and she nearly climaxed again. 'Oh. *Oh, my.*' Talk about an erogenous zone.

'They're so hot,' he said. 'I never thought I'd say that.'

'They feel . . . right.'

'They look right.'

She was a freaking *vampire*! Awesome. 'So, are we going to do this bond thing?'

'Oh, yeah. You've already taken my blood, so your half of the ritual is done.' He threw his head back and closed his eyes. 'Ride me. Ride me hard.'

He didn't have to tell her twice. She began to rock on top of him, felt the electricity build quickly between her thighs. He reached up to cup the back of her head and pull her down. She thought he was going to kiss her, but when he sank his fangs into her neck, she gasped.

And came. The world around her shattered, and she heard a shout, dimly realized it came from her.

He was right there with her. He grasped her left hand with his right, and his arm lit up. Fire shot from her fingers to her shoulder, and a sense of fulfillment poured into her as she collapsed onto his chest. For a long time, they lay like that, tangled up, exhausted, her breath coming in panting spurts.

'I'm a vampire,' she managed a few minutes later. 'Why am I breathing?'

'Eidolon says it's reflex. Like, the body doesn't remember it doesn't need to breathe.'

'Interesting. Guess we've got a lot to learn.' She sighed, because she'd become part of a new world, but in the old one, she had a father whose job description included vampire slaying. Talk about your dysfunctional families. 'I guess I'm going to need to call Val. Let him know I'm not dead.'

'Well, you sort of are. Undead, anyway. And yeah. Call. He's left about a thousand messages on my cell phone.'

'And won't he be thrilled to know I'm a vampire,' she muttered. She drew a harsh breath, remembering Josh's hatred of them. 'What about you? I know how you feel about them. Us.' God, this was surreal.

He tipped her face to his with a finger beneath her chin. 'I don't care what you are. Who you are doesn't change just because you grew fangs and are on a liquid diet.'

'But it's more than that, isn't it? Am I . . . evil?'

He snorted. 'If you believe those Aegis idiots.'

'So, I'm not?'

His hand came up to brush her hair out of her face. 'Becoming a vampire distills certain aspects of your personality into a purer form so you're a little more honest about who you are, whether that's evil or good, but you're still you.'

'I don't understand how you can get past the vampire thing, though, after everything—'

'Stop.' He rolled over and propped himself on one elbow, so she was looking up at him. 'I was totally fucked up and pissed off for so long. What my mother and her clan did to me . . . well, there are no words for it. But I blamed all vampires. Hell, I blamed the whole world. I've got a lot of apologizing to do. Starting with my brothers.'

She cocked her head, watching him, because something was different . . . 'Your face! The tattoo is gone. And you have a new one – no, two – around your neck.'

His fingers feathered over his cheek where the markings had been, and then down his throat. 'One means I'm post-*s'genesis*, and the other means I'm mated.'

She had no idea what the *s'genesis* thing was, but she had lots of time to ask about it. 'Well, I think they're better than wedding rings,' she teased. 'You can't take them off.'

'Smart-ass.' He nodded at her arm. 'That's what you get for being so smug.'

She lifted her left arm and watched in amazement as a replica of his tattoo began to set in her skin.

'You're mine now,' he said. 'No getting away.'

'You think I want to get away?'

'Hope not, because I'm a hunter, remember? I get what I want.'

She smiled. 'And what do you want? Right this minute?'

He showed her. Right that minute.

ᘐ

Wraith waited until Serena fell into a deep, exhausted sleep before he climbed out of bed and left her to recover from the feeding, the sex, the bonding, and the little thing of changing from human to vampire.

Leaving her was the hardest thing he'd ever done, but he had a few things to do, like arrange for his vampire torture and find his brothers. Considering what he needed to say to Shade and E, the torture sounded like fun.

He found them just down the hall in the staff break room, door open. They met him at the threshold.

'Everything okay?' Shade asked, and Wraith punched him in the shoulder.

'You know it is.' As incubi, they would have sensed sex taking place nearby.

'So Serena's all fangy?'

'And bonded.'

E cocked an eyebrow. 'Yeah, the lack of the facial *dermoire* was pretty much a dead giveaway.' He clapped Wraith on the back. 'Congratulations, man. It's good to know you're happy.'

'Yeah, about that.' Wraith moved inside the room. 'I owe you both an apology. More than that, but I don't know how I can make up for a lot of years of hell.'

His brothers just stood there, either stunned or not buying a word. Probably the latter. He'd never given them a reason to trust anything he said or did.

'So, ah . . . I'm sorry. You guys have bailed me out of a lot of shit situations. I can never make it up to you.' Wraith had to smile at his brothers' silence, because now they weren't meeting his gaze. The male sappy crap was embarrassing them. Good thing, because he'd hate to be alone in that.

'It's all good.' Shade's voice was low and rough with emotion.

Eidolon nodded. 'I think we're all good.'

'Bullshit.' Wraith swiped a couple of oranges out of Gem's basket on the counter and beaned his brothers with them. 'I put you through hell for a lot of years, and a sixty-second suck up job isn't going to erase that.'

'Well, hitting us with fruit isn't going to help!' Shade shouted, returning fire. The orange veered to the left, splattering on the wall.

'Hello,' Wraith taunted. 'Charmed.'

'Don't you have more sucking up to do?' E said, but his mouth was quirked in a half-smile.

'I do.' Wraith made a beeline for the coffeemaker, needing to take his mind off how much it bit dick to beg forgiveness. 'But it'll take a lot of time. I'm willing to do what it takes to make it up to you guys.'

E and Shade had fallen silent again.

'Look, why don't we change the subject?'

His brothers nodded vehemently.

'Okay, then. How's Tayla?' More than a change of subject, Wraith really did care. He'd wanted to kill the slayer in the beginning, but he couldn't deny that she was perfect for E. 'The Aegis dudes didn't take her demon thing well.'

'They wanted to execute her,' E growled. 'Kynan made them see the light.'

Shade smirked. 'Now that you made him the most important human on the planet, he threatened to walk if The Aegis didn't let Tayla stay on.'

'Ah, blackmail. I always knew that human had it in him.' Wraith would have loved to see that scene. 'So, did they welcome Ky back, too?'

'They made him an Elder.' Eidolon grinned. 'That sonofabitch is now in charge of the whole damned organization.'

Now, *that* was funny as hell. 'What about Gem?'

'She's moving Kynan into her place as we speak.' Eidolon bent to retrieve the orange Wraith had thrown at him.

'Good for her,' Wraith said. 'So what's with the new brother? And why was he able to bring back Ky?'

'A mating with a human gone wrong,' Shade said. 'His gift is all fucked up. He kills everything he touches, but apparently, he can bring the dead back within a brief time window—'

'And only if they aren't dying of a demon-inflicted disease,' Wraith finished, still slightly bitter about that. 'Where is he?'

'Gone,' Shade said. 'Guess he had some things to do. People to kill. Dunno.'

E tossed the orange into the basket. 'I think he's overwhelmed by the instant family. He'll be back.'

'Speaking of family,' Wraith said to Shade, 'when can I meet the nephews?' There was a long pause, too long, and Wraith added quickly, 'I won't eat them or anything. I swear.'

Shade went rigid. 'Why now?'

'I want to belong to a family,' Wraith blurted before he could rethink sounding like a candy-ass. 'I mean, I have Serena, but she's a vampire, which means she can't have kids. . . . ' He felt bad for that, not just for her, but strangely, for him. With her beside him, encouraging him, he knew he could be a good father. 'I was just thinking that maybe if we could, you know, just all hang out . . . fuck, I don't know. This is stupid. Never mind.'

Shade and Eidolon exchanged looks, as if they had a secret

between them. For a moment he was tempted to get inside Shade's head the way he always had and find out what they were hiding from him. But Shade hated that, and violating his brother's mind would make his pretty plea for forgiveness yet another lie.

'I get it.' Wraith backed toward the door, bumping against the frame. 'It's too late—'

He couldn't picture himself barbecuing hot dogs and playing fucking family board games anyway.

'Wraith, it's not that,' Shade said.

'Doesn't matter. Serena's waking up. I need to go to her.'

Shade called his name as he left, but Wraith just held up a hand to cut him off, and kept going. They might not trust him to be a functional member of the family yet, but they would. He'd earn their trust eventually, but right now, his focus was all on Serena.

She was tying the drawstring on a pair of scrub bottoms when he walked in. 'Hey,' she said, tilting her head to the side as she studied him. 'It's so weird seeing you without that face tattoo.'

'I figure I'll be in for one hell of a shock the next time I look in a mirror.' A good shock, though, like he'd had when he saw that his hourglass glyph had been set right again. He took her hand and pulled her against him, reveling in the feel of her soft curves against his hard body. 'You feeling okay?'

'Never better.' She smiled, and the points of her fangs peeked out from her parted lips. It was so freaking sexy Wraith wanted to throw her down and get inside her while she sank those hot little teeth into his throat.

What a difference a day makes. He was really starting to understand her hard-on for vampires. He was getting one himself. Literally. 'Babe, we *so* have to get out of here.' His swelling cock was way onboard with that plan.

'Where are we going?'

Such utter trust. Her faith in him tugged at his heart and at the same time scared the crap out of him. What if he broke her trust, failed her?

'You won't,' she said softly.

'How did you know what I was thinking?'

'I felt your fear. Didn't take a genius to figure out what it was about.'

He groaned playfully. 'This bond is going to be a pain in the ass.'

'Really?' She reached low and cupped him. 'Because I can feel your arousal, too ... and it's definitely sparking mine.'

Oh, yeah. He could feel it coming through the bond like an erotic drumbeat. 'So, maybe the bond won't be that bad.' His words came out on a moan thanks to the stroking action she'd started.

'So ... you were saying?'

'Right. We're going to my place ... ah, Gods, keep that up, just like that.' He arched into her touch. 'And after I ravage you, I'll start teaching you about life in my world. Are you all right with that?'

She flicked open the top button on his fly. 'Do the lessons have to start right away?'

'Probably a good idea,' he gritted out, but then she dropped to her knees. 'Lessons? What lessons?'

'That's what I thought.' The look in her gaze, the erotic promise, the trust, the love, brought him to his knees in front of her. She meant the underworld to him, and in that moment, he knew.

He would never fail her.

And the faith in her eyes said she knew it, too.

THIRTY-THREE

'They're here!' Serena forced herself to walk calmly to the front door, even though she wanted to sprint. Runa, Shade, and their babies would be on the other side – and she and Wraith would be meeting them for the first time.

It had been nearly a week since she and Wraith had arrived at his place – a very male bachelor pad in Manhattan – and after days of doing nothing but enjoying each other, they'd decided it was time to enjoy his family.

Especially because *her* family had already come and gone.

She'd called Val the moment she and Wraith left the hospital, and he'd been so happy she was alive that the fact she'd become a vampire hadn't bothered him. Much. He'd come to visit yesterday, and though they hadn't had enough time to work out all the issues they faced, from the relationship he'd had with her mother to his reasons for keeping the truth from her, to David, to Wraith's deception and her becoming a vampire ... well, truthfully, it was still a mess.

But Val was willing to repair the damage and heal all wounds. Chances were that he and Wraith would never bond over a game of golf, but she figured it wouldn't be long before they stopped eyeing each other warily over the rims of their whiskey glasses. The fact that they hadn't tried to kill each other was a start.

As for David ... she had a feeling things would never be right between her and her half brother. If he was ever released from Aegis custody for betraying the human race to a fallen angel, anyway.

Wraith – she'd finally gotten used to calling him that – met her in the foyer. 'You ready for this?' He took her hand. 'Because we can do this another time. They'll be at Kynan and Gem's wedding.'

That had been fun news. The pair had dropped by this morning to invite them to Hawaii next week – a wedding beneath the stars, a night ceremony so she, as a vampire, could attend. Wraith had groused and grumped about being asked to be Kynan's best man, but she'd caught him smiling for hours after Ky and Gem left.

'I'm ready.'

He'd warned her that his brothers and sisters-in-law could be overwhelming, but the little ones made her far more nervous, and he knew it.

She'd always wanted children, but as a vampire, she'd learned she was unable to conceive. The maternal ache drilled deep, but she couldn't complain. She was healthy and alive. *Sort of,* as Wraith liked to tease her.

'Let's meet the family.' She opened the door, surprised to find only Shade standing there with a squirming, blanketed bundle in his arms, Eidolon next to him.

'Runa's going to be pissed that you lost some kids,' Wraith drawled.

Shade's dark eyes sparked with an emotion she couldn't place. 'All three of our babies are home with Runa.'

Wraith and Serena stepped back to allow his brothers to come inside. 'So, what,' Wraith said, 'you just picking kids up off the street now?'

'It's yours, bro.'

'My what?'

'Kid.' Eidolon tugged on the blanket, exposing the child's right arm and the *dermoire* that marked it. 'It's yours.'

Serena wasn't sure who got it, who really *got it,* first, Wraith or herself. He stared at the baby, a little wild-eyed. She just stood there, afraid that what Eidolon had just said wasn't true. That this was a sick joke.

Wraith had made a baby with someone else, a fact that might have upset her if he hadn't explained his breed, his past ... and if she didn't understand how committed to her he was.

But somehow she just couldn't see this innocent life as anything but a wonderful gift and an answer to her prayers.

Shade hefted the infant closer to his chest, gently, protectively, and she turned to Wraith, who was still watching the baby as though unsure what to do.

'Hey,' she said, softly. 'You okay?'

He nodded numbly.

Surrounded by silence, Serena approached Shade. The baby stilled, his big brown eyes taking her in with that wisdom all infants seemed to be born with. He was beautiful, with Wraith's nose and mouth, and in an instant, she fell in love.

'May I?' she asked, and though Shade hesitated, he handed the child to her. In her arms, he felt right, and her heart swelled. She walked over to Wraith, slowly, afraid she'd spook him, because he still had that half-feral look in his eyes. 'Look at him. Look at your son.'

He swallowed, locked his gaze with hers. 'My ... son. I never thought ...'

'Just look at him. He's gorgeous.'

The moment his gaze connected with his son's, his expression softened, became one of wonder. 'The mother?' he murmured, and Eidolon cleared his throat.

'Suresh.'

Wraith's hand shook as he very carefully offered his finger to the baby, who wrapped his tiny fist around it. 'You'll be able to teleport someday, little guy.' He glanced at Serena. 'I'm sorry. This must not be easy for you. The female—'

'It's okay,' she said, and she wasn't lying. 'I know what you are, and what you were before we met.' She put the baby in Wraith's arms. He held his son as if the child were made of glass. 'He's yours, and now he's ours.'

Wraith closed his eyes. 'Are you sure? Because . . . I'm afraid.'

'Don't be. We'll learn about this parenting thing together. You'll be wonderful. Your heart is so big.'

He hooked his arm around her neck and brought her in close, so they were all sharing one big embrace. This was the moment she'd lived her entire life for. The one she wanted to hold onto and never forget.

'I love you, *lirsha,*' he murmured. 'All I ever had before you was nightmares. But now I dream. Because of you.'

'I've always dreamed,' she whispered. 'But I never thought they'd come true.' She pressed a tender kiss to the infant's forehead, and then brushed her lips over Wraith's. 'I have everything I've dreamed of and more.'

And when Wraith smiled down at her, she knew he felt the same way. For all eternity.

Demonica: a Demon Compendium

by Larissa Ione

Contents

The Introduction

People often ask me how I came up with the concept of a demon hospital. Basically, I've always been a fan of both the paranormal and emergency medicine, and one day, while watching an episode of *Angel*, the idea popped into my head. See, Angel (a vampire, for those who have never watched the super-awesome show) got hurt, and he needed medical attention right away. But really, where could he go? Where could any supernatural creature go?

Clearly, there was a need for an underworld hospital, and Underworld General was born.

When I started to write the first book in the Demonica series, *Pleasure Unbound*, I knew right away that the Demonica world was going to be extensive. Keeping track of it meant lots of notebooks, computer space, and brain space. I'm not the most organized person on the planet, but I somehow managed to put together not only a glossary, but an inventory of demons.

As the list of demons grew, so did an idea . . .

See, I've always been a big fan of Dungeons and Dragons (when not writing, I'm glued to the computer and playing the fantasy role-playing game!) and some of the best D&D guides are the monster compendiums, which provide backgrounds, vital statistics, and descriptions of the monsters you might encounter in the world.

So I started on the Demonica compendium, and with each book I wrote, the compendium grew larger. Then I decided to include information about the hospital. And the key players.

And as readers wrote to me, asking questions about the characters, their pasts, and their futures, I found that I wanted to explore the world even more and give readers some extras. So I wrote a short story to show how Eidolon, Shade, Wraith, and Roag met . . . an event that shaped all of their lives forever.

'The Reckoning' takes place before Underworld General was even a spark in Eidolon's thoughts, and before Roag went completely mad.

And here we have it. More of the good, the bad, and the really, *really* ugly.

Hope you enjoy!

The Demons

Note: Most demons are invisible to humans unless they want to be seen, the humans are trained to see them, or the humans possess either magic or some inherent ability to see them. The notable exceptions to the invisibility rule are ter'taceo – *demons who, by nature, look like humans, or who can take on human appearance. Seminus demons, for example, are* ter'taceo.

*When any non*ter'taceo *demon dies in the human realm, it disintegrates within moments unless it dies in an area specially designed to prevent disintegration, an area built by demons, or some underground locales.*

Most demons spend the majority of their lives in Sheoul, *the demon realm deep inside the earth. When demons die, their souls are sent to* Sheoul-gra, *which is, in essence, a holding tank where souls wait to be reborn.* Sheoul-gra *is also where evil human souls are sent to either serve demon souls waiting to be reborn, or to be reborn themselves . . . as demons.*

All demon species and breeds can be classified by their Ufelskala *score – a number ranging from one to five on the scale of evil, with a score of five being the evilest of the wicked. It is important to note that the* Ufelskala Scale *judges 'evil' by a species' or breed's love of pain, suffering, and death, but also on its awareness of its own behavior. So a demon animal that eats its prey alive, causing great suffering, may only score a two on the* Ufelskala Scale, *while a demon that doesn't kill, but instead merely torments for fun, might score a four.*

Humans, for the most part, are unaware that demons walk among them, and that is the way most demons – and most humans – like it.

Acid Sprite – Delicate, rat-sized, moves faster than a human eye can track. Winged and colorful, they can be seen by human children who believe the sprites are fairies. They inhabit very dense, very wet European forests, where they hunt small rodents and make the most of their mischievous natures by tormenting human travelers. A favorite game is to ensure that campers and hikers become lost in the woods. While rarely fatal, an acid sprite's bite is toxic to humans and is often mistaken for a spider bite. **Ufelskala Score: 2**

Alu – Rare, ghostlike demon who appears to humans in the shape of a black dog. It has been known to carry diseases such as bubonic plague and leprosy. Usually found haunting graveyards. **Ufelskala Score: 4**

Baruk – Wrinkled, white-skinned creature that feeds exclusively on Umber demons. They inhabit caves worldwide, where they can hibernate for centuries until an Umber demon moves in. Though humans rarely encounter the baruk, when they do, the results are . . . messy. **Ufelskala Score: 3**

Bathag – Mine dwellers, violet eyes, pale skin, silver/white hair. They possess power over the Earth and can cause earthquakes, volcanic eruptions, and mine collapses. They like to live deep in gem and mineral mines, where they cause minor accidents to feed off the energy of those in pain. **Ufelskala Score: 2**

Bedim – Very attractive, sensual humanoid race. Dark skin, dark hair. Males keep females in harems. When harems grow too large for one male to service alone, harems are often shared with friends or 'rented' out in order to keep females sated and calm. **Ufelskala Score: 1**

Bone Devil – Three feet tall, carnivorous. Lives in forests all over the world. Eats its prey (usually deer) alive. One of the few demon species that exists exclusively in the human realm and never enters Sheoul. **Ufelskala Score: 2**

Charnel Apostle – A race of demon born into the Charnelist religion, which celebrates pain, violence, and bloody sacrifice. All charnel apostles top six feet tall as adults. Gray skin, black eyes, and hair composed of porcupine-like quills that extend down their back and along their broad, flat tail. They make their home high in the Mongolian mountains, using their magic to conceal their existence from humans. **Ufelskala Score: 5**

Croix Viper – Giant demon snakes with horns. They exist exclusively in Sheoul unless brought aboveground by another demon. **Ufelskala Score: 2**

Croucher – Three-eyed, scrawny creatures. The size of a small man, they live near dwelling entrances, waiting to pounce. Though they are invisible to humans, as most demons are, they are capable of powerful evil. They harm by bringing bad luck to a house, thereby causing bad illnesses and accidents, from falling down stairs to sudden death. **Ufelskala Score: 4**

Cruentus – Skeletal chests, thorny fingers, blunt, hairless snouts. Extremely vicious race that feeds only on fresh meat. They will hunt anything, including each other. **Ufelskala Score: 4**

Daeva – Harmless to humans unless threatened. Thin, tall, and pale with lidless, glowing eyes, they appear more frightening than they are. They exist mainly in the darkest reaches of Sheoul and come aboveground to the human realm only at night, to gather trash for food and entertainment. **Ufelskala Score: 1**

Darquethoth – Very large, ebony-skinned demons with glowing orange eyes, mouths, and thick slashes in their skin. They live in the hot, inner regions of Sheoul, feeding off prey species who also reside there. A warrior race, they can be hired for any job that promises violence. **Ufelskala Score: 4**

Drec – Hunchbacked creatures with slimy gray skin and long tails. Loners, they live near lakes and streams, where they can easily catch their main source of food: fish. They are extremely cowardly, making them perfect minions for more evil demons who capture and force them to labor as slaves. **Ufelskala Score: 1**

Drekevac – Spindly, long-limbed, oversized head, fangs as long as a human's forearm. They enter buildings through open windows and sicken humans with their breath. **Ufelskala Score: 4**

Fallen Angels – Fallen angels fall into two categories: those who have entered Sheoul, and those who have not. Angels expelled from Heaven face two choices – they can enter Sheoul and become the most powerful of demons and lose all hope of ever returning to Heaven, or they can reside in the human realm and pray to someday earn the opportunity to return to Heaven. **Ufelskala Score: Varies except for those who have entered Sheoul – these fallen angels are ranked as a 5.**

False Angels – Males and females alike are flawlessly beautiful. Highly sexual, they enjoy pleasures of the flesh, but they are very particular in their choice of sex partners and will only engage in sex with the most attractive humans and human-appearing demons. A cunning and easily bored species, they make life interesting for themselves by tricking humans into thinking they are true angels, and then leading the humans astray from their chosen religion and into another. **Ufelskala Score: 3**

Gargantua – Massive, rare demons that live in the deepest ocean trenches and come onto land once every hundred years to mate. Mostly, they scavenge the carcasses of large mammals and fish that sink to the ocean floor, but they have been known to hunt squid and octopus, as well as to sink ships and devour the crews. **Ufelskala Score: 2**

Gerunti – Thirty feet tall, T-rex jaws and claws as long as a man. Only a handful are believed to be in existence still, a result of long gestation periods and high infant mortality rates. They live underground in mountainous regions in the human realm, coming above ground to gorge themselves on humans and animals once every fifty years. **Ufelskala Score: 3**

Grim Reaper – Very little is known about the Grim Reaper, except that he lives in a realm of his own, inaccessible to most. **Ufelskala Score: Unknown**

Griminions – The Grim Reaper's servants. Believed by some to function for demons as angels do for humans ... escorting the souls of dead demons to Sheoul-gra. **Ufelskala Score: Unknown**

Guai (gwah-eye) – An Asian species, approximately four feet tall, stocky, and resembling a wild boar on two legs. Omnivores, these demons hang out near rice paddies, where they raid rice fields and eat the occasional snake or rat. **Ufelskala Score: 1**

Harpy – Best described as a 'winged woman,' or as a cross between an eagle and woman. The size of human women, harpies have the legs and talon-tipped feet of eagles, and wings instead of arms. Clawlike hands extend from the tips of their wings. Harpies are social creatures, living in groups in large wilderness areas, feeding on demon prey species. When females reach maturity at the age of one hundred, they can take human form once every ten years to mate with a human male. She will then lay a single egg, which will hatch two years later. The eggs, believed to impart immortality if eaten, are highly prized by some demon species and have become a black market commodity. **Ufelskala Score: 1**

Hell Stallion and Hell Mare – Black, horselike creatures the size of Clydesdales. These demon equines are carnivores that spit fire and kill with razor-sharp hooves. Few species can tame and ride hell stallions and mares, but once these horses give their loyalty, it is given for life. **Ufelskala Score: 2**

Hellhound – The size of a buffalo, hellhounds are massive black canines with paws the size of dinner plates, glowing red eyes, and a mouthful of bloody teeth. Unlike earthbound canines, hellhounds have catlike retractable claws, which they use to devastating effect. Their main method of killing involves first raping their prey and then disemboweling it and feasting while it still lives. Notoriously hard to control, hellhounds must be handled only by a professional – hellhounds are known to turn on their handlers with terrifying frequency. **Ufelskala Score: 3**

Huldrefox – A seasonal and social demon that emerges from Sheoul in the fall to raid farmers' fields that are ready to harvest. They especially enjoy gourds. They are a fragile, nonviolent breed, but with six-inch fangs and clawed hands and feet, they are capable of defending themselves when necessary and are extremely protective of their young, *flossa*, which emerge from eggs after six months. **Ufelskala Score: 1**

Imp – Around three feet tall, these demons are the worker ants of the underworld. By far the most common demons, they are treated more like beasts of burden than equals. They are thin, hunched over, with big heads and eyes that are disproportionately large for their faces. They eat anything they can put into their mouths. They breed like rats, giving birth to litters of four to eight young, many of which fall victim as meals for other species. Harmless to humans. **Ufelskala Score: 1**

Judicia – Justice demons. Humanoid in appearance, with dark hair, green skin, and white antlers. Males always wear long beards. Females shave theirs. Some Justice demons work within the Sheoul penal complex. Others are summoned by private individuals or species and breed councils for matters of justice. Justice demons possess the power of mind to inflict painful punishment as they see fit. **Ufelskala Score: 1**

Khilesh Devil – Looking like a cross between an alligator and a gorilla, this predatory species hunts in packs, often killing more than necessary. Their favorite food are Umber young, but they will kill any helpless demon unlucky enough to cross their paths. Khilesh devils live in Sheoul, but usually hunt in forests above-ground. **Ufelskala Score: 3**

Khnive – Summoned demon tracker bound by its master to do his bidding until the spell times out. They smell strongly of decay and resemble giant, skinless opossums. When not being forced to track, khnives roam Sheoul in packs, scavenging for other species' leftover kills. **Ufelskala Score: 1**

Lava Beast – Elephant-sized demons that live within volcanoes. They are the only known species that can survive exposure to hot lava. Orange/red and black in color, they can blend into cooling lava flows. Thought to be the physical incarnation of evil humans killed in natural disasters, lava beasts feed on the negative energy produced by a volcano's destruction. **Ufelskala Score: 3**

Leonine Beast – Believed to be the first demons created as a cross between humans and animals. Some demon scholars are certain leonine beasts are the result of a failed attempt at creating lion shapeshifters. Whatever their origins, they resemble lions but are capable of walking upright. None exist in the wild – these creatures are kept only as pets by the most wealthy and powerful demon lords. **Ufelskala Score: 2**

Mamu – An Australian desert-dwelling species of man-eating, shapeshifting demon. These tall, pointy-headed ugly demons hunt for solitary humans. They either attack with large clubs or they wait quietly, disguised as an inanimate object, small animal, or another human. **Ufelskala Score: 5**

Nebulous Demon – These rare, malevolent spirits suck souls out of humans. They are shapeless, appearing as patches of fog or steam. Some breeds take only the souls of those who are comatose, while others prey mostly on children, the mentally ill, and the elderly, leaving them with no sense of right and wrong. The human souls are stored within the demon, providing it energy for as long as the human body lives. The souls can only be freed by killing the demon. **Ufelskala Score: 4**

Neethulum – An extremely intelligent and cruel race who breed, raise, train, and sell other species as slaves and food. Their uncommon beauty has given rise to the rumor that they are descended from fallen angels. They reside wherever they want to within the vast confines of Sheoul. **Ufelskala Score: 5**

Nightlash – Humanoid, with clawed feet and sharp teeth. Very tall, often topping seven feet. They will eat anything they can catch, and they hunt in family packs, mainly because they are all inbred. There are no social taboos with these demons. They reside only in Sheoul, usually the colder regions, but they consider all of earth their hunting ground. **Ufelskala Score: 4**

Obhirrat – Among the most hideous, vile demons in existence. At around seven-and-a-half feet tall, these snouted beasts have foot-long claws they click together when agitated, beady, red eyes, and snakelike tongues. Their skin is transparent, revealing their primary means of defense: live-flesh-eating maggots that squirm constantly beneath the skin. Few can look upon an Obhirrat without becoming nauseous. **Ufelskala Score: 3**

Oni – These rather stupid demons are troublemakers. The party animals of the underworld, they eat, drink, and have sex to excess. Onis may live in the human realm or the demon one, but they are always present at the sites of natural disasters, and they love to hang out in places where diseases reach epidemic proportions. Ranging in size from half the size of a human to three times the size, they also vary in color, from pale peach to bright pink to blue. Their three fingers and toes on each hand and foot end in sharp talons. They boast three eyes, a flat face, and a gaping mouth full of fangs. **Ufelskala Score: 3**

Ramreel – Rumored to have been created from human and goat stock, these burly, small-eyed demons with curled horns tend to make their living by hiring themselves out as guards. As small kids, they train with blade weapons, giving them a head start in the crowded but lucrative security market. **Ufelskala Score: 2**

Rusalka – Freshwater species that can shapeshift into fishes and frogs. Rusalkas are female, pale green in color, with green hair.

They are perpetually lonely, and they lure human men into the water to mate with them. Unfortunately, their partners always drown after they give up their seed, leaving the Rusalkas lonely once more – that is, until their eggs hatch nine months later. Despite the fact that they always kill their partners, Rusalkas are not evil; they never intend to drown their partners, and they always forget that it happened, so they can't learn from their mistakes. **Ufelskala Score: 1**

Seminus – A rare, specialized breed of incubi. Members of the breed are exclusively male. As a *ter'taceo* species, they appear human. As incubi, they are always attractive, and their sexual pheromones can loosen up even the most prickly females. At one hundred years old, Seminus demons gain the ability to shapeshift and impregnate females of other species. Because individual Seminus demons are raised by different species, their Ufelskala scores vary wildly. In addition, after their second maturation cycle at the age of one hundred, they often lose any sense of compassion and rationality they might have had before the *s'genesis*. **Ufelskala Score: Varies**

Sensor – *Ter'taceo* demons who live and work with humans in order to seek out and destroy the infant half-breed offspring of humans and demons. Though their natural form is humanoid, their skin begins to deteriorate after too much time in the human realm. They must return to Sheoul every six months to endure a two-week regeneration ritual. **Ufelskala Score: 2**

Shapeshifter – Shapeshifters (as their own distinct species, as opposed to a demon who can shift his shape) differ from weres in two main ways: shapeshifters turn into true animals, not human-beasts, and shapeshifters can shift at will and are not affected by the full moon. All true shifters have a telltale birthmark, a red, star-shaped mole behind the left ear. According to the Daemonica, the demon bible, shapeshifters, like weres and vampires, have human souls. **Ufelskala Score: Varies**

Silas Demon – The mercenaries of the underworld. These pale white, eyeless demons live in Sheoul, in large communities where no other species is allowed. They sell their war services to the highest bidders as groups, not individuals, and they will destroy anything and anyone they are paid to kill. Their clothing is made entirely of the hides and skins of their victims. **Ufelskala Score: 4**

Slogthu – Apelike demons with long, tufted ears. They often have exaggerated underbites, overgrown lower fangs, and patchy fur. A cold-weather species, they live high up in mountains or in icy regions of Sheoul. They are extremely dexterous, famous for their finely woven garments and rugs. Omnivores, they prefer their meat cooked. **Ufelskala Score: 1**

Sora – Red-skinned, attractive, black hair, and tiny black or white horns that change shade with their mood. Often described as looking like cartoon devils. Very sexual beings, they rarely form pair-bonds and usually have multiple partners composed of several species, though they can only breed with their own kind. **Ufelskala Score: 1**

Soulshredder – Both feared and respected throughout Sheoul, Soulshredders are vicious even by demon standards. They feed off pain, misery, and terror. They rarely kill outright, instead spending years, even decades, haunting and torturing their victims. They resemble skinned gargoyles, with membrane-thin wings, serrated talons on red, scaly paws, and barbed penises. **Ufelskala Score: 5**

Spiny Hellrat – Similar in size to muskrats, these scavengers populate Sheoul by the millions. Supposedly tasty, they are considered by many demons to be food only ‘poor demon trash’ would eat. Their spines, about as long and thick as a hedgehog’s, are venomous, as is their bite. **Ufelskala Score: 1**

Trillah – A sleek, catlike species. Tall, toned, and graceful, they have bronze skin in the summer and a velvety coat of golden fur in the winter. One of the few non*ter’taceo* species visible at all times to humans, they were forced into Sheoul when the human population grew too large for Trillahs to remain out in the open. Though Trillahs are not evil, they resent mankind for their banishment to Sheoul. **Ufelskala Score: 1**

Umber – Humanoid bodies with gray skin, charcoal hair, and gunmetal eyes. Very gentle, cave-dwelling species. They are good judges of character, having a natural ability to sense evil and good inside someone, and depending on their level of skill, Umbers can lessen or even remove the darkness/guilt that weighs an individual down. **Ufelskala Score: 1**

Vampire – It is believed that vampires were created from fallen angels. Any vampire may turn a human into a vampire, but after a population explosion in the Dark Ages, followed by a vampire civil war, the Vampire Council was formed, and rules were created to regulate not only turnings, but behavior in general. Many of the popular vampire legends are true, but vampires do not believe that their souls are doomed. They live with the belief that if they willingly walk into the morning sun, their souls will be carried to Heaven for judgment before God. However, any vampire killed in any other manner is doomed to suffer eternal torment in *Sheoul-gra*. **Ufelskala Score: Varies**

Viper Ghoul – Illtempered, nasty, man-sized reptile that resembles a cobra that has been dead for a month. Viper ghouls are easily controlled by sorcery and are often summoned by humans who play with black magic without fully grasping its power. The results can be deadly. **Ufelskala Score: 2**

Werebeasts – Weres are humans who shift only during the three nights of the full moon. They turn into large, two-legged, furry beasts with both human and animal features. Only a few species of were-creatures exist. Werewolves (who call themselves wargs), werebears, and wereleopards, though werewolves are the most common. There are two classes of werebeasts: those who are born weres, and those who are turned after being bitten. Born weres, especially wolves, tend to live in packs, while turned wolves usually lead solitary existences. There are rumors of a rare breed of werewolves called dark weres, who change during the new moon instead of the full moon. **Ufelskala Score: Varies**

The Hospital

Underworld General Hospital (yes, that would be UGH) is a medical center that sits beneath the streets of New York City. Built by demons, it is part of the human realm. The decision to erect it under human noses instead of in Sheoul was one Eidolon, Shade, and Wraith argued about for months. Ultimately, the decision to build outside Sheoul came about because many of the spells needed to protect the hospital function only in the human realm, and because Eidolon knew he'd need to employ humans, and humans couldn't use Harrowgates to travel to the hospital if it were located in Sheoul.

Underworld General uses the same modern equipment, supplies, and techniques known to human medicine. Eidolon stays as current as he can, and he actively recruits *ter'taceo* to attend human medical schools to ensure he always has enough staff. Educated, trained staff members are responsible for training those who can't pass as humans in medical schools. Because most demons can't attend medical school – and because some demons are natural or mystical healers – he doesn't require his staff to have medical degrees to work at UG, but he does require that they be adequately trained and skilled.

Demon medicine provides a challenge unlike any other. Every demon species' physiology is unique, and every doctor's talents and skills are just as unique. For the most part, Eidolon and his staff are learning as they go.

To aid in the learning process, every new species or breed that is admitted into the hospital is given a thorough examination, X-rays, blood and genetic tests ... basically, Eidolon insists that every demon be catalogued and studied. All demons are also asked to donate blood for the bank.

Running an operation such as Underworld General is expensive, as one would guess. Though Eidolon was able to raise funds for the initial costs through his family connections, coming up with additional funding required creativity ... and Wraith.

Wraith's suggestion to 'squeeze the patients' was immediately met with resistance, but Shade had quickly come around. Though most demons can't pay with money, they can pay with favors specific to their breed or their occupation. The barter system works, but it brings in only a small percentage of the income needed to run the hospital.

A large percentage of funding comes from a by-product of Wraith's job, which is to gather ancient artifacts and magical items for hospital use. Extras and anything that can't be used to cure patients is sold on the legitimate and black markets.

Wraith's other suggestion, to 'squeeze wealthy fucks,' was one Eidolon agreed to right away. The human world is crawling with *ter'taceo* who use their underworld connections to gain wealth and power, and after a little of Eidolon's convincing and Wraith's 'squeezing,' they've been more than happy to donate to a worthy cause like Underworld General.

The Key Players in the Demonica World

Eidolon (EYE-duh-lawn) – Head of Underworld General Hospital, a medical center he built with brothers Shade and Wraith. Born to the Judicia, demons who serve as judge, jury, and executioner for all demon races. He was bestowed with judicial powers and served with the Judicia as a Justice Dealer for decades, until he made a choice that changed his life forever: he attended human medical school and became a doctor in order to make the most of his healing gift.

Hair: Short, dark brown/black
Eyes: Dark brown
Height: 6' 4"
Profession: Physician
Species: Incubus
Breed: Seminus demon
Identifying marks: Tattoolike symbols extending from tip of right fingers to shoulder
Personal Seminus symbol: Set of scales on throat

Gemella Endri – Raised by Sensor demon parents, Gemella was expected to follow in their footsteps and destroy infants born to human-demon unions. Instead, she followed her own path and became a doctor, working in a human hospital in order to root out medical issues with supernatural/demon origins.

Hair: Length and color change frequently. Usually shoulder-length and black with streaks of blue, red, or pink.
Eyes: Green
Profession: Physician
Species: Half human, half Soulshredder
Identifying marks: Pierced tongue, eyebrow, ears, navel. Long-stemmed rose tattoo running the length of her left leg. Dragon tattoo on her abdomen. Tattooed Celtic bands around ankles, wrists, and neck.

Kynan Morgan – Former Aegis leader of the New York City cell. Joined The Aegis after being injured by a demon while on a mission as a United States Army medic in Afghanistan.

Hair: Short, spiky, dark brown
Eyes: Navy blue
Height: 6’ 2”
Profession: Aegis Guardian
Species: Human
Identifying features: Gravelly voice from vocalcord damage. Scarred throat.

Lore – Born in 1880 to a human mother who believed he was the son of Satan and raised by his maternal grandparents, Lore never seemed to fit in. Fitting in became more of a problem when, at the age of twenty, he went through a strange transformation. By the time it was over, he’d gained a tattoo on his right arm and had killed several people with nothing more than a touch. Unable to control his cursed ability to kill, he hid away in the mountains of North Carolina, where he existed as a hermit until the day he was forced into the life of an enslaved assassin.

Hair: Short, black
Eyes: Dark brown
Height: 6' 6"
Species: Half human, half Seminus demon
Identifying marks: Tattoolike symbols extending from tip of right fingers to shoulder
Personal Seminus symbol: None

Luc (Lewk) – Born in 1896, American-born son of French immigrants, he joined the army when his father left his mother and fled to France with a mistress. Luc requested assignment in Europe and was granted the assignment to fight in France during World War I. Before he could locate his father, he was bitten by a werewolf. He has spent the time since trying to hold onto his humanity.

Hair: Shaggy, black
Eyes: Hazel
Height: 6' 6"
Profession: Paramedic
Species: Werewolf

Reaver – A fallen angel who has never entered Sheoul to complete the fall, Reaver is stuck between two worlds, caught between a rock and a hard place. Without the power of Heaven or Sheoul to draw on, he's weakened, physically and mentally, and he's in a constant battle with his baser desires.

Hair: Long, to the middle of his back, pale blond
Eyes: Blue

Height: 6' 6"
Profession: Physician
Species: Fallen angel

Roag (Rogue) – Roag, the oldest surviving brother of Eidolon, Shade, and Wraith, grew up in true hell – in the Neethul slave pits. Born to a Neethul mother who kept him with the intention of selling him later as a slave, he learned early to fight dirty. He made his first kill at the age of four, when he slit the throat of a sleeping slave in order to steal his food. Roag's mother, proud of the son she'd intended to sell off, decided to keep him close, and it wasn't long before he was running his own slave pit. After his first maturation cycle at the age of twenty, he escaped Sheoul to live in the human world, where fragile humans were easier to trick, brutalize, and kill. He never expected to like any other being, but against all odds, he developed a fondness for Eidolon, who was the only person who has ever been able to influence Roag at all.

Hair: Shaved, dark brown/black
Eyes: Dark brown
Height: 6' 3"
Species: Incubus
Breed: Seminus demon
Identifying features: Tattoolike symbols extending from tip of right fingers to shoulder. Irish accent.
Personal Seminus symbol: Snake swallowing its tail

Runa Wagner (RUE-nuh) – Grew up with her older brother, Arik, in a volatile household with an abusive, alcoholic father. When Runa was a teenager, her father left and her mother committed suicide, leaving Arik to raise Runa. She dated Shade during a hard time in her life. His betrayal led to even harder times.

Hair: Shoulder-length, caramel brown
Eyes: Pale champagne
Species: Werewolf

Serena Kelley – Serena loves life, adventure, and danger. She possesses an uncanny ability to locate anything she's looking for, and someday she'd really like to take a stab at finding the Holy Grail.

Hair: Long, blond
Eyes: Brown
Profession: Treasure hunter
Species: Human
Identifying feature: Necklace she never removes

Shade – Born to an Umber demon mother, and raised in a cave in Central America. Thanks to a curse placed on him at the age of twenty, he avoided attachments, especially with females, for years. Has a fondness for leather, Harleys, and, until he met Runa, one-night stands.

Hair: Shoulder-length, dark brown/black
Eyes: Dark brown/black
Height: 6' 3½"
Profession: Paramedic
Species: Incubus
Breed: Seminus demon
Identifying marks: Tattoolike symbols extending from tip of right fingers to shoulder. Pierced left ear.
Personal Seminus symbol: Unseeing eye on throat

Tayla Mancuso – Tayla spent her entire childhood and most of her teenage years in foster care thanks to a drug-addicted mother who was unable to care for Tayla. Eventually, Tayla's mother gained custody of her, but the happy reunion was cut short when Tayla witnessed her mother's torture and death at the hands of a demon. After that, Tayla dedicated every waking moment to killing demons, and until she met Eidolon, she believed that the only good demon is a demon with a stang buried in its brain.

Hair: Red
Eyes: Green
Profession: Aegis Guardian
Species: Half human, half Soulshredder

Wraith – As a demon born to a vampire, Wraith is an anomaly. A childhood of torture at the hands of vampires gave him an intense hatred of the entire race, and he spent his entire adult life killing them for sport. His horrific younger years left him with a strange quirk: he won't feed from or have sex with human women. All other females, however, are fair game – a game he plays several times a day. Unlike most Seminus demons, Wraith was born with the red-eyed glare other Sems gain around the time of *s'genesis*.

Hair: Kept between chin- and shoulder-length, bleached blond
Eyes: Blue
Height: 6' 5"
Profession: In charge of acquisitions for UG
Species: Incubus
Breed: Seminus demon
Identifying marks: Tattoolike symbols extending from tip of right fingers to shoulder
Personal Seminus symbol: Hourglass on throat

The Reckoning

Reckoning (noun) – An unpleasant or disastrous destiny

Chicago. 1928.

They were coming.

Wraith lurched across the floor of the abandoned brewery, one leg dragging. He'd yanked the dagger out of his thigh, but the damage had been done, because his leg wouldn't work right. Hell, it wouldn't work at all.

Dusty equipment and trash littered the huge warehouse, slowing him down even more. He ducked behind a giant vat, but if he believed he was hiding, he was fooling himself. Even if he wasn't leaving a blood trail a blind man could follow, the bastards on his tail were vamps. They'd track him by scent.

Pain radiated up from his leg, competing with the burning in his lungs for attention. Wincing, he put pressure on the puncture wound, which did nothing to stanch the blood.

He was in trouble.

Two years of running had gotten him nowhere. His mother's clan had finally caught up with him. They'd chased him from

California to Texas, and from there to Canada. Then Alaska. Now he was in Chicago, thinking he should have forced someone to teach him about the Harrowgates instead of traveling on foot, following the odd, ever-present feeling deep in his chest that told him he had family out there.

Then again, he hadn't been overly enthused about finding those mysterious relatives. Not when the only family he'd ever known had tortured and abused him, and who were even now entering the building to finish what they'd started the day he was born.

In the moon's silver light streaming through the broken windows, he caught a glimpse of his reflection in one of the vat's metal panels. His dark hair hung in ropes around his shoulders and his face was caked with dirt and blood. Only his eyes looked the way they'd always been – the color of mud and just as murky. A vagrant had once told Wraith his eyes were dead.

Wraith had eaten the guy for that, but the homeless man had spoken the truth. Inside, Wraith was an empty shell, and he had no idea why he kept fighting.

'We know you're in here, boy,' Dick, Wraith's uncle, called out. 'So why don't you come out from hiding like the rat you are and face your justice.'

Justice. Funny. Wraith had been in a kill-or-be-killed situation with his own mother, but that was of no consequence to people who had kept him in a cage his entire life. Wraith's mother had been a fullfledged vampire, while Wraith was nothing more than a demon. Didn't matter that he had to drink blood to survive – he wasn't a true vampire, so his life had been deemed worth less than an insect's, and her clan intended to squash him.

He glanced around wildly for a way out, but three vampires he didn't know blocked the exits. Looked like good old Uncle Dickhead had found some locals who were eager for a little bloodsport.

Wraith dug into his pocket for his knife. This was the end of the line, and he knew it.

Maybe the afterlife would be better than this one, because it sure as hell couldn't be worse.

ↂ

'Hell's bells.' Shade clutched his leg, nearly falling on his ass in the middle of the living room of the Queens row house he shared with Eidolon. Little bursts of pain rode his nerves from his leg to his skull. 'I'm starting to not like this brother of ours.'

Eidolon lit another oil lamp, but the ugly brown wallpaper seemed to absorb the soft glow. They'd just moved in, and the damned lighting didn't work. Worse, the stench of the lantern smoke made Shade gag.

'You've said the same thing about Roag,' Eidolon said. 'I'm beginning to think you wish you were an only child.'

'Not true. I like my sister.'

One corner of Eidolon's mouth quirked in a smile. 'The real mystery is why Skulk likes *you*.'

'Glad you find this so amusing,' Shade said, as he hobbled across the room. 'Because I sure as hell don't.'

Eidolon swiped a bottle of twenty-five-year-old Scotch off an end table. 'So, do you think we should head west? See if we can find him?'

Shade sank down on a chair, rubbing his thigh. They'd sensed this unknown brother all their lives, but over the last couple of weeks they'd felt him growing closer, slowly, which meant he wasn't using the Harrowgates. Still, there was a sense of panic about the movement, and Shade got the feeling the guy was moving east for a reason.

He was coming to find his brothers.

'He's in a lot of pain. We should see what the trouble is.'

Eidolon caressed the neck of the bottle like a lover. Growing up with privilege and wealth had given him a taste for only the finest liquor. Not that Shade couldn't appreciate the expensive stuff, but cheap rotgut got you just as warm.

'Let's find Roag,' Eidolon said, as he poured a drink. 'He'll want to go.'

'Let's not and say we did,' Shade muttered, and E leveled an annoyed look at him. Shade rolled his eyes. 'Come on. You're not the one with fire shooting up his leg.' E could sense the existence of his brothers, same as Shade and Roag, but it seemed as if only Shade had gotten saddled with the ability to feel this mysterious brother's physical pain.

'It won't take long.'

Shade shoved to his feet. 'Fine, but if Roag is at another opium den, you're the one going in to get him.'

ᘏ

Roag wasn't at an opium den. Eidolon could have dealt with that. Instead, he and Shade found Roag in an Irish demon pub. A demon pub full of horny females. Eidolon and Shade had made the mistake of entering, and they'd become stuck for two days, unable to leave until the last female was sexually satisfied.

Only the fact that their youngest brother was in so much pain that even Eidolon could now feel it forced them out of there. The needs of their sibling overrode the needs of the females, and they were finally free.

Exhausted and on the verge of collapse, but free.

They dragged their sorry asses to the nearest Harrowgate, where Eidolon studied the panels etched into the glossy black walls. He sensed the need to head west, but he couldn't pinpoint more than that. It was Shade who fingered the crude map of the United States.

'Illinois?'

'Chicago.'

Roag yawned. 'How the hell do you know?'

'Dunno.' Shade was looking a little green around the gills, and Eidolon knew it was more than exhaustion and a sexual hangover. He was feeling the effects of their brother's pain ten times stronger than Eidolon was. A couple of times at the pub he'd even collapsed on the ground, writhing in agony. Roag didn't seem to be affected at all.

The Harrowgate opened up into a rundown factory district. Low, gray clouds obscured the sky, and smoke billowing from tall stacks turned the autumn air heavy with gloom, as if the very city felt their sibling's misery.

Eidolon definitely felt it. Now that they were close, his skin tightened to the point of pain, and a throbbing ache settled low in his gut.

Shade went taut, his head swiveling as he zeroed in on their brother. A heartbeat later, he shot down the street. 'This way.'

They moved quickly through a bustling section of town, where street vendors hawked cheap food to the factory workers, and when they passed a prostitute hawking her particular brand of wares, Roag stopped.

'I'll catch up,' he said, his Irish accent thick with lust.

Damn him. Eidolon knew arguing wouldn't do any good, and Shade was already out of sight. With a juicy curse, he jogged ahead. The cavity in Eidolon's chest where brotherly sensation centered grew warmer as they approached a more sparsely populated area. The heat exploded into an inferno when Shade darted through the side door of a building whose faded sign indicated it had been both a textile mill and a brewery.

Inside, the windows had been covered with tarps and wood, and eight vampires stood around a broken, naked body hanging from the ceiling. Various tools lay scattered like bones on the floor – hammers, blades, pliers. But what froze Eidolon's blood in his veins was the blowtorch one of the male vamps was holding.

The stench of burning flesh permeated the air.

Rage nearly turned Eidolon inside out. 'You sick bastards,' he snarled, and the vampires spun around.

The vampire with the blowtorch moved toward them with the slinky grace of a snake, and the others followed. 'Who are you?'

'We're his brothers.' Shade seized an overturned chair and smashed it against the wall. Wood shrapnel showered them all. Shade snagged one thick shard out of the air and gestured at the bloody demon with his makeshift stake. 'And we're only going to ask you once to clear out.'

The vampire laughed. 'You're risking your necks to rescue *Wraith*? Why?'

Eidolon had never had a problem with vampires . . . until now. 'Did you miss the brother thing?' He swept up a broken chair leg and tested its weight in his palm. It took every ounce of restraint he had not to plunge the pointy end into the vampire's heart right then and there.

'Do not interfere.' The lone female vamp eased up next to the big male. 'This is a vampire matter—'

'He's not a vampire,' Eidolon bit out, because by now, he'd had it with these assholes.

'As much as I hate to say it,' the male with the blowtorch said, 'the whelp *is* a vampire. Leave us. This is your last warning.'

Frowning, Eidolon studied the body swinging from the ceiling. His *dermoire* was visible under the layers of caked and fresh blood, so this was definitely their brother, and he was definitely a demon. Eidolon had no idea what this madman was talking about, but really, it didn't matter. They had come prepared for a battle, and in addition to his chair-leg stake, Eidolon had an arsenal of weapons stashed beneath his long wool coat.

No doubt these vamps had decades, if not centuries, of experience on Eidolon and Shade, but they weren't completely helpless. Shade could scramble anyone's insides with a touch, and Eidolon's Justice Dealer background had given him a unique perspective on pain and injury.

Wraith's low, drawn-out moan drifted through the factory like a ghost. Eidolon moved forward. These bastards were going to die.

൭

Four vampires were dust. Two had run, and two were now hog-tied and propped against the factory wall. One of them was the asshole who had threatened them, but sitting there, bloody and missing a few teeth, he didn't look so threatening anymore. Shade didn't think so, anyway.

Shade kicked the male, who'd said he was Wraith's uncle. 'Why can't we kill them?'

'Because Wraith should have that honor,' Eidolon said, and Shade supposed that was a good point.

Dropping their weapons, E and Shade crossed the room to Wraith. Shade pushed his brother's hair, matted with blood, away from his face.

Oh, Gods. 'E . . . oh, fuck.'

Eidolon's face went ashen. 'Those *bastards.*' His voice sounded as if it had been dredged up from the pits of hell. 'They gouged out his eyes.'

And that was only a small part of what they'd done to him. Among other brutal acts, they'd opened him up from groin to sternum. In several places, broken bone jutted from between shredded muscle and tendon.

Shade bled fury through his pores. 'Get him down,' he rasped. 'Dear Gods, get him down.'

'Hey, boys.' Roag's voice drifted through the building.

'Where have you been?' Shade snarled, as Eidolon began lowering Wraith's shattered body from the ceiling, the chains that held him clanging.

Roag sauntered toward them, kicking through the piles of vampire dust, looking calmly at the two left alive. 'You two handled things well enough.' He jerked his chin at Wraith. 'Looks like you found our longlost little brother. Not much left. Leave him. We'll go find the whore I just balled.'

'Just keep an eye on the vamps,' Eidolon snapped, his patience with Roag nearly as frayed as Shade's.

They lowered Wraith slowly and carefully. He didn't move, and the only reason they knew he was alive was because Shade had channeled his gift into his brother and felt his heart beating weakly. His pulse had been too faint to feel with their fingers.

Wraith lay on the floor of the warehouse in a pool of his own blood. Eidolon's *dermoire* glowed as he gripped Wraith's wrist, but after a moment, he looked up and shook his head.

'He's too far gone.'

Shade knew that, could feel it, could see it in the massive injuries that should have killed Wraith long before this. 'We have to try. Maybe we can find a doctor who won't ask questions.'

Roag shrugged. 'We could nab one from a hospital and force him to help. Kill him later so he doesn't talk. Want me to go get one?'

He made it sound like he was going to stop in at the corner grocer and pick up a loaf of bread.

'No human doctor can do what we can do.' Eidolon's shoulders slumped. 'But it doesn't matter. He's not going to make it another five minutes.'

Roag picked up the blowtorch. 'Can we kill the vamps now?'

'Hell, yeah,' Shade spat.

He shifted, prepared to rip the assholes apart, but froze when Wraith's finger touched his knee. Not just his finger, but his whole hand. Somehow, the guy had found the strength to move his shattered arm and grip Shade's pants. Shade brought his hand down on top of Wraith's.

Wraith's skin was icy, his hand shaking, but he managed to squeeze, and in that slight motion, he conveyed his message.

He wanted to live.

Shade's gaze met Eidolon's. 'We're going to save him. Damn it all, we're going to try.'

Eidolon didn't hesitate. He thumbed Wraith's swollen upper lip, revealing two fangs. 'He really is a vampire.' He turned to their captives. 'Does he feed?' When they just stared, he snarled. '*Does he feed?*'

Uncle Vamp nodded grudgingly.

'Roag,' Shade said, 'go fetch that prostitute.'

Roag grinned. 'That's the spirit.'

'Not for sex, you fucking lackbrain. We need her for blood if Wraith needs to feed. And find us a doctor. You can adjust his memories afterward. Go!' Shade expected Roag to argue, and for a heartbeat Shade thought he might have gone too far. Roag was prickly, generally listening only to Eidolon. But maybe the two days of nonstop sex at the pub had taken the piss out of him, and he finally nodded sharply and headed out.

'Shade,' Eidolon said quietly, as though he didn't want Wraith to hear too much, 'can you get inside him and keep his blood moving while I try to mend his bones?'

'Have you done that before?'

'Once, when my sister broke her arm. But this is . . . '

Eidolon shook his head, and Shade understood. He hated feeling helpless as much as Eidolon did. He'd never done anything like this before. If he screwed up . . .

'Come on, Shade.' Eidolon lay his palm on Wraith's thigh, over one extremely nasty burn. 'We have to do this.'

Cursing, Shade gripped Wraith's hand and channeled his gift into him, searching out his organs, probing for injuries and weaknesses. E's *dermoire* lit up, and the snapped shin bone jutting through Wraith's skin began to knit together and ease back into place. Shade knew for a fact that E's healing gift was extremely painful, but Wraith didn't even stir. His heart stuttered, but Shade forced it into a strong rhythm, and gradually, it began to beat normally on its own.

When Eidolon was satisfied that he'd healed their brother's bones, he gently tipped Wraith's face up, fury darkening E's expression as he studied the empty eye sockets.

And then, with the coldest smile Shade had ever seen on anyone, he turned to the vampires. 'Eeny meeny, miny moe,' he said, one finger going between the two, and ending on the dark-haired one. Smoothly, deliberately, he picked up a shard of wood and crossed to the vamps.

'Looks like today is your lucky day,' he said, and stabbed the dark-haired vamp through the chest. He didn't even wait for the male to start flaming before he moved to Wraith's uncle, whose face was etched with terror.

Eidolon crouched and roughly gripped his jaw, tipping it up so Eidolon's dark eyes locked with the vampire's blue ones.

And Shade knew exactly what was about to happen.

൭

Consciousness came to Wraith in bits and pieces, which was pretty much what he felt like. He didn't wonder what had happened, because his nightmares had played the events of his capture and torture over and over. The only question he had was how long he'd been down.

He opened his eyes. Blinked a few times. *Eyes*. He had some.

'Hey.' A dark-haired male peered into Wraith's face. 'I'm Shade. Your brother. You're at my place. Well, it's Eidolon's place too. He's right here.'

Another male moved to the side of the bed. 'How are you feeling?'

Wraith swallowed. His throat hurt. 'Like some vampires strung me up and tortured me,' he rasped. Swallowed again. 'Why . . . why'd you save me?'

Eidolon seemed stumped by the question. 'You're our brother.'

'So?'

Shade swore and cast a glance at Eidolon. 'Great. Another Roag.' He turned back to Wraith. 'Roag's our other brother. He's not here. Wasn't there while we were putting you back together in the factory, either.'

'Shade . . . '

'What? Fucker dropped off the doctor and a whore and took off to find another prostitute.'

'Doctor?' Wraith lifted his head, but when pain clanged in his skull, he dropped it back onto the pillow.

Eidolon nodded. 'It took some persuasion to get the doctor to help, but once he stopped blubbering and praying, he pitched in. He had to tack your intestines into place and transfer some of Shade's blood into your body, and that pulled you through. Hate to say it, but if not for the doc, you wouldn't have made it.' He looked down at his feet. 'Shade and I couldn't have saved you without his help.'

Wraith still didn't get why they'd saved him, and hell, he wasn't even sure he was grateful. 'What ... what happened to the vampires?'

Shade bared his teeth. 'They're dead.'

Good. Wraith hoped their deaths had been slow and painful.

'We're going to let you get some rest,' Eidolon said, and Wraith felt a slow burn of panic, followed immediately by shame that he was afraid to be alone.

Somehow, Eidolon knew. 'We'll be in the next room. One of us will always be here.' His gaze locked with Wraith's. 'No one will hurt you like that again, brother. You have my word.'

No, no one would. Because once he was on his feet again, he was going to spend every waking moment training. To kill. And then he was going to hunt vampires until their kind was extinct.

'Hey,' Shade said softly. 'I recognize that look. Too well. Just concentrate on getting better, and know we have your back.'

Wraith's brothers left the room, and as he watched them leave, a strange, churning sensation filled his chest. Hatred and bitterness took up the majority of the space, but woven in there was something else ... something he'd never felt. Gratitude? Affection?

Maybe not the latter, but he appreciated what his brothers had done. And no matter what, he couldn't deny that, for the first time in his life, he didn't feel so alone.

Also available now from Piatkus

FIRED UP

Jayne Ann Krentz

More than three centuries ago, Nicholas Winters irrevocably altered his genetic make-up in an obsession-fueled competition with alchemist and Arcane Society founder Sylvester Jones. Driven to control their psychic abilities, each man's decision has reverberated throughout the family line, rewarding some with powers beyond their wildest dreams, and cursing others to a life filled with madness and hallucinations.

Jack Winters, descendant of Nicholas, has been experiencing nightmares and blackouts – just the beginning, he believes – of the manifestation of the Winters family curse. The legend says that he must find the Burning Lamp or risk turning into a monster. But he can't do it alone; he needs the help of a woman with the gift to read the lamp's dreamlight. Jack is convinced that private investigator Chloe Harper is that woman. It doesn't take long for Chloe to pick up the trail of the missing lamp. And as they draw closer to the lamp, the raw power that dwells within it threatens to sweep them into a hurricane of psychic force.

978-0-7499-5266-2

Do you love fiction with a supernatural twist?

Want the chance to hear news about your favourite authors (and the chance to win free books)?

Keri Arthur
S. G. Browne
P.C. Cast
Christine Feehan
Jacquelyn Frank
Larissa Ione
Darynda Jones
Sherrilyn Kenyon
Jackie Kessler
Jayne Ann Krentz and Jayne Castle
Martin Millar
Kat Richardson
J.R. Ward
David Wellington

Then visit the Piatkus website and blog

www.piatkus.co.uk | www.piatkusbooks.net

And follow us on Facebook and Twitter

www.facebook.com/piatkusfiction | www.twitter.com/piatkusbooks